COVET ME

IMMORTAL VICES AND VIRTUES: HER MONSTROUS MATES

KEL CARPENTER

AURELIA JANE

Covet Me

Aurelia Jane and Kel Carpenter

Published by Raging Hippo LLC

Copyright © 2023, Raging Hippo LLC

Cover Art by Trif Book Cover Design

Map Art by Etheric Designs

Y'all were a few hours away from not having this monster of a story on time. For that reason, we dedicate this book to strong coffee, DoorDash, grocery delivery drivers, anxiety medication, our author support group, Disney movies and soundtracks, and our husbands who make us dinner.

And to all you lovelies out there that want to fuck the dragon. Go put on some Barry White, grab a glass of whatever you fancy, and read on.
This one is for you.

ACKNOWLEDGMENTS

Please buy it. Please read it. Fuck, we hope you love it.

This book was a beast.

We are tired beyond words. That wasn't supposed to be a pun. Those come later.

Some personal things in life fell apart right when we began this book. That happens. We expect it because, you know, that's life. There will always be something.

Normally, one of us can pick up the other's weight. That's what partners do. We're best friends. We fight, we cry, we get mad at each other and argue, we laugh, and we love each other without measure. Even if we complain about it, we pick the other up so we can cross the finish line.

But wow, we got kicked *hard*. Kel's health deteriorated badly and one of my kiddo's health declined. It took months for Kel to have one decent day—and she's not better yet. I'm still in the deep end with my kiddo. While one of us can normally carry the burden of two, it looks a *whole lot* different when we're both limping the entirety of the race.

But here we are, uploading this monster in the eleventh hour—and that's not a joke.

To our friends: Jessica Wayne, Heather Hildenbrand, Annie Anderson, Jen L Grey, Lexi Foss, Everly Frost, Amanda Pillar, and Heather Renee...

You are our lifelines. No words can express what your

friendships mean to us. How <u>valued </u>you are. How much we need you, and how utterly grateful we are to have you in our lives.

Welcome to Season II of Immortal Vices and Virtues, readers. We can't wait to share this incredible 2023 lineup with you.

Happy Reading,
    Aurelia and Kel

P.S. A shout out of thanks to our behind-the-scenes team of PAs. Our husbands. AJ's mom for managing the tyrants for 10 days. The party host that managed AJ's 9-year old's birthday party. Our Amazon & UPS delivery drivers. Kel's housekeepers. AJ's housekeepers. Fucking everyone the last six months, honestly. And last but not least, our readers. Thank you.

You can't break someone who found strength within their own destruction.

- Unknown

- ⦿ Portal
- ☐ No Man's Land
- ▦ Fire & Flourite
- ▦ Air & Amethyst
- ▦ Spirit & Sapphire
- ▦ Sea & Serpentine
- ▦ Death & Diamond
- ▢ Blood and Beryl
- ▦ Gold & Garnet
- ▨ Earth & Emerald

IMMORTAL VICES AND VIRTUES

The Houses
House of Blood and Beryl
House of Air and Amethyst
House of Earth and Emerald
House of Spirit and Sapphire
House of Death and Diamond
House of Fire and Fluorite
House of Gold and Garnet
House of Sea and Serpentine

No Man's Land

No Man's Circus - Portland. Oregan

Supernatural Syndicates
New York City
Manhattan – The Wards – Shifters
Brooklyn – The Roses – Fae
Staten Island – The Outcast Coven – Witches
Queens – The Divine – Angels & Demons
Bronx – Clan Tepes – Vampires

CHAPTER I
NIKKI

I READ A BOOK ONCE WHERE THE PEASANTS BANDED TOGETHER AND fought back against tyranny. Those in charge took everything from those they deemed beneath them. They didn't care about the suffering caused by their actions. The common people in the story didn't take it lying down. They formed a militia—a movement—to take back their kingdom and everything the tyrant king had stolen. Even noblewomen and children joined in the crusade, hoping to make the world a better place. Rob from the rich and feed the poor.

The songs were catchy too.

Okay, so maybe I didn't *read* it. And maybe it was a Disney movie. And maybe the people weren't actually people. More like foxes and bunnies and a bear . . . and I was pretty sure the friar was a badger. Whatever. The point was they did something about the shit soup they'd been served.

They inspired me. Which is why I was slinking around on Brooklyn rooftops by the waterfront of the East River in December. At midnight. In the freezing cold.

I can't say the world has ever been a good place, but it is worse now than ever before. Magic had always existed, but now it was public knowledge on a global scale and had been for over fifty years. Portals to other worlds had stayed hidden for millennia, until one decided to rip a hole in the fabric of space and time, right smack in the middle of downtown Portland. Naturally, panic ensued. Chaos. All the craziness you'd expect from an apocalyptic event.

It changed everything—who had power, who had control—the basis of society itself was toppled. While we weren't in a cartoon version of medieval England, we were in what amounted to a twisted dystopian world that ran on magic and technology.

The supernatural syndicate ruled New York City. Each of the five boroughs were controlled by a different species. Mafias fighting for territory only cared about themselves, and unlike the movies I watched, there was no greater power to keep them in line. No heroes to change things.

This was the only life—the only world—I'd ever known.

Brutal. Savage. Desolate.

Someone had to step up to make it a better place. There was no reason that someone couldn't be me.

I learned the single universal truth at a young age.

What couldn't be bought *was taken*—and no one could do a damn thing to stop it. The syndicate leaders would do anything to keep every bit of power they'd stolen.

My father included.

He ruled Manhattan with an iron fist and zero mercy, as was the shifter syndicate's way. At least under his rule.

That made me the Maid Marian in the story. Except I wasn't all that foxy. Or a fox at all. More like an awkward mythic shifter with ninety-nine problems—

"You're distracted."

An elbow nudged my side, bringing my attention back to the real world.

"Hmm, what?" I stole a sideways glance at my best friend. Sam sat with one leg propped up and the other dangling over the edge of the rooftop. Covered by a glamour and dressed in all black and gray unisex clothing —to disguise any distinguishing features—you'd never know the woman beneath was blonde haired, blue-eyed, and frankly, a total babe. Once upon a time, she'd wanted to be a dancer in a traveling troupe. Like the rest of us, she'd dreamed of a better life in that way that only children could. Instead, she became one of my father's top enforcers and my own personal guard.

"I said, 'you're distracted'," she repeated with a sigh.

"Just thinking. That's all."

"Thinking . . ." she mused. "So you're daydreaming grandiose thoughts that we're vigilante forest animals in *Robin Hood*. Again. Am I right or am I right?" She smirked, overly smug at guessing my thoughts. Like that was an accomplishment. Pfft.

She's been with me for more of my life than she hasn't. I'd be offended if she couldn't guess right.

"Ass," I griped. Sam knocked my shoulder playfully. "You know, sometimes movies have great strategies. You just have to think outside the box. Go with what no one will expect."

She shook her head, huffing a small laugh. "Only you, Nikki."

"It works. They're so crazy that normal, boring people like my brothers don't stand a chance. They get caught up in what's expected. I know you all think I have a few screws loose, but that's the beauty of it. Being unexpected is the

3

perfect strategy. If we don't know what we're going to do next, neither do they."

"Last time we went with one of your 'strategies', you got jumped by pixies on the subway. They would have robbed you blind and left you for dead if Gavriel wasn't there. Thank god you're a phoenix. If your dad saw those injuries, he would have reamed my ass for letting you get hurt—and that's before he started looking into how it happened. The Movement was almost jeopardized."

"But it wasn't," I sniffed. "I healed. We got the kids out of those cages and to the safehouse. It was *fine*. You're being dramatic."

"Oh yeah? What about the time you were humming your own theme song so loud the vampires heard you from a quarter of a mile away—"

"I was *supposed* to be the distraction," I insisted. "That's hardly a fuck up when I did my job perfectly."

"You weren't supposed to become the new target," Sam said, fighting to suppress a laugh and failing miserably.

"Well, being a badass doesn't exactly come with a manual."

"You were pretending to be Kronk. Let's not oversell what you were doing there."

"Everyone made it home in one piece . . . well, mostly. I'm not taking responsibility for Lima's missing finger. He should have known better than to point at something with fangs." He wasn't exactly the brightest crayon in the box, if you know what I'm saying.

Sam chuckled. "I'll give you that one, but answer me this. If this is a supposed 'strategy'" —again with the air quotes— "what was the purpose of egging on Foxtrot by singing "I'll make a man out of you" while scouting last weekend? Hmm?"

Well. She might have had a point there. Not that I'd admit it.

"He needed motivation. Dude thinks he's so big and bad because he's a croc shifter, but he can't admit his weaknesses and he can't climb for shit."

"Uh huh."

"Someone's gotta give the wannabe badasses a dose of reality before they get hurt. Why not me? I'm doing them a favor, really."

"I rest my case."

I pursed my lips. "Do you now? Do you really?"

She shook her head at me, hiding the way her lips tried to curl into a smile. "You're no longer bouncing your leg like it's hooked up to a car battery. So yeah, I'd say my work here is done. Wanna talk about what's really bothering you?" The transition from snarky to sweet wasn't unusual for her. At least not with me. Sam knew better than anyone how to get me to open up when I'd rather be lost in my head.

"New moons just make me jittery, that's all."

"You've been out on new moons before and not been so restless," she said gently.

"It's nothing." I added a grin for effect, but I'm pretty sure she didn't buy it. Rubbing my hands together for friction, I released a sigh. "Bad time for my mind to start wandering. Thanks for pulling me back."

Sam rubbed my back and then reached over to grab my gloved hand, holding it in hers and squeezing tight. A shadow of warmth reached my palm through the fabric. "It's just reconnaissance tonight. In and out. They'll never know we're here."

Nodding, I kept my eye on the pier in the distance. I knew tonight was just listening in on the meeting about to occur. Sam and I weren't even the two directly in the line of danger this time. We were back up more than anything.

Still, something about being out on the night when my power was at its weakest was nerve-racking, also stupid. If anything went wrong, I was about as useful as a human. Slightly faster, resistant to fire, and able to heal from anything—but whatever strength my shifter genes lent me was zilch. I wouldn't let that stop me. This city needed all the help it could get, and I wouldn't hide in my bedroom. Passivity was a luxury, and I was one of the rare few who could afford it. I refused to indulge when I could be part of the solution.

Still, telling myself all of that did nothing to stop the creeping dread that was taking over the longer I watched the two supes in the distance.

They stood beside metal shipping containers with their backs to us, talking to each other while waiting for my dad and my brother to show. Alexander was the second oldest. He had a tough, no-nonsense demeanor, but he was also the calm and collected one between my father's preferred sons. Neither a pushover nor easily ruled by his emotions, he knew how to be the face of the syndicate.

My other two brothers were as different as night and day. Gavriel was warm and gentle—too gentle for this world or the family we were born into. I loved him with all my heart, and he reminded me that good still existed. If Sam was my best friend, Gavriel was my lifeline. He gave me hope on my darkest days and was sometimes the only reason I could drag myself out of bed to play the part of a perfect Mafia princess.

My father thought him weak. A disappointment. He had a formidable shifter form, but his temperament was better suited to, well, me. He was a peacekeeper and knew when to keep his mouth shut. While he couldn't escape the family business, he was given duties that many would consider humiliating for a son of the greatest crime lord this city has ever seen.

My eldest brother Ty was another story entirely. Wherever he went, blood followed. Along with sweat, piss, and strewn limbs.

There was a reason they called him The Sadist.

He was the heir to the shifter syndicate, should dear ol' dad ever retire.

My father was . . . well, my father. He loved his family deeply and took care of us. But he was also a syndicate leader, and they were all ruthless to the core.

Headlights shone in the distance. Cars pulled up to the pier.

Sam looked at the watch on her wrist. "Twenty minutes late. Right on time." I snorted. It was very much a Ward power play.

Dad liked to say that it established dominance.

Personally, I thought it just made him look rude.

"Here we go." Flinging my legs over and dipping behind the ledge, I pulled binoculars out of my small bag. They were old, but functional. Most supernaturals had good eyesight, and I was no different. But we were far enough away that the extra boost was necessary. Spotting the duck shifter floating in the water, I smiled. "Lindsey is in position."

Sam hummed in response, inching off the ledge and tucking herself behind it to stay out of sight. Crouched beside me, she peered through her own binoculars, checking for our other lookouts and making sure they were where they needed to be. She grinned when she found Lindsey near the docks. "Look at her cute little duck butt."

"She's a duck . . ."

"And?"

"Mates are weird," I mumbled, and she huffed a small laugh.

"You'll find yours again one day." Sam nudged me with her elbow reassuringly. I wasn't so sure. Not when I refused his rejection before he ran off. If I were smart I would have accepted it, letting the bond break.

Apparently I was a glutton for punishment in more ways than one.

"I won't hold my breath. If fate has any kindness left in her, she'll leave me alone." My heart had been broken once already. I wasn't in a rush to feel that again. Staying single and having cats for company was a safer route.

"Fate gave you me as a best friend, so she can't be that bad."

Rolling my eyes, I sighed. "Fine. Point to you. Fate managed to not screw up one thing for me."

"Here he comes," Sam whispered while we watched my father exit the vehicle and talked to the two strangers. A few moments passed. Alexander still hadn't arrived. "Where's your brother?"

None of the cars were his. I scanned the docks to see if he had ridden with someone else. "Beats me. He said he'd be here with dad. I tried to get as much out of him as I could, but you know how tight-lipped he is about family business. When the most he would tell me was they're meeting with the fae syndicate at night, it didn't give me warm fuzzies."

Peering through the lenses, I tried to focus on the two fae my family were meeting with. One cracked his neck, and a chill went down my spine. Tingles spread through my fingertips, and anxiety zipped across my nerve endings.

Why watching them elicited that reaction in me, I didn't know, but it couldn't be good. The magic beneath my skin felt itchy. Restless. Terrified.

My power should be nowhere near the surface. Not tonight.

Whoever these strangers were, they were more dangerous than I wanted to admit. That thought coupled with my brother's absence was enough to make every instinct in my body scream at me to leave.

Sam grabbed my arm, making me jump. With one hand, she held her binoculars and the other gripped me for support. The way her fingers dug into shoulder while her breath stuttered made all the alarm bells in my head scream.

"We have a big problem," she whispered.

Scanning the pier and looking through the foot soldiers that were standing around, my heart dropped into my stomach when I saw what had caused her to react that way.

Not what, but who.

"Fuck," I cursed between clenched teeth. "What the hell is Ty doing here?"

CHAPTER 2

ADRIAN

"They're late," I mumbled, shoving my hands into my pockets while I scanned the old greenway, searching for signs of the shifters we were supposed to be meeting.

The waterfront and piers in Brooklyn had once been teeming with life. A center for conducting commerce and trade, with vessels moving in and out daily. Walkways and parks, lively and bustling with city residents as they strolled, taking in views of the bridges and lower Manhattan.

That was no more.

The new world wasn't as simple.

Supernaturals had been revealed, and we populated the earth, reigning over spliced territories worldwide. Magic bled into humans, giving them low-level powers. With each generation born, true humans had become less and less. They were almost extinct.

The piers were now open concrete docks, filled with discarded materials and large metal shipping containers. Though the boat traffic had slowed down significantly since portals had erupted globally, there were still smaller ships and ferries that were used for a variety of purposes.

Parks and walkways were ghost towns after sunset—as they should be. There was almost always a more sinister supernatural in the shadows, and the predator-prey hierarchy still very much existed.

Niall casually leaned against one of the containers, cutting slices of an apple with a pocketknife. One after the other, he'd lift the piece to his mouth, eating it off the blade.

"They're not late. They're making us wait to prove a point," he said without looking up.

"What point is that? That they're late and wasting our damn time?" I kept my voice low, barely above a whisper, to avoid any nearby shifters from making out our conversation, but I could see my breath in the air.

"They're in control. It's a power move." He shrugged, eating another apple slice.

"Comparing dick size is no longer considered an acceptable power move, huh?"

"They'd lose," he said with a grin, flicking a seed away.

I chuckled. "Whatever they need to do to convince themselves. I just wish they'd power-move themselves here so I can go the fuck home where it's warm."

"Patience is a virtue, Adrian." The whirring of a boat sounded in the distance, getting closer. He glanced at me for a brief moment before focusing his attention on the waters of the East River. Manhattan was on the other side, equally as gloomy and quiet. It didn't emit the light pollution that it used to, but the buildings still stood high.

New York and the outer boroughs had always been heavily populated, long before the supernatural syndicate ruled New York City. Some areas had been poverty stricken;

11

others dripped with so much wealth the streets may as well have been plated in gold. Most of its inhabitants had lived somewhere in-between. Now? The middle didn't exist.

"No, it's not," I scoffed, looking around again. If the boat was approaching, then the Wards should be close. "Why does everyone say that, anyway? And who the hell cares about virtues? You look around lately? Virtues will get you killed in this world. So will vices, but lust is at least worth a conversation." I smiled wide, winking at him.

"Yes, we know. Everyone that knows you, *knows*."

"Have to find something to do with my time in this shit-hole city."

"Going on a date with me isn't enough?" He nodded toward the dinner boat that was almost to our location.

"Only if you promise to cuddle afterwards."

Niall began to respond, but a shiver came over his body as he tilted his head to the side and cracked his neck. As I started to ask what happened, a violent chill hit me, and I did the same, feeling a strange sensation suddenly crawl over my skin. It had nothing to do with the cold.

Whatever it was called to my senses, tugging at deeper and baser instincts. The scent of the water became stronger. The taste of the air on my tongue heightened. As an earth fae, I was always in tune with nature, but this was something else entirely. An invisible force pulling me away from this place and in another direction, enticing me.

"Did you feel that?" I whispered, taking my hands from my pockets and rubbing one over my arm where the hair stood on end beneath my clothes.

A frown formed between Niall's brows as he looked down, seeing the same physical response on his body. A wave of iridescent color shimmered across his hands before returning to normal. He hummed in what seemed like agreement, but also in question as he tossed the apple aside, then pulled gloves from his pocket and put them on.

"Yup." He smoothed out his coat around the wrist, clearing a spot in his throat while he looked down the corridor of shipping containers. "We'll have to analyze it later. They're here."

As he said the last word, several cars appeared around the corner and headed toward us.

"About fucking time," I muttered. "I hate dealing with syndicate assholes."

Niall cocked an eyebrow. "Says Adrian Rose, the Prince of Brooklyn."

I didn't care if Brooklyn was ruled by the fae syndicate. It was still a title I didn't want.

"Piss off." My best friend only chuckled in response.

Being a Rose had its perks, but I couldn't care less about the families and the syndicates. I didn't want to be involved with the 'business' and I had no desire to lead a bunch of criminals. Thankfully, being the middle son, I wouldn't have to. Not unless I challenged my older brother, and that wasn't going to happen. Just because I had the power didn't mean I wanted to use it. I didn't even want to be doing the deals with Niall, but someone had to represent the family and he didn't have the blood to do it.

He was a shifter hybrid with no family, no pack, no House, and no affiliation to speak of.

In other parts of the world, if he didn't find sanctuary in one of the eight Houses, he'd be on his own in No Man's Land—an area with no jurisdiction or protection from a House. That's what New York was now. Just one big No Man's Land ruled by the supernatural syndicates. We bordered territory with the House of Earth and Emerald, and syndicate leaders already had plans in motion to expand.

I didn't want to be involved in the inner workings of a Mafia run city, but I was born into it—and I wasn't stupid. I could see the writing on the wall. One day they'd start a war. I just hoped I was dead and gone when it finally happened. Earth and Emerald had territory on almost every continent. They had allies. Access to nearly every portal. They had more members with power than the whole of the boroughs combined. The syndicates changed allegiances like the wind changed direction.

Which is why Niall was the only asshole I trusted in this place.

He was brilliant, but a bit fucked in the head at times. His loyalty was absolute, and his ambition made up for my lack thereof. Still, no matter his intelligence or raw power, he was a half-breed in the eyes of the other supernatural syndicates, especially the shifters.

While many hybrids were accepted there, Niall was far from welcome in the Wards' territory. The prejudiced fucks thought he needed to earn his place first. An impossible demand if there ever was one, but that didn't stop Niall from reaching for it. While Phaon saw him as an abomination, my family saw opportunity. We were the dream team when it came down to making deals.

My name went a long way and got us in places he couldn't go on his own otherwise. Which was good because I got us where we needed to be with a modest amount of effort on my part, and his ingenuity gave the Rose syndicate what they wanted.

Control. Power. The usual.

From the outside looking in, one would think Niall wanted the same. The reality was he just wanted to see his mate again, and everything we did was to get him closer to her—including the deal we were making with the shifter don, Phaon Ward.

Me?

I wanted the bare minimum.

In no particular order: An unrealistic romantic comedy film. Aged whiskey. A good lay. Cake.

And to be left alone.

Right now? I'd settle for getting the fuck out of here.

The dinner boat cruised in next to the docks, then anchored itself, waiting for the rest of the party to arrive.

"Could they drive any slower?" I said through clenched teeth. "This isn't a power move. It's just fucking rude."

Their cars pulled to a stop near us, and the doors opened.

Phaon Ward exited the back seat of an SUV, buttoning his long overcoat and adjusting his cufflinks before he approached.

Cufflinks at a midnight meeting. What a prick.

"Adrian Rose," he said in greeting as we shook hands. He glanced at Niall, nodding once but not touching him. "Niall."

"Phaon," he responded casually as though neither of us had noticed the leader of Manhattan was almost twenty minutes late. "Pleasure, as always."

Pleasure, my ass. Niall had it out for the Mafia leader more than he had it out for those that had wronged him in his past.

His mate was Phaon's daughter, and he wanted nothing more than to be near her again. The years of separation had significantly strained his power and control. All supernaturals that had mates were pulled to them, but shifters had a connection to an animal—and animal desires ignored logic. I didn't know how any of it felt. I didn't have a mate.

I'd promised my best friend that I would do anything I could to help him get to her again. Including working deals to give us intel and leverage on Phaon and the shifter syndicate. Every move we made was calculated.

Tonight's exchange was no exception.

"There's been a change of plans, gentlemen," the Mafia leader began, gesturing to the vehicle fleet. "Alexander couldn't make it tonight, I'm afraid."

It didn't take me long to figure out there was more to his statement, and I groaned internally.

Niall's nostrils flared when the car door opened, indicating he'd caught the scent.

Ty Ward was here.

Most of the time, we dealt with Alex, and while neither Niall nor I liked any of these people, we preferred him. He was still a Ward, but he was the more levelheaded of the brothers. Ty on the other hand . . . well, I could go a lifetime of never seeing him again and it would still be too soon.

"I didn't realize he was needed to complete our transaction, Phaon. Are the shifters losing trust in the Roses?" I asked, trying to understand what game he was playing.

"Of course not," Phaon answered with a crooked smile. "That would imply there was trust to begin with."

Touché, motherfucker.

"Evening, boys," Ty drawled, shutting the door after he exited the car. The sound echoed around us, lacking any tone whatsoever. Half a dozen of his foot soldiers got out of various vehicles and followed.

"Ty," I greeted, walking toward him. "Been a long time. Didn't expect to see you here."

"Well, you know how much I like surprises." Extending

his hand to shake mine, I reluctantly accepted, then inclined my head in the direction of the men that came with him, acknowledging them as my form of hello.

"Don't we all?" Niall said casually, shaking his hand and looking at Ty as though his presence wasn't thoroughly unwelcomed.

I didn't like surprises.

I hated them.

And I despised this one.

Niall didn't care for it either, but you couldn't tell from his calm demeanor.

Whatever weird sensation that had happened right as Phaon showed up began buzzing across my skin again . . . Niall's too. He tilted his head to the side as though he was stretching his neck, but I saw the action for what it was.

The feeling crept over my body, keeping me on edge in an already twisted situation.

"Incoming," Niall muttered under his breath. The final car arrived, completing our dinner party.

Its occupant was another reason I hated dealing with this group. No, I didn't like this particular pack of shifters. I didn't like anyone in the syndicates. And I especially didn't like the fae I had to be involved with. More specifically, *this* fae.

Seconds later, I caught her scent.

She'd exited the car and came toward us, her hand in her back pocket. Her bright red, high ponytail swished as she walked.

A high fae with stunning cheekbones and cruel eyes.

An ex.

"Jackie," I greeted her through clenched teeth.

"Adrian. Niall." She winked at him when she walked by, her associate following her footsteps.

KEL CARPENTER & AURELIA JANE

Her scent had once appealed to me, but now my body reacted in a new way. It wasn't pleasant. It was repulsive and visceral.

The humming sensation on my skin felt like it was pressing deeper. Tiny needles, stabbing. Revolting against her sickly-sweet scent.

"Right. Shall we?" Niall asked, heading toward the boat, and not wasting time for small talk.

The electric humming over my skin worsened like the adrenaline rush prey felt when they realized a predator had spotted them.

But this was beyond the sense of being stalked.

Make no mistake. I knew we were being watched. I just didn't know by who. Or why. Ty being here made me think it was an ambush. I had to assume I wasn't the only one making that connection.

It would be a fucking mistake on the Wards' part, but not all that surprising.

After we'd boarded, Phaon's foot soldiers followed, and everyone spread out to their respective posts.

Follow the plan. Make the exchange. Have dinner. Leave.

That was all we needed to do.

The drug we had would give them an edge for a little while. For us, it was just a means to an end. Not addictive, but one hundred percent sketchy all the same.

It was a formula Niall had worked out that when used, would leave the user in a state to be temporarily controlled. We'd led them to believe it could be altered to be long-term, but it wasn't true. We were all monsters, but some of us were worse than others.

By the end of the night, we'd have more leverage against this shithead.

Like the drug, we'd have temporary control over them. They just didn't know it yet.

I leaned against the railing at the back deck, looking at lower Manhattan, then perusing the water's surface.

It was mostly calm. A duck floated nearby, moving along with the current. Odd for the time of year, but not unheard of. There would be no reason to give it a second glance, were it not for a brief metallic reflection beneath its feathers.

A sense of wariness crept over my body. I kept my mouth shut, scanning the rooftops and shipping containers nearby.

Everything felt wrong about tonight.

I wasn't the only one that noticed either. Jackie stood nearby, and she was laser-focused on the bird, though she didn't speak.

"We have company," a guard said, snapping his fingers and pointing toward the water.

Those three words sent everyone on the dinner boat into a battle-ready defense. The man Jackie had brought with her threw his hand out, controlling the water where the duck was floating. As it scrambled to get away, it found itself fighting against an invisible force before being enveloped in a liquid cocoon. The water fae lifted his arm, pulling the river out and into an arc, and the duck came crashing down with it.

Right before hitting the deck, it shifted.

A woman landed on her side, the thud resounding as she grunted on impact. Her face shimmered with a glamour, though I knew I was the only one who could see that.

Earth fae didn't often have that ability, but I did. My affinity for the earth grounded me so that I could only ever see the true nature of things. While I couldn't see behind the glamour, the unnatural presence blocked her features.

"What do we have here?" Phaon said, walking up to her as she sputtered water. He picked up the device that was attached to her side and inspected it. Satisfied with his assessment, he dropped it back on the ground and crushed it beneath his heel.

"Not one of yours, then?" I asked. The hairs on the back of my neck lifted, sending electric vibrations down my back. Whatever was watching us was still there.

"Not yet," Phaon said, a cruel edge entering his voice.

"She can be of good use to us. Bring her inside." A wicked smile crossed Ty's face as he spoke. The water fae grabbed her, yanking her up and dragging her as she tripped over her feet, still trying to catch her breath.

"What the hell for?"

Everything we had set up was simply leverage against Phaon Ward. While we couldn't guarantee no casualties, we were trying to side step them as much as possible. Getting this woman involved? Not part of the plan.

"To see what's so special about your supply. You'll inject her and prove it works." Ty shrugged. As he began to walk away, he added, "Why not use her for a little quality control?"

"The quality is good," Niall interjected, grabbing Ty's bicep to stop him. As he looked down where Niall held him, his features turned dark.

Under normal circumstances, I would be the one to calm Niall before he started getting angry and overreacting, but now, I was on edge. The feeling of whatever was nearby watching us was overwhelming, and it was distracting me. The tension brewing between them had gone on long enough.

I placed a hand on Niall's shoulder, gently squeezing as if to say *let it go*. Niall inhaled, nodding once. He released Ty's arm.

Ty postured himself in front of Niall, speaking in low tones. "Grab my arm again and I don't care what deals my father has in place with you. I'll take both your hands off before I take your head."

Phaon barked an order at his son, but Ty stared Niall down for a few seconds longer before he walked away.

Niall's body vibrated with rage, and I applied a firm pressure where I held him, digging my fingertips in.

Get in. Do the deal. Get out.

One step closer to his mate.

One more mark against Phaon.

That is all we needed to accomplish.

After sniffing, he nodded, tilting his neck to the side to crack it. Then we walked toward the cabin where they'd taken the woman.

She sat in a chair, a goose egg forming on her head and a bruise already showing on her cheek.

I stared at her, watching the shimmer of her glamour start to flicker. She had minutes before she'd be revealed. What the hell was she doing here, besides getting herself caught? The Wards would blackmail her into pledging allegiance, using her however they could. Her life would be a wreck, and if she had family, they'd suffer the consequences of her actions too.

That's how the syndicates worked.

They owned everyone, one way or another. If they didn't have their claws in you, it was only a matter of time.

Phaon broke the silence, addressing me and Niall. "The terms are still the same. There's no need to discuss it here."

21

We nodded, and Niall pulled a small leather bag from his coat, handing it over.

Jackie took it, sitting at a table to inspect the contents. She rummaged through a separate bag, pulling out a pouch of some sort before unfolding it. Syringes and needles.

When it was prepared, she flicked it with her finger a few times, then handed it over to Niall.

Seconds passed before he reluctantly accepted it.

"Go on," Ty urged. "Inject her."

The woman's eyes creased at the corners as concern filled her, but she refused to speak. As the needle punctured her arm, she inhaled sharply, turning her head away.

Phaon watched carefully, keeping equally as silent while he observed.

A glaze slowly appeared over the woman's eyes, and Ty smiled.

Leaning down and coming face-to-face with her, his grin widened. "Go drown yourself."

She stood up obediently and turned to the nearest exit.

Niall and I exchanged glances.

"What's the purpose of making her kill herself?" I asked, heading toward the deck before the woman made it there.

"Dead people can't talk." The lack of emotion in his voice was unnerving.

"Wouldn't you rather keep her on? Find out what or who she knows?" Her methodical steps echoed as she walked out of the cabin.

"Not really. She's more useful this way." Ty followed her movements, tilting his head to the side. "More enjoyable too."

If I'd hated Ty before, I hated him more now. Sick fuck.

I couldn't believe Niall's mate was related to these

people. It made me wonder if she was as screwed up as they were, but everything our sources said made her seem more like a bird with clipped wings. I understood why Niall was willing to go to such lengths to get her back. If they hadn't tainted her yet, I could only imagine what was going on at home. Phaon claimed to be a family man, but what father kept his daughter's mate away for eight years?

My hands tightened, rage rising from my gut to my chest.

Niall shook his head at me, reminding me that we had arrangements in place. We were one day away. One.

So fucking close to ending the mind games.

As the duck shifter came to a stop in front of me, I realized he was right. The moment I stepped out of the way, the creeping feeling buzzed over my skin, intensifying. An invisible line hooked into me, urging me to turn around.

I didn't know who or what it was, but every fiber in my being demanded I find out.

On a rooftop in the distance, I saw her. Hunched down, holding a bow and arrow.

As she let that arrow loose, I grabbed Niall.

"Time to go."

CHAPTER 3
NIKKI

SAM AND I HUSTLED IN THE SHADOWS, KEEPING OUR FOOTSTEPS swift but light as we headed to where we had two other lookouts.

Delta and Echo were stationed at an abandoned building closer to the pier.

"Here—"

A soft voice startled me, causing Sam and I to dodge to the left, away from the voice. I swung blindly on instinct. My fist connected to a chin with a thud.

Pain exploded in my knuckles right as I saw Delta's face. He swallowed his grunt, glaring at me and obviously trying to keep quiet so we didn't give away our position.

"Oh shit—crap—I'm sorry," I mouthed, grimacing and shaking out my throbbing hand.

He stepped back into the darkness, and Sam and I huddled next to him. Delta placed a finger over his lips, choosing to use sign language so we could communicate without being heard.

Why is Ty here? he asked.

Shaking my head, I signed, *"I don't know. He wasn't supposed to be."*

"We saw him and came over here as quickly as we could," Sam added.

Delta nodded. *"Did you see Jackie arrive too?"*

Sam and I exchanged worried looks. No, we hadn't. This just kept getting worse and worse.

"Ty plus Jackie means we should go," she said.

Delta's face contorted in frustration, showing his displeasure. *"We still need the intel, Sam."*

"It's not worth it. This just got bigger than we expected."

Delta sighed after a moment, agreeing reluctantly.

Sam looked around, then signed, *"Where is Echo?"*

"On the roof," he answered, glancing above him.

As soon as he said it, a pebble hit the top of my head, and I shielded myself with my hands as I looked up.

Echo leaned over the edge, her eyes wide, motioning for us to come to her. She signed for Delta to stay as a lower lookout. A frown formed between my brows, and fear coiled within me, constricting my insides.

Delta's lips pressed into a hard line, but he dipped his chin and brought us over to a hidden entrance to the three-story building. We ducked down to enter, then found the nearest staircase, running up two steps at a time until we got to the top.

Echo was crouched near the ledge, out of sight from anyone near the docks that could be looking this way. She waved us over and we shuffled toward her, keeping our bodies hunched down.

The corner of Echo's eyes twitched. She stared at Sam intensely. Placing her finger over her lips, she handed us binoculars and gestured for us to look.

It didn't take long to see what the problem was.

Through a window into the cabin, Lindsey sat in a chair, and one of the unknown supes they'd been meeting with stood in front of her, holding something in his hand.

Sam released a choked breath and began shaking. Her heartbeat thundered so loudly, I could hear it.

"Don't shift, do you hear me?" I whispered harshly, holding her shoulders. "We don't need you tearing through Brooklyn in a rage right now."

"They have my fucking mate, Nikki."

"And you are the only known shifter that turns into a saber-toothed tiger. If you out yourself as a member of the militia, they're coming for your entire family. The kids included. Death would be a gift if Ty got ahold of them." I hated the truth of the words. I didn't want to say them, but a harsh reality was needed to keep her in check. Softening my voice, I added, "Sam, they don't know who she is yet. Her glamour is still intact."

"Barely," Echo said quietly, peering at the scene through her binoculars. "She looks dazed, you guys. He injected her with something. If you have a plan, now's the time."

We needed a way to get her out without revealing ourselves, and the only way I could do that was a distraction.

I mentally ran through the list of stuff we had on hand. We couldn't get too close to the boat or we'd be caught, so this distraction needed to happen from afar.

I leaned over slightly to get a good view of the docks. There were rows of metal shipping containers.

Multiple cars.

The dinner boat.

Minimal targets.

"She's walking toward the edge of the boat." Sam's

voice wavered as she quietly updated me. "She's under a spell or something."

Kneeling down, I opened my backpack, rummaging to find two very small explosive devices. They weren't big enough to level a building or anything, but they were enough to cause some damage.

Thoughts of fire and flame ran through my mind. Given my shifted form, I might have had a small fascination with things that went boom. The music to *Mulan* started to play in my mind, as though I'd had a plan already and my subconscious decided to share it with me.

There wasn't a firework supply to blow up, but I'd packed two explosives with me.

Sam and I made eye contact, and though fear was riding her, I knew she trusted me—even if she didn't like half the ideas I came up with.

"I need your bow," I whispered to Echo. Her brows pinched together.

She handed it over, giving me her quiver, but I waved my hand in a "no" and held up a finger for two. Tilting her head, she looked down to my bag as I pulled out the two small explosives and understanding hit her. I only had two chances.

"Aim higher to account for the weight," she said, while mimicking the motion. "Like I taught you."

Sam placed a hand on Echo's shoulder. "Grab Delta and get out of here. We'll meet you at the rendezvous point. You have a head start, but don't slow down. The second those charges go off they'll be coming for us. You need to be out of range."

Echo dipped her chin. "Good luck," she mouthed to me before she crouched and ran.

Sam looked at me as she quickly strapped the explosives to the arrow. "Where are you aiming?"

"First shot, by the boat. I don't want to kill everyone on board. I need to rock it and blow a hole in the side so Lindsey ends up in the water again. Hopefully she can take advantage of it and go from there."

"The second?"

I shrugged. "I don't want to hit the pier or one of the cars and deter them from leaving. That might encourage Ty to stick around and try to find her again."

Peering over the ledge, she ducked back down. "There's an old trash barge about a hundred yards from where they are. Hit that. It's half sinking already, so it should be empty."

"Got it." I tested the weight of the arrow so I could try to mentally calculate how to adjust the arc. "Two quick shots, then we bolt."

Sam nodded.

Closing my eyes and taking a deep breath, I steadied myself. "Okay," I breathed out, moving into position. Lining up my shot, Sam lightly touched the device, moving her finger in a quick pattern to activate it.

As I set my aim, one of the two strangers at the meeting turned around. He stared right at me as though I'd lit a beacon and called to him. Even through the dark and the distance, he'd found me.

But he didn't move. Didn't raise the alarm. He just watched.

Maybe he didn't see me, after all.

The arrow arced high in the night sky, crossing the space between us and my target while I quickly grabbed the next arrow and loaded it.

A tiny splash in the water sounded before a thundering

blast boomed beneath the surface. She repeated the activation process, and I aimed for the barge, letting that arrow loose as quickly as I could.

The dinner boat rocked hard to the side. Ty, my father, and his men were scrambling in the chaos. Someone had been knocked into the water and a fae was wielding their magic to pull them out. As the bomb hit the barge, it exploded, sending shrapnel in every direction.

I didn't see Lindsey amid the chaos, but hopefully no one else did either. The syndicates were focused on me, just like I wanted.

She was a duck. She had either taken flight or was swimming to a hiding spot.

"Go!" Sam whispered harshly as we took off across the building rooftop and ran down the stairs. In the distance, we could hear the commotion as Ty and my father shouted demands.

We hustled, putting as much space between us and them as we could, trying to get to the nearest safe house.

Sweat beaded down my back. My lungs burned. The heavy weight of my backpack smacked against my back with each step.

Then my skin felt like it was on fire.

I gasped, tripping over my feet when the overwhelming intensity of the sensation distracted me.

Sam came to an abrupt halt, grabbing my elbow and hoisting me up.

At that moment, we heard it. Voices. And they were getting closer.

Shit.

I met Sam's eyes, and she gave me a hard glare.

"Split up," she whispered harshly. "You. Walt Whitman park."

I nodded, taking off while she went in the opposite direction. My feet pounded against the concrete, and I hoped like hell no one was out right now that would give me away to anyone that might follow my path.

The homeless populations lived in warehouses and abandoned buildings. Not that those locations were safe, but they were safer than staying outside when the syndicates patrolled the boroughs.

A crawling sensation made its way over my arms and up my neck, and I picked up speed.

My pursuer was easily as fast as me, which wasn't exactly hard. I was quick for a shifter, but not exceptionally so. Fae were even faster. I was cursing myself for being out in the open on a cold, winter night. Slowly that itch on my skin began to tickle the edge of my thoughts, finding a way to whisper in my head as though it was a real entity, but I couldn't make out the words.

I clapped my hands over my ears like it would stop whatever magic was trying to creep in.

Nope.

I was noping out of this weirdness.

I wasn't going to make it to the park, but I needed speed to put distance between us.

As I approached my turn, I looked at my watch and changed directions, instead heading toward the High Street station. I had one minute until the next train arrived. Then I had a very short ten seconds between those doors opening and closing.

Anxiety thickened in my throat. I hated the subways. They were their own sort of territory within the boroughs that no syndicate could control. Instead, rogues and gangs claimed them, which made hitching a ride on one a bit like Russian roulette. I never knew if I'd get robbed or murdered from one stop to the next. They were never a first choice for travel, but I packed with this emergency exit in mind after being jumped in the past. I could pay for safe passage, if needed, though it would cost me dearly.

That was the least of my concerns.

I hated being confined in a magic rickety metal tin can. Trapped. Speeding through a tunnel under the East River, completely out of control of the situation.

I was a phoenix. Confined places terrified me. Add in small, dark, and dangerous? Yeah, no thanks.

Nausea and dread filled me, but my choices were limited. I had to get away from whoever was following me. If they caught up before I reached the station, there were good odds I wouldn't make it on that train.

Best case scenario would be that they weren't with the shifter syndicate, and they'd try to kill me. Worst case, they were shifter syndicate and they'd drag me back to my father and brother. I was well and truly screwed if that happened.

My brother loved me, but his cruel streak ran deep. While I'd never been the subject when his viciousness was at the forefront, my other brothers had. There was a first time for everything, right? I didn't want to find out how Ty would react if he knew I'd been involved tonight.

Subway it was.

If I could get there.

I heard whoever was behind me catch up, their foot-steps echoing between the buildings.

The thundering noise of the next train approaching rumbled through the enclosed station as I ran toward it. Holding the railing while I took the stairs so fast my feet barely touched the steps made me feel like I was flying.

Wheels screeched as the brakes forced it to an abrupt

halt that wasn't exactly safe, but it's not like there were laws in place to prevent that anymore.

I pumped my body as hard and as fast as I could, desperately sprinting for the subway car.

Something knocked my shoulder, sending an explosive burning through my veins as my legs felt like they crumbled beneath me. I rolled onto the ground, mere feet from my escape.

My pursuer caught up.

"Fuck," he growled, crouching down on one knee, breathing through pain as though I had somehow used my powers against him.

But I hadn't. *I couldn't.*

My power was tied to the sun. Underground in the subway stations without even the moon to give me a sliver of power, I was utterly useless.

Had it been a good decision to come out on a new moon?

Probably not.

Did it stop me?

Nope.

Did I have questionable intelligence?

Maybe. It was definitely worth a debate.

The fact remained I hadn't used any of my powers because they simply weren't available to me, and yet the heat that seemed to burn through my veins was there.

I scrambled up, trying to find purchase and give myself the momentum I needed to cross those last few steps to the subway car. The countdown until the doors closed had started.

Ten.

Nine.

"Wait," he said, getting up.

His deep voice sent intense vibrations through me, coating my skin in warmth, making my core constrict.

I ran through the doors, then pivoted to see where he was.

The answer was right behind me.

He stood, chest heaving, looking down at me. His sheer size dwarfed me and I wasn't just meaning height. He had a good foot over me, but his wide shoulders and thick arms more than hinted at his strong physique.

I'd never seen him before, but he definitely wasn't one of my dad's soldiers. Or even a shifter for that matter, despite his impressive size.

He was fae. Specifically the one meeting with my family on the pier.

Bright blue eyes practically burrowed in my soul. He was handsome; his sharp jawline shadowed in stubble. His curly black hair shimmered under the poor lighting, just a fraction of an inch from falling in his eyes. Contrary to myth, not all fae were pale and he was no exception. With sun-kissed skin that reminded me of the beach, I wanted to stand here and bask in him. His strength. His presence.

His beauty may have stolen my breath away, but it was the feeling that ran through me that made every part of my body and mind take notice. All the way from the tips of my fingers to the soles of my feet, heat that I've only experienced once before grounded me, stealing my ability to move.

I must have been alone in that because I stood there like a complete dumbass while he reached up and tried to pull off my glamour, as though it was some type of ski mask, and I felt the protective shield struggle to stay in place. My thoughts screamed in my mind. He shouldn't have been able to do that. This wasn't natural.

The moment his eyes met mine, his pupils dilated, and my breath whooshed out as a whole new reality slammed into me.

Three.

I panicked, trying to reorient myself as seconds counted down.

I had to get away from him.

Two.

While he stood there staring at me, I shoved him in the chest as hard as I could. He stumbled back two steps. That's all my push had accomplished, but it was enough.

One.

The doors slid closed, creating a barrier between us.

He looked at me through the window, startled, searching up and down the line of subway cars to see if he could get on one of them.

I placed a hand on the glass as the cars jolted forward. Our eyes met once more, before the subway disappeared into the tunnel. My breathing slowed as the train picked up speed, carrying me, and only me, away from Brooklyn.

Away from my mate.

CHAPTER 4
NIALL

COLD NIPPED AT MY SKIN. I WOULDN'T HAVE REGISTERED THE slight sting at all, if not for the fine mist of ice that melted the second it touched me.

My beast was raging. Livid.

After everything I'd lived through, very little had the ability to make me truly angry. No single moment or action was capable of pushing me over the edge. Not with the tight leash I had been forced to keep on my magic.

I couldn't deny that my beast was more than a little peeved after the explosion on the boat.

My kind were known for explosive anger, but that wasn't a luxury we could afford. Not since we'd been hunted to all but extinction. I was only here because my hunters thought it better to cage me—use me—instead of killing me.

That was their mistake.

One I made sure they could never make again. There was no way to stop others from following in their footsteps. It was why tonight had been so risky to begin with.

If anyone found out *what* the drugs I'd been selling actually were . . . I shook my head. Damp strands of dark hair stuck to my skin as I tore through the streets of Brooklyn with a single-minded purpose.

Find whoever caused the explosion.

Then make them talk.

The anger wasn't so much about the explosion itself or the inevitable fallout I'd have to deal with considering our exchange was blown to bits—literally and figuratively. The anger was due to the reason why I was even willing to work with the shifter syndicate in the first place.

Tonight wasn't about money. The product I was selling them was worth far more than the shitheads would ever pay, but that wasn't the point.

The negotiations. The terms. All of it was a ruse, but also necessary so they would believe this was a legitimate deal and not question what it really was for me.

Leverage.

With the explosion, my safety net to ensure that their leader, Phaon, didn't double cross me on another, far more important deal, quite literally went up in flames.

Adrian said it was a mistake to even attempt this. That the risk it posed to my beast being discovered outweighed any possible benefit.

He wasn't wrong that it was a high-stake deal.

He was just wrong that it wasn't worth it.

She was worth all of it.

Every bad deed I'd committed in the last four years. Every asshole I killed. Every casualty that got caught in the middle of it.

I knew that the Wards, the leaders of the shifter syndicate, would try to find a way to screw me over. They'd done it before.

But neither of us planned for such subtle subterfuge.

Where the fae weren't above such trickery, the shifters used brute strength. Most of them despised cunning. A duck in the water recording everything we said wasn't their style. But the odds of it being a lone shifter or group of rag tag thugs seemed too easy to be true.

Coincidences didn't exist.

Still, I couldn't argue that Ty seemed just as shocked as we were before and after the bomb went off. I didn't like him, but the bastard ran a tight ship. Very little went on in his syndicate without him knowing, or so I'd thought.

If that wasn't the case . . .

I couldn't let myself believe that. Not yet. Not without any sort of proof that made him all guilty or just less guilty. There was no such thing as innocent.

Not for men like us.

He either planted the duck shifter and was a better actor than I gave him credit for, or he didn't. In which case, there was a new party entering the scene in New York City's No Man's Land—and the timing couldn't have been worse.

I swallowed hard, tasting phantom blood on my tongue from the cold rage I was holding at bay. My feet thudded along the concrete streets. Shades of gray passed me, blustery from an icy mist.

I missed nothing as I surveyed my surroundings.

A piece of trash moved a few feet when the winds grew stronger. Open doors to abandoned buildings smacked against their frames in warning.

The high-pitched shriek of the incoming storm suppressed whatever noises the unknown figures might have made as they ran from the scene.

I cursed under my breath. Wherever the non-descript assailants had gone—I'd lost them.

The trail had run cold.

Beneath my feet, the ground began to shake and rumble.

A subway train was passing. The faint shrill of brakes grinding against hard metal rails told me it was incoming. We weren't far from a station.

I pivoted mid-step and took off toward the nearest entrance on a hunch.

Up ahead of me, two figures practically flew toward the stairs that led down. I recognized the curly black hair of the pursuer, even from a distance.

Smoke scented the air as I approached the gaping entrance of the stairway. Then a cloying aroma hit me, sitting on my tongue, lingering like warm spices. The scent felt familiar somehow, but I couldn't identify it when the sickly sweetness of oranges was attempting to scramble my senses.

They had to be wearing a scent blocker of some sort. Maybe even an expensive glamour, which added to the growing suspicions that we'd been set up. It was unlikely that some random people off the street could pay for a decent glamour, let alone one that could block scent. Over ninety percent of the boroughs were poor. Only those in power had the means to acquire such things.

Unless we caught one of them, it would be my word against the Wards. The shifters would be able to paint this however they liked because the word of a bastard with no name, no family, and no syndicate was worth about as much as dogshit.

Footsteps echoed from the underground tunnel. I sprinted after, taking the stairs two at a time. My chest seized as I inhaled deeply, trying to place where I recognized that underlying scent from. To pin it to a face or an animal or even a type of supernatural, if possible.

I rounded the corner just as the train doors snapped shut. Standing on the edge, shoe tips hanging just over the side of the platform, was Adrian.

The person he'd been following stood right on the other side of the reinforced glass. I didn't get a good look at their features, but the longer I tried to think about it, the more they shifted and changed in my memory.

Cold clarity made my muscles tense.

That wasn't just a half-assed glamour. That was the real deal. To not only fully disguise whoever the mystery person was while masking their scent was no small feat. But it went a step further. Whatever object they were wielding packed enough magic to leave even me disoriented and confused when trying to recall their face.

We weren't dealing with some petty thugs. These were professionals. People with enough money and power to cause a serious problem.

Yet another sign pointed to a syndicate, although I couldn't fathom what their endgame was. Anyone with the kind of money and resources these people had to afford a glamour like that didn't make it by keeping your hands clean. It wasn't possible. No one could.

So why ruin the product instead of stealing it? They were obviously aware of our meeting. If it was the shifters, wouldn't they have attempted to take the product before bombing the boat?

I shook my head.

There was something missing. A piece of the puzzle I couldn't see.

Focusing on Adrian, who was staring at the empty tracks, I walked up to his side.

"What the hell was that?" I demanded; a growl infused my words, making them sound more animal than man. "You had them. They were within reaching distance. Why didn't you grab them before the door slammed shut?"

Adrian didn't trip over himself with excuses or even attempt to defend his actions. On the contrary, he didn't respond at all.

With a posture as stiff and unmoving as the frozen concrete all around us, he stared into space where the subway had been moments ago. His face, which was normally set in a carefree mask, now showed fractured edges of emotion that I'd never seen before.

Thirty seconds passed before he finally spoke. The words came out in a deep rasp, as if it took all of his will to pull them from the place that he'd gone.

"My mate."

Shock stole my breath for a moment, followed by the closest thing to joy that I could muster. I couldn't feel it, not really, but I could feel *something*. To find one's mate was no small thing. It often took years, decades, even centuries.

Adrian was young for a fae; only eighty years old.

He'd lived long enough to remember the world as it was before. When humans still thought they ruled. Prey living their lives, completely oblivious to the monsters that surrounded them.

I was older than him by a few decades, but I'd never experienced the world before. I'd only heard about it secondhand or watched it in movies. The idea of a world that was a nicer, kinder place—even if only because it lived in ignorance—was little more than a daydream.

Then again, so was the thought of finding my mate. Until the day it happened.

It was almost like divine intervention. I was so incredibly close to giving up when she was dragged into the facility where I was kept. It was the happiest and hardest day of my life.

That was four years ago, and I hadn't been *allowed* to see her since.

Resentment blossomed whenever I thought about her. Bittersweet in the knowledge that she was here, in this city, but still out of reach.

"Did you recognize her? Him?" I prompted. Torn feelings trailed on the heels of being happy for him. Whoever they were, they were part of a group that ruined the deal I'd set in motion months ago.

And they'd struck at the most inopportune time.

"Her," he said, voice thick. "I—she—" He tried to talk but seemed to be struggling with the words. I understood that feeling. "I've seen her before, but I can't remember where. It's like the more I think about it . . ."

"The more you forget," I surmised. "She had one hell of a glamour on. Unless she was fae?" I only felt the slightest tinge of guilt for pushing him when he was still reeling from what would be one of the single most important experiences of his life.

"No, she—" he groaned, scrubbing a hand down his face. "Fuck. I don't know. I don't think she was, but I can't remember."

"Definitely a glamour then." Fae or a witch were the most likely if she was powering her own. To be Adrian's mate, she'd be powerful. No doubt about it. While he liked to play off his abilities, he was far more dangerous than he let people believe, particularly his parents.

"I think I would know it was her if I saw her again, but I

have no idea how to find her." Another emotion thickened in his voice. This one I was painfully familiar with.

Loss.

Adrian sympathized with me over the years because I'd struggled with my emotions surrounding my mate. She was drugged when we met. Out of her mind with terror. Then grief. Her father sent me away. Told me to become a man that he could respect. One that could take care of his daughter, if I ever wanted a hope of bonding with her.

Logically, I knew she was barely an adult at the time and I was more animal than man, but it still hurt that she never sought me out. That she never went against him. That she was right across the fucking river, but I couldn't have her.

Adrian made banal remarks that it was better to have one and know she's alive than not. He was right, but that didn't stop me from being pissed with him all the same over it.

I didn't believe in karma or cosmic justice, but the irony wasn't lost on me.

I clamped a hand around his shoulder and gave it a firm squeeze. I wasn't particularly good with affection or comfort. Having never experienced it myself, I struggled to give it to others. But for him, for this, I would try.

"Then we return to the docks. See if we can find any clues about who they were."

"And when we can't?" he asked, stiff with rising anger.

"Then I guess it's a good thing the trials will be announced tomorrow. Soon that pretty face of yours will be everywhere, and I'm sure your girl will make an appearance then."

Adrian was quiet for a moment. "She pushed me. She

ran. I wouldn't be so certain she's going to come looking for me."

"Well, when we have Earth and Emerald under our thumb, we'll use their resources to look for her. She might run, Adrian, but she won't be able to hide. Not for long."

CHAPTER 5
NIKKI

Twenty-four hours had passed and all I could think about was his face.

My mate.

The way he looked at me . . . he was certainly stunned, but he knew it too, right? He seemed like he did. That's how finding your mate worked.

Except, it shouldn't have. Not for me.

My mate—my *first mate*— had rejected me six years ago. Every time I thought about it my heart hurt. Malachi. My best friend. How could you spend your entire childhood with someone, grow with them, love them, and then just reject them when you find out they're your mate?

I could understand if he hated me or if I'd done something, but he didn't, and I hadn't. He even claimed the rejection process was just as painful for him as it had been for me, but that was hard to believe given he went through with it and then left.

Malachi had wrecked me.

The moment those words came out of his mouth I was

44

utterly devastated. My breath felt like it had been stolen. A future. A life.

Possibility. It had all been ripped away from me that day.

I hadn't accepted his rejection. I'd refused to believe it. What we had was real, and I knew that deep down.

But I was wrong.

Over time, I'd started to question if it had always been a one-sided love between us, and the thought of being my mate was too much for him to bear. Even if he didn't feel the same way before, the bond should have changed his feelings from platonic to very much *not*. We were best friends who could have been so much more.

But he walked away from all the possibilities we had and never looked back. I hadn't seen him since, and my heart still felt the phantom pains.

I just wish I knew *why* he'd rejected me.

I wanted to ask him one day, but the coward ran off after I refused to acknowledge his dismissal of what we were. Who knows how he'd react anyway. My brain told me I'd be a confident badass, walking up to him like I didn't care, and giving him a verbal smackdown.

It was nice to think about, but I was pretty sure that wouldn't be how it went down. My heart and mind still battled each other. I wanted to punch him and kiss him, but I wasn't sure which I wanted to do first.

Malachi aside, I just didn't get how I was able to have a second-chance mate when I hadn't severed the bond with my first. That wasn't just unusual. It was impossible. I needed answers, but there was no one to ask.

When I confirmed both Sam and Lindsey made it home after our wild chase through Brooklyn, I failed to mention some of those details about my escape. It wasn't something I wanted to chat about via text—encrypted or not.

Bringing it up to the rest of my family wasn't an option either.

I could talk to Gavriel, but the truth of it was that I didn't want to share it just yet. I wasn't in a place to process it. I just wanted straight answers. If I went to my favorite brother, it would turn into twenty questions.

Gavriel: *Where did you find your mate? Why isn't he here?*

Me: *Um . . . well, see, I went on that mission you told me not to go on because I couldn't help myself.*

Gavriel: *I told you, blah blah blah. Insert lecture about listening to my oh, so wise older brother.*

Me: *You were right that I was going to be caught because my power wouldn't work, but I'm not going to concede because I'm stubborn as a mule and would rather eat gravel than admit I made a mistake.*

Gavriel: *Sighs dramatic AF. How does your mate play into this?*

Me: *Turns out he was one of the fae making a deal with dad. Funny story right? So, I shot a homemade bomb at the boat they were on because they captured Sam's mate and injected her with some kind of mind control drug that made her try to drown herself. Anyways, shit kind of hit the fan. Some dude chased me down and was able to see through that really expensive glamour you got, and that's when the mate bond snapped into place, even though I never rejected my first one. Who knew? But don't worry. I didn't leave a glass slipper behind when I shoved him out of the subway car and ran.*

Gavriel: *I can't with you.*

Me: *Honestly, me neither right now.*

I snorted at the ridiculousness of it. So yeah, no, I was keeping that info close to my chest for now.

"Who's Nikki's escort tonight?"

"Hmm, what?" I asked, refocusing my eyes when I heard my name.

Alexander side-eyed me and shook his head slightly. Crossing my arms, I rolled my eyes.

He didn't want me to speak unless I was spoken to.

Figured.

Totally planned on throwing his favorite candies in the dumpster. I knew where he kept his hard-to-find favorites. Maybe I could put bread rolls in the bag to weigh it down. Or better yet, rocks.

I sat between him and Ty in the backseat of the SUV while one of my father's drivers took us to the annual winter solstice celebration, though I had no idea why we were going. The House of Earth and Emerald was hosting, but we were syndicate. While we were exceptionally well-known, we weren't recognized as anything official. Our presence at such an event wasn't expected, or even generally welcomed as far as I knew.

As if my nerves hadn't already been shot by coming face-to-face with my second-chance mate, hearing my brothers tell me we were going to this event was almost enough to give me a heart attack.

Were we party crashing? Because that sounded like a terrible idea. Maleficent party crashed in *Sleeping Beauty* and look how that turned out for her. She ended up looking like roadkill. Let's be real; some members of my family weren't above cursing babies—and I wanted no part of it.

"No escort. She's solo, and Sam is her bodyguard," Ty said, answering my brother's question. "Gavriel is escorting Mom."

They wanted me *solo*? And *Mom* was coming?

"Why are we going to this solstice celebration?" I

blurted out, ignoring Alexander's earlier suggestion to keep hushed.

"It's an election year for Earth and Emerald, and we've been invited to attend. Tonight they'll announce the candidates for the election trials."

"C'mon, Ty, you gotta give me more than that. In all the years we've been neighbors with them, none of the syndicates have ever been *invited*. Why us? Why now?"

While some Houses were ruled by gods, others were ruled by royalty, or even passed down their leadership through familial bloodlines. Earth and Emerald was the only democratic House, governed by someone elected to the position, advised by a council approved by its citizens.

Of all the places I had dreamed of running away to, that was the House. Not because we bordered one of their territories, but because it made the most sense to me.

Choice. Freedom. Having a say in how you lived your life.

"How would you know that?" Ty asked, raising an eyebrow. The car turned a corner, and I could see a building lit up a few blocks away.

"Common sense," I answered with a shrug. "And oh, I have these two things called ears that dad encourages me to use. Weird, I know, but they haven't heard anything about being invited to a single event hosted by *any* of the Houses in the last twenty something years, so . . . why are we going? You're not answering my question."

Ty's lips curled into a cruel smirk as he patted my knee. "Stop worrying. Like I said, we've been invited." If anyone else tried being that level of smartass with him, they'd need to sleep with one eye open. Ty might not be my favorite brother, but I was arguably the only person aside from our mother who was exempt from his wrath.

"I'm not worried."

Alexander snorted. "You're a terrible liar, you know that?"

Better liar than you think I am.

Just as we pulled to a stop, I huffed, acting as though they were right.

"Look, just do what Dad says, and tonight will go along fine, okay?" Alexander said quietly, and I turned to see him giving me a stern look that was somehow mingled with brotherly affection.

"I—What?"

Just as I started to speak, the doors opened on both sides. My brothers started to climb out, but as I scooted toward an exit, my father was standing at the door, and he slid in the back seat, closing the door, leaving just the two of us.

"Nikki," he said softly, smiling at me.

"Dad . . ."

"You look so beautiful tonight." I took a breath to respond, but I didn't get the chance to. His next words were a knife to my gut. "Just like your sister."

Wow. He had to go there.

We all missed Marissa. Every day. No one more than me. She was my twin. We'd shared a bond that no one else could understand. My soul had irreparably fractured the day she died. A piece of me had been lost and it could never be returned.

"Thanks . . ." I hesitated, biting my bottom lip, but deciding to push. "I don't understand why we're here. Ty and Alexander wouldn't tell me."

Grabbing one of my hands, he held it reassuringly. "That's why I wanted to talk to you."

"Okay . . ." My voice trailed off, waiting for him to say something more.

"Ashton Ward secured an invitation for our family to be here."

"Ashton is syndicate, though," I said, stating what he already knew. It was more a reminder for myself as I tried to understand. That sort of thing where you talk aloud to try and make sense of a situation.

He nodded. "Ashton's cousin is on the council. The syndicates felt strongly that since we neighbor Earth and Emerald, it would be beneficial for us to be involved with each other. Officially. We've co-existed peacefully for some time. We even provide a level of service when they need access to something we have, and oftentimes don't even charge them for it. It's time we do proper business with each other."

I wanted to scoff. The syndicates charged for everything. They wouldn't give anything away for free. The fact he was trying to play it off otherwise was insulting, but it wasn't my place to correct him.

"So . . . tonight is about a business deal," I said carefully. A business deal during their election year. Earth and Emerald would be announcing candidates after the solstice celebration. My entire family had been invited. And then it clicked. Closing my eyes, I sighed. "Which one of my brothers is running?"

My dad barked a laugh. "You've always been so keen," he said, squeezing my hand and patting it on top. "Alexander is going to join the trials. He'll be making his announcement tonight."

That didn't really come as a surprise. He was so level-headed and charismatic. He knew how to be a business-man. Or at least what I imagined a businessman would be.

You know, if we weren't syndicate and our idea of doing business with someone wasn't just chopping off a hand or blackmailing to get what we wanted. Torture was our motto. Not really, but it may as well have been.

My father didn't value Gavriel at all. He thought he was too much like our mother. Too soft. Too *weak*. Dad would never support him being in any position of power. And Ty was a psycho. Which brother had been chosen for this task made sense, but there were still several factors that didn't.

"I don't understand how Earth and Emerald is allowing this. We're syndicate. We aren't members of their House. I can't see how they would accept any of us joining the trials. If we made it through, they'd be running for their election."

"The syndicate leaders and I have taken care of some of those finer details. It's nothing for you to worry about."

"Other syndicate leaders are in on this as well?" I was getting all sorts of good intel right now. I couldn't wait to tell Sam.

"This move has been in play for a long time, Nikki. Longer than you can imagine." Dad's eyes became unfocused for a moment, as though he were lost in thought, but I couldn't afford for him to get distracted now.

"If Alexander is entering, does that mean that the other syndicates have someone running as well?"

"Of course; though, not all syndicates were willing to play nice."

Duh. We took our own territories in a world ruled by Houses. We weren't known for playing nice in the sandbox. Honestly, if anything, the syndicates were like spoiled children, more likely to throw sand at each other as opposed to sharing.

For the first time since forming the militia, the hopes I'd had and the progress we'd made felt imbalanced. We had ideals for change. That we could make a difference. The realization that we knew so very little was a daunting prospect. If the syndicates had this deal working behind the scenes for years, I'd missed it. We all had.

"There's like twenty-something candidates, right? How can you even guarantee that Alexander is going to win?"

"The syndicates and I have placed three other candidates in the competition. One of them will win." Of course they would. This was rigged. The other candidates didn't have a hope or prayer.

"And if Alexander doesn't win," I hedged, wondering which three we'd be dealing with. "Wouldn't that just be giving greater control to the other syndicates?" If my father disliked the idea of being ruled by a House, he hated the idea that another syndicate would have any say over him.

From what little he'd said, his plan was incredibly flawed and risky. I was surprised. He usually had a much better grasp of risk assessment. This seemed like a foolish grab for more power.

"That's where you come in."

Aw, crap.

Well that was an ominous response, and I didn't care for it. I held my breath. It felt as though minutes were passing rather than seconds.

"What do you mean?" I said, finally finding my voice again.

"You'll marry the winner."

My heartbeat stopped. Or did it pick up speed? I wasn't sure. My mouth fell open a little bit, but no words came out. The silence was deafening, but at the same time, I could hear the blood rushing through my veins.

"You've got to be kidding me," I choked out.

"When have I ever made jokes about business, Nikki?"

"You can't be serious. You want me to marry someone I don't know just because you've made a deal with some syndicate leaders?" I shook my head without thinking. "They won't even be a shifter, and we *both* know how you feel about that. What about finding my m—"

"Your sister knew that this was going to be her role one day. But she's not here. None of us were able to protect her." He stared at me intensely and I felt the weight of his words crushing down on me, as though her death was my fault. Like I hadn't tried to save her.

"She knew about this?" I whispered, taken aback.

"Of course she did. We prepared her."

"Then why didn't you prepare me?" I bit out. "You're telling me this now. Before we go *inside*. Even yesterday would have been better than *right now*."

"Fathers make mistakes sometimes, Nikki. I realized that all too late. Your sister knew for a long time. She knew our expectations. After everything that happened... I didn't want to burden you with the prospect of your future. Not when you were working so hard on trying to get over your past. I just wanted you to live in the present for a while."

"Then why would you do this? Why would you be willing to give me away to someone I don't know?"

"Because sometimes we're forced to make decisions that are difficult to swallow. You won't enjoy everything you have to do in life, but you will live and flourish because you're a Ward. Your hand in marriage will secure the alliance we need."

That was easy for him to say when he wasn't the one being auctioned off like a prized cattle. Probably a better idea if I kept those thoughts to myself.

"Which other syndicates are you working with?"

"The Roses and The Divine."

The Roses were the last name of the family that ruled the fae syndicate; their territory covering all of Brooklyn.

The Divine was the name celestial beings took to represent the angel and demon syndicate that ruled over Queens. Normally that group never got along. New York City was the exception.

I was honestly surprised. He was a speciest. He didn't value any other species or race. In his mind, shifters were superior in every way. The idea that he'd want me to marry a fae, an angel, or a demon instead of a shifter? It went against his own moral code. Looks like it was okay to lack the strength of his conviction as long as it got him what he wanted. Power.

It hurt to think about what my worth was as a woman in this family. He may not care for Gavriel, but my brother wouldn't be auctioned off. None of them would. He may emotionally abuse him, but having a dick between his legs granted him more worth than me, even though we were both family.

The truth stung, but there wasn't much I could do about it. No matter what I said, I knew I wouldn't be able to talk him out of it. I was just another pawn that had to do what he said. If my sister were here, she'd be doing it too, apparently. I would have held her hand through it, but there would be no one to hold mine. "Who are they? The candidates."

"The fae have put forth Adrian Rose and Niall Thorn."

I didn't know either of them, so I didn't know what to think. Adrian Rose was second in line to power in the fae syndicate. I figured if he was that high up, he was likely just as big an asshole as the rest of my family. I had a lot to look forward to. I hadn't heard the other name. Thorn was the surname of nameless orphans to the fae. Roses were also protected by their thorns. "Who is Niall?"

"The Roses' top enforcer. He's a shifter hybrid."

"What kind of hybrid?"

"Does it matter? His better half is shifter. His hybrid status renders him unable to take over any syndicate. He's high-ranking, Houseless, and loyal. That's all we need."

So that was Niall's bartering chip. He was a no-one in the supernatural syndicate. But if he won this election, he got to take over Earth and Emerald and he gained power within the syndicates. The bonus? He got me as a prize. Real winner right there. Whatever pity I might have felt for him being an orphan was diminished by the reality of the bargain he'd entered. No good man did shit like that.

This sucked. We were two for two on winning personalities.

"And The Divine?"

"Malachi Duarte."

If I lived a hundred lives, I never would have expected him to say that name again.

"The fuck?" I sputtered, forgetting myself for a moment. "He's gone. He left years ago . . ."

"He didn't leave; he just went away for a while. I knew where he was."

I had countless questions, but the only thing I could manage was blurting out in panic. "Why? Why would you do that? You never liked him. You *hated* him."

"As I said earlier, sometimes you're forced to make difficult decisions in life. Concessions had to be made for this to work. This is mine."

Oh, why didn't he say so? This makes it so much easier knowing he'd made a compromise and it was hard *for him.*

I wasn't a violent person by nature, but I felt like it right then.

My father had no idea that Malachi was my mate and that he'd rejected me. *Left me.* He had no idea the hurt and pain Malachi had caused, so there was no way he could know how much hurt and pain he was causing me now just by telling me I'd not only see him again—tonight—but that I might have to marry him.

For power. My stomach churned as bile threatened to climb up my throat.

"Where has he been since he left?" I asked quietly.

"Queens. The boy finally realized where he belonged and crossed over six years ago, then started moving through the ranks of The Divine. He's finally made something of himself, good for nothing half-breed that he is."

My dad's venom wasn't shocking. While terrible, it didn't hurt me the way it once had to hear him talk like that about my childhood friend. He'd never liked Malachi. But learning where he'd been all these years . . . I thought when he left that he'd truly escaped, maybe even traveled to another continent or world. To find out that fucker had been basically next door in Queens the whole time? Betrayal was an understatement.

"I don't want to do this."

"This election matters to me very much. Its outcome will change borders," he began, taking both my hands and cupping them between his. There was a firmness to his grip that didn't have a loving quality to it. "Your sister loved this family. She never questioned what was best. Do it for her, Nikki."

Those words didn't have the effect that he thought they would. Instead of touching that part of me that ached when I heard her name, it peeled back layers of an open

56

wound. I'd had four years to "heal"—whatever that was supposed to mean. What no one seemed to understand was that losing my twin sister was something that I would never recover from. That wound would always be there, a gaping hole in my chest that I had learned to survive with. Not live with, really. Just exist. By bringing her into this, he called attention to that hollowness and now I was angry.

No, my sister never did question him. She never questioned anything. Never went against the grain. My sister was the good girl. She fell in line, submissive and agreeable while she tried to earn our father's love and respect. She was born a void. Someone without real magic but one that could also stop others from using theirs. She had no animal and was closer to a low-powered witch. She tried so hard to be the perfect daughter and make up for something she had no control over. And look what good that did her. It was because of who we are that we were taken. Our family name is what got her killed.

As though my father could tell that my emotions were starting to ride me, a dark expression crossed his features. "All three of them are being announced tonight. I expect you to put on a smile." The silent threat of *or else* didn't need to be said. Hell would be enjoyable compared to my life if I defied him on something this important.

He dropped my hands and rapped twice on the window with a knuckle. One of his enforcers opened the door to let us out. After he exited, I followed. Sam waited for me by the door. Shoulders back and posture straight, she clasped her hands in front of her body. As my father passed, she dipped her head in respect.

A swarm of foot soldiers and enforcers surrounded him as he entered the building. My brothers followed Gavriel as he escorted our mom. Sam stood by my side as we trailed at the back of the pack silently.

As we walked through double doors into a grand room, my family began to filter out, doing the rounds. It was a political machination I was well acquainted with, given they'd raised me to listen and learn while wearing a smile.

"Oh look, food," I said, a little too loudly while I started walking toward an hors d'oeuvre table. Sam glanced at me but stayed by my side.

"'Oh, look, food?' That was the best you've got?" she asked, suppressing a smile.

"Shut up, I'm processing a lot at the moment," I mumbled, getting a plate and stacking snacks on it without paying attention to what I was grabbing. "My father just informed me that Alexander is going to join the trials to run for the chancellor seat in Earth and Emerald and it's being announced tonight."

Sam jerked her head in my direction. "What? How?"

"Oh, it gets better," I added, picking up an item from my plate and shoving it in my mouth. Something broke between my teeth, followed by a course and leafy sensation scraping my tongue. I grimaced and chewed through it painfully while looking at my plate. "What the hell did I just eat?" I ground out.

"A whole chocolate covered strawberry, green top included. And a toothpick."

My eyes widened while I chewed. "Is anyone watching me?"

Sam looked around. "A few."

"Mmm, so good!" I said, smiling and giving a thumbs up.

"Not helping," she muttered from the corner of her mouth. She raised her hand as though she'd made eye

58

contact with someone, then pointed across the room. "Now."

With a quick glance to see that people were looking at whatever they thought she'd pointed at, I sucked in a deep breath, and aimed at dark curtains nearby. With a low thwapping sound, I spit out the mouthful of toothpick skewered strawberry.

I was done before anyone saw me, wiping my lips on a napkin. This time, I properly inspected another berry before plopping it into my mouth.

"Want to tell me what happened that has you so jittery you just ate a stick?" Sam said, leading us away from people.

A waiter walked by, and I spied rock glasses with light pink drinks in them. Shoving my plate of food at Sam, I snatched a glass off a tray, then reached to grab another before the waiter walked away.

"Nikki, stop it. Your dad is going to kill me if you get wasted in public," Sam chided, trying to take one of the drinks out of my hand but I twisted away from her. "You said Alex is running for this election and now you're double-fisting drinks? What the hell is going on?"

"Nothing too terrible. Alex is running for the election. My dad has been working with The Roses and The Divine." I slammed one back and coughed, handing her the empty glass. Her lips parted in shock. "Oh, and apparently the deal he made for their alliance included me marrying whoever wins the fucking election. Cheers!"

I slammed back the other drink before she could stop me.

"This is vodka. I hate vodka," I coughed, then looked around. "I need another one."

Sam reached over and set the plate and glass on the

high table. Turning to me, she took my elbow and pulled me in a different direction. "You don't need another one, and you're drawing attention to yourself. Try to chill for a second and explain to me what you mean by 'you're marrying whoever wins?'"

"It's rigged, Sam. Under the table deals have been made. Someone in Earth and Emerald is helping to pull the strings. The syndicate are going to win, one way or another. And if Alex doesn't, I'm supposed to marry whoever does." I held my stomach, feeling nauseous. "Ugh, this is like a movie, but the kind that doesn't have a happy ending. It's the kind where you are left slack-jawed and trying to figure out what you just wasted two hours of your life watching."

Was I having a panic attack? I thought I was starting to.

"Who are the candidates?" She looked around casually, but I knew she was taking in the entire room with one sweep, keeping guard.

"The fae are putting in Adrian Rose and some enforcer named Niall Thorn." I inhaled through my nose, exhaling through pursed lips.

"Adrian Rose, as in the second son?" Her eyebrows shot up in surprise.

"Yup. That's the one."

"What about The Divine?"

I'd been tracking a waiter's movements and seeing him come closer, I reached over and grabbed another glass of what I assumed was vodka as he passed us by.

"Nikki," Sam hissed, trying to take it from me as I tilted my head back and drained it in one go. "That isn't going to help you at all."

"Fucking Malachi," I ground out in a thick voice. Thick from swallowing a burning liquid. Definitely not thick with emotion.

Sam's arm dropped to her side, and she was no longer concerned with me taking drinks. "*What*? Malachi is back?"

"Funny thing—ha ha—he never left. He's been in Queens the whole time."

Sam's features softened, and she rubbed my arm. "Shit, Nikki. Are you okay?" I side-eyed her while trying to take deep breaths. "Right. Stupid question, sorry."

"I don't know what to do, Sam."

"We'll figure it out. Together. The trials last a while before they declare a winner," she said in a barely audible whisper. "Maybe it's time we considered"—she sighed —"Operation Sunnyside."

I knew it pained her to repeat what I'd affectionately named our backup plan. Operation Sunnyside was our escape from Manhattan. Permanently. It was similar to when the toys escaped the Sunnyside daycare in *Toy Story 3*. It was costly, and so dangerous it was more like a loosely drafted story outline than what I would consider an actual "plan." I had fun thinking about it, and I had fun naming it, but it wasn't really something we thought we'd use. For once, I was willing to entertain it.

I nodded, smoothing out my dress, and bringing my shoulders back. "Yeah, maybe. You're right. We have time. I just have to smile and get through the announcements. Not like I'm getting married tonight. I can do this."

"Exactly." Sam rubbed her palm over my back in a soothing motion as we walked through throngs of guests. "Just ease up on taking whole drinks as shots and try to look before you end up eating a houseplant."

Chuckling softly, my lips turned up in a smile as I looked at her. "I'm glad I have you as a best friend. I don't know what I'd do—"

My body stiffened when I spotted a familiar face across

61

KEL CARPENTER & AURELIA JANE

the room. Tingles spread over my skin, ice cold and fiery hot all at once.

"Oh god. Oh, shit . . ." Panic attack returning. "He's here."

"Is it Malachi?" Sam asked, scanning the room.

"No, the guy that chased me to the subway last night." I swallowed thickly, my mouth going dry. "My mate."

"Your fucking *what*?" A waiter walked by, and Sam grabbed a pink drink, slamming it back the same way that I had earlier. She gripped my hand pulling me toward an exit. "Start talking. Now."

CHAPTER 6
MALACHI

I ABSOLUTELY DESPISED PARTIES.

While they were an opportunity to schmooze and find allies, they also served as a brutal slap in the face, showcasing the opportunities and luxuries I'd been denied in my childhood.

Standing tall at six foot five with my cropped ears on display and wearing a custom-tailored suit that was specifically made to accommodate my tail, you'd never know that I was once little more than an abandoned orphan, starving on the streets of Manhattan. That I'd been five feet tall until I turned sixteen, then I suddenly sprouted like a weed. It was about that time that I noticed the occasional looks Nikki would give me. I pretended not to. Now, I wished I hadn't. I wondered if we'd be here today if I didn't play it so safe.

We'd never know.

"Stop staring like that," Tylea said.

"What?"

"You're staring like, hella hardcore. You look two seconds away from murdering someone," she chided.

"That's not going to do you any favors. You're supposed to be schmoozing, remember?"

Schmoozing. Yeah. I think I hated that word almost as much as *moist*.

Internally, I cringed.

"I am." Sort of. Not really. I was existing. Wasn't that close enough? Getting to know these people didn't matter all that much. I was here for one reason and one reason only.

To throw my name into the fire and run for Chancellor of Earth and Emerald. Was it a position I wanted? No.

It was a position I *needed*.

Regardless of how nicely I played with the other members of the House or even the leaders of other syndicates, their opinions would matter little to none. When it came down to it, Earth and Emerald was run democratically.

The people decided the chancellor, and whoever got the majority vote won. It really was as simple as that. Phaon was firm in the belief that he could somehow sway the election. I wasn't so convinced.

Earth and Emerald had been around a long time; almost as long as the Roses had been in power. They were one of the oldest and most affluent families in the western hemisphere, which allowed for an easy transition from wealthy elites to No Man's Land mobsters once the human government fell apart.

Earth and Emerald came along about the time that America had been "discovered" by the Europeans and they had established themselves strategically as the colonies gained their independence. Yeah, I know those things had an almost three hundred-year gap in-between, but when dealing with immortals, three hundred years was a blink of the eye.

My point was, I didn't need to get on with all of these supernaturals. I just needed to win.

"Uhh huh," Tylea said under her breath. "Well, you're not going to be winning anyone's vote by standing there, glowering at people. Even if you're not going to make nice with the leaders, you should at least look charming. Approachable. People always rally around someone that's charismatic."

My second was a true pain in the ass. But she was my pain in the ass.

Yes, I was annoyed at what she said, but that didn't make her any less right. That was the reason I had appointed her as my second, after all.

"Fine," I grumbled, swallowing the last bit of whiskey neat. I barely felt the burn that followed. "Do the rounds. See what you can overhear. I'll go play nice and fetch us more drinks."

"Mine's not empty," she said, holding up the gin and tonic. I took it from her and drank the rest in one gulp. She crossed her arms and shook her head at me.

"Now it is."

"I can't with you."

"You can. That's your entire job. Now go do it."

She sniffed haughtily and turned on her heel in mock offense. I saw the smirk peeking through that showed she wasn't all that peeved. Her long red hair trailed down her back as she walked away. I caught several people staring at her as she passed, openly ogling her unique appearance. She wore a dress with a low cut back, allowing her one black feathered wing to be unrestrained while showcasing the heavily scarred tissue where her other had been ripped out of her back.

Many angels would have died from such an injury. Most angels would prefer to kill themselves rather than remain flightless. Tylea was a child when the incident happened, but instead of caving to what her kind told her she should feel—she chose to take a different path.

Some people hid their scars, but not Tylea. She didn't treat them as if they were a weakness. She treated them as if they were a story. Her story.

A glamour would have let her fit into supernatural society without all the looks and whispered judgments, but she never wanted to cover herself up to make others more comfortable. She'd already had her wing stolen, she didn't deserve to lose her identity for someone else's sake.

I admired her for it. Especially on nights like this, when the rumors would be as strong as the alcohol they served. I watched her pretend to bump into someone. One of the Earth and Emerald council members.

An owl shifter, if memory served.

The councilor turned to excuse her apology when she caught sight of her wing. Pity crossed her features. Tylea pretended not to notice, using the opportunity to capitalize on the woman's softness for our gain.

I let out a low chuckle and shook my head. As I started for the drink table, the atmosphere thickened. A charge I hardly recognized stirred to life after remaining dormant for too long.

My breath caught in my chest when the most stunning sight caught my attention, literally stealing my breath away.

A woman so beautiful, her face could have been carved by a goddess. Long lashes framed eyes so dark, they appeared black. I knew from experience that if I got closer, I'd actually see changing colors in their depth. Blue like the deepest ocean. Green of the darkest forest. Red that was only a touch darker than blood. Her eyes changed like the shifting of the wind. Wild and unpredictable, much like her.

Her hair was longer than the last time I'd seen her, but still the exact same shade of dark chocolate. It framed her face in loose curls, soft and feminine.

Then her scent hit me. Frankincense. Cinnamon. Cloves. Heavy, warm spices. It might feel overpowering to a lesser being, but it called to me, unlike many females that smelled sweet or sugary.

Nikki Ward was anything but.

She stood off to the side of the room, speaking to a remarkably tall young woman with long blonde hair pulled back into a tight ponytail, dressed in a simple yet fitted suit. I vaguely recognized her face from before I'd left the shifter syndicate, but I couldn't place it. Her bodyguard, I presumed.

The way she angled herself toward Nikki speaking in low tones while surveying the floor for danger told me my guess was right.

I hadn't laid my eyes on her in six years, and they were the longest years of my life. I stood there staring at her dumbfounded with leaden feet. They weighed me down as if I were strapped to concrete. My emotions warred.

Awe filled me as I took in the woman she'd become, but it was followed by irreparable sadness that while she was clearly the same Nikki, she also wasn't. There was a strength to her eyes that she didn't have before. A guarded expression. Her jaw was more angled now; the last bit of innocent roundness that had filled her young cheeks had diminished as the years had passed.

She was sharp angles and hard edges.

I'd heard about Marissa. I knew that her twin had died, and I had to assume that was the reason why she'd changed so much. It killed me not to come back when I'd found out, but I stayed away because her family told me to. Gavriel said it was better that way.

I didn't ask Phaon. He would have killed me if I'd set foot in his territory again. No matter what I wanted, I didn't need to cause her more problems when she was grieving.

Gav was her favorite brother. She trusted him—and she never was the trusting type. Though I didn't put my faith in any of the Wards, her closeness to him meant he was reliable. He seemed to love her more than anything, so I took it to heart when he said I shouldn't show my face. That she was too distraught. Too fragile.

If she had been that weak at the time, you'd never know it looking at her now.

The woman that surveyed the ballroom like it was a pit of vipers was not the soft, wild child that I knew. Wrapped in a delectably sinful dress that showcased the arc of her breasts and wide hips—she definitely wasn't the girl I'd left.

Nikki turned and walked away from the blonde without seeing me. I couldn't help but follow her, never taking my eyes off her.

The last time I saw her she was newly eighteen. Still so young; barely an adult. She was filling into herself. Finding herself. Figuring out the world.

While she'd always had a lovely ass, it never looked quite as good as it did now, hugged in the black satin of her gown. Just below her hip all the way to the hem that barely dragged the floor, it flaunted the curve of her thick thighs. My hands curled into fists, unable to stop myself from imagining what my fingers would feel, digging into her skin.

The sleeveless dress left her arms and neck bare. Light scars peppered her skin that weren't there before. I didn't like them. Not for vanity reasons, but because I hadn't been there. The only thing marking her body should be *me*. I wondered what caused them and if it had anything to do with the significant muscle gain that wrapped her form.

I'd find out soon enough.

Nikki turned down a hallway and toward the women's restroom. I followed after her, not giving half a fuck that I wasn't supposed to be allowed inside.

The door closed behind me. She was already in a stall and hadn't seen me yet. This was good.

I barely noticed the woman at the sink washing her hands. She tensed, eyeing me warily in the mirror.

I shook my head silently. My eyes flashed yellow with power.

She swallowed hard and hightailed it out of the bathroom without a word. My gaze swept over the line of stalls. They were empty, save one. Tiny feet donning black heels with red bottoms. I clicked the lock in place behind me right as the toilet flushed.

My heart rate sped up.

Anticipation clogged the air.

I didn't hear the bathroom stall swing open, but the sharp inhale of breath made me turn around.

Gripping the frame like it was all that stood between her and the floor was the mate I'd rejected.

Desire slammed into me so hard I took a step toward her without even realizing it. My skin buzzed with an undercurrent of anxiety. It pushed me to take her, claim her, undo the wrong I'd done.

I might have, if not for the way she was looking at me.

Desire was likely the last thing on her mind.

"Get. Out." She exhaled the words quietly, but her chest rose and fell with a silent fury. Her plum-colored lips pressed together and in the fluorescent light of the bathroom I could have sworn her eyes turned red.

"Please, hear me out—"

"No." The short, apathetic word struck me. It would have hurt less if I'd taken a punch to the throat.

My hands clenched into fists, and I fought my own baser instincts that urged me to go to her. To calm her. To fix what made her so angry. *So hurt.*

Except I was the cause, and I didn't know how to fix it.

Nikki used my silence to quickly dart to the sink furthest from me and wash her hands. She scrubbed them roughly. Aggressive even.

Fuck, this wasn't at all how I planned for it to be. Who was I kidding? I didn't plan. Sure, I'd spent six years thinking about what I'd say when this day came, but it wasn't careful planning that urged me to follow her into the women's bathroom like a fucking creep. I was in here because of my inability to stay away from her once I had her in my sights.

"I made a mistake, Nikki."

She froze. Her hands stopped moving. In the mirror, her dark eyes collided with mine. Unreadable. The anger in her voice, however, was not.

"Too late," she choked out.

"I take it back," I said quickly. Fear gripped me. Fear of the rejection I *deserved*. "I don't reject you."

Her lips parted. For a split second, I thought I saw the

briefest flicker of possibility. A moment later, it died a sudden terrible death to the fire that had just roared to life, metaphorically speaking.

"You don't reject me?" she repeated. She huffed a laugh, but there was no humor to it. She bit her lip hard, eyes shimmering as she shook her head. The panic eating me alive didn't let up.

"Please, Nik," I said gruffly. My voice was thick with too many unsaid things and not enough time to air them. "I—we—I never wanted to leave you. It was *always* my plan to return. Always."

"Don't call me that," she said, tongue flicking out to wet her bottom lip, soothing where she'd pressed too hard. "My friends call me that. And you?" She motioned between us with an open hand. "You aren't my friend."

Fuck. It hurt to leave, more than she ever knew, but being confronted with her—the new her—the woman that came out of her hurt, out of her grief, out of six fucking years of distance . . .

I'd made an even bigger mistake than I realized. I should have never let her go. Consequences be damned.

"You're right," I said. The smallest wince made me feel a spark of hope that I didn't deserve. I didn't want to hurt her, but damn if she could still be hurt, that meant she cared. Hurting was better than nothing. I could fix the hurt. I could win her heart again. What I couldn't change was indifference. "You're right. I'm not your friend. I'm your best friend, and your mate."

Nikki shook her head, like she was in denial. Or maybe she was trying to convince herself of it. I knew she hadn't rejected the bond. She didn't then, and even if she did now, it wouldn't snap. Not after I took back my own rejection.

"You're not. Not anymore." She swallowed hard,

appearing conflicted about what she wanted to say next. "Friends don't leave. Mates don't reject you and then disappear for *years*. You . . . I don't know what you are, but I know that you're not mine."

Damn if those words didn't kill me a little inside.

I buried my own feelings because she didn't know yet. Not about what happened, or the deal I made with—

"And I don't care what deal you made with my father. I *will not* marry you. Not now. Not after the election. Not in this lifetime."

She turned away from the sink and marched right up to me. I wasn't sure if she realized it, or if it was simply a reaction to her anger. She'd always had a temper, but this was so much more. Nikki didn't touch me, but she stopped close enough I could confirm her eyes had indeed turned red.

Tension filled the air, creating a charged and heady cloud around us. I was struggling to keep my hands to myself. It wasn't time yet. I knew that. She wasn't ready, that was obvious.

If I were an addict, she would be my drug of choice. Her mere presence was my addiction. My craving. Now I was standing in a pool of obsession; bathing in it.

It was why I'd stayed away. Why I hadn't returned to visit. Why I'd never even checked in.

I couldn't do anything half measure, especially not when it came to loving Nikki.

But it didn't matter. I was seeing that now. If she knew about the deal, it stood to reason she knew everything. *And it didn't matter*.

"I know I hurt you, and I'm sorry, Nik. I didn't want to. This deal with Phaon wasn't my idea, but I didn't have a choice—"

Hurt vanished from her place in a second. I wasn't sure

what I'd said, but the guarded expression she threw up might as well have been a fortress.

"Everyone has choices, Malachi. And yours—" She cut off when her voice cracked, inclining her head for her to take a second and steady herself. She brushed past me, reaching for the door. It didn't budge.

I turned to unlock it, just as the metal clacked.

"I'm not giving up or walking away this time. Even if you reject me, I'll be here."

Her hands shook as she threw the door open. It would have hit the wall if it hadn't bounced off the door stopper.

She took one step and then looked over her shoulder. I wasn't sure if it was a second or a minute, but time passed as she seemed to consider her parting words. I braced myself for the impact, but it wasn't enough.

"I wish you would have stayed away."

And fuck if that didn't hurt.

CHAPTER 7
NIKKI

THE NERVE OF THAT MAN.

After seeing Subway-Mate in the crowd, I'd successfully dodged his line of sight just to end up locked in a restroom with my former best friend and unrejected mate?

Fate—the bitch—was on a roll tonight. Two for two, she was.

For years I'd dreamed of the moment where I could confront Malachi. All the conversations I'd thought of went smoothly, and always in my favor. In my imagined scenarios, I was on fire. Engulfed in confidence and ready to respond to anything he threw at me. Shooting witty comebacks with ease, not the slightest bit flustered. Then I accepted his rejection and walked away forever. Take that, you jerkwad.

The reality was *nothing* like the rehearsals in my head. Then again, none of my rehearsals involved him stalking me in a women's bathroom at a party.

I didn't even know how to explain it, but it was such a Malachi thing to do.

The flood of emotion from seeing him ranged from

resurfaced heartache to full-on rage. It was a lot to process. I didn't get to accept his rejection, and even if I wanted to scream it first, my brain and mouth didn't always coordinate well together. This happened to be one such occasion. He'd retracted his rejection before I could even think. Was that a thing? Could you do that? It wasn't like I was an expert on the rules and guidelines of fated mates.

As I zig-zagged my way through random guests, the past—our past— came crashing down, and memories flashed before me.

Stolen kisses. Falling asleep with my head on his chest while we watched the moon reflecting on the river. The way he'd look at me like I was his entire world. I'd loved him so deeply . . . and I knew I'd never stopped.

Nope. Seriously, Nikki? I couldn't think like that. Not now. There was so much happening in such a short span of time, and it was all out of my control.

"Whoa, whoa, whoa," Sam said as I approached her. "What just happened? You're stomping through here like Godzilla."

"Malachi just happened." Mocking his apology with whiny voice and air quotes, I filled her in. "He thought trapping me in the ladies room while he groveled, going on about 'he made a mistake' and 'he always intended on coming back' was a good way to win my affections."

Sam's mouth fell open. "He didn't."

"Yup."

"Did you give him the tongue-lashing he deserved?" Her face changed as though a thought had occurred to her. In utter seriousness, she lowered her voice and added, "Or is there a body I need to take care of?"

"No on both accounts," I answered with a smirk. "None of my witty smackdowns came out. I was so confused because I wanted to fuck him and strangle him—maybe even both at the same time. But I do get bonus points because I didn't cry. Not even angry tears." I sucked those fuckers right back in where they belonged.

She held up a hand for a high five. "Hey, there's my girl. Finding the silver linings."

Chuckling, I smacked her hand. "I'm a fucking wreck, Sam. The prick unrejected me, so that's a thing, and I can honestly say I didn't see that coming."

"Wait, can he do that?"

"I don't know, but that's what he did. I know jack-all about mates, but I apparently have two now, so I should probably find a book or something."

"A book?"

"Yeah, so I can learn how to get rid of them," I mumbled. "Maybe all I need is a poisoned apple."

"C'mon. Let's get out of here," Sam said with a roll of her eyes, turning my body to face away from her. Placing her hands on my lower back, she gave me a gentle nudge. "Walk. There's a western facing balcony through those double doors over there. You need fresh air."

Moving quickly through the crowd, Sam stayed behind me.

"Thanks for being willing to hide his body," I said with a wink as I looked over my shoulder.

"Wouldn't be the first time, though you're hardly dressed for the occasion." Sam grinned, a glint of mischief in her eyes.

"Think my wedding dress would be better?" I snorted at my joke. "But seriously. Maybe black widows and praying mantises have it right." Sam chortled, and I turned to look at her, but I didn't stop walking. "If they think for one second I'm going to fu–"

Oh, that? That was me slamming into a hard body. That's what I got for not looking where I was going.

Sam had grabbed my hips to stop me from falling, and the person I'd just plowed into held my upper arms to keep me steady.

"I'm so sorry, please excuse me, sir—" All words jumbled together in my head when I came face-to-face with the stranger and looked into the depths of his eyes. I tried to speak, but my lips were as numb as the rest of me as I stood there unmoving.

The faint hint of smoke tickled my nostrils. A hazy memory pressed on the edge of my psyche, but it was more like a lost daydream. Or a nightmare. A smudged and unclear picture flashed in my mind, but all the images were distorted the way impressionist art is up close.

He didn't speak for a moment, but his features held me captive all the same. Dark, but not traditionally beautiful. Striking. Compelling. He radiated savagery. There was no question in my mind that people feared him. Common sense told me I should fear him too.

"Niall," he said, his deep voice washing over my skin.

"Wait, what'd you say?" Hearing his name shook me from my frozen state and made me forget decorum. Funny how shock can render you completely unable to have a polite conversation.

"You can call me Niall."

"Okay . . . Niall." I stepped back from him, rubbing my arms where he'd touched them in an attempt to break the chill . . . and maybe because I was a little weirded out. Sam stood at my side, and we glanced at each other briefly.

"It's good to see you again, Nikki," he added, not at all creepily.

My surprise at meeting Suitor Number Two waned, and

absolute confusion took its place. Judging by the way he looked at me, there was no doubt I had it written on my face. I glanced at Sam and shook my head slightly when she gave me a questioning look.

Taking another step back, I tried to put distance between me and the stranger. "You must have mistaken me for someone else. We've never met."

I wanted to tell him I was sure I'd remember the face of one of the assholes that made a deal with my father. Call him out for being the guy that wanted to increase his status in this world while my father could control him through me. Was he so stupid he didn't realize that was my father's entire play?

They all wanted leverage, and they were using me to get what they wanted.

A whisper of uncertainty teased my memories, but I quickly brushed it off. My heart had been racing for too long while I tried to suppress the anxiety that was consuming me. Adrenaline and fear coupled with anger were playing mind tricks on me.

Apparently that wasn't the response he'd expected. Niall's hands clenched into fists at his side. Pressing his lips into a hard, thin line, a frown formed between his brows. His body language was intense, and it made me want to get the hell out of here.

"It has . . ." He paused, looking as though he was searching for the right words. "It's been a long time. Maybe—"

"Nope. I'd remember you," I said, instantly cutting him off. "Niall, like the river in Africa. I'm good with names and I never forget a face." *Certainly not one like his.* A dark shadow covered his features, making it clear he didn't like my dismissal of his advances.

"Why are you acting this way?" he asked, looking between Sam and me.

"I don't know what you're talking about. As I said, you must have mistaken me for someone else. That or you think you know me because certain . . . deals have been made. Rest assured, you don't," I answered, feeling more uncomfortable in his presence now that he was turning into a psycho. "My bodyguard and I were just heading somewhere else. By ourselves."

Please, for the love of the gods, leave me alone so I can go panic about this moment in private.

He didn't move, but anger radiated from him. Though he remained silent, he inclined his chin, and I took that as my cue and managed to pivot around him quickly with Sam at my side. Glancing over my shoulder as we walked away, I saw Niall standing where I'd left him. He watched me through a narrowed gaze, and it sent a chill down my spine.

"What the hell was that all about?" Sam muttered.

"Dunno. My guess is he thought I'd play along because of my dad. That or he really does have me confused. Which bodes well given I could end up shackled to him for life, but ya know . . ."

We hustled, moving through the throng of supernaturals until we found a double door opening onto a wide balcony. It was an incredibly cold night and it looked like we had the entire terrace to ourselves.

"The way he looked at you . . . It was intense."

"You mean the way he looked at me like I was a piece of meat? Because that's all I am. Every single guy that made a deal with my father is going to look at me like I'm the trophy at the end of the race." The thought made me nauseous.

"No, I mean the way he looked at you like you *belonged* to him," she said quietly.

"Oh my god, do you think he's a stalker? Maybe he's stalking me . . . No, he can't be. Dad's security is too tight for that and none of the militia would rat me out like that. It doesn't make sense."

Sam looked at the doorway again, seeing that no one had followed us. "I've seen him before," she said in a whisper so low, no one could possibly hear.

"Wait, so he *is* stalking me?"

"No, drama queen. Really? You think that'd be something I'd fail to mention to you?" She shook her head at me in exasperation. "Some bodyguard I'd be."

"Fine, he's not a stalker. Probably." I fidgeted with my thumbs, picking at the nail with my index finger. "Where have you seen him?"

"Last night," she mouthed. "He chased me."

"What?" I meant for the question to be light and quiet. Instead, it came out in a hiss.

"Keep it down." She scanned the perimeter again, then motioned with her hand, palm down in an effort to accentuate her statement.

"He was the other one on the pier?" I whispered.

Sam nodded. "I didn't get a great look at him when I was running because I needed to hightail it out of there, but that's definitely him."

"First Malachi, now this guy? I haven't even met Adrian yet, but it's not like I have high hopes he won't suck too. And I'm trying to dodge Subway-Mate-the-Shady-Brooklyn-Criminal, wherever he is now." I waved my hand around in a wild gesture while I word-vomited.

"You're rambling, Nikki."

"You're damn right I am. I deserve a good ramble. Have

you looked at my life the last twenty-four hours? Hello shit show, meet the dumpster fire. All I wanted was to be free of all the bullshit politics that come with my family. Now I'm being thrown into the fire headfirst by my own dad who's decided we're going to do what all the archaic assholes in the middle ages did by marrying me off. Like my vagina is supposed to somehow make whoever wins loyal to him. Hasn't he seen Frozen?" I demanded as Sam's mouth popped open. "Hans *betrays* Anna and tries to get rid of her and Elsa so he can have the crown to himself. It doesn't take a freakin' genius to see that I'm next."

"First, this isn't Frozen—"

"I know. Anna and her family were good. Mine deserve to be screwed over, but *come on*. Did they really have to drag me down too?"

"Second," Sam continued, ever the picture of patience. "I won't allow that to happen, and neither will you." I heard her. I really did. But the rationale didn't register. My brain said sheer panic was the better choice. "Just take a breath."

"You take a breath!" I grumbled, rubbing my temples. "I'm okay. Just losing control of my sanity. Preparing for my future as an ice block. Quite possibly having a nervous breakdown. You can have one at twenty-four, right? There's not an age requirement for that?"

"You're not having a nervous breakdown."

"Guess we just need to wait a little longer and see, right? Every single supernatural at this horrid party will get to watch me lose my mind." Heat crept over my skin, and I fanned myself. The world started spinning. Bending over, I braced my hands on my thighs to keep myself from tumbling over. I gulped in mouthfuls of air while I felt my lungs constrict. "Bet Earth and Emerald didn't know they'd be getting dinner *and* a show tonight!"

"Nikki," Sam said with a gentle tone. It was the tone she used on her kids. A maternal, kind, and reassuring reminder that she was present, and I was safe. Crouching on one knee, she met me at eye level. "Look at me. You aren't going to have a nervous breakdown. You've been through entirely too much to let *this* be the thing that gets you, do you hear me?"

Her words struck a chord in me. It didn't take away the intensity of everything that was happening, but it was enough to pull my head out of the funk I was falling into. She was right. I closed my eyes and nodded.

"They don't own you. They only think they can have you. Show them nothing. Give them nothing. You are in control, even if they don't know it," she said, trying to encourage me. "You go in there and own the room like the godsdamned phoenix you are."

I chuckled, standing up and putting my hands on my hips. "I feel like a godsdamned platypus."

"Okay, well, I don't know if a platypus can really command a room or if they just grab attention because they're weird looking, so maybe fake it till you make it?" Sam patted my shoulder with a grin, and I let out a small laugh.

A loud voice carried onto the balcony, announcing the upcoming presentations.

"Fake it till I make it." We smiled at each other and nodded, leaving the terrace and entering the ballroom again.

I made my mental checklist.

· Fake it. *Check*.

· Get the hell out of here as soon as the candidates are announced. *Soon*.

· Go home, have a nervous breakdown, then pull up my

big girl panties and plot my escape from New York. *Coming right up.*

It was a solid plan. Did most of my plans go accordingly? Not historically, no . . .

But there was a first time for everything, right?

Right??

CHAPTER 8
ADRIAN

AWARENESS BUZZED ALONG MY SKIN. A PRICKLING SENSATION THAT was now familiar. Heat that was a little too hot to be comfortable raced through my veins.

She was here.

My mate was *near*.

"Are you all right?" I faintly heard the queen of Blood and Beryl's soft voice. She was a young immortal, and a rare one at that. A shifter that couldn't shift, turned vampire; the rumors that surrounded her were almost as crazy as the truth.

I turned my head, scanning the crowd for any signs of my mate. I didn't remember what she looked like, but I felt certain I would recognize her when I saw her again.

"He's fine, Danni. Probably just bored of hearing all about Cappadocia and hot air balloons." Her sister's snarky comments would normally make me laugh, but not tonight.

The two sisters looked nothing alike. Both were beautiful in completely different ways, but like the sun and the moon—they were opposites as best I could tell. Adora had been adopted by Dannika's family when she was born, as I understood it, and they were incredibly close.

"No," the queen, said lightly. "That's not it. He's feeling anxious—frenzied, even. It's like—"

"Danni." The deep rumble of her mate's voice made her stop talking, not that I was paying much mind anyways.

Where was she?

"Sorry." The queen blushed; her face turning red with embarrassment. "That was rude of me. Your emotions are just very . . . distracting. I usually have an easier time distancing myself from them."

I grunted in acknowledgment, not that I particularly cared. Normally I despised supernaturals who had the ability to manipulate emotions, but they were often fae or demons. The wolf queen was an empath that came into power when her mate turned her. Unlike the vicious beings that liked to toy with emotions, she was young and untried. Her core nature was pure. Innocent. I ran into her and her mate several months prior and found myself intrigued by a couple that was powerful and yet, not cruel.

We'd kept up in passing over the months and they were going to be some of my biggest supporters during the election. Members of Earth and Emerald liked seeing their candidates allies, especially when it came to co-mingling and working amicably with other Houses.

In truth, I should have been focused on them.

But for the life of me, all I could do was search.

The scent of clove and cinnamon touched me, making my heart pound.

A man stepped in front of me, blocking my view of the party. I blinked, focusing on the long dark hair and sharp eyes of a god.

Quite literally.

"Is there something we should know?" Pan asked. He inclined a brow while wrapping an arm around his mate's waist, pulling Adora close to him. While he dressed for the occasion, there was a ruggedness—a wildness—that was unmistakable, even in a three-piece suit.

"It's not danger," Danni said calmly. "He senses his mate."

My head whipped to the side as I regarded her.

Her pale features were flushed again. She had an arm wrapped around her king's waist as she leaned into him. Her other hand was settled on his chest.

"I remember the feeling," she said, answering my unspoken question with a half-smile. "It's like someone injected adrenaline into you. The high is like a drug. So is the obsession." That last part was murmured.

The vampire king, Elias, fisted his hand in the blood red material of her dress before whispering something I *definitely* had no business hearing. Adora groaned, waving her hand in annoyance.

"Jesus Christ, and I thought they were bad before. The stairs are *right there,* you two. Go back to your room."

Pan chuckled, pressing a tight kiss to Adora's temple. "That doesn't sound like such a bad idea to me. I vote we leave the man to his business and go back to the cabin. The city is *stifling*. I promise to make it worth your while."

Fucking mates.

I couldn't hear any more of this when my own was here and still just out of reach. "Elias. Dannika." I turned to say goodbye, but they were already starting for the stairwell. The queen glanced back and smiled brightly as her mate dragged her through the crowd. A white wolf walked right behind her, growling at anyone who got too close.

"We'll speak tomorrow, Adrian. Good luck!"

Under different circumstances I might have been annoyed they were leaving before the main event had even started, but I was in no less of a hurry to get it over with and find my mystery mate.

Spinning on my heel, I gave in to the urge to follow that divine scent.

Niall's back profile became center point the closer I got. I paused when he turned, revealing the beautiful petite woman in front of him.

Electricity struck me.

My blood fizzled and *burned*.

It was her.

Without the effects of a glamour affecting me anymore, I could recall her dark hair she'd worn in a ponytail last night. Her light brown skin practically glowed in the warm lighting of the ballroom. I devoured every inch of her with my eyes, taking in her curves and edges. Every line was beautiful. Stunning.

I took a step toward her just as she walked away, in the opposite direction. It was only when she was out of sight that some of the mating frenzy cleared, allowing me to think.

To understand.

My mate. The mysterious girl from the subway. The woman that ruined the deal with the shifter syndicate— was none other than Nikki Ward.

Fuck me.

I needed to backpedal. To find a quiet corner where I could process. Before I could do just that, Niall spotted me. In quick, restrained strides he closed the distance between us.

"She doesn't recognize me."

His words conflicted with my thoughts. "What?"

"Nikki doesn't recognize me. At least she claims not to."

My mouth opened, then closed. Niall couldn't tell I was having my own internal crisis about the situation we had found ourselves in, because he didn't know. It wouldn't stay that way for long, but I needed to wrap my head around it before bringing it up.

There was no way to prepare him for that shock. While I knew that he was my best friend and wouldn't kill me, I couldn't guarantee that his animal might not start posturing and lose its shit at the perceived threat.

When it came to pretty much anything, Niall was a stone-cold bastard that operated on logic. Except when it came to Nikki.

She was his kryptonite, and she just became mine.

"Why would she lie about that?" I asked after a suspended beat. Niall didn't notice my pause, too consumed with his own demons.

"I don't know," he growled, a sliver of his animal coming out in his voice. I didn't have to tell him to tamper it down. The looks we were getting spoke for itself. He tightened his fists as he locked down the monster, keeping it away from the public eye.

"Are you sure she's lying?"

That was the wrong thing to say.

"The alternative is she *forgot me*." It had been four years since he'd walked into my life by accident. In all that time, he'd only once used that cold, angry, wrathful voice; when he told me about the fire.

"She can't just forget you. Her biology—"

"Is either as broken as mine, or she lied. There's no other possibility. Phaon said her trauma was too much. . ." I could sense the dark thoughts circulating through his mind.

"We'll figure it out," I said, working to keep my own possessive tendencies at bay. He didn't know. The situation was delicate enough as it was without my instincts running rampant, whispering that he was competition. That I should eliminate him. Fucking mate bond hormones were going to be a big fucking problem if I didn't handle this right.

"I never should have left," he said quietly. "If I'd taken Nikki instead of handing her over—"

"You have no idea how it would have turned out. For all you know, she would have hated you. Her family would have hunted you both to the ends of the earth, so there's no point going down the road of 'if only.'"

His jaw tensed. I could tell he wanted to argue, but not because he really believed that was the better option. It was because he was hurt. He needed to rage and purge the negative emotions from his psyche so he could focus on the topic at hand.

That wasn't exactly possible right now.

"She knows about the deal," he said quietly. "I'm getting the impression she hates me already."

The deal.

It was bad enough when I made it for him. That I was now just as complicit, and it turned out she was actually my mate too . . .

Part of me was tempted to turn and walk out.

To forfeit and try to get her on my own terms.

As much as the idea appealed to me, I knew Niall would never go for it—and mate or not—he and I were together through thick and thin.

I just hoped he saw it that way when he learned the truth.

CHAPTER 9

NIKKI

WHILE WITCHES AND OTHER VARIOUS MEMBERS OF EARTH AND Emerald stood on stage, giving thanks to Mother Earth and honoring the winter solstice, I sat and waited for the inevitable. The commitment ceremony of the candidates.

My entire family was seated at a large, round table near the front of the stage. We were stage left, The Divine were center, and the Roses were on the right with ample space provided between each family. The Outcast Coven were seated behind the Roses. They were placed as far from us as possible. Contrary to popular belief, vampires and shifters weren't always the bitterest of enemies. In the case of the syndicates, it was actually the witches and the shifters. I wasn't surprised in the slightest they hadn't gone for this sham of an alliance, given how much the coven despised my father and vice versa. They inhabited Staten Island, which at least made it easier to not be near them often.

Clan Tepes were seated next to the Outcast Coven and behind The Divine. Of all the syndicates, the vampires and The Divine had the best rapport. Ty liked to claim that it was because angels and demons mixing was so unnatural that they'd confused the vampires as one of them. I didn't believe that for a second, but I also wasn't sure what the actual reasoning could have been. My father had always been the wariest of the vampire syndicate. While he viewed the witches as weak, I suspected he begrudgingly respected the vampires for how they ran the Bronx with a cutthroat mentality.

Sam stood off to the side of the room, keeping watch with other bodyguards, enforcers, and soldiers. Some of them were ours or other syndicates, a few belonged to different Houses, but most were Earth and Emerald—made obvious by the emerald stone they all wore in some form or fashion. Our people blended in well, but everyone knew they were there and what they were capable of.

Black ties and fancy party dresses weren't enough to camouflage the wolves amongst the sheep. Earth and Emerald may not have been entirely innocent in this, nor were they entirely corrupt. They had a few bad apples that got into bed with my family.

Because my best friend had a part to play and a job to do, I had to sit by myself, festering in the uncomfortable weirdness that consumed this entire evening.

Gavriel sat next to me on my left, our mom sat silently on my right. Alex, my dad, and Ty circled in the remaining chairs at the table. The latter three huddled in hushed conversation.

"Nik," Gavriel whispered.

"Mmm?"

"It's going to be okay."

I jerked my head in his direction. "You knew about this?"

He shook his head. "I just found out a little bit ago. Mom told me."

"Lovely," I muttered. She knew, and yet she'd never said anything to me. Why would she do that? I wanted to ask my mother why she never told me, but not until we were in private. I wanted her truth.

My entire life I'd felt loved. Even if I didn't like the syndicate dealings, that part of their life didn't extend to the confines of our home. I hadn't questioned the love my brothers or my parents had for me. Not once. That changed when my father tossed me in as a signing bonus for a backwards Mafia deal. A reverse dowry. Instead of them paying my father for my hand, they win an election, win me, and he gets to control both of us.

Hard to feel loved when you've been reduced to nothing more than a commodity.

Gavriel sensed my unease and wrapped an arm around me, bringing me in for a side hug. "Just get through tonight."

I glanced at him and gave a tiny smile. He knew me well, and he knew Sam. He was one of us. It wouldn't take much for him to deduce our plans. I took comfort in knowing he would do anything for me. We'd have to talk about it later, but I wouldn't leave him behind. He had to come with us when we left. That was non-negotiable.

Ty glared at both of us from across the table, as though he knew we were conspiring despite not having said a single word that would give us away. Gav noticed too, and he let his arm fall from my shoulder.

"Is there a problem?" my father asked, seeing that Ty had stopped paying attention to him.

"No, just making sure Nikki is okay. She's looking a little jittery," he answered, not taking his eyes off me.

When my dad looked in my direction for clarification, a

logical explanation wasn't the first thing that came to mind. "I ate a toothpick earlier," I blurted out.

"You . . . what?" Alex asked, cocking an eyebrow and trying to suppress a laugh. Ty remained unchanged, and my dad looked at me incredulously.

"I mean, not on purpose, obviously. Who would do that?" I cleared my throat. "But yeah, I just can't get the taste out of my mouth. Gav was just telling me to get through the rest of the night and then I can go brush my teeth."

My father shook his head and Alex flagged down a waiter, telling him to give me one of the pink drinks.

Since I'd already chugged three of those, my stomach flipped the moment it was set down in front of me.

"There. Kill your tastebuds with that," he said, gesturing to the rock glass.

Ty sighed, crossing his arms and leaning back in his chair, and my father chastised Alex for encouraging me to drink.

A twenty-four-year-old woman, being told what to do by her father and her brothers. It was humiliating.

"Good evening." A deep voice filled the room. "On this evening's winter solstice, we gather together with neighbors as we open our doors and welcome five New York families that have come to join our celebration. The Roses, the Outcast Coven, The Divine, Clan Tepes, and the Wards." The speaker motioned to the front tables and polite applause followed. I just kept my head down as best I could. "Never has Earth and Emerald allowed another House or faction to engage in our election process until now. Members of these families have worked diligently with our council to create a peaceful and rewarding co-existence. As a symbol of that good faith, we're allowing select members to join Earth and Emerald tonight if they would like to run for chancellor."

I noticed how he never used the word syndicate. It was clear by the buzzing in the room that this came as news to several Earth and Emerald members in attendance. *Just wait,* I thought. *That's not even the real surprise. The syndicates are about to infiltrate your entire governmental structure.*

" . . . oath is binding." The speaker on stage pointed to a basin with magic flames burning in mesmerizing and unnatural purple and teal hues. "Your commitment to join the trials is sealed when your blood burns within the fire."

One by one, various members of Earth and Emerald stood from the tables, announced their names, and walked toward the stage. As each individual approached, they paid their respects to the speaker, and pressed their hand to a sharp pin before squeezing the blood into the fire basin.

Crackles and pops of magic sounded with each new entry. The last members of their House completed their commitment, and my heart began to race. My nails dug into my thighs as I pressed my hands on top of them in an effort to prevent myself from shaking.

I carefully glanced at Sam, and she gave me a forced smile.

We're almost done. It was as if I heard her voice.

Taking in a shaky breath, I prepared myself for the next few minutes. It was almost over.

Moments passed as the applause died down, and the speaker from Earth and Emerald held his hand out toward the front row of tables.

Malachi stood up, tall and proud—the asshole—and spoke with confidence. "Malachi Duarte from The Divine." His swagger was on full display as he walked onto the stage, then he drew blood on the pins and squeezed it into the fire. Turning to look at me for a moment, I felt the heat of his dark gaze before he walked to the other side of the stage and stood by the other candidates.

My father tapped the table to get my attention, sending a stern look my way. I hadn't spoken a word, but I guess my face was speaking for me.

The adrenaline was back in full force now too, so that was cool. Not at all unnerving. The vampire representative had gone up while I was too busy trying not to have a mental breakdown. I didn't catch his name as the witch representative went next. "Ayla Whelan from the Outcast Coven." Her black hair swayed on a phantom wind as she tossed her blood into the fire.

Then Niall stood up following the same steps onto the stage. "Niall Thorn in honor of the Roses."

When Niall glanced at me as he finished, I looked away. Why did he keep doing that? Like Sam said, give them nothing, and that's exactly what I tried to do.

Just two more to announce and the night was over.

Until a familiar face stood up and my world turned upside down. It was Subway-Mate. I tried to inconspicu-ously slide down in my seat, attempting to make myself smaller so that no one would see me. So that *he* wouldn't see me.

How could it be my luck that he would be a candidate in this shitshow election?

Then it dawned on me. He just got up from the fae syndicate table. He was . . .

In a panic, I looked over at Sam and she stared at my subway-mate with eyes wide. Her lips parted slightly in shock.

"Who is that?" I asked Gavriel quietly, fearing I already knew the answer.

He opened his mouth to respond, but was silenced when the man in question spoke first, his voice projecting as he claimed his place.

"Adrian Rose of the Roses."

Heat flushed over my skin. Nausea climbed up my throat and I swallowed it down.

My mate was Adrian Rose.

Adrian Rose who'd made a deal with my father.

Adrian Rose was the mystery man meeting with my brother.

Fate was a backstabbing bitch.

If I ever met her, I'd punch her in the face.

A strangled gasp escaped my lips before I could rein it in. My mother reached over to grasp my hand, giving it a tiny squeeze.

I met her eyes, expecting to see encouragement. Support. A proud and firm matriarch. Despite her painted smile, I saw how much sadness filled her features. "It's just marriage, Nikki," she whispered softly. "There are worse things in life."

Not exactly the most uplifting speech. There was no strength behind her words. No conviction. It was dull and flat. Emotionless. It sounded like a mantra she had repeated to herself for years. What she had to tell herself to make it through the day. I don't think I'd ever seen that side of her before. Or maybe it was there all along and I just never thought to look.

That was the moment I realized she didn't have control of her life any more than I did mine. None. I'd overlooked that detail as I grew up, so consumed by finding my own path in this world, I never stopped to look at hers. I'd always thought my father loved her. He showered her with affection, and she seemed to love him in return. Then again,

I was misguided and thought I was loved too. Now? Seeing the way she looked at me painted a different picture. The melancholy in her gaze spoke volumes. She didn't have a choice in which path she took.

And neither did I.

My future was her past.

A panic attack was coming on with the energy of a tsunami.

In slow motion, I watched my subway-mate prick his hand before I heard the sizzle when the magic accepted his entry.

Adrian walked to stand beside Niall . . . who stood beside Malachi . . .

My three suitors, competing for my hand.

Just like Merida in Brave, I thought to myself.

Just like Merida . . .

I knew what I needed to do.

I glanced quickly at Sam, and she dipped her chin slightly.

My heart pounded in my chest so hard, I swore everyone could hear it. Sweat beaded and dripped down my back. It was only a matter of time before my deodorant would fail me.

Alex placed his hands on the table to scoot his chair back and I looked at my mom. *Really* looked at her.

At the dark circles. The tight smile. The painstakingly perfect makeup which was meant to show everyone what she wanted to see. No, scratch that. What my father wanted them to see.

I couldn't do it.

I wouldn't live her life.

My chair shot backwards, and my legs snapped straight, thrusting me into a standing position. Each member of my family whipped their heads in my direction, eyes wide.

"Nikki Ward for the Wards," I blurted. Okay, maybe it was more of a light shout. Or just a shout-shout.

Moving quickly, I practically ran up the stairs. I could see the look of shock on my brothers' faces out of the corner of my eye, but they weren't my concern. The man—the monster—I called my father was fuming.

"Nikki," he hissed. "*No*."

Before anyone could stop me, I slammed my hand down on the pin pad. Blood pooled in my palm, but I didn't flinch. That pain was the least of my worries. I practically threw my hand over the basin.

Malachi, Niall, and Adrian stared in my direction with varying degrees of surprise. A small smirk appeared on Malachi's face. Niall just looked infuriated. And Adrian seemed conflicted.

Me too, Subway-Mate. Me too.

The teal and purple fire crackled and sizzled deeper and longer than it had with any of the candidates. Sparks shot out of the fire when I was accepted, burning brighter. Flames licked at my hands without hurting me, curling around my wrist like it was a living, breathing entity, caressing my skin in a desperation to mingle with my blood.

For some reason, the magic more than just accepted me. It called to me.

That was definitely unexpected.

But so was my throwing my name into a proverbial (not)goblet of fire.

Too late now.

CHAPTER 10
NIALL

WHAT THE ACTUAL FUCK WAS SHE THINKING?

Better yet, what was Phaon thinking?

Of all the things he would do to get out of his side of the deal, having his daughter run for chancellor wasn't one I'd ever considered.

If not simply due to his own misogynistic viewpoints, then because of the risk associated with the trials. Candidates died every election. The trials that preceded the election were beyond taxing. They were flawed and dangerous.

The council made a point to push every candidate to their mental and physical breaking point, and then some. While Earth and Emerald wanted a good leader, the trials were as much about the ability to lead as they were survival. They valued physical strength. Brutality. They wanted to know their leader could withstand a war and come back swinging. That was the world we lived in.

I didn't know if Nikki could do that because I didn't *know* her.

But I wanted to.

Needed to.

99

The fire wrapped around her nimble fingers, blue and purple along with some fascinating color in between. It touched her skin but didn't burn.

There were whispers of what kind of shifters Phaon's children were. His prejudice of other species was renowned, as was his frequent boasting that his family were all shifters of lore. While what he and Ty could shift into wasn't exactly hidden, the others were less obvious. But very few shifters could withstand fire, let alone have it wrap around them intimately.

Adrian's parents had asked me a dozen or so times what I knew about Phaon and his family. They didn't even know if I was from his territory, but as a shifter in the boroughs, it was assumed. I lied out of absolute loyalty to my mate, even if I couldn't have her yet. Nikki was the rarest form of shifter; more of a myth than anything. While the other members of her family didn't keep their shifted forms as much of a secret, my mate seemed to have hers on a tight leash. Much like me with my own. I suspected what we went through had changed her.

And yet, she seemed to stand there a moment too long with her hand in the flames. Or perhaps, it was the flame that clung to her.

The violet fire seemed to move as she pulled away, trying to pull her back.

Nikki stepped to the side. She blinked her dark eyes, as if coming out of a trance. A slight shudder ran through her as she took in the stage and the candidates.

"Final nominations," the announcer called out. Nikki jerked before walking to Adrian's other side. He was all that stood between us. "If there are no further nominees, we will proceed to—"

"Typhaon Ward the second."

If I weren't so schooled in keeping my emotions under lock and key, I might have snapped at Phaon's audacity. He was supposed to have Alexander enter the race. Not her, not Typhaon, not Gavriel—*only* Alexander.

My eyes narrowed, moving from the man starting for the stage then shifting to the father seated in the front row. The lights were glaring down on me, which made it harder to make out his features, but I could see the firm set of his lips.

If looks could kill, his son would be dead. Maybe Typhaon wasn't supposed to be running. If the glare he shot Nikki afterward was anything to go off of, neither of them were meant to be on stage.

Which made me wonder, was my mate not quite as obedient as Phaon made her out to be? Or did she simply despise the possibility of marrying me that much? Was she willing to risk her life to avoid it?

Bitterness coated my tongue. Frankly, it seemed the more likely option between the two because this wasn't the agreement we made. First, the previous night went to shit, and now this evening was shaping up to be almost as bad.

Ty approached the stage in long, competent strides. His dark eyes were focused on Nikki as he ascended the stairs.

He slapped his hand down on the needle much like the sister had. It was only meant to prick, except Nikki seemed to have done it out of desperation. There was something deliberate about how Ty let his blood coat every inch of the metal and stand. He didn't grimace or make a sound as he held his weeping wound over the flames. The fire touched his skin for only a fraction of a second, but where the flame called to Nikki, it seemed repulsed by him.

The scent of burning flesh lifted into the air before he snatched his hand back.

Well this was certainly a change of events . . . and not at all welcome.

Ty crossed the room swiftly, standing closer to my mate than I would have preferred as he took up a protective stance. Yeah, he was her brother. But I didn't really care. I wasn't a fan of anyone, male or female, being that close to her.

It reminded me that my own presence wasn't welcome. *She didn't remember me.*

The thought flashed through my mind again. Yet another unwelcome reminder. Bitter resentments clung to me, whispering lies that if I had only claimed her four years ago as my instincts told me to, we wouldn't be here now.

Thoughts like that would get me nowhere. At least in that, Adrian was right. I hadn't claimed her. But like it or not, I would now.

I wasn't the same man as I was back then. I didn't know how to live in this world, or what to do with a broken mate. I was no longer an experiment, and while phantom nightmares haunted me—they didn't have the power to drag me back.

Four years had taught me a lot.

And this time, I wasn't letting her go.

CHAPTER II
NIKKI

WELL THAT JUST HAPPENED.

Not only had I jumped the gun and run on stage, but the wrong brother did too. I didn't see that coming. What the hell would have possessed Ty to take Alexander's place? It's not like I could ask him. Even if I could, it wasn't really a conversation I wanted to have. Whether I liked it or not, that unpleasant chat was coming soon because he was going to ask me the exact same thing.

Now I had to think up an answer.

Minor detail.

The announcer prattled on about the importance of the trials, about the democratic process within the House of Earth and Emerald, and how tradition had kept them strong for centuries, blah blah blah.

That wasn't what caught my attention.

Gavriel was holding our mom's hand for support, and she looked petrified. As Alexander moved to stand, dad gave a slight shake of his head, indicating that he wanted him to stay. I could see my brother's reluctance. Alexander pursed his lips, twisting them to the side. With a glance to where Ty and I stood on stage, he looked back at our father, acquiescing with a slight dip of his chin before sitting back in his chair fully.

While others may not have been able to see my father's aggravation, I knew him well. Although his features were stoic, I could feel his rage radiating. Alexander was no different. This was not the plan, and that man lived by rules and checklists and organized strategies. My brother loved me, and he had always protected me, but I'd be lying if I said I wasn't a tiny bit concerned that he might strangle me and forget to let go before I ran out of air.

I clenched my fists and kept my focus straight ahead. Breathe in. Breathe out. The lights on the stage were bright, and it helped block out the audience so I couldn't see the faces of those beyond the first row of tables. The syndicate tables.

They were all looking at us, and there was no mistaking the confusion some of them were experiencing.

That wasn't even the worst part.

I was wedged on stage between Adrian the Subway-Mate and Ty. There was nothing in this world that was strong enough to stop the intensity of some stupid inexplicable instinct urging me toward my mate while my brain said "absolutely not"—all while having my pissed off brother stand next to me. I knew he was glaring at me from his periphery. I could *feel* his rage as easily as I could feel my father's.

They seriously need a spa day or something so they could relax.

If shifters weren't so good at healing, their anger issues and stress levels would give them a heart condition.

Not that I was much different at the moment. Adrenaline had me completely frazzled. I had just jumped up on stage and committed myself to a magically binding bowl of fire and agreed to go through the pre-election trials.

"Each candidate will have the opportunity to bring a second. Their second can be their lifeline. This individual will provide assistance; they will strategize together, and at times will compete with their second by their side."

Shit. What? I was so lost in my own thoughts that I hadn't been paying attention to what the announcer was saying anymore. Had he been going on about the rules? That was probably important information. I didn't know that we had to pick a second. Who was I kidding? There was a lot I didn't know about this. What else had I missed?

"Your second should be someone you trust with your life." The announcer stepped back gesturing to the line of candidates to begin. "Choose wisely."

Since Earth and Emerald candidates had been named first, I was expecting someone at the beginning of the line to step forward and start naming their seconds. So consider me surprised when Ty stepped forward.

My heart thundered, pounding in my chest.

"Jackie Storm." Ty took a step back.

Of course he would choose her. Twat.

Silence.

Oh shit. It was my turn.

This was what I missed. The announcer had been saying we were going to go in reverse order, so I had zero time.

Pretty sure I couldn't ask them to skip me and come back around. This wasn't a game show.

My brain could barely process what was happening.

Oh my god. Oh my god. Oh my god.

Panic was my go-to when faced with a last-minute decision and no time to think about the consequences.

With one foot forward I stepped out of the line. My voice was hoarse. I needed water. I couldn't swallow without feeling dry spots, making me feel like I was going to choke on sand. "Samantha Lowe of the Wards."

My best friend stood against the wall, still at her guard post. The glare of the lights didn't block me from seeing her, nor did it block the look on her face. The color had drained from her skin, and her lips were parted as though I had stolen her breath. Which, to be fair, I probably had.

Had I really just done that? Yes, but I had no one else I could trust. The trials were hard, and I couldn't ask Gav. Other members of the militia movement might be outed if I called their names. Too many questions about why I had chosen a particular person. Some of them were part of the syndicates, but no one needed to know that I was cozy enough with them to ask them to be my second. Sam made the most sense. She was my bodyguard. One of my father's top enforcers. She was the one assigned to me all the time. They wouldn't question why I said her name.

So really it wasn't panic that made me say her name. It was a logical decision.

Yeah, we're gonna go with logic.

Sam was going to kill me.

Adrian stepped forward, and said, "I do not choose a second."

Son of a bitch. That's what I get for not paying attention. If I knew I didn't have the option of choosing someone, I would have kept my damn mouth shut.

Also, why would you not choose a second? I knew why *I* wouldn't choose a second. I was flying by the seat of my pants. Adrian was part of a strategic deal. Wouldn't you set yourself up for success by having a second? Now I just questioned his intelligence.

Niall stepped forward, and said the same damn thing that Adrian had. No second. Shocked whispers filtered through the crowd.

The audience could be surprised all they wanted. I just thought they were idiots.

Malachi stepped forward, glanced to his left and scoffed at the two before him. As much as I loathed to admit it, he and I were in agreement in regard to their choice, or lack thereof. "Tylea Amon of The Divine."

As each member of Earth and Emerald stepped forward, they named their chosen second. Only a few others chose to go without, and I just mentally included their name in the pool of morons.

The announcer came back to the podium and adjusted the microphone. This time I forced myself to pay attention before I missed out on magic beans, magic wands, or some other packaged deal we might get.

"Will the seconds that have been named please come to the stage and stand next to your candidate."

As the others approached, Sam stepped away from her post and slowly headed towards the stairs. With tentative steps, she came to me and stood by my side in silence.

"Supernaturals, I present to you the candidates for this year's election."

The room stood up and applauded. A few hoots and hollers from Earth and Emerald tables sounded, but the bare minimum of polite clapping came from my family's table. Forced and fake.

The applause grew louder, thundering in the room.

The stage was incredibly crowded, and as other candidates and their seconds moved around and shaking hands with fellow House members, Sam and I inched our way towards the back of the stage and out of my father's line of sight.

Jackie and Ty didn't follow me, thankfully, and there was simply too much going on for anyone to pay attention to us.

"What are you doing?" Sam asked in a harsh and hushed tone.

"Taking control of my life," I whispered.

"By trying to get yourself killed?"

"No, by not letting my father marry me off. You remember that movie I made you watch? About the Scottish princess? I'll be shooting for my own hand, you know?" With a grin on my face, I nodded in hopes she understood the reference.

Instead, she stared at me blankly. "This isn't archery. This isn't a movie. We had a plan, Nik. We were going to get you out. You weren't going to marry anyone."

"Yeah, I got freaked out, okay? I kind of forgot about the plan." I winced at my admission. "Adrian is the Subway-Mate, Sam. Niall thinks he knows me. And Malachi ripped my heart out once and I'm terrified to give him a part of it back. I was about to have an anxiety attack at the thought of being handed over to any one of them."

A crease formed between Sam's brow, but her eyes softened. "What about my family, Nik? If something happens to you, your dad will blame me and then he'll kill them as my punishment."

"I . . ." My mouth hung open, but no words came out. Sam continued to look at me, waiting for my explanation. The problem was, I didn't have one. "That won't happen. I don't know. I'll think of something."

"Like you thought of this?" She crossed her arms, shaking her head.

I flinched at her disappointment. That hurt when I realized what I'd done to her. I'd dragged her into this, and I'd put her family at risk.

Straightening my posture, I spoke firmly. "I won't let them get hurt, Sam. I swear it. Operation Sunnyside was going to get us all out. Now it's just for them, okay? I'll take care of your family. I promise. We'll get them out."

"Getting them off our shithole island was the plan all along, I suppose. Now we'll need to move fast."

"With my father's attention on me and now Ty, they won't focus on your family just yet. Gav can get them out." A mental image of his face flashed before my eyes. "As soon as he comes to terms with the fact I just joined the trials, then he'll be right as rain. Then we'll skedaddle when no one is looking and join them. It'll be easier to escape Earth and Emerald territory than Manhattan."

Sam nodded. "This isn't like our missions in the past. It's not covert. We don't have a team. It's you and me. All eyes are on us, and they'll know we're coming."

Grabbing Sam's hand, I squeezed it. "You're right about one thing. All eyes will be on us. They're going to be watching our every move."

"But?"

"But they have no idea what's coming. I have an entire arsenal of movies, books, and cartoons in my armory, and I can guarantee that not one of these assholes is half as crazy as me."

Sam stared at me blankly. "Are you seriously planning to escape these trials using an Acme rocket?"

"If I did, they wouldn't see it coming, would they?" I grinned.

"Oh my god, we're gonna die."

"C'mon, Sam. Have a little faith. Show a little enthusiasm."

She gave a saccharine smile and with a peppy voice repeated, "Oh my god, we're gonna die!"

"That's the spirit." I held my hand up for a high five.

"Fine." She smacked my open palm. "Just get my family out of here before they become a target."

"Don't worry. I'm already working out some details in my head."

"Please tell me that plan doesn't include tunneling underneath the city like a rabbit?"

"Don't be ridiculous," I chided. "That's not even practical."

"Good—"

"Maybe a slingshot, though," I muttered, ignoring the way Sam pinched the bridge of her nose.

CHAPTER 12
ADRIAN

NIALL STOOD IN THE CENTER OF THE BROOKLYN BRIDGE, MOPING —though he'd never call it that.

It should have been a cloudy night, filled with the dim glow of city lights. Instead, we were standing on the edge of a hurricane. Wind and water batted at him at the apex of the bridge, unwavering despite the intensity of the weather. A weaker person might have flown right off the bridge and into the choppy waters never to be seen again. There was nothing lesser about Niall, except maybe the occasional pity party he threw himself.

I approached him from the side, walking slowly, making sure not to startle him. After the events of the evening, it didn't take much to guess that he was in a very dark place. So much had changed in little more than twenty-four hours. More than he even knew.

Part of me wished that I didn't have to come here; that I didn't have to have this conversation with him; that I could put it off—even though I never would. The reality was that we had one day before we would be magically whisked away to camp. They didn't really call it camp, but it was the equivalent of Earth and Emerald's supernatural Camp David. Swanky residences with underlings to do our bidding, all located on a massive compound that no one had access to unless they were in the trials.

I suspected that Niall's thoughts weren't about the election or strategy, or anything that would probably be useful to ponder the night before we left.

Instead, he was thinking about her. Nikki, *our* mate.

I stepped up beside him, a few feet away, wrinkling my nose in distaste as icy water battered at my side. I fucking hated the cold. He did too, for that matter.

But for some reason, whenever anything was tough, this became his go-to spot. It was the same place I'd found him four years ago; alone and unsure about what to do. When faced with a difficult choice and he needed to weigh his options, he'd stand on the Brooklyn Bridge just as he was now. Rain or shine, stormy or clear, night or day; Niall would be here when he needed to think.

"We need to talk," I said.

If I'd shaken him from his memories or cycling thoughts, he didn't show it. Not a jerk or twitch or any acknowledgment that he registered I was present.

"What's there to talk about? Tomorrow we'll be at some undisclosed location. My mate will be there, and she doesn't even know who I am. I'm not sure she even recognizes that we're mates. She certainly didn't act like it."

I frowned, though I'd suspected this was where his train of thoughts had taken him.

It was still difficult to hear. I felt for him. I really did. But it could be a lot fucking worse. He'd been on the other side of the city, away from her for four long years.

Did he really just expect her to welcome him with open arms? Honestly, I didn't think he'd actually thought it through. If he had, he would have acted by now instead of letting Phaon lead him around with a carrot on a stick.

The truth was, he wasn't ready to take a mate when he'd first escaped.

She was trapped in there with him and he got them both out, but he didn't know her. He wasn't even with her for a full day before her family found them and demanded her back. That's all it took.

He handed her over just like that, and even though he hesitated, he still did it.

He still gave her up because at the end of the day, Niall wasn't ready back then. No one could blame him for that. He'd been imprisoned and kept as an experiment for half a century. He had shit he needed to work through, but now that he had, he was ready for her—and he wasn't happy that Nikki didn't seem all that ready herself. I'd never say it to him, but who could blame her? We'd all made a deal with her father and didn't give her any say. It was archaic and as backwoods as it got.

"There's nothing to say," he responded. "She'll be there and we'll be there and I'll win her back. I'm pissed, but we'll get past it. I'll make sure of it."

Well, that really wasn't the best approach to the situation.

Before I learned she was my mate, I probably would have let him just go at it this way. He was like a bull. When he decided to charge, nothing would stop him. Including me. The only difference this time was the red flag waving in his face was my mate—and his approach would alienate her. I'd be collateral damage, and that wasn't acceptable. So while the bull was going to charge, I needed to make sure that he missed, or perhaps tripped, if necessary.

Even if I had to stick my own foot out to do it.

This was going to suck.

"My mate from the subway was there tonight." There wasn't exactly an easy way to go about this conversation. Last I'd checked, no one had written a handbook on how to tell your best friend that the woman he had been pining after for four years was also your woman. I figured softening the approach was probably ideal, but wasn't sure beyond that.

"Really?" he asked, idly staring ahead. Under different circumstances, he might have been more interested.

I knew that he had been more than frustrated to learn that my mate, whoever she had been, was somehow involved in turning our deal sideways the night before. That deal was important in getting him one step closer to his mate. He'd still attempted to be happy, which I appreciated, but this time he didn't have it in him. I wasn't all that offended. Hard to be, when I was fixing to rock his world.

"Yeah, I did . . . and I recognized her." I sounded like a damn idiot. "I knew I'd seen her face before. I just didn't realize how or when, or where ..." I slowly trailed off.

"I'm glad," he said, his tone not matching his words. I chuckled.

Eyebrows lifted, he turned his head away from the dark water to look at me.

Now or never, I told myself. I really hoped we'd make it through this.

"It's Nikki."

"What?" he said, not understanding. At least I was pretty sure he didn't since he didn't seem to be upset. Or more upset, rather. I didn't have a lot of experience with shifters outside of those in the fae syndicate that had either defected from the Wards or were stragglers like him.

"It's Nikki," I said again, repeating it slower this time. "Nikki Ward is my mate."

Niall blinked slowly, as if he were in a trance of some sort, and coming out of it. Then the spark of anger came. His hands tightened to fists and literal fire shone in his eyes, making him look more like a demon than a shifter.

I gave it sixty/forty odds that my admission would be my famous last words and they'd be on my gravestone.

Forty percent leaned toward Niall drowning me in the river and I didn't have a gravestone at all.

"You can't be serious. She's mine. My mate. I've known she was mine for four years, and I *never* rejected her. Even if she rejected me and never told me, I would have to accept it to break the bond. I won't. Ever. I am her mate." The very ground shook beneath us, and I drew in a breath. We were on a bridge. It didn't need it to shake. This was the closest that he'd ever come to losing his temper.

"I'm aware," I said slowly. I didn't step away because that would anger the predator in him and make him want to pounce, but I also didn't draw closer.

Rabid dogs couldn't be blamed for biting. While my best friend kept himself on a leash, I still knew who and what he was.

"I'm not saying she's not your mate. All I'm telling you is the girl in the subway was Nikki. I saw her face. I knew I'd seen her somewhere, but I couldn't remember where it was. Once I saw her again, without the glamour, it clicked. The pictures of her that you've gotten from Alexander over the years. I saw her in them. And I saw her again tonight. I felt it, Niall. The bond is there and she feels it too."

Niall's jaw tensed and he looked away

"I don't know what to say."

"Well, speaking to me is a start," I replied.

Despite the difficult nature of this conversation, one corner of his mouth tilted upward. He was still glaring at me, but any inkling of a smile meant this was going better than I'd ever expected. I'd convinced myself I'd be dragon chow.

"Son of a—"

A hard fist slammed into my gut. The air rushed out of my lungs as I hunched forward. Clearly, I thought too soon.

"What the fuck?" I wheezed. "You were fine two seconds ago."

"That's for being her mate," Niall said. The thunderstorm scattered his water-logged hair all over his face.

I glared back at him. "It's not like I had much choice in the matter."

"No," he agreed. "But you're not rejecting her, are you?"

"Of course not." I would take the punch, but I wasn't walking away from Nikki. For years, I'd wanted to find my mate. Decades, even. A great many fae had laughed at my expense because I was young for one of my race. I didn't have a problem finding pretty women for sex. They couldn't understand why I would want to settle down when so many of my kind waited at least a hundred years before looking for their one and only.

What no one realized was that I was afraid I'd be forced into a loveless marriage. Trapped, just like my parents.

I didn't know if they'd been good people at one time, but I could guarantee the last three hundred years together hadn't helped either of them. When they weren't fighting, they were frigid. With one another. Unhappy with his marriage and bitter that he never found his true mate, my father drowned his woes in drugs and pussy at the Madame Dupont's. My mother wasn't much better. She kept a harem of indentured servants she'd fuck anywhere and everywhere, including in front of me and my siblings. Her favorite place to have an orgy was in the center courtyard of the Rose mansion, where her voice echoed off the four walls and the statues could watch.

Sometimes she'd even fuck herself on the statues.

My mother wasn't sane, but I was told she hadn't always been that way. Once a young heiress with power and potential, she'd accepted my father's hand for the prestige—turning down and rejecting her common-born mate when she did.

Sometimes I wondered if she'd regretted that decision. I'd never asked, but I'd heard his name echoing through the house when she got off. That felt like enough of an answer.

"All I've wanted is to find my mate. I didn't think I would, certainly not in the same woman as you—but I won't turn my back on her. This may be unconventional, but if she'll have us both, I'm willing to make it work." It was late, well past midnight. The storm had finally begun to die away; its rumbling reduced to a dull roar. "Will you?"

Niall waited a moment, thinking about his answer.

I wasn't backing down. He had to realize that. If we weren't together in this, we were against each other—and it would make Nikki's life much harder.

And truth be told, I didn't want to be against my best friend.

"You won't try to get in the way?" he finally asked, uncharacteristically vulnerable. "You won't take her from me?"

I bit back the urge to tell him he had to have her first for anyone to take her. Smartass comments, while second nature, would end in my spleen being *outside* my body. I wasn't about that, and I wouldn't shit all over his feelings.

"You're my best friend, Niall. Dickhead or not. Do I like

the idea of sharing my one and only? No. I won't pretend that I do. But you two are the people I care most about in the world now. It would hurt you both to try to do this any other way. If not for our friendship, then for her sake—I will do everything to make this work. Not just for me, but for you too."

"You mean that?" Niall said; emotion he couldn't hide was prominent in his tone.

"Nah, I'm just fucking with you," I said dryly. "I planned on stabbing you in your sleep the first chance I got."

"You shithead." He punched my shoulder lightly. He laughed a little and everything in me breathed easier.

"So, are you with me?"

"Yeah, asshole. I'm with you. Now we just need to get Nikki on board."

One down. One to go.

While I was mildly worried about telling Niall and having him kill me, something told me that my spitfire mate was going to be the harder one to convince of the two.

I'd always enjoyed a good challenge.

CHAPTER 13
NIKKI

SINCE I HADN'T REALLY PLANNED TO JOIN THE ELECTION TRIALS, I didn't know what to expect. When I was *actually* paying attention to the announcer, I learned we'd have twenty-four hours with our families before we'd be magically whisked away to an undisclosed location deep within Earth and Emerald territory. Just "poof" and we'd disappear from wherever we were located, whether we were ready or not.

This was good since it gave me time to talk to Gavriel.

This was not good because it gave my family time to talk to me.

At home.

Did I mention I was with my family?

Things weren't going well, as one would imagine.

So there I was, calmly sitting at the dining room table and keeping my gaze focused on what was unfolding before me while my dad ripped into Ty for going against him. It was only a matter of time before it was my turn.

"What the hell were you thinking?" my father yelled.

"I was thinking Nikki is going to get herself killed and I

did exactly what I was supposed to do as her brother. Protect her."

"This is exactly why you weren't chosen in the first place. You make rash decisions without thinking about the consequences. Alexander was supposed to be running. Now the one person in this family that needed to be there isn't because you couldn't think things through."

"I'm meant to take over the syndicate," Ty argued.

"The syndicate, Ty. I needed you here. Alexander is more suitable as a candidate. He knows how to talk to people. He knows how to charm them. He knows how to think before he speaks. For fuck's sake, if I wanted someone to screw this up, I would have chosen Gavriel." Our father threw his hands up in the air.

Reaching over, I grabbed Gav's hand beneath the table and patted it. My brother had said that he wasn't affected by the way our father regarded him, but I sometimes found that hard to believe. There were only so many times you could be told you're worthless before you started to believe it, right? He was anything but.

Gavriel took my hand and turned it over placing his into my palm and began to sign slowly so I had time to thoroughly understand.

Why did you do it? he asked.

It's complicated.

Try.

I don't want to marry any of them.

That's not complicated.

I want out. I saw a window. So I jumped.

The trials are dangerous.

I'll be okay. Trust me. But you have to do something for me.

What?

Use Operation Sunnyside to get Lindsey and the kids out.

120

He paused, not turning his hand and placing it into mine for an answer. When he finally did, I felt the sheen of sweat that had developed. *Operation Sunnyside?*

Yes. ASAP. Swear it.

Another long pause spanned between us. The attention wasn't on me at the moment, and I felt like if I stayed totally still, no one would see me there. Like my dad was a T-Rex or some equally angry bird-lizard whose vision was based on movement. I took the risk and turned my head to look at Gav. He angled his head down as though he was looking at his lap, then turned slightly and glanced at me from the corner of his eyes. With a long blink, he dipped his chin a fraction and squeezed my hand.

As I began to sign a response into his palm, the dinosaur saw me. Now his ire was directed my way. "And *you*!"

My body jerked in response, and I let go of Gavriel's hand.

"You have no idea what you've done. The deals I made are now at risk. If I could make you take it back I would, but there's no way around the binding magic of the fire."

I was entirely aware of that fact and how it worked in my favor, thank you very much.

"Why did you go against me?"

"I don't know . . ." I probably should have thought something up before now. Too late.

My father pounded the table with his fists and a crack appeared in the wood. "You better come up with a better answer than that, Nikolette Aset Ward. Those families think I am reneging on the deal we made. I've already been accused of sabotaging them by letting two of my children enter the trials, especially the daughter who's hand they are supposed to win. You're a woman. I thought you understood the role you play for this family."

"There are other women in the trials," I grumbled, and my mom shook her head at me as a warning to not fight back. "If Alex won, he didn't have to marry anyone in the syndicates. My competing is no different. If I win, you still have the power of Earth and Emerald but I wouldn't need to marry anyone then. I don't see the problem, Dad."

My father scoffed a condescending laugh. "Do you actually think you are capable of winning?"

"The thought had crossed my mind, yeah." Alex shot me a look. It was one I knew well, and it was telling me to shut the hell up. Don't dig the hole deeper. Ty pinched the bridge of his nose.

Dad's features darkened and a deep crease formed between his brows. "You will drop out of the trials when you reach a point that I'll no longer look incompetent as your father. I can't risk you getting kicked out in the first round and having the other syndicates question my power."

"Thanks for the vote of confidence." My blood began to boil. I grit my teeth clenching my jaw so much it hurt. The threat of tears stung my eyes, and I dug my nails into my thighs.

This was a means to an end. The first chance I got, I was escaping, but he didn't need to know that. I had no intention of winning, but part of me wanted to now, just so I could throw it in his face.

"Your sister knew how to keep her mouth shut and do as she was told. You should learn to do the same."

"Phaon, *please*. Don't bring Marissa into this." My mother's words were pleading and not at all chastising, but that didn't matter.

My father spun, the back of his hand cracking against her face. Gavriel and I gasped, clutching each other's hands beneath the table.

Alexander stepped forward, his voice deepening into a growl of warning. "*Don't.*"

My dad held his hand out to stop Alexander from approaching, but my brother didn't halt until my mom looked at him and shook her head. She palmed her cheek and water filled her eyes while my father glared at her, spewing his venom in anger. "This is your fault. You let her watch those ridiculous movies with imprudent girls. They made her believe she could defy me. I tried to put a stop to it, but you asked me to stay my hand. You said they were just movies. When you let her read whatever she liked, you insisted it would be an outlet so she wouldn't act out of line. Now look at her."

My mother stood straighter, somehow strong yet broken at the same time. "They were children. I won't apologize for giving them time for imagination before the reality of this world set in." She kept her voice even and calm, meanwhile, I wanted to rage. "Don't do this, Phaon. Husband. *Please*. Not now. Our baby girl is leaving us for these trials because she thought she could please you. She made a mistake, but people in the election every time."

"I won't let that happen, Mom," Ty interjected.

"Stop talking. You've done enough," my father said, pointing at him before aiming at mother. "I should never have listened to you. You didn't want to tell her. You wanted to wait until the last minute. Look what good that did us."

"She was grieving! We all were!"

"She wouldn't have been grieving if she would've saved her sister and not left her to die," he spat.

Alexander's lips parted in shock, and he glanced at me. Gavriel's grip on my hand was firm, unyielding, as if trying to feed me strength and support. Ty just stood there, watching it all unfold, wearing a mask I couldn't read.

None of it mattered. I felt like I'd been stabbed in the gut. Never once had I been directly blamed for my sister's death. We'd both been taken. We'd both been tortured. We both tried to escape. So many of the details of that experience had been blocked from my mind. I was told it was a trauma response. My brain attempting to protect me from my past. Sometimes it was just shapes and shadows and fuzzy outlines of people. But one thing always remained solid. The last time I saw my sister's face.

Burning.

I dreamed of her often and I could still hear her voice— her screams—but I couldn't remember what her last words were to me. Over the years the dreams had become clearer, like my mind was ready to process what happened. I assumed it was the truth breaking through my mental block. I couldn't remember everything about that night, but I didn't need all the memories to know I never left her to die.

To hear my father say as much crushed me. He was a cruel man, yes. I knew that. But I had never seen this side of him. It had never been directed at us. At me. Had he always blamed me for Marissa's death?

My body began to vibrate in outrage. Fire licked beneath my skin, begging to be released. I stood up, my chair scraping against the floor.

"She died because we're Wards. We were taken because of y—"

His hand wrapped around my throat, cutting off my air

124

supply. "Finish that sentence, daughter. Say it," he said in a deadly whisper, pressing his fingertips into my flesh.

My brain screamed at me to let it go. To not say it. I'd never seen him like this. He'd never hit my mom. He'd never laid a hand on me. He'd never threatened me.

I'd never so outwardly defied him either.

Guess there was a first time for everything.

From my periphery, I saw Gav. He was shaking his head, pleading with me not to say the last word. Alex and Ty froze while they held my mom back.

I tried to swallow, but couldn't. His hand was squeezing too tight. I closed my eyes, conveying that I wasn't going to push further.

"That's what I thought," he said, letting go and shoving me toward Gav. My back slammed into his chest, and he caught me as I stumbled.

Air filled my lungs and I coughed. My mom rushed to me as my brothers let her go.

"The deal still stands. You're going to lose exactly when I say so, do you understand?" I nodded, not trusting my voice. "In the meantime, try not to fuck this up any more than you already have."

As he went to exit the room he stopped in front of Ty. "That goes for you as well." Seconds passed where no words were spoken. Then he clocked Ty across the jaw unexpectedly. "I expected better of you. Don't disappoint me this time."

It's not like I didn't know what my family was. I loved every one of them even when I didn't like them and a part of me always felt guilty for that. That was before tonight.

Gav tended to my mom's cheek, putting ice into a napkin and holding it against her face. "Don't fuss over me, Gav. It'll heal in about five minutes."

Alexander sighed and put his hands on his hips while looking at me. "You okay?"

"Yup," I responded while rubbing my throat, the word coming out scratchy and gravelly.

"Good. I hear the trials start immediately after arrival. I suggest you get a good night's sleep. It'll probably be your last chance for a while."

Ty rested his hand in the middle of my back. "I won't let anything happen to you, Nikki, but I expect you to do as I say so I can protect you."

"Ugh, stop it," I mumbled, shimmying away from him and his touch. "I heard everything dad said, loud and clear. I don't need to hear it from you too."

Alex started to leave the room, and he caught Ty's bicep as he was walking by.

"Get the fuck off me," Ty snapped, jerking his arm away.

"I have to try to repair some of the damage the two of you caused tonight. You're coming with me." With a final glance in my direction, he added, "Bed. Now."

They left the room without another word, and it gave me the opportunity to leave. I stormed out, heading down the hall, ignoring my mother and Gavriel's calls for me. I needed to be alone.

When I reached my bedroom, I grabbed a pillow and screamed into it until it felt like my throat was raw and bleeding. Then I threw it across the room.

Staring out the expansive window of our high-rise, I took in the view one last time. The city was massive. The people that lived here were forced into submission. Living their lives in fear of the syndicates; following rules they had no voice in making. Phaon Ward expected obedience without question, no matter who you were. Everyone here did as they were told knowing if they didn't, they'd answer to whatever leader would bring hell upon them for defying their orders.

My mom was no different. Marissa had been no different.

If my father wanted obedience, he had another thing coming. That trait died with my sister.

Taking out a phone, I typed a message to Sam in code.

"G is taking care of the family."

Little dots appeared instantly. "They're ready. I've already moved them to the safehouse. Thank you, Nik. Tell G."

"Of course. I always keep my promises."

"I'll see you tomorrow. I can't believe you got us into this mess. The fucking Earth and Emerald trials."

"About that . . ."

" ???"

"New plan."

"No. No new plans. Stop making new plans!"

"You'll like this one."

"I highly doubt that."

"I'm going to win this election, and you're going to help me."

" . . . I'm listening."

"And then I'm going to dismantle the syndicates brick by brick."

"Now we're talking."

CHAPTER 14
NIKKI

THE PORTAL SWIRLED BEFORE US; A MYSTIC COMBINATION OF colors mingled on the edges, creating a glittery effect. Earth and Emerald had territory all over the world—more than any other House, unless you counted Sea and Serpentine, because you know, water. We could only guess where this portal would lead, or what our final destination would be. What we could see on the other side was beautiful, and such a stark contrast to life in Manhattan.

Tall, green trees framed an open meadow, providing a picturesque and tranquil view. The setting sun painted the sky hues of pink and orange against a backdrop of mountains in the distance.

The location of the trials were kept a closely guarded secret for obvious reasons. No family or friends were allowed to interfere. And in this case, no syndicates. The only assistance we were allowed would come from the person we'd chosen as our second.

That's how it was *supposed* to be. My father said that he would contact me and tell me when it was time for me to " lose the trials" so that I didn't embarrass him. I didn't know how, but I fully believed he had a way to reach us. It was just another reminder of how corrupt this world was.

Sam stood next to me, our arms touching. We simultaneously gave each other a nudge of encouragement; nothing to give away that she was anything more than my bodyguard. I didn't know this place, and I didn't know who was watching.

When the magic took us from our home, Ty and I had been sitting in my father's study, getting another earful about our behavior and what he expected from us. Then "blip". We were gone while he was mid-sentence— taken immediately to wherever we stood now.

Alone.

And I couldn't have been more grateful for it.

A little bit of sadness crept over me as my thoughts drifted to my mother, and I wondered if we'd just shared our final hug. I wondered if that would be the last time I saw her. If I couldn't win the trials and win the election, I was leaving. Opportunities like this didn't come along often, and I wasn't going to miss it. Gav had the contacts to follow me out, but couldn't do it for all of us. Not without our father finding out.. I loved Alexander, but he lived the syndicate life, and he could take care of himself.

No matter what, this was going to change everything. I'd never go back to New York, and with the exception of the few items I had in my backpack, I was leaving behind everything I had ever known.

"Ready?" I asked Sam.

"Do I have a choice?"

"Nope." My voice was steady despite my nerves, and I marched forward. "Let's go."

The portal was wide enough that Sam, Jackie, Ty, and I could walk through it side by side.

It was also deceiving.

It looked like we were going to walk through, and our feet would immediately hit the ground on the other side. That's not how it happened. That portal was a good six feet *off* the ground.

I should have let Ty and Jackie walk through first. Or you know, listened when Jackie told me to stop. Instead, with my head held high, I dragged Sam through. When my foot hovered over the air, I realized entirely too late that there was nothing below it. Sam and I tumbled out, landing in a pile on top of each other.

"Well, that's just fucking rude," I mumbled through my groan.

Sam lay on the ground next to me. "Did anybody see that?" she croaked.

Jackie looked around. "No. We're the first ones here."

Well thank fuck for that.

Ty just looked pissed off that I'd fallen. He wasn't used to embarrassing situations. Not like me. I lived that life constantly. Even through his scowl, he extended his hand out to pull me up. "You okay?"

"I'm fine, you don't need to coddle me."

"I'm supposed to protect you, Nik." He offered a hand to Sam, and she took it warily as he helped her up.

I didn't want his help. Ty's definition of protection varied. On the one hand, he didn't want me to get hurt. I could understand that. On the other hand, I knew who he was, and he wouldn't think twice about snapping somebody's neck because they looked at me the wrong way.

How did I know? Because it happened before.

I really didn't want another unnecessary death on my conscience.

"I noticed that you didn't fall, Jackie," I said casually while dusting off my pants.

"Of course I didn't. I'm half fae," she said haughtily before turning away. "Honestly, I thought you had better eyesight than that."

Thought wrong, I said to myself.

Multiple other portals were open, waiting for other contestants to arrive. Jackie and my brother were watching all of them, sizing up the competition as some literally face planted in the same way we had.

As other candidates arrived, I kept my focus on the two portals that no one had come through yet. The chatter and buzzing amongst the newly arrived became background noise while my pulse quickened.

Malachi was first. Standing at the edge of the portal, he cocked his head to the side, assessing the ground below. His dark eyes narrowed, and rather than taking a step through the portal, he jumped, landing on his feet. With a swift move, Tylea followed suit, and landed next to him.

Fucking demons and their good eyesight.

Shifters were supposed to be better, but I wasn't buying it. Nope. That would be way too inconvenient for my argument.

Niall and Adrian appeared at the last portal. My mysterious subway-mate walked through it casually without falling. He didn't glide like his element was air. The way the ground called to him with a magnetic force, and he landed so effortlessly suggested he was an earth fae.

Which made sense.

I remembered the way he smelled when he caught up with me in Brooklyn, and goosebumps erupted on my skin, sending a reminder to my body that he was supposed to be mine. Not *supposed* to be. He *was* mine. I clenched my thighs together and grit my teeth to suppress the sudden desire to go to him.

Niall jumped through next, landing with an echoing thud so heavy that it didn't quite make sense for his stature. Hybrid, I'd been told. But hybrid what?

Moments later, a representative from Earth and Emerald walked through another portal.

"Candidates. Welcome to the trials," she began, smiling warmly as she looked at all of us. "My name is Courtney. I'm Hekate's primary personal assistant. You might be wondering why her most important assistant is here with you, and the answer is that I am to be Hekate's eyes and ears throughout the trials. Think of me as Hekate during this time. I am her, and she is me. Now, I'm well versed in—"

"She sent her assistant? Are we not worthy of her presence?" the vampire from Clan Tepes asked.

The woman looked instantly irritated, and responded in a way that said that was right on the mark. "Right now, no. You're all a bunch of plebians as far as she's concerned. Prove yourself and make it to the election, and then you'll be *worthy of her presence*, though I assure you, rudely cutting people off while they're speaking won't put you in anyone's good graces."

The vampire pursed his lips, but managed to keep his mouth shut.

"Does anyone else have any stupid questions they'd like to get out of the way?"

I snorted, and Sam elbowed me.

"Are you able to tell us where we are?" Ayla asked, the witch from the Staten Island coven asked. She had pretty features. Smooth taupe skin and dark eyes. Her black hair was straighter than an arrow, despite the humidity. She was dressed in business attire befitting of a chancellor, with heels to match. Despite her soft appearance, I got the impression she wasn't someone to mess with.

"No, but I can tell you it doesn't matter. We aren't staying here," she said after appraising the speaker. Her response was kinder, and you could tell she appreciated the way Ayla conducted herself in comparison. "Anyone else? No? Good. Follow me."

Everyone began walking toward the portal she'd just come out of, but this time, I waited. No way was I going to be at the head of the line, just to eat dirt again. I'd let these other people walk through first. If they fell, or landed upside down, or were sucked into a vortex, I'd get to watch that happen first. Mind you, if it were a vortex and I was going to die, that would suck to know it, but—I did not want to be the embarrassment my father said I was.

Unlike the other portals that showed what was on the other side, this one was a mirror image of where we were. I expected it to change once we stepped over the side, but that didn't seem to be the case. I leaned over to Sam, whispering, "Is this a trick? The first trial, you think?"

"What? No. Well, probably not." She sniffed the air. "No, it's definitely different. Colder. The temperature is two and half degrees lower."

"Could just be because Jackie's here. She's a cold bitch."

Sam stifled a laugh, scrunching her eyebrows together in an effort to remain serious, but Jackie heard me. She gave me a hard glare from the corner of her eye, but I shrugged my shoulder. She worked alongside Ty and knew damn well what I thought of her. How could she not?

"Welcome to the compound. This property is where you'll be staying. There's a main house with community dining hall, meeting rooms, theater, and gym with full access to weapons for training. And it's also where you'll find us," Courtney said, gesturing to multiple supernaturals that were standing on the property. "We are all representatives of Earth and Emerald, and we will hold each of you to the same standard. Break any rules, and you're out of the trials."

Someone raised their hand and she pointed at them, seemingly pleased that another person had the forethought to use manners and not interrupt her.

"Where will we be staying?"

"There are buildings located throughout the compound, and that's where you'll be housed. Your chosen seconds will have their own accommodations separate from you on another part of the property. As the trials begin, you'll understand why." I glanced at Sam with concern. This was not what I'd expected. "Each house is equipped with three bedrooms that have en suite bathrooms, a full kitchen, and a library so you may study for the trials. Your seconds will be able to visit you and act as a liaison with the outside world, but that's all. There is no electronic or magical communications for the candidates after this point.

"To our guests from New York, you will be put up on the west end of the property. As your families are new to the trials, we only have two houses available for you to split. You may choose whichever you want to stay in."

What did us being new have to do with anything? They should have had enough housing no matter what. Doing quick mental math, I stepped forward. "Did you say that each house only has three bedrooms?"

The representative looked at me knowingly. A small smirk pulled at the corner of her lips. "Yes, I did."

Adrian and Niall stepped forward, forming the start of

one group. Ayla, the witch, and Rude-ass, the vampire, stepped forward and formed another. There was one spot left in each group. I glanced at Adrian. And he gave a little head tilt as he looked at the empty space next to him, beckoning me to come.

Yes. Mine. My mate. My body and cavewoman instincts pulled me in that direction.

My brain said don't go. I wasn't ready to address the mate situation. I wasn't ready to admit how scared I was at the prospect of how much I wanted him. I wanted to belong. I wanted to know I would have the person that would never, ever leave me. Like Malachi. Like Marissa. Niall was next to him, watching the exchange between us. He looked tense; his jaw tight.

My gaze shifted over to Malachi. He raised an eyebrow, then walked over to stand with Niall and Adrian.

Ty made his move over to the vampire/witch group. "Come on, Nikki. You can share a room with me."

Dread coiled within me. I had no desire to share a room with my brother. I didn't even want to share a house with him most of the time. He was just too apathetic about everything. His cruelty knew no bounds, since it was the only time he seemed to feel anything. Even though it had never extended to me, the fact remained, it was who he was —and I didn't like it.

I couldn't try to win this and get away from my family if he was my constant protector and shadow.

My alternative was putting my lust-driven self in the same house as my incredibly gorgeous subway-mate, my lickable—and frustrating—ex-mate that unrejected me, and a dude that looked at me like I was a goddess denying him the right to breathe.

I thought there was only supposed to be shit at one end of the stick.

"Can I just stay with Sam?" Courtney looked at me, arching a displeased eyebrow. "Right. That was a stupid question. Got it."

"Nikki," my brother hissed at me.

With a quick side glance at Sam, I could see she approved of what I was about to do. I closed my eyes and inhaled deeply. Then I walked over to the group where Adrian, Malachi, and Niall stood.

Ty was fuming.

Before he could argue, Courtney clapped her hands and said, "So it is done." A little fizzle of energy crackled through the air, as though magic had just bound us to these houses.

And it had.

No take-backsies.

I really just hoped I'd chosen well.

When they had described it as a house, I kind of pictured it more as like a small bungalow. What it really was a grand lodge style cabin with a huge porch wrapped around it. It was beautiful. Two stories with luxury furnishings and a warm, inviting feel on the inside. The main room had high ceilings with big windows that gave a front row seat to the forest. The phoenix inside me began to feel a sense of calm and peace. Nature tended to do that to me, but it was so rare that I got to experience much nature living in Manhattan.

If I put some thought into it, I couldn't remember the

last time I'd felt peace. I longed for it. For my world and my head and my phoenix and my body to just . . . *be*.

I stood in front of the window, soaking in the silence. Part of me wanted to stay here forever. Sneak off into the woods and disappear. Screw the trials. This was heaven.

My momentary serenity was ripped apart the moment I heard Malachi's voice next to me.

"Hey."

I sighed and rolled my eyes. "What?"

"Just wanted to come say hi. We're staying in the same room, after all."

"Presumptuous much? We're staying in the same *house*. That's not the same as sharing a room."

"That's actually what I meant," he said quickly, the words stumbling out in rapid succession. "I wasn't trying to insinuate that you were going share my—"

"What makes you think it's your room and not mine?"

He looked around, unsure of how to answer. "I don't know. I don't know why I said that. You can have the room. There's a couch in the living room. I'll just sleep there."

While a part of me loved watching Malachi so flustered, it didn't change the fact I was mad at him. "No, that isn't going to happen," I scoffed.

Niall walked into the living area. "Well, now, I can't have you being all chivalrous and giving her your bed without offering mine. So, Nikki, you can have my room, and I'll sleep on the couch."

I glanced between the two of them. "You have to be kidding me right now."

"Nikki, can I please talk to you?" Malachi asked.

"No, Malachi, you can't. I told you at the solstice cele-bration that I didn't want to talk to you. I haven't changed my mind in the past twenty-four hours."

"All I'm asking is for a chance to explain."

All the hurt began to resurface. When it coupled with my anger, I felt the heat rising inside. "What makes you think you deserve a chance?"

"I don't deserve a chance. I won't argue that. But I'm still asking for one."

"No. Request denied." Only minutes before, I'd been on the brink of feeling fully at peace, but now, my mood had soured.

"You have every right to be mad at me. I won't pretend otherwise. I just want you to know the truth."

"I don't want your truth, or whatever version of the truth you believe. Literally an hour before you accosted me in the bathroom last night, I learned that you'd been in Queens for the past *six years*. I didn't even know if you were alive anymore because you didn't tell me anything after you rejected me and then walked away. You *left me*, Malachi," I said, holding my voice as steady as I could despite the emotion thickening. "And you never looked back. Allow me to return the favor."

Niall glanced at Malachi, looking him up and down. "I think she said her piece, mate." And he let out a chuckle. The sound teased at some sort of faraway memory, like it was reaching for something, but I couldn't understand what. Like maybe I'd heard his laugh before? Like an echo from another time. It was a weird moment of déjà vu, and it made this uncomfortable situation even more so.

Adrian had walked into the room at some point during my tirade. With his arms crossed, he leaned against the door frame and appeared to have been listening to our conversation.

"I suppose you're going to offer me your room and tell

me you'll sleep on the couch as well?" I said with a snarky tone.

"I hadn't planned on it, no."

Looking between Malachi and Niall and back to Adrian. I pursed my lips and nodded once. "Good. Then I'm sharing a room with you."

All three guys raised their brows in surprise. Niall looked confused by my choice, and he gave Adrian a hardened glare. Malachi looked like he was at a loss for words.

I adjusted my backpack and walked down the hall, not saying a word to any of them. Then it occurred to me I didn't know which room Adrian had come out of. After stopping and looking down the hallway, I came to a halt. Internally I groaned, not wanting to turn around and ruin my perfectly executed exit, but now I was going to look stupid if I went into the wrong one.

Adrian casually said, "Third door on the left."

Bless.

He so got brownie points for that. I nodded and headed that way.

The room was massive. I supposed they all were. A long green velvet couch was centered in front of a stone fireplace. A small fire had been lit, warming the space perfectly. A four-poster king-sized bed was nestled between two large windows. Thick drapes hung on either side. Overall, the decor was simplistic. Nothing really that flashy had been added, and of course it wasn't personalized. Despite the grandeur and quality of the furnishings, it was a few steps up from the necessities.

Standing in front of the fireplace, I held my palms over the flames while I listened to the crackling of the wood. Its heat licked at my skin, and a tendril reached out, trying to wrap around my hand like it had at the solstice celebration.

The fire nestled between my fingers, never burning, but pulling at something I'd suppressed for reasons I couldn't bear to admit. Closing my eyes, I stepped forward, letting the flame curl around my arm as I relished its touch while whispers in my mind begged the fire to consume me...

"Hope I'm not interrupting anything," Adrian said, startling me.

"Son of a Baptist preacher!" I shouted, yanking my hand away from the fireplace so hard, the momentum turned my body, and I tripped over my own feet, landing on my ass with a resounding thud. Some supernatural I was.

Adrian's lips twisted in amusement while he looked at me on the ground.

"You know, you could clear your throat or something benign like that to let a girl know when you've walked in the room," I complained as he extended a hand to help me up.

"I didn't intend to sneak up on you. You're a shifter. I assumed you heard me down the hall." He released my hand and shrugged, walking over to the side of the bed.

"Well, I am, but I wasn't paying atten—"

He lifted his shirt, pulling it over his head, and words were lost on me.

Holy wow.

Seeing Adrian without his shirt on sent desire straight between my thighs. He was sculpted. Lean. A tree of life tattoo covered his back; branches twining around his biceps. The center trunk was morphed into the body of a beautiful woman. Mother Earth.

While I wanted to marvel at the artwork and ask the story behind it, I couldn't stop gawking and wanting to see more of him—just with less clothing.

Clearly it had been a while since I'd been with someone.

Syndicate Princess meant I was frequently under some-one's watch. Any relationships that I'd had after Malachi were few and far between. At first, I dated some of the enforcers. Those hook-ups were always safe, and keeping it on the down low wasn't a point I had to drive home. It's not like they'd out themselves to my family. Me? I'd get chewed out. They'd just end up dead. For that reason, there wasn't much action to be had. Was I worth the repercussions? Most thought not, and who could blame them?

After that it was other members of the militia. Delta and I'd had a thing for about six months. He was great, but I couldn't get too attached. I could never get too attached. Not that I'd ever expected to be married off in some syndi-cate exchange-for-power program, but I knew I couldn't settle down with someone my family didn't approve of. And after Malachi left, I wasn't really sure that I wanted to.

Sex was different. I didn't mind having sex. But I wasn't willing to lead someone on. We had to be in it for the same reasons. And usually, their reasons morphed into some-thing different. At which point, I cut things off because I wouldn't string them along that way.

So here I was, ogling hardcore. I checked to make sure my mouth had stayed shut. It wasn't and I cringed. At least there wasn't drool. I think.

"Well, you may not have been paying attention earlier, but you seem to be paying attention now," he said with a smirk, pulling a clean shirt over his head.

"Well, look, I'll be honest, I wasn't expecting you to start stripping." My cheeks flushed. "So yeah. I noticed *that.*"

"Like what you see?"

"I'm not entirely sure how that's relevant," I said lightly, walking past him.

"Are we going to talk about this?" he asked, gesturing between us.

"You mean what happened the night before at the subway station, and then what happened yesterday at solstice celebration?"

"Yeah, that's exactly what I'm talking about." He looked relieved that I wasn't pretending it didn't happen.

"Oh, then in that case, no," I answered while opening a window.

"What are you doing?"

"What's it look like?" I asked, pointing outside.

"It looks like you're about to climb out the window in the middle of a conversation."

"Nailed it. Five points to Gryffindor," I said, giving him finger guns. "I'll be back later."

Internally, I groaned. Oh my goddess, I'm a walking embarrassment to women. Who gives finger guns to a sexy fae that just took off his shirt and wants to talk to you? Or better yet, bang you?

Broken phoenix shifters that are trying to avoid humping their mate without even having a formal introduction, that's who.

"You know, there's a door here," he said, signaling behind him.

"The window is also a perfectly acceptable option right now." Mostly because I'd already declared my intentions and would look stupid if I backed down now. Nope. I was doing it. Sticking one foot out the window, I tested the strength of the awning. On the bright side, I healed super fast if I did bust my ass.

"Care to tell me where you're going?"

"Sam's house, wherever that is." Sliding my body between the open pane, I straddled the windowsill.

"Okay, well I prefer to sleep on the right side of the bed, just in case you get back before me."

I froze. "Wait, what? What do you mean "your side of the bed?""

"I mean we're sharing, Nikki. I told you I wasn't offering you my bed while I slept on the couch, and you said good. So you can have the left side of the bed."

"I'm not . . . I can't . . ." *But you want to.* Flashes of his hands on my body played in my mind.

"You can't what?" He leaned against one of the posts on the bed, his hands casually tucked in his pockets.

"I can't sleep with you."

"Wow, really jumping ahead there, aren't you?" My lips parted, but no words came out. "You aren't sleeping *with* me. You'd be sleeping *next* to me. There's a very big difference."

"How do I know you're going to stay on your side?"

"How do I know you're going to stay on yours?" he countered.

"What do you mean?" I spluttered. "Why would I come to your side? I'm not the guy in this situation."

"So are you saying because I'm a guy that I would automatically be the one to cross boundaries and come to your side without invitation? Wow, Nikki, that's pretty sexist."

"I . . . That's not . . . Usually, yes . . ." My mouth fell open and I didn't know what to say. "Fair enough. You stay on your side; I stay on mine?"

"That's the plan." Pressing my lips together, I nodded in agreement, then continued to drag myself out of the window opening. "Oh, and Nikki?"

I stopped. "Yeah?"

"You are *invited* to come to my side. If you did, I wouldn't say no." He sent me an appraising look and

143

winked. Before I could respond, he walked out the door, leaving me standing there in an awkward, crouched position with one leg in the room and one leg on the roof.

Another shot of desire pulsed between my legs, throbbing against the windowsill, and I stifled a moan while my body begged for friction.

This was going to get dicey, especially since I wasn't entirely sure I'd say no either.

I just hoped he didn't sleep in the nude.

Or maybe I did hope that.

I was undecided.

CHAPTER 15
NIALL

When it became clear that Nikki wasn't coming back anytime soon, I retreated to the one place that I'd found solace in, no matter the location.

The library.

This one was large, though a bit sparse for my liking. At least it was part of the house and it was easily accessible without needing to go anywhere. There were few things I despised more than seeing people.

Most of the titles here had to do with pre-portal politics, things like the Cold War, Vietnam, European and Asian history. Roman military tactics. Blueprints for monstrosities called tanks.

I skimmed over them, not all that interested in reading about one of the many, many wars that humanity had fought.

As I moved farther along the mahogany bookshelves, the topics changed from history to a range of eclectic nonfiction. The topics weren't something I expected, nor were they particularly relevant for the vast majority of people. I skimmed titles, feeling more confused the further I went.

How to Keep a Pet Raccoon.

Why? They were wild animals that shouldn't be kept.

Acing your SATs.

I wasn't sure what a SAT was, but I was fairly certain it wasn't some forgotten art of sitting.

Psychology for Dummies.

Surely that wasn't a textbook.

What Your Horoscope Says About You.

Just, no.

The books became more absurd the farther I went.

The hardwood floors squeaked every other step, no matter how quietly I walked, and the thick rug did little to cover the noise. Toward the back of the room, dark brown leather seating surrounded a grand fireplace. It was actually an aesthetic I found agreeable.

I'd just come to the fantasy section, ready to skip right over it—the whole three shelves that it was—when a hearty chuckle sounded and broke my train of thought.

Adrian watched me from the end of the row, leaning one shoulder against the case, with his leg bent and the tip of his shoe pointed down to balance himself.

"I didn't know you were a romance reader." He tilted his forehead toward the shelf in front of me where barrel-chested men were plastered on the front of every cover.

"It's not my first preference. Particularly this brand of romance."

Titles like *The Duke's Temptation*, *Throbbing Manhood*, and *Aching for Him* were among the mildest of the selection. A winged man covered in scales caught my eye, and I picked up a co-authored title called, *Dragon Unleashed*.

I had no idea anyone wrote novels about dragons . . . in

romance. I scanned the names on the front, wondering if Jessica Wayne and Heather Hildenbrand were dragons as well.

It wasn't exactly what I'd be reading if I were back in New York City. Then again, when we were in the Roses territory, there wasn't much time for me to do anything beyond plot, scheme, conduct shady business deals, and beat up the occasional person.

I enjoyed reading but hadn't gotten to do much of it the last four years. In the facility where I was raised, one of the assistants had helped me learn to read. She snuck me books to practice with, until the head scientist found out. I never saw her again, but instead of being angry about it, they'd decided to use it to force my cooperation.

If I was *tame*, they gave me new books.

If I wasn't, I'd have nothing but four walls and a thin blanket to keep me company for weeks.

Books were the only thing that kept me sane, before Nikki.

My hands clutched the worn paperback a bit too tight.

"What? Gasp. You don't want to read about your brethren getting laid?"

Adrian's joking helped me disperse the tension in my shoulders. One corner of my mouth lifted. "Brethren?"

"You know, the big scaly bastards looking for a lizard mama—"

I chucked the book at his head. Adrian ducked, narrowly missing getting hit in the face.

"You're ridiculous."

Adrian chuckled. "What I am, is surprised that you left her alone. Once you had her in your general vicinity, I thought you might try to smother her."

"Yeah, well she's made it perfectly clear that she has no

desire to be around me. That doesn't mean I'm giving up. But I may have to rethink my strategy for how to approach her."

Adrian nodded, motioning to the leather chairs just behind him with his head, and I followed him over to the seating area

"I know it sucks," Adrian said quietly. "But I think you're doing the right thing here, giving her some space. She'll be living in the same house with us for the next few months and we don't want to overwhelm her with too much, too fast."

My animal snuffed at him in a haughty manner, not at all interested in what my best friend had to say. The dragon couldn't understand why Nikki didn't feel the same. He felt like we should claim her, and then she would understand and be happy about it.

I might be emotionally stunted, but even I knew that wasn't how it would go down.

If the years since I've found her had taught me anything, it was that not only were women fickle, but trying to make her see things my way would only backfire.

It bothered me that she didn't seem to remember me or feel any sort of pull. Meanwhile, I was burning in lust for her. My skin was hot and tight. I was perpetually hard because just the smell of her had my hormones in full rage and my blood pressure rising.

It was very much a "me problem."

Being around her had already become the sweetest torture.

"I need to talk to Robert and see what the council has planned for the first trial." I sidestepped away from my own self-pitying thoughts. "I'd rather not go in blind when I have her to think about."

"Agreed," Adrian said. "She hasn't rejected me, which makes me think she's at least somewhat open to the bond. I'm hoping that I can use that to get her to let me in. The easiest way to protect her is by being her mates. Until then, we'll just be fighting an uphill battle."

Bitterness coated my tongue, tasting of ash. I felt my nails sharpen to talons and quickly quelled the urge to shift. My beast may not be thrilled, I wasn't either, but we'd agreed to make this work for everyone's sake. We were both going to have to get used to it.

Double doors opened on the opposite side of the library. The leader of The Divine slipped through silently before shutting the door behind him with an audible click.

"Can we help you?" I asked. It didn't sound sincere. If anything, it came across as passive aggressive. One corner of his mouth curled up in a self assured smirk.

"We need to have a conversation."

Adrian leaned back on the leather loveseat, bracing one arm across the back of it. He tilted his chin and asked him in a bored, placating voice, "About?"

"Nikki."

While I had no reason to know why, his topic of choice wasn't exactly unexpected. It hadn't escaped my notice that Adrian and I weren't the only ones she seemed to be purposely avoiding. She may have chosen our house over the other option, but it wasn't exactly like she wanted to stay with us. There were only two available. And according to her, Ty was the worse of the two evils. Being the lesser evil when the other was nicknamed The Sadist wasn't a high bar to reach.

"What about her?" I asked stiffly, not caring for the direction that this was going. Then again, I'd rather not discuss Nikki with anyone, outside of Adrian.

149

"We need to get a few things straight," Malachi said as he walked into the room, crossing his hands behind his back. His shoulders were strong and his biceps flexed. His locs swayed slightly as he approached. "As much as I'd like to believe otherwise, I know Phaon cut a deal with you too."

Adrian and I exchanged looks.

"Don't know what you're talking about," Adrian said flippantly.

He was good at pretending to be a shallow playboy prince with little depth or emotion.

Malachi snorted. Stopping a few feet away from us, his gaze was sharp. Intelligent.

"So, I was imagining the pining looks that you've both been giving her since yesterday evening?" he asked. Neither of us answered. "Well, if that's so, this should be simple. She's off limits."

"Excuse me?" Adrian asked, his lazy smile turning thorny.

"I know your hearing is fine, Rose. So unless we have something to discuss, you'll stay away from my mate."

The floor was ripped out beneath me. If I weren't sitting, I would have fallen. I barely even noticed he'd begun to walk away.

Adrian's smile flatlined. "What did you just say?"

Malachi halted mid-step, then looked over his shoulder.

An unhappy smile barely masked his displeasure as he stared back at us. "So you do know what I'm talking about."

He turned and walked back over, taking a seat in the armchair between me and Adrian.

"You're mistaken," Adrian stated firmly.

"About?"

"Nikki," I answered in a near growl. "She can't be your mate. She's *mine*."

150

"And *mine*."

That bitter smile grew, feeling all too familiar to my own. "That explains a lot."

"Come again?"

"Phaon," Malachi said. "I don't know of a man in their right mind that would agree to his little bargain if they didn't have a reason for wanting her. Not with who you both are."

"You're taking this very well," Adrian said slowly.

"As are you," Malachi replied.

"Trust me, I'm not."

"I'm aware," Malachi said, propping his ankle over his knee as he leaned back in the armchair. "I'd heard rumors that Nikki had found her mate but that her father sent him away. They couldn't be about me. The timelines didn't match. I was hoping they were wrong . . ." He rubbed at the stubble on his jaw.

"When did you meet her?" Adrian asked.

Malachi lifted his eyebrows. "When I was ten years old. We grew up together. You?"

"She, uh, was on the subway."

Malachi frowned. "Subway? Her father would never let her—"

"How do you know?" Both Adrian and Malachi turned to me. The darkness in my tone made the hairs on their arms stand straight. "How do you know she's your mate?"

"The same way both of you do, I would assume." He gave me a strange look and cocked his head. "I was eighteen when the bond snapped into place. She was younger and didn't feel it yet, so I kept it to myself. Later when it did . . ." He looked away.

"You haven't claimed her." I couldn't hide the glimmer of hope in my voice.

"No."

"Why?"

"Why haven't you?" He shot back with a quirked brow. "We all have our reasons. Our own relationships with her to manage and work through."

"Right," Adrian drawled. "If that's the case, why are you here? You don't need us—"

"That's where you're wrong," Malachi interrupted. "We share a mate. Unprecedented as that is, our futures were all merged when we found her. Our individual relationships with her may have nothing to do with one another, but claiming her? Living a life with her?" He looked between us as his word settled in. "We may have just become lifelong roommates in a complicated living situation."

"Welp. He's not wrong," Adrian said, getting to his feet. "I'm going to need a drink for this conversation."

I was just getting used to the idea of her having a second mate when a third one showed up. One that existed *before* me. "Might as well bring the bottle. I think we're all going to need it."

"That's the spirit," Malachi said with fake cheer. He clapped a hand on my shoulder in solidarity. It was only due to this newfound revelation that I let him keep that hand.

It was going to be a really long fucking night.

CHAPTER 16
NIKKI

SAM AND I STOOD OUTSIDE OF MY NEW PRISON-MANSION WITH our arms crossed, looking up at the window that was now closed with drapes drawn. I was contemplating how to get myself back inside without being detected.

"Why don't you just use the front door?" she asked.

"And have another confrontation with my betrothed? Betrothed-s? Is that a word?" Sam gave me a skeptical look, pursing her lips. "Either way, no thank you."

"So what's your plan here? You're gonna swing from the tree to the roof like Tarzan?"

"No, do you see any vines here?" I said, waving my hand toward the trees.

Sam chuckled and shook her head. "There are no vines in Manhattan either, and yet, I vaguely recall an incident involving you, rope, and the Brooklyn Bridge."

"And it worked, Naysayer! But I don't need anything that elaborate." Pointing to a large oak next to us, I continued. "I'm just going to climb the tree like in the movie Pollyanna, walk across that branch, and make it to my window."

"You do remember in Pollyanna, that she fell out of the tree and broke her back?"

"I said, *like* the movie. I didn't say that the execution was going to be exactly the same."

"I've heard that before," she teased.

"Well, if you're right—which you aren't—then it's a good thing I have incredible healing abilities," I said in a chipper voice, and she laughed. "Makes up for my shit hearing and sense of smell," I added while finding my footing against the tree and climbing.

Sam stood below me with her hands on her hips, watching like a disappointed mother hen. "I won't catch you if you fall."

"You're a terrible liar, Sam," I said, grunting as I hoisted myself onto the thick branch. Inching my way across, I stepped onto the awning of the porch roof and slid the window open. Looking back down at Sam, I winked and blew her a kiss.

Sam wrinkled her nose and waved me off. "I'll see you tomorrow for whatever shitstorm they have coming for us."

"I'll bring the umbrellas."

Shitstorm was probably an understatement. Alexander's warning about the trials starting as soon as we got there never left my mind, but I'd opted for emotional support and comfort, choosing to stay at Sam's for as long as I could.

It wasn't all to get away from the guys. I was intent on winning now. In order to do that, we had to come up with some strategies and ideas. She really wasn't on board with a few of my movie-inspired tactics, but I still had hopes that I could change her mind.

It hadn't taken much to find the house where the seconds were staying. Sam was sharing a cabin with Tylea and Jackie. It was smaller, but that didn't mean it was shabby. It was remarkably cozy, and they each got their separate rooms—which was more than what I had been given.

With that thought, I ducked down and crawled through the window.

I'd been gone for hours. I'd expected—hoped?—to come back and find Adrian asleep. Instead, the room was dark and empty. The only light was the flickering glow of the fireplace. Part of me felt a twinge of disappointment that I was here alone.

The bed was still made, and his shirt from earlier was strewn on top. A mental image of him getting undressed immediately flashed in my mind and a shiver went up my spine.

I walked to the bed, but I didn't go to "my side." Rubbing my hand over the comforter, I let the smooth fabric glide beneath my palm. My fingers grazed his shirt, and I stopped, picking it up.

You're a creep, Nikki. You're going to smell his clothes. That's what a total weirdo would do.

Doesn't count if it's technically your mate, right?

Oh well. I'd come this far. Arguing with myself had its perks.

I always won.

Just like a fucking creep, I held it up to my face and inhaled it with the enthusiasm of a Grade A stalker.

His earthy scent was beyond captivating. The mate bond pulled taut inside me, sensing that its other half was near, shooting through my limbs and pulsing in my core. I dropped his shirt back on the bed, startled at the sudden intensity of the feeling.

I had some seriously conflicting thoughts about Adrian.

He appeared to be charming. He was incredibly attractive. For the record, I had never been anti-mate. I was anti-having my heart ripped out—and that was the only mate experience I'd had thus far.

As best as I could tell, he didn't anticipate finding a mate any more than I did.

My phoenix and I were never against the notion of being bonded. After being rejected, I'd just accepted that was my lot in life. I wouldn't have a mate, and my love life would be stifled and confined to sneaky short-term 'relationships'. Maybe eventually go a little batshit crazy without a mate to ground my magic just so I could add a little excitement into the mix.

The desire to find your one, to find your partner—to find that person made for you, who completes you—that was buried deep within us. Shifters, fae, demons; it didn't matter. That biology was ingrained in the fabric of our being—and it never went away. Not after heartbreak. Not even after rejection.

I'd know.

Low voices caught my attention, and I turned, going to the bedroom door and opening it. Curiosity drove me to see if someone was coming, but more importantly, I didn't want to get caught sniffing Adrian's shirt.

I stilled as I listened, trying to make out where they were. It was all three of them talking to each other. But I couldn't hear what they were saying. My nosiness wanted to listen in. Maybe it would give me a little bit of insight into who they were. After all, they were each syndicate and they'd made deal involving me, but I knew next to nothing about them.

I tiptoed further, and the floors were blessedly quiet.

The chattering grew closer, and I began to hear parts of the conversation.

"I don't understand how this happened."

"Phaon's a liar, that's how."

"I can't believe he separated you. He's a bastard but to do that to your own daughter?"

As the voices got louder, I came close to a set of wooden double doors. I would have stopped, but the delicious and distinct scent of paper and leather pulled me in.

I knew it well. It was one of my favorite places to be. If I couldn't have nature, it was the closest to peace that I could feel.

I walked around the corner and found myself in complete awe. It was a two-story library. The walls were floor-to-ceiling mahogany shelves, filled to the brim with books. Rolling ladders were strategically placed so you could reach the top rows with ease.

"Just like Belle's," I whispered to myself.

"Who is Belle?" Niall asked, coming up behind me and making me jump.

"Geeez, you three need to wear a collar so I know when you're coming." Shuddering, I continued. "Just a woman who likes to read, but she ends up trapped in a castle with a beast." I crossed my arms, turning to them in a defensive stance. "Or you know, in my case, three."

"If I recall, Belle ends up marrying the Beast," Adrian said, joining the conversation. My eyebrows shot up before I had a chance to school my features. "I have a sister," he offered as an explanation.

"She does marry him. By her own choice. Not because

her father made some shoddy business deal with other syndicates that involve the trade of a *person*."

The three of them exchanged glances. *That* was what they were talking about. Got it.

"Nikki, there's a lot we have to talk about," Niall said.

"What do you wanna talk about? What you two were doing on the pier the other night in Brooklyn?" I said haughtily, looking between Niall and Adrian. Shifting my gaze to Malachi, I added, "Or maybe what you've been doing in *Queens* for six years? Or maybe you would all like the opportunity to tell me what kind of guys you are, like we're on some antiquated bad dating show. Show off your muscles and talents and embellish your accomplishments? Suitor number one, do you want to go first?"

"I think it's an excellent question. What were you doing on the pier that night?" Adrian ignored my snarky comments, choosing to go in his own direction.

I narrowed my eyes. "Nope. Denied. Suitor number two?" Niall stared at me blankly and said nothing. Then Malachi began to laugh.

"What's so funny?" Niall asked.

"She's shooting for her own hand," he muttered, attempting to suppress a smile.

"I don't know what that means." Niall looked to Adrian for an explanation, but he just shrugged.

"It's from an old movie she loved to watch. A princess is told she has to marry one of three guys from different neighboring clans. She's a badass in her own right. An archer, and damn good at it."

"What does that have to do with anything?" Niall asked, still just as confused as ever.

"The princess throws herself into the competition against the guys so she doesn't have to marry anyone. It's why she took it upon herself to join the trials and run for chancellor," he answered.

I clenched my jaw, staring at my ex-best friend. My ex-rejected mate. I hate that he still knew me so well.

Niall and Adrian looked at me, but my focus was still on the ex. "Yes. I don't want to marry any of you." I looked at Malachi, assessing him up and down. "*Especially* you. So I took matters into my own hands."

"Phaon didn't put you up to this?" Niall stepped forward with intrigue.

"I can assure you he didn't." I chuckled humorlessly. He really had no idea of much my father hated what I'd done.

"What about Ty?" he continued.

"What about him?"

"It was supposed to be Alexander."

"You're all syndicate, right? Isn't that part of the deal? You just stab each other in the back to get what you want. Don't act so surprised. You should have known what you were getting yourself into. Alexander's levelheaded. He would have done well here. Ty is a hot mess and made a rash decision to protect me. He has no idea how to think things through, and he acts on impulse, plowing through anyone that gets in his way. If you've heard a rumor about him, it's probably true. But you already know what kind of person he is since you were meeting with him the night before the solstice celebration."

"Listen, there's more to it than that," Niall said, his voice tense as he gestured between Adrian, Malachi, and himself.

"No, *you* listen. I know you *think* you know me, but you don't." I looked at Malachi. "The guy I knew six years ago? My friend—the one who was supposed to be my mate? He wasn't syndicate. He *hated* the syndicates. He wouldn't have joined The Divine, so I *definitely* don't know who you are anymore."

"I'm the same person I've always been, and I'm still your mate."

"You are not my mate," I said between clenched teeth, glancing at Adrian for a moment. He gave away nothing, but now he knew this was more complicated with whatever weird double mate situation we had going on.

"You never accepted the rejection, *and* I unrejected you," Malachi countered. He kept his frustrations out of his voice but I could see it growing in the way he held himself. He did not like me renouncing his claim on me.

Payback's a bitch.

"I'm still not sure that's a thing. It's on my To Do List to investigate how that works—and how to get rid of it." Turning on a heel, I prepared to leave.

"Nik, don't walk away from me, please," he pleaded. "I'm sorry I wasn't' here when Marissa died. I wanted to be with you. I'm so sorry—"

"Don't," I whispered harshly. I turned around, glancing at him from over my shoulder. "Don't say her name to me *ever* again." Then I kept walking until I made it to the room I was sharing with Adrian. Shutting the door behind me, I let out a quiet sob.

Tears stung my eyes, but I didn't want them to see. It was times like this I missed my sister the most. I missed her smile. Her laugh. Her presence. I missed the way she just knew when to let me cry and quietly comfort me. We did that for each other instinctively.

Here I had two mates that should technically be able to provide that support to me—even if one of them had been the cause of my pain. Yet here I was, pushing both of them away.

It was just too much, all too fast.

I stared at the bed, feeling anxiety at the prospect of being in bed with Adrian, while simultaneously itching for him to come so I wouldn't be alone—which just confused me more because I was essentially wanting a stranger. The mate bond was a lot to process.

Could I trust myself, or trust that my feelings were my own? I didn't know, and that made me come to the conclusion I'd opt for the couch. It was comfortable, warm by the fire, and it was more than adequate space wise. It would do just fine.

Not even bothering to undress, I laid on the couch, taking the throw blanket and wrapping myself in it as I let sleep overcome me, praying my dreams would be blissfully silent.

Rough hands curled around my biceps, pressing me into the couch cushions.

"Bind her feet," an unknown man said, and my body jerked.

"What the he—" I yelled before a calloused palm closed over my mouth.

My heart rate spiked. Adrenaline and anxiety flooded my senses, and fire licked beneath my skin.

Kicking out, my foot cracked against someone's jaw with a pop and a painful grunt. I tentatively let the heat take over, digging deep for the flames inside me, but keeping it just below the surface. I didn't need an explosion. I just needed to get their hands off me. Pushing it forward, I let the magic leak out so I could have a fighting chance against my captors.

But they just continued to wrap my legs, and I fought the restraints.

I tried again, but their hands didn't burn.

No matter what I did, nothing happened. Not even when my clothes themselves started to burn did the assholes let go. Putting the fire out, I bit down on the hand that bound my mouth. When it retracted slightly, I screamed.

"Nikki?" Adrian's muffled voice sounded in the room, but I was too disoriented to know which direction it came from. My stifled attempts to yell back reached him, and he rushed to speak. "It'll be okay. Stop fighting it. They're voids."

"Voids? Seriously?" Just because our magic wouldn't work on them didn't mean I had to give in to whatever was going on. These people just busted in my room and—

I felt a pinch on my thigh, and the energy reserve I had to fight back began to drain. But my fear of being confined and trapped again didn't. My mind took me back to a place I never wanted to be again, and I couldn't help but wonder if that's where I was headed now. If that's what was happening again . . .

Taking gulps of air, I tried not to hyperventilate.

Adrian's voice started to sound far away and slow. "Nikki, just breathe. I'm here."

A burlap hood slipped over my head, and the world turned dark. My heated breath blew back into my face in rapid bursts. My heart pumped loudly, the sound of it echoing in my ears. I'd lost all sense of direction as they carried my bound body.

I survived this once. I can do it again. I can escape.

162

But Marissa didn't. . .

My sister's face flashed before me, and I let out a strangled sob.

"Nikki," Adrian mumbled through what sounded like a gag. "Breathe. I'm with you."

In through the nose, out through the mouth.

Repeat.

My body shook as I tried to soothe the terror coursing through me. Then it clicked.

Voids had captured us.

In our secluded and secret cabin at an undisclosed location.

Adrian was calm.

That meant one thing.

The trials had begun.

CHAPTER 17
MALACHI

Iʀᴏɴ sɪɴɢᴇᴅ ᴍʏ ꜰʟᴇsʜ.

The scent of burning skin made my nose wrinkle in distaste.

Manacles bound my wrists and ankles. I was half demon, but my father was a fire fae. Real fire couldn't burn me, but iron? That was another story entirely. Still, the pain I was in had to be nothing compared to what Adrian was experiencing. He came from a pure line. Iron would be hell for him.

The blindfold was ripped from my eyes, revealing a bright, sterile room.

Every candidate was bound to a chair like mine as other voids pulled the hoods from their heads. If not for the chains and lack of clothes on half the people, I would have thought we were about to have a group therapy session.

Over a quarter of the group was fully naked. Half were in boxers or undergarments. Only two of the twenty-six candidates were fully dressed. Niall, in sweatpants and a T-shirt, and Nikki in the clothes she was wearing yesterday.

Standing in the center of the circle was our no-fucks-given assistant, Courtney. She was bright eyed despite the early wake up call. Not a hair was out of place. Even her features were schooled into pleasant nothingness as she looked around the room at us.

"Welcome, candidates." She clapped in mock excitement, setting a grim tone. "Today you are being gifted the grace of the witch goddess's presence. Lucky you." After a suspended moment when no one responded, she set a crystal on the ground and muttered a few words in Latin and an image of Hekate appeared.

"I would say good morning, but I'm aware your morning has not been all that pleasant. Nonetheless, one of you will be the next chancellor. Look to your left, then to your right. By the end of this week, one or both of those people will be gone."

She spoke with distinction. Importance. It wasn't a trait that could be taught easily, but as a goddess, she was likely born with it. Most of the old gods were.

"Earth and Emerald values strong leaders, but strength comes in many forms. Your first test is one of endurance. It's important to remember that no matter how strong or how unkillable you believe yourself to be—there is one simple truth. No one is infallible. Given enough time and pressure, every person will eventually succumb to pain. Whether it happens in twenty minutes, two hours, or ten days from now—eventually, you will break."

She looked around the group of us, despite not being here. I wondered if this was a recording or if she was actually transmitting a live stream to this crystal.

"Being leader of Earth and Emerald is a dangerous position. You will become one of the seven most powerful people in the world—in charge of governing, protecting, and enforcing laws over millions of individuals. That sort of power comes with a price. You and your weaknesses are now worth something more valuable than any stone. The power you will hold as chancellor is coveted. The threat to your life, imminent. Every single day, there will be someone trying to kill, kidnap, or blackmail you.

"Obviously Earth and Emerald will do its best to protect you, but no protection detail is perfect. Inevitably someone will slip through, rare as it is. Today, we're going to test how weak of a link you would be to this House.

"Your mind and body will be put through significant pain, the likes of which many of you have never experienced before. Your job is to hold out as long as possible. We don't expect you to last forever. As I said, everyone has a breaking point. We expect to find yours today.

"There have been many studies throughout the years. A team of researchers have managed to deduce the average amount of time it takes for help to come when the chancellor has been abducted. You have to withstand the pain for this amount of time if you wish to move forward in the trials. You can't fight it. You can't attack, and you can't subdue it when you've reached your point. All you need to do is say mercy, and the pain will stop. You'll be escorted from the room to wait for the others."

My eyes sought out Nikki.

Her lips pressed into a firm line as she listened to Hekate.

The trials for Earth and Emerald candidates were notoriously difficult, oftentimes more akin to torture. I had a feeling that was going to be the first of many like that.

"Okay, let's get started." Hekate clapped. Gold effervescent magic exploded between her palms as she weaved a spell. It wasn't like any that I'd seen before. Every witch did magic in a different way, but Hekate was as much a goddess as she was a witch. The spell she wove through the crystal was more complex than the greatest of the witch hybrids in The Divine were capable of.

I stared in mild bafflement, hoping like hell that my slack-jawed expression wasn't being broadcast all over the world right now.

A moment passed like a suspended beat.

Then the pain came.

It started with a crawling sensation that prickled, then began to itch. I twitched in my seat involuntarily. The slight pinching morphed into a sting, as a thousand fire ants started biting me.

I was being stung, bitten, eaten alive by something I could not see.

Magic.

It took a turn for the worse when my nerve endings suddenly burned. I was on fire. Invisible flames licked at my skin.

Several people gasped. A few were starting to tear up. None of the syndicate candidates, mind you. Unlike the privileged few of Earth and Emerald with enough power and influence to get here, we were born a different breed. Raised in Hell's breeding den instead of a civilized House with rules. Savageness ran in our veins.

Draco, the vampire from Clan Tepes, wore a stony expression. His entire body was stiff. The witch from the Outcast Coven was similar. Ayla had her lips pressed together and white knuckled fingers where they clenched into fists in her lap. Ty's nostrils flared as he breathed harshly. I hoped they'd accidentally burn him to death.

Beside me, Adrian sat in his boxers. The scent of his skin burning turned my stomach more than the fire itself. His curly dark hair was tousled from sleep. I couldn't read the expression on his face, given the angle that it required me to hold my neck.

His eyes were shuttered, but he didn't move a muscle under the assault.

Nikki and Niall surprised me the most. Out of all of the candidates, syndicates included, they both appeared almost . . . bored.

A creeping feeling rose up in my mind that their unique and similar responses to this torture had nothing do with their shifter genes or a high pain tolerance. I had taken my fair share of beatings and broken bones. The magic currently eviscerating my body went beyond that.

They were experiencing the same burning, the same pain, but neither of them seemed bothered by it in the slightest.

They could be watching a movie for all that either of their faces revealed. While I didn't know Niall well, that wasn't what I expected of Nikki.

Seconds ticked by, turning to minutes.

The quiet cries became moans. Writhing bodies moved in almost every chair as they tried to escape the internal burning. It wasn't fire that caused it, and no amount of movement or pressure would make it let up until Hekate wanted it to.

I wasn't sure how long had passed when the first person spluttered out a pathetic sob and whispered, "Mercy."

Neither Hekate, nor Courtney gave away anything for how long had passed and whether he made the cut off or not.

Voids undid his chains, one by one. When the final manacle fell away he exhaled heavily in relief.

Only a second passed, then that relief turned to regret.

There was no way our time was up, and he'd just proved he was too weak to take it.

A few more, all from the Earth and Emerald called mercy in the minutes following him.

When we were down to fifteen people, the pain started to change.

The burning subsided. My nerve endings still felt raw, even though it was a phantom pain. When the next sensation came, it wasn't fire that was ruining me, but ice.

My insides were freezing over.

There was no time to adjust or adapt to the new shock. My throat seized up like I had been thrown into a frozen lake. My chest constricted painfully as I struggled to breathe.

Logically, I knew that we were still sitting here. We hadn't moved. This was all part of the spell. But knowing did little good when it felt like I was drowning. Darkness edged around my vision, threatening to steal my consciousness.

My heartbeat pumped louder. The blood in my veins was moving slower somehow, like it too had frozen, and my heart was having to work double time to push it through my veins.

I clung to reality, focusing on the only person that could possibly make this worth it. My mate.

Not the other candidates, certainly not Ty; just her. I didn't care what happened to the rest of them, and they weren't my lifeline.

Time pressed on, and there was nothing to stop the inky blackness from reaching for me.

My arms began to shake as my vision went dark.

I was only hanging on by a thread, the smallest part of me still cognizant of what was going on.

It could have been minutes, hours or seconds for all I knew when I gasped, and the process of drowning started all over again.

Water filled my eyes involuntarily. I quickly looked around the circle while I still had enough mental presence to pay attention.

We were down another five people.

Again, none of those that failed were syndicate.

We were outnumbering them when I drowned again.

Then again.

The third time that I gained consciousness, more candidates had been removed.

My bleary eyes focused on Nikki, using her as the piece that grounded me. That reminded me why I was voluntarily going through this.

Pain itself wasn't horrible. In some situations, it could even be enjoyable. Drowning wasn't under any circumstances to me, and if I had to guess this was very similar to being waterboarded.

I couldn't block out the pain when it was so absolute and all consuming, so instead I focused on it. On the air leaving my lungs, on the explosion in my chest, on the stabbing pains setting into my fingers and toes.

In some ways, focusing on the pain made it easier. It almost lessened it. I still wanted it to end and wasn't sure how much more I could keep up.

I couldn't believe that Nikki had lasted this long. That she was still in this room. She had no idea how proud I was, even if I hated that she put herself in this position. I didn't like the thought of her being in pain, but her strength to endure and withstand the same thing was the only reason I was still sitting here.

I blinked through watery eyes to focus on her features.

Her lips were pinched, and her forehead was damp with sweat. She was suffering, but she didn't seem to be struggling the same way as the rest of us.

Adrian was now shaking uncontrollably.

By contrast, Nikki's eyes weren't watery from being choked. Her muscles weren't stiff like every other person's in this room. She was tense around her eyes, but unlike the rest of us, her body wasn't fighting it.

She was relaxed.

The earlier whisper of dread rose again.

Why wasn't her body fighting it?

While in the syndicate, she wasn't a gutter rat that rose to a leader, like me. She wasn't an enforcer who had no doubt had his body put through hell on the regular, like Niall. She was closest to Adrian, who albeit, was disadvantaged the most thanks to the iron they'd used. Nikki wasn't a fighter, though. Not physically.

Her response to this made no sense when as far as I knew, she'd never been through anything nearly this painful.

I didn't understand, but I would soon. I'd make sure of it.

The cold started to ease very suddenly. Air entered my lungs. I gasped, panting hard and doing my damnedest to breathe after god knows how long of being pushed to the edge.

We must have lost another person while I'd been staring at Nikki, because we were down to thirteen, including myself. I made note of the Earth and Emerald people that were left.

They were worth watching if they could make it this far.

I didn't get a chance to think about that more before the next round began.

First, we were encapsulated by fire.

Then we were frozen, followed by drowning.

While physically we were unmarred, mentally this trial was taking its toll.

The third round of torture went a step further.

A series of sickening cracks echoed through the room, one after another.

I'd heard the sound enough times to know that it was bone being snapped.

Hekate had upped the ante.

I grunted when it was my turn, and my pinky broke in half. One of the tiny finger bones jutted out grotesquely. Blood spattered at my feet as droplets rained down from the open wound.

When it was Niall's turn, I watched his wrist bend at an odd angle against his will, snapping by an invisible force.

Bile swirled in my gut. Nikki was next.

She handled the other things beautifully, but this was different. It wasn't the illusion of pain. It wasn't a mind trick.

This was real.

Except Nikki didn't respond. At all.

I thought it had ended somehow, sparing her, until Ayla's ankle cracked.

My eyes widened in shock.

Nikki's fingers and toes were all in place. Her wrist wasn't hanging at an odd angle like Niall's. Her legs were straight. There was no blood.

It was only by staring at her for several seconds that I noticed her breathing had become labored.

Her injury was internal.

They'd snapped something we couldn't see, likely a rib if it was hurting to breathe. Yet she hadn't said anything. She didn't utter a sound. She didn't cry or moan.

There was incredible pain tolerance and then there was *this*.

Once again, I was so absorbed in watching Nikki that I didn't realize it was my turn again.

I didn't have time to brace. My forearm cracked in half. The bone splintered unevenly, breaking the skin.

I bit down on my cheek.

When the person after me lost her knee, she screamed, "Mercy!"

The voids released her as Niall went next, his elbow joint popping grotesquely. I winced, unable to help myself.

Nikki grunted when her head flew back. The skin split down the middle of her forehead. Horror filled me.

They'd gone for the skull.

Crimson bled into the whites of her eyes.

A bloody tear leaked out.

I couldn't stand to see her subjected to this. The sooner we quit, the sooner it would end for her. The word left my lips before I could think of swallowing it back down. "Mercy."

Ty let out a shout when his back bent in half and his legs went slack. "Mercy!"

The vampire read the writing on the wall. These breaks were getting worse each round.

"Mercy," Draco snapped while two voids untied me. His head whipped around to look at them, as if to say, hurry the fuck up and let me out of here.

As I was escorted out, the witch, Ayla, followed suit. "Mercy."

There were only three of us left in this room.

Adrian. Niall. Nikki.

Ty was carried out, and I was pushed into a room with two-way glass. We could still see them, but they couldn't see us. Adrian and Niall locked eyes. They didn't have more than seconds to act if one or both of them didn't want to end up incapacitated.

Nikki's determined, bloodstained face said everything. She wouldn't back down if it killed her.

She'd sooner bleed out than admit defeat.

Stubborn. Stupid. Woman.

"Mercy," Niall and Adrian yelled in unison, coming to the same realization I had.

Hekate smiled, knowing and amused.

The magic around her winked out.

CHAPTER 18
NIKKI

THE PAIN HAD FINALLY CEASED, THANK THE GODS.

Just because I could manage it didn't mean I wasn't screaming on the inside.

I tried singing to myself. Catchy pop songs like "Wannabe" from the Spice Girls. When that wasn't doing the trick I turned to musicals. "No Good Dead" from *Wicked* seemed particularly relevant—and dramatic. Lastly, I turned to my tried and trues. Disney.

"Almost There" from *The Princess and the Frog*.

"How Far I'll Go" from *Moana*.

"I Can Go The Distance" from *Hercules*.

Everything. *Anything* to keep my mind off the agony and torment lancing through my body as I felt my head crack from an unseen entity.

It was all I could do to keep my focus. To not succumb and beg for mercy.

I'd felt pain before. I'd been taken and held against my will. I'd felt the grief of losing my twin as a result of it, so fuck Earth and Emerald for starting off with this shit sundae as the first trial. Not that they knew my past—no one did—but I could still be mad at them for it.

My entire being was spent; mentally, emotionally, and physically.

The end came quickly after my head cracked. When my brother's spine snapped, shouts of "mercy" filled the room. Malachi backed out on my behalf. Niall and Adrian did it simultaneously because they knew I wouldn't give in.

It touched some vulnerable part of me, even though I didn't want it to. At least for two of the three.

An attendant walked toward me. The iron chains unlocked and dropped to the ground as Hekate disappeared from the crystal she'd been broadcasting out of. I did everything I could not to flinch. I wanted to curl into the fetal position and cry, but I wouldn't let them see how they had affected me. As my head tilted forward, and my labored breathing filled the silence in the room, the woman's shadow hovered over me. I couldn't make out her features..

"Congratulations," she said.

"Eat glass," I mumbled, wheezing as soon as my broken rib sent sparks of pain into my chest. The bone was mending itself, but it wasn't healed yet.

She smiled, and I could only tell because I saw the white of her teeth. "Such vigor. You could have taken more, it would seem." I glared at her with hate-filled eyes, though no words came out. "Relax, Nikki Ward. You're our reigning champion. For now."

"Super. And what do I win?" I asked. Breathing was becoming easier, but my throat was as scratchy and dry as my humor.

"Drink this," she offered, pulling a small bottle from her robes. Waving her hand over me, my bindings loosened, freeing me completely.

Eyeing the bottle with unease, she gestured it forward. "What is it?"

"You'll need it to get out of here, as that is your next task. The others won't be so lucky."

"What do you mean my 'next task?'"

"It's time to find your way out of our facility. It's every man—or woman—for themselves."

"Of course it is," I whispered, more to myself than to her and whoever was watching us. Angling my head in the direction of the bottle, I asked again, "What is it?"

"It's a potion that will allow you to heal faster."

Staring blankly, I waited for her to tell me this was a joke. The advantage I was given for withstanding what felt like days of torment was . . . faster healing? The *one thing* my shifter magic provided me in spades beyond what any other supernatural possessed.

My eyesight was average.

My hearing was poor at best.

My sense of smell *and* taste were truly abysmal. Worse than *any* shifter I'd ever met.

But healing—that was my one real gift. And a good one considering my awkward sense of balance and some of the stunts I'd pulled on missions.

A laugh bubbled in my chest and the puzzled tone in the woman's voice was clear. "What's funny?"

"Nothing." I had no intention of showing them all my cards. "Can I exchange this for vitabrew? I'm exhausted."

"A what?"

"You know? Vitabrew. Stronger than coffee, less than cocaine. Keeps me awake. I'm tired after being ripped out of my bed and then used as a pin cushion. I'll even take a coffee if that's all you have. It's not as potent, but it'll do the trick." When she didn't answer, I took her bottle, but I also chose not to drink it.

The attendant stepped back, and I got a quick glance at her. She looked at me with a cocked eyebrow and a slight smirk. "Good luck, Nikki Ward."

She disappeared and I gave a half-hearted salute with minimal enthusiasm.

"Thanks, lady who didn't introduce herself." Leaning forward, I rested my elbows on my thighs and dropped my head into my hands. I was so drained.

Adrian moaned, then coughed. "Didn't even bother with prep work. They just bent us right over the table and went for it."

"I know caffeine is hard to come by, but lube isn't," I muttered, offering the bottle to Adrian. "Here. My skull is throbbing, but the bone is already knitting back together. You need this more than me."

He shook his head. "No, you—"

"Stop. Healing is one thing I am really good at." When he looked at me with uncertainty, I added, "If you don't take it, I'm going to drop it on the floor. I don't need it. Stop trying to be chivalrous. You're fae. I know it takes you longer to heal than me." After a suspended moment, Adrian got up and took the potion, drinking its contents.

"Thank you," he said quietly, and I could see the change in his skin color almost immediately.

I dipped my chin and gave him a thumbs up.

I stood, wobbling on my feet. Niall put a hand to my back, bracing me.

"Are you okay?" he asked. His voice teased at the edge of my mind, echoing and taking me to another time and place.

As I looked up at him to answer, our surroundings shifted, and words failed me. We weren't in the trials anymore. Orange and red flames roared in the background; its menacing heat tickled my skin, threatening to devour me as it engulfed everything it touched.

Fire couldn't hurt me, but I was afraid. A soot-covered face was dangerously close to mine. Even with blood red eyes, slit like a reptiles, I recognized Niall. Anger and fear were consuming him. He called my name and begged me to hold on. Hold on? I tried to look down but couldn't. I was a passenger in my own body. Able to see, to feel, but not control anything. Not even a slight tilt of my head.

His voice sounded distant, like some far-off dream.

Yet, it *felt* real. As if we had been transported, and this was our new reality.

"Nikki!" he shouted, bringing me out of my stupor.

Clear liquid pooled on the floor, getting my knee and pants wet since I'd remained in the same spot during whatever episode I'd just been experiencing. It took a few moments for my brain to fully process that something bad was happening.

Water was rising up from the ground, filling the closed off room. Panic set in, paralyzing me as my logical brain threatened to shut down in the wake of such extreme stress.

The second task was getting out of here, but they weren't letting us do that on our own time. They were forcing us out.

It's every man or woman for themselves.

Banging sounded in the room, though it was muted. I stared at the two-way glass, knowing the other candidates were on the other side.

Malachi. Ty.

My brother may have had his spine snapped, but I'd never underestimate his beast to not heal him in no time

179

flat. He was the most indestructible creature out there, beside me.

Neither of them would leave me here, but I was fairly certain magic reinforced the mirror. Otherwise, this would be all too easy.

Adrian ran to the door only to find there was no knob. "Fucking magic, are you serious right now?" He pointed at the window. "Use the chair. See if it'll break."

Niall was already there by the time Adrian had finished speaking. The metal chair hit it with a thud, bouncing off. It didn't even make a mark. While Niall continued to swing, this time using his fists, Adrian assessed the room.

"Where's the water coming from?" I asked, turning and looking for the source. Spinning in circles, nothing stood out. Fucking magic.

Adrian ran his hands along the walls, closing his eyes while he tried to feel for a hidden seam, but he found nothing. As he looked up he saw a vent and gestured to it. "There. That's how we get out."

The vent was easily wide enough to allow passage and we assumed that was the purpose. That was the only exit.

My skin crawled and I felt a tightening in my chest. I hated confined spaces. They sent me into panic attacks. It was hard enough to ride in the death tube on the subway, but now they wanted to put me into a long metal tunnel and not know where we were going or if we'd ever get out.

My heart started racing and I shook my head no. "There has to be another way," I said, clenching my fists as I stood in my spot, frozen.

Niall had stopped trying to break through and had put the chair underneath the vent. He held out his hand, but I couldn't move.

Adrian came over to me and grabbed both of my shoul-

ders giving me a slight shake. The water was at my knees. "
Nikki, we have to go."

"I can't," I whispered, trying to take a step back as the
water reached my mid-thigh. "I can't go in there."

"You have to. We don't have much time."

"You don't understand. I can't. I can't be confined
again."

Adrian looked at Niall for help. He had a firm set to his
lips, almost like he felt pity for me. Under normal circumstances, it would have bothered me. I didn't want their pity,
but I also really didn't want to go in that vent.

Freezing water rapidly filled the room. Once it reached
my torso, I began to shiver.

Adrian gently cupped my face in both hands, looking at
me with softened eyes. "Nikki, I have you. We both do. We
aren't going to let anything happen."

"You don't know that. You couldn't stop them from
taking me or cracking my head like an egg. What if we get
stuck? What if we don't come out?" I asked with a panicked
breath.

"You didn't just endure all that pain to stay here and
drown. You didn't just show your family and everyone
behind that mirror how incredible you are, just to let this be
the thing that beats you." His thumb caressed my cheek as
he spoke.

"I don't know if I can do this."

Instead of continuing his attempts at convincing me or
giving me a pep talk, he pulled my face towards his and
pressed his lips to mine. My fingers curled into the shirt
around his bicep as my body shook. He kissed me with
fierce hunger, but there was a tenderness to it somehow.
The intimate touch sent electricity through me reaching the
end of my fingertips. His earthy scent filled me with a sense

of calmness similar to the peace I'd felt when we'd arrived at the cabins. It was the same stillness that consumed me when I breathed in crisp air on a quiet autumn morning when the mist covered the ground. Visions of my future—a future with him—appeared in my mind.

When he pulled away, I jolted back to reality. He looked me in the eyes, speaking with urgency. "This is the only way out. You don't know me yet, but I need you to trust I would never do anything to hurt you. Niall's going to go in first, then you, and I'll be right behind. All you have to do is follow him. Can you do that?"

Taking a deep breath I nodded in agreement. "Okay," I whispered.

The water was too high for me to walk through it, so we had to swim over to where Niall stood on the chair. He'd already removed the vent opening and had dropped it into the water. If we weren't supernaturals, I can't imagine this would've worked. He jumped up slightly, grabbing the edge of the vent and hoisted himself up.

My heart hammered against my chest. At any moment, I was sure it would burst. I had to climb in that cursed vent and trust that Adrian and Niall would help me find my way out. My feet touched the chair, but I didn't have Niall's height. Adrian gave me a boost so that I could grab the edge of the vent and pull myself up. Niall had already moved forward to give me space, and we moved forward a bit more to allow room for Adrian to jump in. It was cramped and uncomfortable, but they helped hold the worst of my anxiety at bay.

Niall glanced at the vent and then looked down the air duct tunnels. "Let's go before the water reaches the top and pours in here."

Another surge of panic filled me. Drowning in this

confined space wasn't something I had considered before. New fear unlocked.

We crawled through the metal maze, twisting and turning in different directions. Every now and then we would stop, and Niall would sniff the air. Adrian did as well. They consistently agreed on which directions to take, which made me think scenting my way out would've been an option if I didn't have a terrible sense of smell and an overwhelming dread weighing me down.

I just wanted out.

Breathing became harder, and I was struggling not to hyperventilate. Flashes of memories I'd long suppressed were beginning to resurface. I'd always feared this day would come, but the timing was absolute shit. Why was it when the mind tried to protect you, it locked away traumatic moments in your life but then chose to fuck you over at the worst possible time by allowing you to remember it.

Trauma unlocked trauma.

Ain't that some shit.

We came to a large conjunction where multiple air ducts converged. I was so focused on trying to breathe and convincing myself we'd find a way out that I hadn't noticed that Niall had stopped, turned around, and was sitting hunched over. With my head down I bumped into him, tumbling into his lap.

The threat of an anxiety attack loomed close, and as awkward as it was being in his lap, I just went along with it in the name of getting out of here sooner.

"Adrian, take the lead. She's about to crash," he said, stroking my hair. "She has too much adrenaline running through her."

"Try to get her heart rate down."

Adrian took off down the tunnel, and honestly, I didn't

know how much time passed. I laid there with my eyes closed while I counted, focusing on filling my lungs deeply instead of gulping shallow breaths. Calloused fingers stroked through my hair, but Niall said nothing, and I didn't ask him to stop.

Thuds against the metal ducts echoed, drawing closer. Adrian came back into view and crouched next to us. Inclining his head in the direction he'd just come from, he said, "That's the way out. You want to lead again?"

Niall agreed and nudged me gently. "We're almost there."

I nodded in silence, removing myself from the warmth of his lap. As the anxiety waned, so did all of my energy.

I followed them for what felt like forever. We hovered over the new vent opening. It looked like the foyer of a large building, but a wall of proper windows covered one side. This wasn't two-way glass. And we saw exactly what we needed: outside.

Niall kicked the vent and it clattered to the ground below. He jumped out first, landing on his feet in a solid stance. On full alert, he visually searched the perimeter of the empty room, then looked back to me. "This is it. Nice and easy. I'll catch you."

I jumped out, not even caring if he was telling the truth. I'd rather eat a face-full of linoleum than be stuck in this place a second longer. My body dropped, not even free falling before strong arms caught me with one cradled under my knees, and the other holding me protectively at my back.

As soon as the room opened around me, I breathed a sigh of relief when I no longer felt the confines of the air ducts touching me from every angle.

My momentary reprieve was taken away when I looked

up and fire once again flashed before my eyes. Whereas the visions that I'd had with Adrian appeared to be the future, this was different. It was stronger. I felt like I'd lived it already—and forgotten for a reason. Rather than a sense of calmness and peace, it was the polar opposite. This memory was filled with fear, loss, pain—but it wasn't *caused* by Niall. It was almost like we *shared* it. Where I felt like I was drowning in grief and despair he exuded a sense of protection, longing and . . . sadness.

It felt *real*.

Fire still raged in the background, and plumes of black smoke billowed into the sky. He was holding me and running. *"It's over. I've got you,"* he said. *"I promise I won't let go. You're safe now; we both are. You saved us . . ."*

"Nikki!"

Niall's actual voice brought me back to the here and now. No longer in the unknown recesses of my mind, a lobby surrounded us while a deep frown marred his face.

"I think she's going into shock," Niall said, pulling me closer to his chest.

Shivers racked my body. "I'm fine," I said through my chattering teeth, even though I was far from it.

He looked at me with concern. "What just happened? Where did you go?" Still cradled in his arms, I met his eyes, unable to answer. The truth was, I didn't know, but I had some questions of my own.

Glass double doors burst open, and Sam ran in, screaming my name and rushing to me. Niall seemed hesitant, but he set me down just as she got to us.

Throwing my arms around her, I wanted to completely collapse—but I wouldn't. Not here.

Later? Oh yeah. That meltdown was definitely coming.

"They pulled us out of bed and told us they'd started

the first trial. I was on the other side of the glass. I saw *everything.*" Her eyes hardened, even though I could see the slight sheen that glazed over.

"I'm okay." I could barely speak. Emotions I couldn't process clogged my throat, making me sound like I was drunk. "I just want to get back to the cabin and sleep."

Sam nodded, looping her arm through mine. "Ty's on a rampage and he's headed here now. We need to hurry."

A sense of numbness started creeping over me as soon as I took a step forward. This exact feeling had happened three times that I knew of, and I knew what was coming.

The first time I'd been doing reconnaissance and was running on no sleep after picking up a shift for the Movement when one of our members went down. I wasn't thinking straight and fell off a literal building. I'd broken my neck. I'd barely healed before I lost consciousness, freaking Delta and Foxtrot the fuck out. They almost risked taking me to my family because they were so scared I was dead. Then again, I was still a latent shifter at the time so there was a good chance I could have. Still, the stupid caring assholes almost got themselves killed fretting over me.

The second time, I'd forgotten to eat before we had a particularly difficult mission in the Bronx that ended in a gory encounter with a group of vampires. There was a lot of blood and body parts left when we were done and, you know, it was a lot to take in one night, so my body just checked out.

I totally didn't faint from the blood.

The third time . . . well. It was like Bruno. We didn't talk about the third time.

My vision swam, and all the energy I'd had was fully depleted. My feet became heavy, and Sam jerked to a stop.

Pinpricks were exploding across my vision as the ground moved under me.

"Nikki," Ty roared in the distance.

"If he wants to bitch at me, he's going to have to wait a minute," I choked out, dropping to one knee in a forceful thud as I fought against gravity. "Yup." My speech slowed. "It's coming."

"Not again," Sam said, her voice sounding far away. "You have the worst timing, you know that? Maybe worse than the time with the vampires."

"You mean what was left of them," I slurred.

"What's happening?" Niall asked in a hard voice. "What's she doing?"

"Fainting. Duh," I muttered, and my world turned black.

CHAPTER 19
ADRIAN

"You're being an ungrateful brat." Ty's voice echoed through the foyer of the entryway.

She'd been standing at the front door, arguing with him for half an hour. Arguing was a bit of a stretch. He was berating her for not backing out of the first trial way sooner. When that wasn't going anywhere, he turned to being pissed she was staying here with us and not in the other syndicate house with him. Never mind that three rooms were already filled there as well. He still insisted that they could share his.

That was a bit weird to think about, considering they were brother and sister. Ty's need to protect her felt just a hair too close to possessiveness for my liking.

I frowned.

With each passing minute, she'd become more agitated. Her subtle resistance to his manipulations turned into a forceful confrontation.

Niall's hands clenched into fists as he hunched over the back of the sofa. A low, rumbling growl vibrated in his throat, and white, iridescent scales flashed over his uncovered arms.

Thank fuck Malachi was still out with Tylea. It was hard enough suppressing my own instincts while trying to calm Niall. I didn't need a third feral mate in the mix.

I gave him a stern look, conveying that his reaction wasn't going to help the situation. He met my gaze with a surly expression of his own.

"Go," I said quietly, tilting my head toward the hallway.

Another yell from the front door echoed, and it was enough to make both of us shudder.

Ty's alpha vibe coupled with Nikki's internal distress was making it incredibly difficult for both of us to stay put and not intervene.

"He needs to be dealt with," Niall said. "Permanently."

I sighed, not exactly disagreeing. The difference was I understood we couldn't get rid of her family. If he was some random guy that was obsessed with her, or a jealous ex, sure. I'd say he could have an accident at one of the next trials, but he wasn't some nobody. He was Ty Ward Jr., her brother, and Phaon's heir. There was no way in hell that her father would forgive us and hand over his daughter when the trials were over if he found out we'd killed his son.

Putting Phaon aside, I got the feeling that Nikki wouldn't be very forgiving if we killed her family either. Not when she'd already suffered a grief so terrible and twisting it rendered her unable to recognize Niall as her mate.

We weren't positive that was why, but he and I agreed it seemed like the most logical explanation. She wasn't ignoring the mate bond with me, and while she was pissed at Malachi, I also saw the way she looked at him. Even in her hurt and anger she didn't reject him. Nikki had no reason to *pretend*

Niall wasn't her mate. If she truly remembered and found him repulsive, she would have said so. I didn't doubt that. Not after being around her. Nikki was one to speak her mind.

She'd kept relatively calm while arguing with Ty, but that patience was running thin. I heard the strain when she finally raised her voice in return.

"Look. I've had a long day. My skull was smashed open and then I got to climb through the buildings air vents while they flooded the whole damn place, trying to drown me. There's no vitabrew. The food here sucks. I'm *exhausted*, so can you just give me a break? I know it goes against your nature and all your alpha bullshit, but I need you to back off and let me go to sleep. If you're really that insistent on berating me, come back tomorrow."

Ty emitted a growl that had the hairs along the back of my neck rising.

Niall started toward the door, eyes shifting to a reptilian slit.

Dragon.

Fuck.

I intercepted him with a hand on his shoulder, squeezing the muscle hard. "Go. I'll deal with it."

He paused, looking from me to the open hallway where Nikki was just out of view. He did it twice, eyes flickering back and forth between him and his dragon.

"If he hurts her," Niall began.

"Let me deal with this. He won't lay a hand on her. Now go. The last thing she needs after the day she's had is an angry dragon flipping the fuck out and mutilating her brother."

Niall deflated slightly, his shoulders sagging. It was a low blow, but he needed the push to walk away. With a stiff jaw, Niall left for the library.

I walked into the entryway just as Ty exploded.

"You're not safe!" He insisted. "Those fuckers couldn't stop the voids from dragging you away this morning. What's to stop them if something else happens? One of the other syndicates could easily break in here, or one of the other candidates. You won the first challenge, Nikki. They're not just going to let that slide. You're a target now, and you know damn well that there are some things worse than dying. Those three can't protect you like I can. Hell, even your phoenix couldn't protect you."

Nikki froze. Her muscles tightened. Her shoulders snapped back as she straightened her posture, a flinty expression shone in her eyes. "Way to keep a fucking family secret, Ty! Now everyone in the house knows what I am!"

I walked toward them quietly, but not at all silent. Everyone knew not to sneak up on an alpha predator. While I wasn't sure if her phoenix was an alpha, she had the spirit of one.

Today had proved that.

"Nikki—"

"Don't." It was a single word, yet she put so much emotion into it that I felt her anger. Her rage.

We hadn't even completed the bond and I still felt how deep that one word went.

I stopped at her side and placed my hand on her lower back, almost flinching at the contact. Her skin burned, radiating heat like glowing embers.

I fisted my hand in the back of her baggy T-shirt and tugged gently, twice.

"There a problem here?" I asked, looking between the two of them. Ty stood in the doorway, hands at his side, hunched over his sister. He was over a foot taller than her and twice as wide. The dark gleam in his black eyes shone brighter when he saw my hand resting on her back.

"This doesn't involve you, Rose," he spat.

"That's where you're wrong. It involves her, and anything that is Nikki's business is now my business too."

His upper lip curled back in a snarl. "What? You think that because you're sharing a house she's going to be another notch in your belt?" He laughed coldly. "You don't know my sister. She's worth a hundred of you. You don't deserve to breathe the same air, and I don't give a fuck what deal you made with my father, but I can tell you this, Rose: Dead men don't get married."

The hand at my side tightened. My jaw strained as the muscles clenched, teeth gritting together. Everyone thought that I was careless. A playboy. Shallow. Very few realized that it was just the mask I chose to wear.

I felt just as deeply as Niall, but I refused to show it. I refused to give any piece of myself to someone that was insignificant. Having a mate—even unbonded—that intensity to feel shot up to a whole new level.

I smirked, outwardly pretending to be unbothered even though inside I was burning. What's more, the dark-haired vixen at my side burned even hotter with me.

"Back off," she said quietly. Her voice was soft, but there was nothing gentle about her tone.

"Nikki . . ." Ty tried to quell some degree of his anger upon seeing that his words didn't just affect me, but her as well.

"You heard her," I said. "Back off. Be gone. Go back to your cabin. Take a walk. I don't care which. Just get the fuck off *our* porch."

I leaned forward going chest to chest with Ty Ward. He was a big guy, but so was I, and I'd be damned if he towered over her using intimidation to try to get what he wanted.

"Take your pick," I told him. "Next time you think to threaten me, remember the only reason you're still breathing is because of my mate."

Ty's eyes widened. The black in them seemed to bleed out as the ring around the iris shifted to a deep, hazy red.

"Mate?" he repeated coolly. "She never said."

I cut him off by lifting my hands. "Why would she say anything if this is how you act in general?"

He shot Nikki a sharp glare, incredibly displeased that she'd failed to mention this to him. I would have found that amusing under different circumstances.

"He's not your mate," Ty insisted, completely and utterly sure of himself. "I know that you've been lonely since Marissa died . . . that you've struggled to find your way. But he's using you, Nikki. He's abusing your grief—"

"Stop it!"

At a breakneck speed I didn't expect, she shoved Ty in the chest, *hard*. He stumbled back with lips parted, and a stunned expression on his face.

"I told you I couldn't do this right now. Then you try to use Marissa to guilt me. I'm so sick of you and dad gaslighting me; saying that I'm too emotional or incapable of anything because of what happened to Marissa. You think I don't know what happened? *I* was the one that lived through it," she shouted, pointing at herself. "*I* was the one that had to watch her die, and *I* was the one that left there, covered in her ashes. You're only here posturing because you care about me as a *thing*, therefore you think you own me in some way. You don't actually give a shit, Ty. If you did, you wouldn't do things like this. You would respect my boundaries when I tell you that I'm too fucking tired to deal with it right now. So if you'll *excuse me*, I need to get some sleep before I deal with another one of your massive bitch fests that I'm sure will still be waiting for me tomorrow."

She slammed the door in his face and flipped the lock. It's not like that would truly stop him if he wanted to come in, but her point was made.

Chest heaving with exertion, Nikki stood staring at the door like she expected him to open it and come right back at her.

"Nikki—"

She held up her hand.

"Thank you." The words shocked the hell out of me. I expected some sort of fight. Or at the very least, irritation at me for interfering in the argument with her brother. Instead, she had gratitude.

"He shouldn't treat you like that," I said.

"No," she agreed. "He shouldn't. Our father always said if you want something, then take it. Ty is a product of being raised a syndicate heir, and he applies that same mindset to me without realizing that it's not going to work. He wants me to listen to him and do what he wants. He would wrap me in bubble wrap if I let him. But I have no interest in being coddled and hidden away from the world. I never really did."

I swallowed the thick lump forming in my throat, focusing on keeping the emotion from my voice.

"If that's not who you want to be, then why don't you break away from it? Why let your father decide your life?"

The little bit of vulnerability that had been present quickly vanished. "You're one to talk. Adrian Rose, the Fae Prince of Brooklyn." She scoffed, sneering at my name.

My teeth ground together, but I lifted my hands in a placating gesture. "Right. Pot, meet kettle."

One corner of her mouth curled up reluctantly, as though I'd unexpectedly amused her. "Well, at least you can admit when you're being a hypocrite. I suppose that's something."

"Hypocrite?" I asked, clutching my chest where my heart was. "You wound me. And here I thought we were making progress."

Nikki sniffed haughtily. A sort of playful flirtation flitted across her face, but there was no hiding the tired circles beneath her eyes or the strain in her voice.

"I . . ." she paused, as if trying to grasp some words to explain everything, but words failed her as much as they did me in that moment.

I wanted her words. Her truths. I wanted to know her past. I wanted to what she thought of the bond. Whether she was planning to accept it or not. More than anything, I wanted to crush her against me, to fuse our lips, and relish the way she tasted as deep and earthy as she smelled. There was nothing sweet about her scent, and I loved it. I didn't want sweet. I'd spent my entire life having women throw themselves at me using false charm in an attempt to lure me in, and it never appealed to me.

There was a kick to Nikki; a spiciness. And I liked it. *A lot.*

"I appreciate what you did just now," she said, "but I wasn't lying to Ty. I really don't have it in me tonight. Not for him, and not for . . . mate talk."

I nodded twice, holding her gaze and watching her irises switch from a deep magenta to the darkest shade of yellow—if it could even still be called that.

Her eyes fascinated me. I'd never met anyone with color-changing eyes. Apart from Ty and Phaon, but where theirs seemed to change with emotion, Nikki's betrayed nothing. It was possible that I was truly shit at reading her which wouldn't be shocking given how long I'd known her.

Niall had more than enough reason to be emotionally stunted, but he wasn't the only one. I was just better at masking; pretending like I understood how other people felt and behaved.

"I'm not going to push you," I told her. *Not yet, at least.* "We'll talk tomorrow."

Nikki inclined her chin. Her bottom lip curled inward, and two small white teeth poked out, biting into it. My cock hardened. I wanted to bite that lip too. Taste her again— but now wasn't the time.

"Agreed. Right, well . . ." She trailed off awkwardly, then turned to walk away.

"You should sleep with me," I blurted out, and Nikki froze. "Nope, that wasn't it. I'll admit that didn't exactly come out right." I spoke quickly, trying to cover the blunder. "You should sleep next to me tonight. Not on the couch. It's a king-sized bed. You need proper rest. It'll be harder for people to sneak up on you if you're in bed with me."

She slowly looked over her shoulder, cocking an eyebrow.

"Sleep?" she repeated.

"That's it. Just sleep."

Turning to face me, she tilted her head in consideration. "No funny business?"

"Just sleep, Nikki. I'm not going to try anything. I promise." I might smell her hair if she got close enough, but that wasn't the funny business she was talking about.

"Pinky promise?" she asked, holding up a hand and extending a curled pinky finger.

"Are you serious?" I said, scrunching my brows and

looking between us. She remained stoic, waiting for me to answer. "That's a child's—right. Okay, yeah. I pinky promise." I curled my pinky around hers tightly, shaking it up and down three times.

"Good." She smiled, and this time, it reached her eyes. "You know what happens if you break a pinky promise, right?"

"I, uh, can't say that I do."

"If you break the promise, I break your finger," she said, pausing while waiting for me to react. We'd just had numerous bones broken. Not that I planned on breaching her trust, but a single finger was nothing in comparison. "Off," she added.

"Come again?"

"I break it *off*. And I'll keep it too." Nikki turned for the hallway, giving me her back as she walked toward our room. Gesturing to her neck and her ears, she said, "Maybe make jewelry out of the bones or something. Who knows."

I just stared, completely fascinated with my mate—as twisted and wonderfully weird as she was.

My cock throbbed again, and I realized I'd need the time to take care of myself in a cold shower before sleeping next to her.

Lest I break the pinky promise and give my mate a new pair of earrings.

CHAPTER 20

NIKKI

THE SOUND OF A THROAT CLEARING TEASED THE EDGE OF MY subconscious. Drifting in and out of sleep, I blissfully floated not wanting to wake up and leave this place.

Yearning and fulfillment had consumed my dreams, and damn if it wasn't a beautiful place to be. In this space, I was safe and loved. A bond—once lost—had found me again. I wasn't angered by our past. I'd reached a peaceful acceptance and acknowledged how much I'd always loved him.

Yet, somehow, there was this strange piece missing. I couldn't explain it. Even with a mate standing on each side, I wasn't whole.

An unseen but powerful connection pulled at my psyche, but my mind never showed me what it was. Who it was. I never knew if it was meant to harm or help, but every time the presence made itself known, I felt unstable and incomplete.

My only tether in this dream world was Adrian.

There was something about him that was warm and safe. It enveloped me, protecting me from the unknown.

Whatever wanted me to wake up needed to leave me alone. I wanted to go back to the full state of sleep. My dream world drifted further away from me, and I begged to hold on.

Birds tweeted, making me smile against the pillow and I curled into it tighter.

Another throat clearing sounded, and I frowned in annoyance. "Five more minutes," I mumbled.

"I'm afraid I really can't wait that long."

Adrian's voice vibrated beneath my cheek, and my eyes shot open, ripping me straight out of whatever cloud-like place I'd been wandering in seconds before.

My arm was coiled around his muscular torso, and my head rested on his chest. My legs twined through his, holding him tightly.

Honestly, more of me was on top of him than not.

The touch of his bare skin was heated as it pressed against mine—and gods it felt good.

Wait . . . why can I feel his skin . . .

I bolted up, shoving him away from me as I felt over my breasts, my stomach . . . I was naked. My fingers touched fabric just below my navel. No, just topless. I still had underwear on.

"What the fuck?" I said, scrambling to the other side of the bed. "You said you wouldn't try anything. You promised!"

He sat up, flinging his legs over the bed. "The agreement was that I wouldn't try anything—and *I* didn't—but we didn't say anything about me stopping *you* from trying something."

I tore at the sheets, looking for a shirt. "What? You're saying *I* tried something?"

"You stripped that off at some point." He tossed my

shirt to me with a mischievous grin. "I'm guessing you sleep hot?"

"When I'm healing, I do," I said, pulling the oversized tee over my head. I gestured to the bed. "You could have just moved away from me. You didn't have to let . . ."

"A beautiful woman who is my mate press her breasts against me while she slept?" He snorted in amusement like I was crazy. Yeah, I guess he was only doing what any mate would.

Feeling my cheeks heat, I blew out a breath. "Yeah. That."

"I pushed you off twice, because I'm a *gentleman*, and if I moved any further away, we'd have fallen to the floor because not only do you not abide by the same boundaries you set for me, you also latched onto me like an octopus and told me to stop moving because I 'felt good.'" He lifted a dark brow, equally devilish and delicious. I was such a goner. "What else was I supposed to do?"

"I . . . I didn't." *I said that?*

"Indeed you did." He winked at me, then walked to the bathroom. "I let you sleep as long as I could while you healed, but nature calls, and I couldn't hold it any longer."

He closed the door, and I dropped my head into my hands. If he was what I was dreaming of the entire time, I hoped I didn't talk in my sleep. Did I talk in my sleep? I didn't know. Ugh. Knocking around the sheets again, I found my sweatpants and put them on.

When he came back out, I didn't want to make eye contact with him. I probably owed him an apology after making him swear he wouldn't try anything and then I basically plastered myself to him.

"I'm sorry I put you in that position," I began, trying not to watch him get dressed—and failing.

"I'm all for trying other positions we'd both enjoy, preferably while awake," he said, winking at me. "Unless that's a kink of yours. It would be a first for me, but I'm not opposed."

"Uh, that's not what I meant . . ."

"I know." He chuckled, flashing me a warm smile. "But I thought it would be easier to break the ice with humor than watch you stumble through it."

I pressed my lips into a twisted smile. "I do that too. Make jokes when something's awkward or uncomfortable."

"Look at that. Something we have in common."

Huffing a small laugh, I nodded. "Thanks for not making it weirder."

"I kept my word, and as agreed, you have had a good night's sleep."

Thoughts of talking in my sleep immediately came back to mind and I hoped I hadn't shared anything. "How do you know I had a good night's sleep?"

"Because you snored all night, sleeping like a father with a newborn baby."

I barked a laugh, even through my embarrassment I found his comment funny. "Fair enough."

"But also, as agreed, it's time to talk, Nikki."

I sighed. "I much prefer the witty banter, but if you insist, where do you want to start?"

"How about we start at the beginning? What was the reclusive shifter princess doing at the pier that night in Brooklyn?"

"I have the same question for you, minus the princess part."

"And I'll answer it, but I asked first."

"Fine, but we also have to talk about what happens when we hear the truth about each other." Trepidation filled me. We were both syndicate royalty, but I wasn't about that life. What if he wanted to stay in the syndicate?

"I don't understand. Honesty between mates is a bad thing?"

"What if you learn something about me, or what if I learn something about you that's a no-go? People have dealbreakers, you know, lines they won't cross," I said. "Then what?"

"Oh," he said, the pitch of his voice rising slightly as he understood. He raised his brows for a moment while he thought, clearly caught off guard by my suggestion. "Then . . . I suppose you can reject me."

"Or you could reject me," I added softly, hating my vulnerability. I'd been rejected once, and that was bad enough.

"There's nothing you could say that would make that happen. I'm syndicate, Nikki. Whether you like it or not, I was born into this world, just like you. Niall and I were there that night making a deal with your family, playing our part in the syndicate matrix that is New York. I'm not really the judgmental type." The silent, 'are you?' hung in the air.

"What was the deal?"

"Oh, no. Tit for tat. You next."

"I was there spying to see what secretive deal my family was making, and with whom. Usually I know what's going on, but not this time," I said on a heavy sigh.

"On your own? Why would you spy?"

"Nope. My turn. What was the deal that you were making with my family? Alexander was supposed to be there that night, not Ty. He only shows up under. . . extreme circumstances."

"You're telling me," he mumbled with a slight laugh. "I need you to listen with an open mind."

"Okay, that's a bit of an ominous start, but I agree to keep an open mind."

"The Wards came to us looking for a specific type of drug. Niall and I are rather good combining chemistry and magic, and we know a few witches for the parts we can't manage between ourselves. We were able to supply your family with what they were looking for. That night was supposed to be our exchange." He waited for me to respond.

"The Roses made the deal to supply, or . . . you and Niall?"

Adrian pressed his lips into a firm line, telling me what I needed to know. It wasn't an answer I expected, and I wasn't sure how to feel about it yet without knowing more.

"What does the drug do?" He gave me a look, cocking an eyebrow and inclining his head in my direction. "Oh right, my turn. I spied because I don't like what my family does and I want it to stop." When he looked at me with surprise, I added, "Just because I'm syndicate doesn't mean I'm part of it."

"They wanted a drug to control people," he said. "They'd been quiet, but Niall and I have a lot of friends in low places. Word gets around when you're looking for magical mind control, so we approached them with an offer they couldn't refuse." My mouth fell open and a small gasp escaped my lips. That was way worse than what we would have thought, but it explained why Lindsey looked like she was under a spell. When he saw my reaction he made sure to finish quickly. "The drug we delivered wasn't quite what we negotiated. Your father wanted something that would permanently make people fall in line. This isn't that. It's a temporary way to influence the user, albeit-very strongly at first, but it can't be altered to be a long-term means of controlling anyone. It's also not addictive in the slightest."

"But why?" I asked. "Why do it at all?"

"Because one way or another they were going to get their hands on a drug like that. The deal for your hand had already been made. This was buying us time."

"For?"

Adrian sighed. "One of us to win. We were concerned he planned to use it on the entire shifter syndicate to start a war. This would put a wrinkle in that plan because it would never last long enough to do something like that. He'd need far more than he could get his hands on."

He looked at me with something akin to hope, but I could tell he expected me to lash out at him.

"You . . . lied to my family . . ." I paused, taking a deep breath. "And sold them a bad product?"

"That's oversimplified, but yes. I don't like what the syndicates do either, Nikki. Like you, I was born into one, but I've found ways to undermine them along the way."

A few tense moments passed between us while I considered him.

"Have you heard of the Movement?"

Adrian narrowed his eyes. "No . . ."

"It's a militia group that works against the syndicates," I said quickly, blurting it out without stringing the words together thoughtfully. "I'm one of the members."

Adrian blinked a few times, processing my admission, then he tilted his head back and laughed. "That's—those are honestly words I didn't expect to hear. Sort of a relief, actually. I wasn't sure if you were involved in some sort of setup by your brother." He scrubbed his hands down his face.

"Is that why you chased me?" I asked.

"Yes. I'm assuming your father has no idea you're working against him, so it makes sense you ran."

We stared at each other in silence as I pieced together the kind of person that Adrian was.

"So . . . what? You're a syndicate criminal with a good heart?" I asked, curling my lips into a smile.

"Something like that."

"Unexpected," I said, nodding. "But certainly welcomed."

"So . . . you're a vigilante like Batman, but without the cool gadgets?"

"Vigilante like Robin Hood, asshole," I muttered, smacking him in the arm. He caught my wrist, pulling me close, and wrapped an arm around my waist. My hands splayed across his broad chest, and I looked up at him. "Batman is too dark and angsty. And what's with the cape? It's totally impractical. A real badass doesn't need one."

"Of course," he chuckled, caressing his thumb over my cheek. "They much prefer explosive arrows."

I leaned into his touch. It was new and exciting but also comforting. Heat zipped along my skin as desire rushed through me. I had more questions, so the damn mate bond needed to chill out. "What about the deal you made with my dad . . . for me?"

Adrian's body tensed against mine, and I felt him pull back just a fraction. I didn't like that. My phoenix really didn't like that. Distance was bad. People put distance because that made it easier for them to handle it when they hurt someone. "That's more complicated."

"Try me."

He didn't let me go, but he hesitated, struggling with the physical touch between us now.

"Phaon was making a deal with the other syndicates whether or not I was involved. He and a few others went to all the trouble of setting the groundwork so that syndicates could run for Earth and Emerald. Your father is a lot of things, but stupid isn't one. There's a reason the shifter syndicate got Manhattan, and it's because Phaon always gets what he wants. My parents knew one way or another that he would decide the winner in the race. They wanted to be the horse he bet on, so I volunteered. We both did."

I scrunched my brows, trying to make sense of it. "You volunteered? Why?"

He nodded. "Niall volunteered for his own reasons, but my family doesn't trust him the same way they trust me. They never would have let him represent us by himself, and because of our friendship I was the obvious pick to go with him. Besides, I wanted to support my best friend. In doing so, it allowed the Roses the option of putting an heir in the running. They were pleased they'd have two horses in the race, so they didn't care. I didn't know you'd be my mate."

"Mate or not, you still see how shitty it is, right? Both of you made this deal. Just because you didn't know we were mates doesn't mean it was okay to sign on the dotted line and get rewarded with a person."

Adrian's muscles tightened when I started to move away. "I won't claim it was right, but I'm not going to apologize for doing what I needed to do for Niall."

Flashes of smoke and fire speed through my mind. Visions of Niall's face and a phantom voice calling to me while I looked up at a burning sky filtered through my thoughts.

"You seem close with him. Niall. You said he's your best friend. How did you meet?" I asked, hedging carefully.

Adrian exhaled through his nose, bordering on a sigh.

"He came to Brooklyn about four years ago and asked for sanctuary with my family. At the time my parents were also pushing me to take on more responsibility in the syndicate. As a way to sidestep that, I offered to take on Niall. Turns out, it was really him taking me on. He quickly proved himself worth keeping around for the syndicate, but I found kinship in him. We trust each other with our lives, and I honestly can't say that about anyone else I've ever met. Present company excluded."

"Me? You barely know me."

"I don't have to know you. You're my mate. I trust the fates."

"We haven't completed the bond," I countered.

"You haven't rejected it either," he said, though the inflection in his voice made it sound almost like a question. "Unless . . ."

"No, I'm not going to. I want this. Us," I murmured, feeling heat rush through my body at the thought of being with him. Of having a person that was completely and wholly mine, and would never leave or abandon me. Who would fight for and with me. "I'm just still in shock, I think. A lot has happened in a stupidly short period of time—and I somehow have two mates. This kind of thing only happens in books and movies."

Adrian looked as though he wanted to say something, but he closed his lips and thought for a minute before speaking again. "Are you going to reject him?"

"I . . . talk about complicated," I said, blowing out a long breath. "Malachi and I have a history. He hurt me beyond measure the day he walked away. . . but my heart has always belonged to him. I loved him before the mate bond. I can't just turn that off. I don't want to turn that off. I just need to, I don't know . . . talk to him without visualizing myself strangling him. Love is weird sometimes."

"You'd be willing to have two mates?" he asked carefully.

I shrugged, hoping he wasn't going to ask me to choose.

"Like I said, I'm still coming to terms with all of this, but fate wouldn't give me more than one mate if it wasn't meant to be, right?" Images of being sandwiched between Adrian and Malachi flitted through my mind. Both of them adoring me. Coveting me. Filling me . . . Shaking my head before I got too attached to an impossibility, I knew I had to ask what he thought of it. "Um"—I cleared my throat— "Does that bother you?"

"Not in the slightest," he answered without hesitation. "If the fates chose more than one mate for you, who am I to argue whether you have one or three?"

"Three?" I coughed as I said it. Was three a crowd? Not that it mattered, but *wow*.

"One, two, three, ten. Just making my point." He lifted a shoulder casually.

"Well, ten might be too much to handle. There's only so much of me and relationships require work, even predestined ones." I said, laughing at the very notion. "Have you told Niall that I'm your mate?" He nodded in confirmation. "Then why is he still going through with the trials? Trials get us to the election. Election means he could win. You're okay with Malachi because he's also my mate, but I can't imagine you getting on board with me becoming a free for all. I wouldn't be if the roles were reversed. Why hasn't he conceded?"

Adrian pulled his bottom lip into his mouth, biting it, and wincing as he said, "That's a longer story, and honestly, I think he needs to be the one to tell it."

"Why can't you just tell me?"

"Because his secrets aren't mine to share," he whispered.

He looked so conflicted, and I wanted to know why.

I pulled away from him, instantly feeling a level of rejection he couldn't understand. It was stupid to be upset. Niall was his best friend, after all. He'd made that perfectly clear. While he might say he trusts me the same, there's no way it was actually true.

"Nikki, wait," he said, taking a step forward, but I took another step back.

My heart rate increased. I just expected a little honesty where it had to do with me. Was that really such a big ask? Was it because we barely knew each other or was it something else? The mate bond was meant to connect us instantly. I certainly felt connected to him, but this wouldn't be the first time someone claimed to care for me before walking away. What if—

"If he wins, are you going to reject me?"

"No."

"Are you sure?" I asked, taking a step back. "Because you're being really cagey about this and ringing all kinds of alarm bells right now."

Adrian's eyes darkened and his lips parted to speak when a knock sounded at the door.

CHAPTER 21
MALACHI

I SIPPED MY CARAMEL MACCHIATO, IGNORING NIALL'S underhanded comments and looks of disgust.

He could call me a basic bitch all he wanted. The way I saw it, I spent my childhood drinking swill that may as well have been sewer water. I was going to enjoy every last luxury that accompanied being a high-ranking leader in a syndicate.

If he wanted to drink black coffee and feel like a manly man for it, more power to him. My ego wasn't fragile.

I was going to enjoy my coffee and embrace the semi-peaceful ambiance that was created by sharing a house with Nikki.

I'd never gotten to experience that. When I was ten, I'd accidentally fallen asleep at her house. I wouldn't lie. It was way too easy to fall asleep next to her. My life was nothing like hers. I was used to sleeping on hard pews with a bunch of other orphans in a rundown church that was covered in rat droppings. The couch in her bedroom was remarkably comfortable while we watched one of her sappy Disney movies, and I felt safe and loved in her presence. Of course I let my guard down.

Ty nearly beat me to death for it. Probably would have killed me, if not for Alexander stepping in. I hid it from her. I never wanted to let her see how badly he'd hurt me.

No sane person would have blamed me for wanting that comfort as a child, but after that beating, it never happened again.

After that, I couldn't even be under the same roof with Nikki without feeling some level of anxiety that Ty would lash out if he thought I was too friendly. Too comfortable.

It made me angry when I thought about it for too long. Always did.

Back then, I was scared she would side with Ty because he was her brother, so I made a point to never put her in a situation where she'd have to choose between me and her family. That didn't mean it was easy.

For fuck's sake, I was ten. She was eight. We were kids. It was completely platonic. We didn't even understand what it meant to have feelings. That didn't develop until we were teens. I kept my distance then. Even more so with the way Ty was always magically in the same room we were. Like he'd expected me to deflower her the moment we were alone. I scoffed.

I couldn't say that thought didn't occur to me by the time I was seventeen, but I was two years older than Nikki. The mate bond hit me first. I ignored the urges and tried to bide my time; to be patient until she felt it too. It was hard when she didn't feel it at the same age I did. But these things were different for everyone. I wasn't going to push her into something if she didn't want it. She was my safety. My comfort. My home.

She was my everything.

So after nearly three years of wanting her and being unable to do anything about it, it crushed me when I had to leave her.

When she finally felt the bond, she wanted to solidify it right away. After the beating of my life, I knew better than to do the mating equivalent of eloping. Not if I wanted to live. I went to her father to make sure that it would be safe to claim her. I knew I could help with her animal—which she didn't even have at the time. She was latent, and I'd hoped the bond would encourage her shifter form to surface. Phaon was obsessed with bringing her animal out. I thought it might be enough for him to overlook that I wasn't a shifter. I wasn't even 'purebred'.

I just never imagined I'd be forced to walk away from her.

Phaon warned me that if I even touched his daughter, he'd kill me—regardless of the fact that it would destroy her emotionally. He didn't care that the physical destruction of losing a mate would take its toll, maybe even driving her to madness. He swore I'd disappear, and she'd never know what happened, or that he had a hand in it.

The reality was I believed him, without a doubt. Ty had threatened the same thing weekly for a decade. He'd nearly succeeded once. Of course I believed him.

Her ability to live her life normally rested on my shoulders.

All I had to do was walk away.

To be able to sit under the same roof as her now; to know that she was content and safe and alive—that we were *both* alive after all we'd been through—and that there was a chance we could overcome our past? Yeah, it gave me some measure of peace. I was going to fucking enjoy it and not let the asshole hybrid ruin even one second.

"It's past ten in the morning," Niall griped.

I lifted one shoulder in a half-hearted shrug.

"Can you blame her? She had a long day yesterday."

"Yeah, but does she have to be asleep? In his room? *This* late. . ."

Amusements filled me, even though I was also feeling more than a little jealous of Adrian at the moment.

"Isn't he your best friend?" I pointed out. "Between the two of us, shouldn't you be more understanding with this arrangement?"

Niall scoffed. "He's alive and sleeping in the same room as her. Clearly I'm okay with it. That doesn't mean that I'm happy about it. When she still isn't acknowledging my existence—" He cut himself off, not wanting to elaborate further or acknowledge the vulnerability he'd just let seep through his stony exterior.

"Ah." I hummed. "This has less to do with Adrian, and more to do with the fact that she doesn't want to be in your bed. That she doesn't feel comfortable enough to sleep in it, or around you."

"She doesn't remember me." Niall said defensively.

"Oh?" I questioned. "How does she not remember you? If you're her mate . . ."

If looks could kill, I'd be dead on the floor, torn apart limb by limb. He'd probably beat my bleeding corpse with the bloody stump of my arm.

It wasn't about me. I was just a source of frustration, and there wasn't anything he could do as I was one of his mate's mates. I wondered how long it would be before he took a swing. It was bound to happen at some point.

"I'm not sure why," he said through gritted teeth. "But I plan to find out."

Hmm. "Well, good luck with that."

Niall pointedly ignored me as he assessed the breakfast he'd made for Nikki and himself. I had a feeling Adrian and I weren't included, but that was all right. I wasn't sure I trusted his food anyway. While he wouldn't kill me out of respect for Nikki, I wouldn't put it past him to stuff my portion full of laxatives.

He continued to glance back and forth between the door and the pan of eggs, sausage, and cut-up potatoes. He'd mumbled something about them being hashbrowns, but they lacked a certain amount of seasoning for me to consider them as such.

I watched in delight while he debated on going and potentially waking her up. When he finally cursed under his breath and said "fuck it", I turned to watch him as he carried the plate in hand and approached the door.

From my position in the living room, it was a good view of Adrian's room.

The way he aggressively knocked twice wasn't as soft as one would suggest when trying to politely wake a person up. Rather, it was more akin to the way someone pounded before barging in.

"Yes?" Nikki called out.

Her voice wasn't groggy enough to make me think she'd actually been asleep. Which meant she'd been awake, probably for a while. Interesting, the thought ran through my mind and a prickle of the same jealousy that Niall was feeling touched me.

Now I wondered what they'd been doing in there.

"I made breakfast," he said, omitting the fact that he'd made it specifically for her.

Shuffling sounded on the other side of the door, and a moment later, it flew open.

Nikki stood in the doorway in baggy sweatpants and a

214

loose T-shirt—*without a bra underneath*, my sexually frustrated brain noted—with one hand on the frame, the other on her hip.

Her hair was wild from sleep. Not sex hair, thankfully, but sexy as hell all the same. I liked seeing this version of her. Natural. Less put together, so to speak. It reminded me of when we were younger . . . freer and happier. Before who and what we were caught up with us.

She took a long look at the plate Niall had made for her. Awkwardness colored her features, and a slight blush started to stain her cheeks.

"That's . . . really nice of you", she said, then cringed. I had to bite my cheek to keep from laughing out loud. "I'm not very hungry right now, though."

Her stomach grumbled loudly, calling her out like the liar she was.

I lost it. My drink swished, the ice clinking as I doubled over in laughter. Nikki shot me a sharp glare from the doorway.

"I guess I'm hungrier than I feel," she mumbled. Adrian walked up behind her, placing a hand on her hip. The blush in her cheeks deepened against her olive complexion.

"Why do you never make me breakfast?" Adrian asked, yawning.

Niall cocked his head. I couldn't see much of his face, but his muscles tensed.

"You can make your own damn breakfast," Niall muttered.

Nikki snaked out of Adrian's grip and stepped around Niall to head toward the kitchen.

While her attention was focused elsewhere, she missed the silent conversation between Niall and a much more alert Adrian, than he was pretending to be.

I stood from the loveseat and walked into the kitchen, taking a seat at a bar stool instead.

There was no way I was going to miss this.

I watched her poke at the food in the skillet, a grimace marring her pretty lips. Nikki grabbed a small plate from the cupboard. A saucer really. I couldn't even call it a plate. Then she spooned just enough on there to feed a baby bird.

She had to be starving. We'd skipped breakfast and lunch yesterday because of the first two trials. I didn't see her eat dinner, but I assumed she went and got it with Sam.

She scooped a mouth full of the sausage and hash-browns onto a spoon, then plopped it in her mouth in a way that reminded me of someone taking a shot of vodka. Like she knew the taste was going to be horrific, but she was doing it anyway. Her expression flatlined as a mask fell over her. She chewed robotically before swallowing.

When Adrian and Niall entered the kitchen, they both tilted their heads and gave her a questioning look. If only they knew.

Adrian walked around the bar and helped himself to a large portion of the food, much to Niall's annoyance. Given how little Nikki had eaten, it wasn't really cutting into what he'd made for himself.

Adrian took a bite, chewing thoughtfully while watching her.

"You feeling all right?" he asked, as she set down her spoon.

I wasn't sure if she'd realized that she'd chosen the wrong utensil for a meal that traditionally would require a fork, but that was Nikki for you. A little bit odd and out there on occasion.

"Yes," she said, her voice just a touch too high. "Totally fine."

216

She cleared her throat, and awkward silence descended throughout the room as Nikki took another painful bite.

She tried really hard not to scrunch her nose in disgust. I'll give that to her. She really did try. She also failed miserably.

I started laughing, and she swallowed down her second bit. All three of them turned to me with various glares.

Without saying a word, I opened my jacket pocket and pulled out a paper bag, then slid it across the counter toward her.

She accepted the package warily, looking between it and me. Nikki sniffed twice, and I wasn't sure if she was consciously scenting it or if it was an involuntary response. Slowly she opened the bag, and her eyes widened. I could swear a tiny bit of drool escaped the corner of her mouth.

"You brought Reaper chips? Oh my god." She took a bite and closed her eyes while groaning in pleasure.

Adrian and Niall no longer looked annoyed with me, but they certainly had questions.

"Should you tell them, or should I?" I asked her. She paused halfway through chewing and swallowed, licking her lips for every last trace.

Nikki sighed.

"What?" Adrian asked. "You don't like eggs or sausage? It's actually pretty normal not to eat these, at least amongst the fae. I'm kind of an oddity for eating all of this. I love nature as much as the next person, but true nature is savage. Predator and prey. I can respect and honor nature, eating all that the earth has provided to me. That's the cycle of life. I'm just embracing it," Adrian said as he took another bite of hashbrowns.

"It's not that," Nikki said. "I have a different kind of . . .

preference." She stumbled over the words, struggling to explain.

"Nikki thinks normal food tastes like dirt," I interjected. "What's good to you or me; what we consider well-seasoned? She hates it. The only stuff she'll eat that she actually enjoys is so heavily spiced that it's inedible to pretty much anyone else."

A corner of Nikki's mouth curled up. "I wouldn't say it's inedible," she started.

"No, really, Nikki. It's pretty terrible," I said with a laugh, then I turned to Adrian and Niall. "And she is a rotten cook because of it. Truly. Don't ever let her cook for you."

"It's not that bad!"

"You almost killed me with popcorn when you were fourteen. Popcorn, Nikki. All you need is butter and salt. Marissa had to give me the Heimlich after I started choking on the ground dragon's breath pepper you'd sprinkled all over it."

"Fuck your butter and salt." Nikki moved to throw the chips at my head, but stopped, thinking better of it when her stomach gave another loud growl.

I chuckled under my breath.

"Is it because of your phoenix?" Niall asked.

I blinked, taken aback. *Phoenix*. She'd found her animal . . . and she was a fucking phoenix. A beast so rare now, it was nothing more than a myth.

Shock hit me square in the chest. She'd been latent, and so scared she'd be that way for life. Marissa was a void in a family of powerful and legendary creatures—and both girls were reminded of it constantly. Somehow Nikki had found her phoenix . . . and she'd managed to do it without me.

Part of me was so proud of her for that, but part of me was also incredibly sad.

It wasn't that I ever doubted that she could do it on her own, just that I wanted to help her. I wanted to be there with her.

Her brother and father had already tainted so much of our past, and this felt like that was stolen from me, oddly enough. But it also was never guaranteed to be mine.

I'd walked away. I'd had good reasons. But I'd still walked away, and it sucked.

"Heard that when Ty was raging, did you?" she asked, wrinkling her nose.

Niall shrugged.

"Well, that's what I think it is," she said, eating the last chip and licking her fingers. "No one else in my family likes spicy, so probably safe to assume it's the firebird in me."

I had so many questions I wanted to ask. Before I could, the doorbell rang, and Adrian stood up quickly. I'd heard about Ty berating Nikki—though I hadn't heard he'd spilled what kind of shifter she was. I assumed Adrian was about to go tell him to fuck off again. "I'll get it," he said, leaving the kitchen.

Nikki looked at me, raising her brows in hope, but not speaking the question I knew was lingering in her mind.

I rolled my eyes. "Yes, I brought more. And I brought ground dragon's breath as well. I was worried you'd starve without it. Just keep it away from my food."

Her face lit up, and I melted. I'd eat that horrible shit every day of my life if it meant she'd look at me like that again.

Sam and Tylea walked into the kitchen, with Adrian trailing behind them.

"Sam!" Nikki said, excitement in her voice. "Guess what? Malachi brought Reaper chips and dragon's breath!"

Her best friend stood there, forcing a tight smile. "Is that all he told you?"

My gut twisted, and I shot a look at Tylea. She mouthed "sorry" and squeezed her eyes shut.

Oh fuck . . .

CHAPTER 22

NIKKI

"WHAT IS THAT SUPPOSED TO MEAN?" ALL THE ENTHUSIASM I HAD flew out the window. The elation I felt at eating spicy comfort food was now long gone. Sam never spoke in an ominous tone.

Niall and Adrian stood there, frozen.

"It means, not only are Malachi and Adrian your mates, but it seems that Niall here has been keeping a secret." She looked from person to person in the room as she spoke, landing on him last. "He's your mate too."

"What?" I whispered, but I may as well have disappeared.

"You told your second," Niall growled, standing up and knocking his chair over.

"Clearly," Malachi answered tersely. "It's not like I expected it to go down this way. That wasn't the plan!"

Adrian rubbed his temples. "I don't think that's the point right now."

"Et tu, Tylea?" Malachi said. "I told you that in confidence. I thought you knew better than to run your mouth."

The look he gave her was nothing short of pointed and pissed.

"Sorry, boss. In my defense, Sam is really crafty when getting information out of people. I didn't realize until it was too late."

"Fair point. So, what, you're going to bust in here and drop a bomb like that, Sam?" he said, raising his voice to her.

"Eat shit, Malachi. I don't owe you anything. I'm loyal to Nikki and no one else." She crossed her arms, cocking an eyebrow.

"You've known me since we were kids. We were friends too."

"I was also there when you broke her heart," she spat. "I got to pick up the pieces when you walked away. Don't talk to me about 'friends'."

Somehow, I'd been left out of the conversation, and it was starting to piss me off.

"Hey, explain to me—"

Their bickering still drowned me out.

"How do you know this—"

It was hard to hear over the din in the kitchen. It began to echo, and I wasn't having it anymore.

I whistled loudly, bringing the attention back to me. "What in Satan's knickers is going on right now? What do you mean ALL three of them are my mates?"

"You want to answer her, or should I?" Sam hooked a thumb over her shoulder toward the statuesque redhead with one wing.

"Someone had better answer me before I set this gods-damned place on fire."

"Sorry," Tylea said to me with a grimace. I didn't know

her, but she looked genuinely apologetic. That's more than could be said for the rest of them.

"This isn't how we wanted to tell you." Adrian sighed.

"*We*? You knew. . ." Betrayal washed through me. We'd just opened up to each other and had a real conversation about this mate business. He said he trusted me, but he lied by omission. "Are you serious right now? You knew this when we were just . . . not even twenty minutes ago?"

"Like I said; some secrets aren't mine to tell."

Understanding clicked into place, but the truth didn't make it sting any less. "Not even with your mate. I guess you don't trust the fates as much as you claim." Did I believe what I was saying? Probably not. But dammit, I was furious. And hurt.

"Would you have wanted to hear it from me?" he replied, his blue eyes flashing.

"It's better than hearing it like this," I shouted, gesturing to the room.

"I'll give you that, but you deserved to hear the truth from your mate—your other mate." Malachi cleared his throat, and Adrian rolled eyes. "Whatever. Your other *other* mate. Niall deserved to tell you too. It wasn't my conversation to have, Nikki."

I shook my head. "No, this isn't . . . it's weird enough I have two mates, thank you very much. I feel a bond with both of you—even if I'm having serious doubts about it right now." Turning to Niall, I said, "I don't . . . I don't feel that with you. I'm not saying that to be hurtful, it's just . . . the truth. Until the night of the winter solstice, I'd never seen you before. If you were my mate, I would have felt it then. I'd feel it now."

"Unless someone interfered," Sam mumbled, looking everywhere but at me.

I shot her a questioning look. "What's that supposed to mean? Whose side are you even on?"

"Yours, Nikki. I'm always on your side. That's why I came here and told you as soon as I found out. You have a right to know, and not whenever these three douchebags got around to telling you."

"We were getting there," Adrian said through gritted teeth.

"Well, I got you there faster," Sam countered. "You're welcome."

"Does anybody else have any secrets that they want to share? Maybe children I need to know about?" Silence spanned the room, but all three guys shook their heads no. "Am I the lucky recipient of a homewrecker award? Are any of you already married and plan to tell your spouse that you're leaving because you've now found a mate? Which for the record, is shitty of you and fate. I'm starting to think those bitches got drunk when pairing us up."

"You know we're not," Malachi answered.

"I don't know what I know anymore," I said in exasperation. "I spent my entire life believing that my father's love for me made me immune to who he really was, only to find out he sold me as part of an alliance. You disappeared for *six years*, Malachi, and the whole time you were in Queens. You could have been dead or moved on for all I knew. It's not like you ever checked in or gave me even the slightest indication you were there. You rejected me then left. So yeah, asking if you've got a wife or kids isn't all that far fetched." He turned away, jaw tensing. I looked at Adrian. "You were the second chance. The one that didn't hurt me or walk away. I just poured my heart out to you, and you still kept this from me. It's hard not to believe there aren't more things you're doing that with because you can mentally write it off as 'not your secret to tell'. Trust goes both ways. I've been honest with you, but you lied to me by omission. I can't just ignore that—because clearly, I can't trust you. Not like I thought I could." Adrian had the good sense to press his lips together and dip his chin in acknowledgment. I faced Niall. "And now you're also claiming to be my mate, but you've not had the balls to say it to me. What am I supposed to think? This isn't a 'the more the merrier kind of situation'."

Niall struggled to speak, but seemed to be struggling with finding the words. Adrian, ever the best friend, stepped forward. "I think you and Niall need to talk about a few things."

"Go on," I said, waving at him. "Talk. I'm listening."

"It's not that simple," Niall said. "There's a history. A lot has happened . . ." He looked warily at Sam, Malachi, and Tylea—but mostly Sam.

"Perhaps *without* an audience," Adrian interrupted. "I think we need to leave and give them time to have this conversation privately."

Malachi crossed his arms. "No thanks. I'm good. I wanna hear this."

Adrian placed a hand on Malachi's back, nudging him forward. "Not your call to make man. Nikki deserves to be the first to know and process it without us. If they wanna tell you, they can at some other time. Come on. Sam. Tylea. You too."

"I don't answer to you. You might be her 'mate', but I'm her person and second," Sam said. She looked at me for confirmation and after a few seconds I dipped my chin in acknowledgment.

"Go on. I'll call if I need you—or yell. You can come back if you smell smoke."

Sam inclined her head and walked out of the room with Tylea.

Malachi hesitated, clearly not wanting to leave. "You and I still have to talk, Nikki."

"One pain in the ass boyfriend at a time."

Malachi smirked. "Not a boyfriend, but I'll take it as long as there *is* a time." He stepped out of the kitchen. The commotion in the room lessened leaving a rather. . . uncomfortable situation behind. I crossed my arms and sniffed, shifting my weight to the other side.

Every time Niall and I talked it left me on edge. He acted like he knew me and was upset that I didn't reciprocate. I had a feeling this was why.

It made it impossible to have a conversation.

Those visions though . . . they felt so real.

"Do you want me to stay?" Adrian asked, sensing my apprehension. We hadn't completed the bond and he was already so in tune with my emotions. I wondered how much more intense that would get once we did.

"No," Niall said instantly. I didn't care for him answering for me.

Adrian looked pained and cleared his throat. "I was asking Nikki." So he does learn. Smart mate.

"What the fuck for?"

"Because she's uncomfortable."

"What are you suggesting?" Niall clenched his fists, posturing with his best friend. I wasn't a fan of that either.

Adrian held his hands up in mock surrender. "Nothing. I'm just asking her"—he paused, considering his choice of words. On an exhale, he added—"as her mate."

"I'm her fucking mate too."

"You know that's not what I meant."

Niall glowered, his jaw tensing as Adrian stood his ground. It was like two animals about to fight on a nature show, and I was so over it.

"Oh my god, the testosterone in this room is going to kill me. I just want some fucking answers."

When Niall looked away from Adrian and his eyes met mine, they softened a bit, as though he had realized that he was practically banging on his chest. All he was missing was the club.

Niall sighed. "Would you be more comfortable if Adrian stayed?" Hm. Maybe he could learn too.

"That depends. Are you going to keep acting like a caveman?" Niall's lips set into a firm line. His brown and silver hair was pulled back in a short ponytail. Strands had fallen loose, framing the hard cut of his jaw. When he didn't answer, I spoke again. "No? Then we're good."

Adrian nodded, coming over to kiss my temple before leaving the room. Niall glared at him, but refrained from jealous comments.

As soon as the door shut upon Adrian's departure, I looked at Niall. "That right there," I motioned to him. "That needs to stop."

"What?"

"The dirty looks. The posturing. Jealousy won't work in this dynamic."

"I can't help it, Nikki."

"Well, you better start helping it. Malachi and Adrian are both my mates. Granted, I need to work out some shit with Malachi and he has some serious groveling to do—but he's still mine and I'm keeping him. *Don't* tell him I said that. Regardless, I feel those bonds. It was instant with both of them. I know it's real, and neither one of them act like

227

stupid gorillas in front of me, even if they want to. So if you're going to claim you're my mate, start acting like it."

"It's . . . hard for me. I'm trying."

"Why? I doubt they like the idea of sharing me, but they seem to be doing okay. What makes you different?"

"I've known you were my mate for years. I've been waiting for you. At the solstice celebration, I thought you were pretending to not know me and it made me angry. I didn't realize you truly don't remember me. I'm frustrated, but not necessarily with you. It's hard to watch you with two other men, when you don't see it or act the same with me."

"You say we've met before, but I have no memory of you. When did we meet?"

"Four years ago. When you and your sister were—"

"Oh my god. Are you Marissa's mate? That's why you think you know me. I don't know what to say. . ." My heart skipped a beat.

He shook his head. "No. It's always been *you*. I feel it now. I've always felt it."

"How do you know my sister?"

"The same way I know you."

"Stop being so damn cryptic. If I wanted you to speak in riddles I would have said "hey do you think you could be a complicated asshole and answer questions without actually answering any of my questions?"

"I'm sorry." He sighed in frustration. "This is just harder than I thought it would be."

"I don't want your apologies, Niall. I want truth."

"The truth is complicated."

"Why does everybody keep telling me that? You all act like I can't handle it? Like I'm too fragile and might break apart if I hear something I don't like. Do you have any idea

228

what I've been through? I know what difficult is. *I know*. And this?" I motioned between me and him. "It's not all that difficult. Neither is my relationship with Adrian, if I'm really honest. These trials? Barely a blip on the radar—with the exception of the air duct. Difficult is being kidnapped and having no idea if you'd ever get out. It's the anger and resentment or not remembering the most important week of your life. It's grief so overwhelming that you can't get out of bed, you can't go on, because the other half of you wasn't just taken—but murdered. That is difficult."

Niall watched me for a moment, his brown eyes sharpening.

"What about betrayal?"

"Excuse me?"

"What if not knowing is easier? Less painful? What if that anger and resentment only grow when you find the missing pieces? Once the truth is out there, that can't be undone." He tilted his head, considering me. "Then again, maybe it can."

"What the—? What does that even mean? You know what, never mind. I'm tired of this. You have five seconds to start talking, or I'm done."

"Done?"

"If you don't start speaking words that make sense, I'm going to fix this entire situation."

Niall scrunched his brows in confusion. "I don't understand."

"Join the fucking club. We have name tags and T-shirts."

"I still don't under—"

"It means I am *done*. If you don't start talking, I'm going to reject you and any bond we may have. It hurts like a bitch. Maybe I'll feel it. Maybe I won't, but if you're really my mate—it's one of the worst pains imaginable."

"Nikki wait—"

"Five."

"Stop."

"Four . . ."

CHAPTER 23
NIALL

WELL, WHEN SHE PUT IT THAT WAY, IT LEFT ME NO CHOICE.

I wasn't willing to do anything that would jeopardize Nikki accepting the mate bond with me, but I also didn't want to cause her pain that came with making those memories resurface. If she didn't remember what happened, it was because her mind had suppressed it. That spoke to the severity of the suffering she'd experienced. I might have been the same way if I wasn't born in that terrible place, but torture was all I knew. I sighed heavily.

"Three."

"I'll tell you," I whispered. "But you need to be aware; The way we met . . . it was traumatizing for you. I believe there is a reason you don't remember."

"I need to know."

I could understand that. Respect it, even if I didn't want to put her through the pain this would dredge up.

"To understand, I need to go back to the beginning. I was born in a facility run by humans. Extremists looking for a way to fight against supernaturals. This was shortly after the portal to Arcadia opened. The world was still very much unsettled. Governments all over were falling apart. Nowhere was safe for those without magic, but even worse were those *with* magic that were too young and vulnerable to protect themselves. I was still in an egg when this group of radicals got a hold of me."

"Wait a minute, did you say *egg*? What kind of shifter are you?"

With anyone else I would have lied or told them to piss off. Oddly enough, my greatest secret was the easiest one to share with her. "A dragon."

She blinked. "Dragons are extinct."

"Apparently not, since I'm sitting before you."

"Prove it."

I lifted an eyebrow at her. It wasn't like I was going to shift in the middle of one of the most watched places in the world right now. Instead, I blinked, letting my eyes shift to their crimson color with a reptilian slit. I pushed it a step further and white iridescent scales descended on my arms. Her mouth popped open in awe. I expected fear or wariness. This was a welcome surprise.

"I heard dragons were unstable."

My beast retreated before I replied. "I don't know. I haven't met any others. You'll have to tell me if you do."

"Okay, smartass."

"Do you want to play twenty questions about my dragon or walk down memory lane?" I snapped, then closed my eyes and took a deep breath. "I'm sorry. This isn't easy for me, Nikki. What happened to us. . . It changes people. It changed you and you don't even know half of it yet."

"Keep going," she said quietly. "But I would like to know more about your dragon later."

I nodded; my dragon was all about that.

232

"The humans wanted to see if they could create a shifter that could change into any supernatural being. They'd learned from preliminary trials that the subject had to already be a shifter, and a powerful one at that. Otherwise they would die too quickly. They experimented on me before I was born. I was subjected to radiation and slew of other "treatments" that were meant to make me harder to kill later on, when the real changes came. This continued after I'd hatched. My earliest memories are of being sick and nearly dying on the floor of a cage."

"That's horrible," she said through a barely audible whisper.

"I wasn't the only one. For several years there was a water fae that accompanied the cage next to mine. She was also a child they'd kidnapped, but in her case they only wanted her DNA. Her name was Lydia, and she was my first friend . . . and my first mistake. The"—I struggled to find the words. I couldn't find it in me to call them researchers because what they did went well beyond research, but they weren't simply torturing for the hell of it either. "The scientists used my friendship with Lydia against us. If they wanted me to do something, they would hurt her to provoke a response, then do the same to her in return.

"One day they went a little too far . . . Lydia didn't survive." Nikki put a hand to her mouth in silent horror. "Are you sure you want to hear this?" I asked her.

Her fingers slipped away, and she pressed her lips together, nodding tightly "Yes. I need to."

"After her death, I didn't let myself get close to any of the other prisoners. Some of them were there for days; others lasted weeks, months, years. The time blended together. I wouldn't have known how long I was in that

233

place, if not for certain events that helped me date it. To my best understanding, I was held there for about fifty years."

"Oh my—" Nikki broke off, realizing she'd said that out loud. I didn't like the pity in her eyes, but I wasn't going to chastise her for it either. I hated being someone that people could pity, but it was certainly a story and experience that was unfortunate.

"How do you know you were born there?" she asked. "That they didn't kidnap you as a child?"

"Conversations I'd overheard," I told her. "They talked about things that they'd done when I was still in an egg."

"That had to have been so hard," she said softly, empathizing with my situation. I nodded, even if inside I was having to separate myself from the story I had to tell. Distance was the only way I could do it.

"It was and it wasn't," I said. "The facility was all I knew. A cage. Bars. People poking and prodding. I was miserable and depressed, but I didn't realize how bad I had it, or what life could be outside of that place." Scrubbing a hand down my face, I paused briefly before speaking again. "I was complacent. I didn't fight back because I didn't have anything to fight for. But somewhere along the way, I gave up on myself entirely. Freedom was a foreign concept. I didn't have bodily autonomy, let alone any understanding of what happiness was. I didn't have anything . . . until you." Nikki's lips parted. A slight dusky blush rose in her cheeks.

"That was four years ago," she said, and I nodded in agreement.

"Four years. Three months. Twenty-six days. And fourteen hours."

Her jaw went slack, completely in shock.

"You counted?"

I lifted my shoulder in a nonchalant shrug even though I was feeling anything but.

"The day I saw you was the day I took my first breath. I'd never seen the sun shine, and yet I felt like I knew what it was to have its rays on my face."

"I don't know what to say to that," she said slowly.

"You don't have to say anything. In fact, I would rather you didn't. Say what you mean, and mean what you say. I don't need flattery or false assurances."

She swallowed hard and dipped her chin. I took her acknowledgment as a win and kept going.

"You and your sister were brought in and put into separate cages. First, they did the usual tests; measurements and taking blood. You were both unconscious for them. It was when you woke up that the real nightmare started. They tagged you like livestock. You were number one. Marissa was number two."

I hesitated to say her name because I didn't feel I had a right, but she had been Nikki's twin—and Nikki was my mate. Not saying her name seemed like a disservice.

I'd met Marissa. I'd tried to save her, but it wasn't enough.

I wasn't sure if Nikki was alright with me speaking about her, given how she snapped at Malachi for it. Maybe it was different because I was there and she would be glad that I'd acknowledged her sister's existence.

Nikki didn't lash out at me, instead remaining stoic.

My chest loosened a tiny bit.

"They kept talking about a phoenix. They knew one of you was, but they weren't sure which. They said the only way to find out was to force you to emerge."

Her face turned pale and ashen.

"They tortured us," she said, almost asking for confirmation rather than making a statement. "Tell me . . ."

"I'll tell you everything," I said. "Just don't ask me to go into details about how they hurt you."

"All right. I can live with that." Nikki exhaled harshly as she prepared to hear more.

"It didn't take very long for them to figure out which of you was the phoenix and which of you was the void. Once they put together that Marissa repelled magic, they turned their attention to you.

"I tried so hard to control it. To not make a sound or let them know what you were to me. I knew if they figured out you were my mate that it would only get worse. When they burned you alive the first time, I couldn't anymore. Something in me just snapped."

I tugged my shirt down at the neck, revealing a ring of mottled skin. When she saw it, a frown formed between her brows. She didn't look away, which I noticed and very much appreciated.

"For most of my life, I'd worn a collar because I was kept as a pet. The collar ensured that they could control how much of my magic I used. The first time they seriously hurt you, I lost control of my magic. It didn't matter that I was wearing it. It didn't matter that I was in a cage. I just had to get to you. I started to shift right there. It'd been decades since I'd shifted. They'd let me when I was a child, before I was too large to be contained.

"The gap between shifts made the process slow, excruciating. I was too slow to fully change before they started hitting me with electric rods, and when those failed, they escalated to poison darts, silver nitrate—all sorts of things they'd tested on supernaturals over the years. I wasn't just a shifter anymore. They'd already changed my DNA by trying too much with the two dozen or so supernatural creatures they'd wanted me to turn into. It took a lot more to put me down because of it, but they managed. One by one, they loaded enough poison into me that would kill a small army. I blacked out, and when I woke up, I was in solitary confinement."

"Jesus . . ." she muttered, clasping her hands together.

"I could hear you still, and feel you, just not physically. It was all emotional at that point. When I tried to shift, some part of me reached you and I thought I felt . . ." I shook my head. This part sounded crazy, but I didn't have any other explanation after everything I'd learned.

"You felt?" she prompted.

I was good at hiding my feelings; wearing the mask to prevent anyone from seeing what I was experiencing. Something must have slipped through because she reached across the table and took my hand.

"You were in so much pain that you also reached out. Your fingers brushed against one of my scales. I felt our souls touch." Her brows furrowed in confusion. I couldn't blame her. I knew how it sounded.

"When they put me in solitary, I shouldn't have been able to feel you and yet I did. Our bond wasn't complete. While mates supposedly had a connection, I'd never heard of it being that strong? Later, I learned how insane this sounds. But then? I didn't know much, only that what I was feeling—was powerful."

"I don't know if that's because I'm a phoenix, or if there's another explanation," she said quietly.

"I'm not sure." What I did know was that there was an intense connection Adrian felt with her, but his wasn't as strong as mine. We'd talked about it.

I could find her anywhere she went. Her emotions were

237

always there, taunting me like smoke I couldn't grab. Adrian didn't have that. I'd bet a fair bit that Malachi didn't either.

"What happened after that?" she asked.

I wasn't sure if she was uncomfortable about the mate bond itself, or if she was just desperate to get to the end. She was desperate for the truth and I still had more of the story to tell.

"They hurt you a lot. Most of it was fire—at least in the beginning. After a few days, it stopped being effective. You stopped blistering. Then your skin grew accustomed to it. Before long, you wouldn't even burn, no matter how hot the flame. You were getting close to emerging. They talked about it when they visited me. They taunted me, and I . . ." She wanted to ask. It was written all over her face. I shook my head. "They used fireworks. Made you swallow them. I can't go into it more than that, Nikki. What they did . . . was worse than the fifty years of hell I'd been through. They talked about your transition. That you were a perfect specimen to breed me with."

"Breed?" she repeated.

"They'd tried in the past. It was always unsuccessful. The first time I refused. When asking failed, they drugged me." I had to swallow against the dryness in my throat. "I don't remember what happened. They'd created some sort of chemical meant to induce a mating heat. Except my body wasn't meant to go through heat. What's more, they gave it to the female's because it convinced my hormones that I was actually with my mate. After the first incident I begged them not to do it again. I said I'd do it willingly—because I could keep the aggression under control. I could spare the women so much pain, but they told me I'd lost that privilege—" I cut off sharply, taking a deep breath. "The researchers thought I was more inclined to impregnate them—but it made me a true monster. So my dragon took over. We stayed that way for years, with him at the forefront and me in the back. I couldn't handle it. The guilt was overwhelming."

"It wasn't your fault," Nikki said softly. Water filled her beautiful eyes. I reached up to wipe the tears. When she didn't flinch away, it gave me the power to keep going.

"There were miscarriages. Sometimes early. Sometimes not. No matter what they did, the pregnancy never took. It was only when they gave up on the idea of using me as a stud that I resurfaced."

I hated it. I hated it with every fiber of my being.

"It had been over five years since I had last been with a woman when you were brought to the lab. They were oh so gleeful to learn a phoenix was my mate. They were certain that we'd be successful where so many others failed." They had plans to force us together if we didn't comply, but I wasn't going to give her nightmares even more fuel.

Those memories troubled me. I longed to forget them. My worst fears. I would never, ever do that to a woman let alone my mate. And yet those men, those monsters, they made me into one just like them . . .

"It wasn't your fault," she repeated, squeezing my hand gently. The skin on skin contact healed some broken, bleeding part inside me. "And they never got that far. We escaped." I nodded, taking a cleansing breath.

"When fire stopped working altogether and they moved to other methods but you stopped responding to the pain. It's not that you didn't feel it. It was more like you embraced it. You fell into it. You let that become your existence and it took away the power that it had over you."

"I've been able to handle anything since then. It hurts still, like you said, but not the same as it did before."

"It's a rare response to trauma like that, but you're not alone. Their methods stopped being effective on me too. That's why they resorted to drugs. After Lydia died, they didn't have a person they could use against me. Not until you. You stopped responding and were healing too fast to die, but the phoenix wouldn't emerge. That's when they turned to Marissa."

Tears slid down her cheeks as she started to cry.

I couldn't imagine what she was going through, what she had gone through, not the torture, but the pain of having her bond with her twin turned against her.

I knew what it was like to watch someone you cared for hurt, but not die. We may have escaped, but Marissa didn't.

"She died in the fire," Nikki said.

Her chest started to heave with labored breaths. I squeezed her hand tighter and her eyes jerked to mine.

"She did, but you didn't start it. When nothing else worked, they burned her alive in front of you."

"I could have stopped them," she said emphatically. "I should have."

I shook my head at her, understanding the logic but not liking the way she used it against herself.

"Don't go there. Don't do that to yourself. These people were well-funded extremists with magical weapons. I don't even know how many years of experience and knowledge they acquired before me, but they held me captive for fifty years. I can turn into a dragon the size of this house, but I was as powerless as you," I said, trying to gentle my tone, but it still came out like churned gravel.

"I'm a phoenix," she said, shaking her head. "I'm the

rarest shifter in existence. I don't just control fire. I *am* the fire and I should have been able to stop them."

"You did."

Her brow furrowed. "When they were burning Marissa, I remember feeling your pain, your anguish and your rage. I'd felt plenty of those things myself before. But nothing—nothing I've ever felt came close to the ghost of the feeling that I got from you that night." I couldn't save her sister, but I could give her comfort knowing she did her damnedest to save her. "I was being transported to the main lab when they started. There were concerns that if Marissa dying wasn't enough to trigger you, then maybe hurting me would be. But that wasn't needed—"

"How did they do it?" she asked, voice somehow hoarse from nightmares she couldn't remember. "How did they burn her?"

"Oil." She shuddered. "They dunked her in it and then tossed her in the same cage as you before setting it on fire. You were already locked in there together when I was brought in. Listen to me, Nikki, even though you couldn't stop it—you held her through every single second."

Nikki didn't need to hear about the flesh melting from her sister's bones or how she screamed so hard the glass rattled. She didn't need to hear how her sister turned into a charred corpse.

"The fire burned until there was nothing left to burn. In the ashes, you had curled around her. When it went out, I'll never forget the look in your eyes as you stood up."

"The phoenix was born," she murmured. I nodded.

"You erupted. I don't have a better word for it. When you changed, the entire facility—every horrible person inside it—they disintegrated. I'm not even sure you could call it ash. The fire melted the chains right off me, but you released so much power, so quickly, that you tapped your-self out. Between the abuse your body had been through, the grief I could feel consuming you, and the exhaustion—I think it all was just too much for you. You fainted. I carried you out. Had no idea where we were going or what the hell we were going to do. I'd never even stepped foot outside of that building. That was the first night I saw the sky. If I understood anything, though, it was survival. I could smell the river, so I started toward it."

"Wait, my father said they found me where the ware-house was. That they saw the explosion and followed it. He said my fire had killed her."

I couldn't grasp how someone like him, who called himself a family man, could have such cruelty toward his own child. If I'd known what lies he'd feed her once I was gone, I never would have let her go. But the past was the past, and I couldn't change it now.

"That's not what happened. I was with you for almost a day, when your family found us. You were slipping in and out of consciousness at the time, so I found shelter near the Brooklyn Bridge while I waited for you to come out of it. Ty was the first to find us. We nearly fought. Alexander stepped in the middle when he realized I was protecting you and explained who they were. That they were your family. I didn't have a family. I didn't have anything. But you'd just lost your sister. Who was I to take them from you? To take you from them? I wanted you, Nikki. I always have, but I could never do that to you. I tried to convince them to let me come with you and help you heal. I knew next to nothing about you beyond that you're my mate. I didn't know your name, or where you were from, or how old you were. I wanted to be there, with you, more than you can imagine, but . . ."

Nikki stood, her chair dragged against the hard floors loudly. There was a steel in her eyes as she stepped around the edge of the counter to stand right in front of me, not letting go of my hand.

"My father made you leave, didn't he?"

"You were young. I didn't realize how young until I talked to Phaon. Your father was of the belief that after everything you'd been through, it was too much trauma. He insisted I needed to go away for a while. That you couldn't handle a mate and grieve. I resisted at first, but when you woke up the first time and saw me you started screaming. Your hands burst into flames. You were so broken by what happened that I was a trigger for you. So I agreed to stay away for a little while, to let you heal. . . and to heal myself. I didn't know anything about the world I found myself in. I didn't know what kind of man I was, let alone what kind of mate I would be to you. I didn't know how to deal with a traumatized mate when I was still so messed up myself— and I still am. Make no mistake, Nikki, with me you won't get a nice normal guy. I will fight for you. I will love you fiercely. I will protect you with everything I have in me. I will do my best to comfort you and to treat you with respect, because you deserve it. You are the most important person in my life, but I'm not normal. I probably shouldn't tell you that. Given how badly I want this bond and how much I know that you're hesitating. But you asked for the truth and I'm giving it to you. Back then I didn't know what to do, but I knew that me being there wasn't helping. So when he told me to leave until you were better, I did."

It was a lot. More than she was probably ready for, but that was her decision to make. I wouldn't make the mistake of assuming for her or holding anything back.

"The election," she said. "If you left then, that was four

years ago. Why? Why did you stay away this long?" I pressed my lips together in a tight smile that pained me.

"Phaon needed assurances. Six months passed. You were better, but he insisted you weren't stable yet, that you needed more time. Then a year passed. I insisted on trying again. That time, Phaon said that you didn't want to see me. I wouldn't settle for that. It became clear that you weren't ready to meet. That you didn't want to mate yet. That you needed more time. I gave it another six months and tried again. He insisted you still weren't ready and he wouldn't give his blessing if I tried to force it. I backed down, but I didn't give up. Next, it became my position that I was no one, and you deserved better—until I became someone. It was one excuse after the other over the years. So many times I thought about crossing the river and just taking you somewhere we could talk, so that I could hear it from your lips and not his, but then I remembered the look on your face when you woke up and I couldn't do that. I couldn't take you from your family. And if you would rather be with them instead of me, then the only thing I could do was find a way to get your father's blessing—even if it was a carrot that he was dangling in front of me. When he came to me with the election deal, I didn't feel like I had another choice. Not a good one. I called him out on the excuses he'd given these last four years and said he needed to meet me halfway. He agreed you would attend as Alexander's second, so that I could get to know you—and then if I won, he would finally give his blessing. I still expected him to find some way to move the yardstick before the trials ended, but if I got to meet you again, talk to you, be near you. . ." I hesitated out of fear of rejection.

"You thought I'd want to bond."

"I hoped," I agreed. "I couldn't understand why you

stayed away as long as you did. Unless it was that you truly weren't ready. I thought by getting to know each other, you might change your mind—I didn't know that you had completely forgotten me; that you had no memory at all."

"He lied. Not that it should come as a shock. I was never going to be Alexander's second. I don't know who he was going to choose, but it wouldn't have been me."

"I suspected as much once we were there at the solstice celebration."

Nikki leaned closer, and her scent invaded my senses in the best way. I wanted to pull her onto my lap and see if she tasted as good as she smelled.

"If it's true, if we partially bonded, how come I don't feel it?" she asked.

I sighed. "I wish I knew. The only thing that I can even guess is that phoenix's are born differently, which seems incredibly convenient for my argument, even to me."

She smiled. It was slight but genuine.

"Do you think if we were to complete it that I would feel it?" she asked.

I wanted to say yes. The small bit of hope in her eyes was fuel and all it needed was for me to strike the match. But I wouldn't lie to her. "I don't know. I don't know if it's that you're a phoenix and you do things differently or if the trauma somehow suppressed it. The brain is a complicated thing, just like magic. The way that they interact doesn't always make sense."

She swallowed and my attention was drawn to her lips. To the slender column of her throat. To her flawless bronze skin.

It very much wasn't the time for my thoughts to be going there after everything I just said, but the longer she

KEL CARPENTER & AURELIA JANE

stood there, the closer she got, the more I inhaled her—the more I couldn't think of anything else.

"I think . . ." she said, her voice dropping to a husky tenor. My chest stalled when she swayed closer. Her voice was an aphrodisiac, and I didn't need one. "I'd like to try."

"Try?" I asked, having a hard time computing the words with her being so close to me.

My cock was painfully hard.

I wanted to pull her on my lap and rip her sweat pants off. I wanted to shove her on top of me and slide into her over and over again. I wanted to feel her warm heat orgasming around me, pulling me into her, fusing us together as one.

"Mating," she rasped. "I want to try mating with you."

Oh fuck.

CHAPTER 24
NIKKI

MY HEARTBEAT POUNDED IN MY EARS. BLOOD RUSHED TO MY head.

I'd made a split-second decision. A leap of faith, if you will.

Some could say it was a little bit crazy.

After all, you can't marry a man you just met.

But the truth of it was that I didn't just meet Niall. I'd met him four years ago. And for four years, he'd been trying to find his way back to me.

He didn't make the deal with my father because he didn't respect me. He'd made the deal with my father because he wasn't given another way to get to know me.

I might have doubted him more, but if there was anything I'd learned in the last week, it was that my father was an abusive liar.

He wasn't just a bad person to everyone else. He was bad to his family. He hit my mom and tried to force me into a marriage for his own gain. He didn't do that out of respect or love.

No, I was just another bargaining chip. A carrot on a stick.

Alexander had always hinted at it; dancing around what he thought of dad because I'd dismissed him the first few times.

"It's not that bad," I'd say.

"He does it because he cares."

But now I saw what Alexander had been trying to warn me about for quite some time.

Our dad was really fucking shitty.

He'd stolen four years from me and Niall. We should have been able to get to know one another. In another life, we would have fallen in love naturally without all the bullshit. My father took that from us. He put us in this terrible situation where I didn't trust my mates or their motives, when no one had been more hurtful than him.

I had a feeling he had something to do with Malachi leaving, and he would take Adrian too, if given the chance.

Well, I was done. I was done letting him take things from me.

The stubble on Niall's cheek lured me in. I ran my lips along his jawline, feeling just the barest of prickles. I might not feel the mate bond, but that didn't mean I wasn't attracted to him.

Hearing him respect me enough to not just give me my truth, but his own as well—to know that he was willing to do anything to have me?

Yeah, it got me a little hot and bothered.

"Nikki, there is no try when it comes to mating," he said in a strangled voice. "If we fuck—"

"I know," I whispered in his ear, and my hands lifted to his chest.

"There's no going back," he said gruffly.

"I *know*," I repeated, trailing my lips along his neck. I liked his taste. I wanted more of it. My teeth nipped him lightly on the neck, testing the waters.

Niall tipped his head back and cursed under his breath.

"Nikki, I want this more than anything but . . ."

His hesitation made me freeze. A sliver of rejection touched me. I tried to block it out as I pulled back, putting some distance between us.

"You want me, or you don't," I said. "If you want me, we do this here and now. Your dragon is struggling and . . ." I looked away letting my voice break off. I'd been about to tell him that I *wanted my mate*. I wanted the man that never chose to walk away and kept trying. The one that saved me from hell. The one that gave me a choice.

I wanted the person that was meant to be mine.

After losing my twin, I was terrified of losing anyone, but instead of letting that fear rule me—I was making the choice to pull them closer—to keep them safe.

To let them keep me safe.

But he wouldn't get that truth. Not unless he wanted to complete the bond.

"I want you," he growled. "It's *not* that."

A shiver ran up my spine as he reached between us and fisted a hand in the front of my T-shirt, tugging me closer. Not for the first time it occurred to me just how small I was next to him. Tiny.

"I told you that I refused to have sex and so they drugged me, to make me do it. Nikki, I haven't had anyone since I left the facility. I couldn't . . . I wasn't going to sleep around on you when you were recovering for all I knew—

and no, I don't expect that you stayed loyal to me. If you didn't remember," he added quickly upon seeing the change in my expression.

I felt guilty even though I had no reason to. He was right. It wasn't as though I knew about him. And for all I knew, Malachi had run off and met some demoness and had a couple of spawn.

"I didn't know there was someone out there waiting for me."

"I know. I don't like it," he continued. "I won't pretend I do. I'm not super keen on sharing after having nothing all of my life. I want to hoard you all to myself, but I know I can't do that. Much as I hate admitting this, you need Adrian and Malachi as much as you need me. While I am struggling right now, I will figure out a way to make this work for you. That's not what's giving me pause, though. Nikki, I haven't fucked anyone outside of when I was forced . . . our first time we'll need to be very careful."

My lips parted. "Oh."

"Oh," he repeated.

"Careful how?"

"I need control." His hand slid along my stomach, fingers curling toward my side. He squeezed me by the hip. With his other hand, he tilted my chin up, using the side of his index finger. Our gazes locked, too close to be anything except intimate. I sank my teeth into my bottom lip to keep from gasping.

"When you say control, do you mean like BDSM?"

"Not exactly, no. But I will be very dominant in the bedroom with you, and I *need* you to trust me to take care of you, because I will. I would never hurt you, Nikki. I also won't be the mate that can have wild, unrestrained sex without boundaries. At least I'm not now, and I likely won't be for a very long time. What happened to me—to us—it affected a lot more than just my pain tolerance. I need you to give me that control—and to do what I tell you, but I want you to do that because you *want* to. Not because I want it."

I nibbled on the inside of my cheek toying with my next question. "If you haven't been with anyone else, how do you know that's what you need or how to do it?" I questioned. "That isn't something you learn overnight."

"I didn't touch anyone," he said. "But I went to clubs, parties, places with Adrian. I still had urges and needs. I just imagined doing the things I saw to *you*. Over time I figured out my likes and dislikes by watching, and I do like to watch. As I learned what appealed to me, I looked for any information I could find on it. There were books in the Brooklyn library, and what I couldn't find, Adrian was able to. I learned quite a bit about how to manage myself, because when I did come to you, I didn't want to be a broken mate. I wanted to be a man that could fulfill all your needs."

Emotion swelled in my throat.

He was so rough and jagged on the outside, like an uncut diamond forged in fire and pressure. Beneath that hard exterior was something soft and so vulnerable.

"I've never been very submissive," I told him. "Or dominant for that matter," I added a second later. "I'm an in-betweenie, I think. I've never been to any clubs or parties like that. Not because I'm not interested, but because I'd be reported. All my hook-ups were secrets and were kept within a closed circle. My guards. Friends my father didn't know about. The occasional one-night stand with another member of—"

His mouth tightened, but he didn't get angry with me.

He didn't change his hold. He didn't hurt me. I couldn't blame him for not being thrilled about the woman he knew to be his, sleeping with someone else.

"So, yeah, I've tried different things," I continued, feeling emboldened by his response. "And I'd be willing to hand the reins over to you, but you'll have to guide me through it."

A glaze fell over his eyes, dark with lust. He wrapped his other hand around my back, placing it over the curve of my ass. With a strong grip, he pulled me so close that my stomach pressed against the hard bulge between his thighs.

"I can do that," he murmured, staring at my lips with nothing short of hunger.

"Good," I replied, swallowing hard. It was kind of an awkward response, but I wasn't sure what to say. Lacking words, I let my body do the talking for me.

I pressed my lips to his. Desire unfurled its claws inside me the second our skin touched. It pushed at my skin, seeking an outlet. I lifted my arms to his neck, pulling him even closer. So close there was no room between us. My fingers slid into the hair just above his neck as he engulfed me in his arms.

Niall swept his tongue across the seam of my lips in silent request. I opened up to him, giving him what he wanted.

He devoured me.

There was no more accurate way to say it. My brain shut off as if my wet panties short circuited it. I leaned into the feeling, the touch, and pushed up to my tiptoes.

Niall dropped the hand holding my ass to the top of my thigh, lifting it and me with no effort. He slid his hand downward, guiding that leg around his waist. I curled the other around him on my own, straddling his lap.

There wasn't enough bar stool underneath him for me to balance on. So I settled for falling . . . directly against his cock.

Then began to writhe.

A growl rumbled out of his chest that made my blood rush faster.

Niall kissed me until we were breathless. When it started to become difficult to breathe, he let go with a sharp nip to my bottom lip. His hands drifted south, cupping my ass. He stood, pulling me tight against him.

"What?" I was startled, not used to being carried. I wasn't sure I liked the feeling. People always thought short women were like lap dogs, but what those assholes failed to see was that because I was short—I wasn't very accustomed to being tall.

It was an uncomfortable sensation. Particularly because I wasn't the one in control of it, he was.

"Bedroom," he murmured. "When I fuck this pussy, *my pussy*, and bury my cock in you, I want to do it in a bed. Not on a kitchen counter."

That was romantic in a way.

I wasn't necessarily opposed to the kitchen counter, though. I may have loved my princess movies, but I also loved a good, dirty fuck.

A real Prince Charming would have bored me to tears.

"Okay," I said, choosing to trust him—even if I did cling to him like an octopus.

Niall smirked, not bothering to look where he was going on the way up the stairs, to his bedroom.

"It'll get easier," he said softly.

"What?"

"Trusting me."

CHAPTER 25
NIKKI

NIALL KICKED THE BEDROOM DOOR SHUT BEHIND HIM. THE ECHO of the wood panel hitting the frame sent a little thrill through me.

My stomach flipped when he set me down on a black suede couch. Not the bed. Goosebumps rose along my arms when he kneeled in front of me, between my spread legs.

"Tell me about your first." His lips grazed my ear, and his breath was hot against my skin.

The commanding tone of his voice got me. I did just say we needed to tell each other the truth, but I didn't mean this. "My first . . ."

Niall brushed the hair off of my face and wrapped a strand around his finger. "The first time you had sex. How you lost your virginity."

"When I said I wanted us to be honest, I didn't mean—"

"I know." He cocked an eyebrow, urging me to speak.

I sighed. "Like most girls it wasn't all that eventful. About a year after Malachi rejected me, I hooked up with one of my father's guards."

"And? Tell me about it. Did he get you off? Was it painful?" he asked me again. "Was it slow and sweet, or—"

"It was sloppy, but he was older. He knew where my clit was and got me off with his fingers first." I sighed again. I didn't know what he was getting at or why he'd want to know this. It's not like me fucking other people wasn't painful for him to hear about, even if we hadn't met yet. "I didn't love it, but I didn't hate it. We fucked a few more times, until he got attached."

"I see."

Did he? Because I didn't. I couldn't figure this out.

"Tell me about the best sex you've had."

Delta came to mind, and I choked up. It's not that I had feelings for him. We were friends, or friendly, and shared a mutual hatred for the syndicates and what they did to New York. I'd stayed with him for longer than anyone else for two reasons: neither of us were invested, but we had *great* sex.

"It was . . . sex."

He smirked. "Yes, that's what I want to know about."

"We were—he was—we fucked hard." My head started to spin. Of all the possible ways this could've gone, I never would've guessed it started like this. "I liked—like to be, uh, handled, um . . ." At the first sign of a smirk on his face, I threw caution to the wind. If he wanted me to say it so badly, I wouldn't try for the most diplomatic route. "I was hurt. Heartbroken. I didn't want to make love. I haven't had sweet sex because I don't *want* to. The best sex I had was with a guy that used me the same way I used him. That's what I like."

"Was that so hard?"

He tugged on my hair a little, eliciting a sharp tickle on my scalp that made me hold my breath for a moment. I moved my hand to Niall's leg, resting my hand on his taut thigh as I tried to steady my breathing. "Yes. No. I thought we'd kind of get straight to it."

"Like one of your fuckboys?" Each word in the question was punctuated with a tug of my hair. Each tug getting harder and harder. Each tug making me wetter.

The bulge in Niall's pants swelled to an impressive size. I didn't understand why it was turning me on so much, but knowing it was doing the same to Niall only spurred me on.

"I told you, Nikki. I like control. You keeping your fuck buddies at a distance was how you controlled the situation. I'm your mate, not a body to help you get off. I want far more than a quick release and distant relationship. I've waited four years. I'll wait more if I have to, but I won't accept half measures."

I blew out a long breath. It was getting increasingly difficult to concentrate on his words when all I wanted was for him to touch me. "I don't know what to say to that."

"Tell me if you still want this. I won't be mad if you've changed your mind . . . but what we're about to do goes a lot deeper than me asking about your previous sex life. If you don't reject me—once we complete the bond—all your previous partners are a thing of the past. This is a warmup, Nikki. I'm yours whether you'll have me or not, but if you're not ready to be mine, then walk away now, before it gets . . . complicated."

"No."

Using both hands, Niall turned to me and fisted my hair in his palms. He tugged hard and I gasped at the pleasure as it mixed with pain.

"You sure?" he asked again.

"Yes." I could hardly get the word out because Niall started moving his hands down my body. He slipped one down the front of my sweats and my legs automatically widened for him. He skimmed my slit with two fingers then slowly pushed them inside. He found me wet and warm and remarkably ready.

"Then leave your shyness and embarrassment outside this door. It has no place here. You're beautiful. You're desired. You're everything to me. Now tell me who this pussy is wet for." He murmured the words into my neck as if they were sweet nothings.

Oh, *wow*.

"You . . ."

He was hovering over me in an instant and then pushed me back against the backrest of the couch. He hooked his arm under my leg and pulled it up, giving him ample room to rub his clothes-covered erection into my greedy cunt.

"Damn straight. Whose pussy is this?" he asked while pressing against me. "Tell me, Nikki. Whose pussy?"

"I . . ."

I couldn't answer. All I could think about was grinding my hips into Niall's to find just a little more pressure. Just a little more friction. He was going to make me come and he hadn't even taken his clothes off yet.

But then he stopped. He moved off of me. Niall buried his hand in my sweats and quickly found my throbbing clit.

"Whose. Pussy?"

"Yours," I mumbled the word, too focused on his fingers lightly stroking me to care about anything else.

"Good girl." He took a finger and pushed it inside me, then slowly pumped it in and out. "This is my tight pussy that's dripping wet. My pussy that's weeping for my cock." As if to punctuate the sentence, he took his thumb and pressed down on my clit. "I'm going to make you come so many times. Do you want that?" Niall worked another finger inside me while keeping a steady rhythm.

"Please."

"Please what?" He picked up the pace, moving from slow and leisurely strokes, to fast and focused.

"Oh god, yes," I moaned, so close to finding my release.

"Answer me, Nikki."

"Oh. My. Gods." I squirmed under him. "Will you please make me come?" I was so close, my pussy rippled and clenched around his fingers.

"Not yet."

He stopped touching me completely and I whimpered at his absence. My breath came out in heavy pants, all my thoughts centered on getting off. I pushed my sweats down to around my feet and reached down to stroke my own clit.

"Why did you do that?"

Niall knocked my hand away, then pinned my wrist to the couch. I struggled against him, desperate for an orgasm, but then Niall palmed my sex.

"If you want this to stop at any time, just tell me. I will never do something you don't want. All you have to do is say stop."

"*Mmhmm*," I moaned. I didn't give a damn what he said as long as he kept touching me.

"Do you understand?"

I gave him a languid nod while I breathed heavily.

I was burning up with desire.

Everything was burning.

"Say, 'yes, Mate.'"

"What?"

He pinched my clit between his fingers, taking away the pleasure and bringing only pain.

I cried out. "Yes, Mate."

"Yes Mate, what?" he asked, going back to gently stroking my clit.

"Yes, Mate. I understand. All I have to do is say stop, but I won't because I want you to fuck me."

"On your knees, then."

I did as he said, more than a little eager for what came next. Niall reached behind my back and tugged my shirt up over my head leaving me completely naked and him fully clothed. He stood up and stepped back, biting a closed fist as he took me in.

"Don't move."

I didn't. The only movement I made came from my hard swallow of anticipation, need, and a hint of excited fear. Niall stripped, revealing his length, rock hard and glistening,.

"Scooch forward, to the edge."

I did as instructed. Niall guided my head until my lips were only an inch away from the thick head of his cock.

"I want your mouth."

I licked my lips making sure they were fully moistened, then took him in as far as I could. God, it felt good to taste him. I sucked long and deep working him in as far as I could, then pulling him out. My head bobbed up and down, sucking and swirling my tongue as I did.

"Fuck, if I don't want to come down your pretty throat and watch you swallow."

He pushed forward, gaining another inch that my mouth didn't have as he hit the back of my throat and kept going. I swallowed him down and Niall groaned, petting my face gently. He liked that a lot.

Too bad I couldn't keep him there longer. I pulled back, taking him out completely. His tip brushed against my lips, painting them with a salty drop of come.

"I didn't say stop, firebird. You can take more than that."

Niall took my head in his hands and shoved his cock into my mouth. He hit the back of my throat again and I had to fight the urge to gag. He kept going, fucking my throat as if it were my cunt, and after just a few seconds, I didn't feel the need to gag. With each thrust, he hit the back of my throat and I moaned. His eyes became feverish. Sweat dotted his brow from how much he was holding back. I wanted him to be as out of control as I felt, but that's not what he wanted or needed, so I sucked his cock until I felt him swell.

"Stop." He pulled out of my mouth. "Turn around. Knees on the edge. Stick your ass out."

I got into position, and he grabbed my arms and pinned them behind my back, Forcing me to lean forward until my face rested against the suede black fabric. I turned my head, resting my cheek against it. Anticipation built within me.

He entered me in one forceful thrust, and I screamed out in both pleasure and pain. "Yes, good," I groaned out as he moved slowly, entering me fully and then pulling out. He got into a slow rhythm while I moaned wildly. He crossed my wrists over one another and held them in one hand, while he reached around me with the other and found my clit.

"I want to claim you, firebird," he breathed roughly.

"Do it," I said in a strangled voice.

He flicked over my clit with his finger while he drove himself in and out of me at a mercilessly fast pace. His chest touched my naked back as he curved over me. A faint point grazed over the juncture between my neck and shoulder. Before I could tense for the expectation of a sting, fangs punctured my skin. I threw my head back as two worlds collided. Blood and pain. Sensation and pleasure. His thick cock pumped into me while half the bond snapped into place. It was more than I could take. I came hard, spasming around him.

I blacked out. My release was so intense that I'm pretty sure I died again and came back too soon. Niall was moving me. Repositioning me over his lap. He pulled one leg over him, maneuvering my body to straddle him.

I used my core muscles to pull my face off his shoulder. His erection jutted out, the tip bumping my entrance. A moan escaped me as I glided onto him again, letting him fill me up.

"That's right, firebird. Work my cock. Squeeze me."

His hands clasped my hips, helping me as I slowly slid myself up and down his length. Niall groaned, leaning into the shoulder he bit. He licked the already healing wound, sending another pulse of heat through me.

"I need . . ." I grasped his shoulders with both hands, steadying myself. His neck appealed to me, but I didn't have fangs. Biting, while fun, didn't feel like the claiming I needed right now.

My phoenix urged me to follow my instincts.

I let my left-hand snake down his chest, stopping over the center.

There.

That's where—

Fire kindled beneath my palm. Niall's nails turned sharp, biting into my hips. Another orgasm hit me out of nowhere. Niall moaned, thrusting upwards while dragging me down. Our bodies came together. The hard smacks of flesh meeting and stinging skin only pulling us both higher.

Niall erupted inside me. His cock twitching madly as he filled me.

The bond snapped fully into place.

Our emotions merged. Our souls met.

The sheer intensity of it brought tears to my eyes.

Niall leaned forward, still throbbing inside me, and tugged on my hair to lift my head and roughly whisper in my ear. "You're mine, Nikki. Your secrets, your orgasms, your pussy. They all belong to me. There's no going back. Do you understand?"

I was riding a wave of ecstasy, and I wasn't sure if I was still coming, or starting to come again. "Yes, Mate." My hand dropped from his chest to reveal a burned handprint. It left me with a supreme sort of satisfaction to see my mark on him. To know that he wore it proudly. I could tell he felt the same about his bite on my neck.

Higher than any vitabrew could get me, pure ecstasy fueled my body as the urge to come on him, around him, with him, coursed through my veins.

I needed him more than I needed air. Every part of him.

Niall groaned. "Good girl. Now get your sexy ass on that bed and spread your legs. We're just getting started."

CHAPTER 26
MALACHI

THE SOUND OF A HEADBOARD HITTING THE WALL IN A RHYTHMIC motion echoed in the house, keeping time with the frustration that pulsed within me.

The four of us had left Niall and Nikki to talk about their issues. After Tylea and Sam had come in to drop the "you have three mates" bomb, the tension was thick.

That wasn't how we'd planned on telling her. I still had to fully explain why I'd left. I needed her to understand I'd been forced to leave. It was never about not loving her or wanting her. Gods, more than anything I wanted to be with her—which made it all the more vexing to be listening to some other guy fuck her endlessly.

It had been going on for hours, and it felt like it would last forever.

"Seems like they solved whatever issues they had quickly enough," I muttered, gritting my teeth when I heard another loud moan.

"It would appear so." Adrian cracked his neck and exhaled, standing up from the couch where he'd been sitting. He walked around the room, stretching his legs.

Sam had fallen asleep with her arms crossed, leaning against some cushions. Tylea was quietly reading a book about tattoo styles, seemingly ignoring the sounds of Nikki's screaming.

Not long after Niall and Nikki had disappeared, Courtney had arrived with notification of our next trial. There were no notes yet as to what that next assignment would entail, but seeing that we were politely given a heads up to be rested and ready to report to the council, it was safe to say we weren't going to be ripped out of our beds in the middle of the night.

"How much longer is this going to go on?" I glanced at the clock on the wall. "We have to prepare for the trial tomorrow."

"Yes," Tylea said quietly, not looking up from the page she was reading. "I mentioned that already. Twice. You have pointedly ignored me."

She set her book down, giving me an exasperated sigh.

Glancing at Adrian, he nodded slightly in confirmation. Shit. I hadn't been paying attention to her at all.

"Sorry," I said, scrubbing my hands over my face with more force than I meant to.

"The mating frenzy will probably last twenty-four hours," Sam mumbled, cracking an eye open to look at the time. "We're only ten hours in. Gonna be a bit."

"How do you know?"

"I'm meant to protect her. I know everything about her and her animal." Sam said. "But you're right. Someone needs to tell them we got notification of the next trial."

"Not it," Tylea said quickly, shaking her head.

"Not it?" I asked.

"That's right. I don't know them, so I'm not volunteering to go into a mating den and risk getting shredded by whatever types of shifters they are." She picked up her book again and opened it back up. "No, thank you. Keeping myself right here."

I looked at Sam, and with her eyes still closed, it was like she knew. She shook her head. "I'm not going either. She's your mate. You do it."

"She barely recognizes me as her mate."

"That may be the case, but it's only because she's hurt. I always rooted for you to come back and prove to her that you were better than how you acted."

"You rooted for me?" Every encounter I'd had with Sam since returning suggested she'd prefer I took a long walk off a short cliff.

"I have a really good shitbag radar and you never set it off. That tells me your reason for going wasn't within your control. So yeah. I know how much she still loves you. Even if she's still a mad at you."

That explained some of the hot and cold that I'd been getting from Nikki. She hadn't given me the opportunity to sit down and explain what happened, but Sam's words gave me a glimmer of hope.

"Glad to know I didn't set off your shitbag radar."

"If you had, I would have killed you and made it look like an accident."

Tylea snorted, covering her mouth to block her smile.

Adrian walked over and placed his hand on my shoulder. "Come on suitor number one—"

"I thought you were suitor number one?"

"Who knows? Maybe I am. We'll go up there together."

I tried to make eye contact with Tylea, but she didn't look up from the book she wasn't actually reading anymore. You could tell because she stared at one spot.

Traitor.

Not taking her eyes off the page, she gave a thumbs up. Sam didn't bother to open her eyes again.

Adrian clapped me on the back, and I stood up. Walking down the hallway, the sounds of pounding and Nikki's screams got louder. The closer we got, the more I could hear Niall grunting.

Rage pressed against my skin as my baser instincts screamed that another man was fucking my mate. Those same instincts demanded I kill him and take her as mine.

She was mine.

She always had been.

And now she was in a room with someone else as he made her come over and over again.

I clenched my hands into fists, digging the shortened nails into my palm. My claws elongated, and the scent of blood reached my nostrils.

"You okay there?" Adrian asked, glancing down at my hands.

"No, you made us leave the kitchen. So not only do I not know what was said between them, I'm now having to listen to Niall fuck my mate."

"She's his mate too. And mine," he said softly.

Adrian knocked on the door and no one answered. The sound of skin slapping and heavy breathing didn't slow.

Adrian knocked loudly and still nothing.

He sighed. "I'm coming in," he called, then turned to me and added, "I'm pretty sure they still can't hear a word I'm saying."

I held my breath as Adrian turned the knob and entered the room. I had every plan on going in with him, but as the door swung open and I saw Nikki's ass in the air with Niall pounding into her from behind, the only thing I could do was freeze.

Adrian faked a cough and then cleared his throat loudly.

"Get the fuck out," Niall roared, leathery wings sprouting from his back. His back glittered with scales, and that answered a few questions I'd had earlier.

The rumors that dragons still existed were true. It was something I was keen to explore, but I could hardly focus on it.

I clenched my jaw tightly; the monster inside me ignoring the danger of his shifter and instead insisting I rip his heart out.

"Bad timing. We won't stay long. We've been notified of the next trial. It's tomorrow." Adrian looked at a watch on his wrist. "You've got about fifteen hours before we're expected in front of the council."

Niall grunted in response and his fingertips pressed into Nikki's hips as he slammed into her harder.

If she understood what we had just told her, she didn't say. Her hazy lust-filled eyes met mine, and she bit her bottom lip as she moaned deeply.

Her sexy whimper sent desire straight to my cock and I took a step forward.

Adrian's hand pressed into my chest and his eyes met mine, shaking his head tightly. "Not now, man. Now is not our time."

Fighting my instincts, I chose to listen to him, and I couldn't understand why.

When he closed the door behind us, we walked down the hallway to the other side of the house. We needed to get as far away from the sound as possible.

In the library, he walked over to a decanter and poured whatever was in it into a glass, taking the whole thing in one gulp. He held the decanter up to me in question, and I nodded. Pouring two glasses, he then came over and sat it down on a table between two reading chairs.

He fell back into one chair, pressing the heel of his hand into his thighs, grinding from the top of his leg all the way to his knee, repeating the motion like he was massaging his quads. I realized he was taking steady breaths.

He was calming himself down.

"How did you do it?" I asked.

"Do what?"

"How did you stay so chill when we were in there? How did you keep it in check?"

"How did you?" he countered.

"I'm not entirely sure that I did," I admitted, staring at the healing puncture wounds on my palms.

"Well, you didn't try to rip Niall apart. You survived it the same way I did."

"I'm not sure I understand."

"It's just something I had to do. I didn't like it, and I wanted to be with her, but it wasn't the place and time."

"But you didn't look like you were struggling." He glanced at my hands, seeing the dried, crusted blood.

"I was struggling. But I also have to think about what is best for her. She's my mate, and every cell in my body knows that. Her scent is the purest form of nature that I've ever experienced. As an earth fae, I had no idea it would be that incredibly calming to be in my mates presence. I've never had a mate, so I didn't know what to expect. Every minute that I'm away from her, it hurts. Every minute that I'm not touching her, my body screams for that connection again. Knowing that every sound she's making right now is being caused by my best friend and not me is torture."

"I understand that more than you realize. You feel the same mate desire I do, but I don't know how you handle it."

"If the fates chose for her to have three mates, then who am I to argue that? I want her. I want to spend eternity with her. If that includes two extras in her bed, then so be it."

"I hadn't thought about it that way."

He shrugged. "You're still young. I've been around a lot longer than you, but I've still never had a mate before, so at least we're new at this together."

"I shouldn't be so new at this. She's been my mate since I was eighteen."

"The difference is you walked away from it for a while. You threw that rejection out into the world, and your attachment began to fray."

"I didn't mean it when I rejected her. I was trying to save her."

"I'm not saying you don't love her. I know you do. Whatever your reason for leaving, your love is what brought you back to her. Once you were with her again and you acknowledged her as your mate, the bond started to knit itself back together. That's why it feels new. Probably like when you first figured out she was your mate, right?"

I huffed a laugh. "Right."

"There you go."

"I never expected to have to share her," I admitted. "Honestly, and stupidly, I thought I would come back and claim her as my mate and she would accept me."

"And you'd live happily ever after?" Adrian added, a smile curling up one side.

"Yeah," I chuckled. "Something like that."

"I never imagined I'd have to share my mate, either, but I'm okay with the arrangement. If you think about it, it could be a lot worse."

I scoffed, still hearing Nikki's screams in the background. The image of her being fucked from behind was seared into my memory. "Yeah? How?"

"When you're mated, you're family forever right? This isn't too bad of a set up. She's mated to my best friend, and you seem like an all-right guy. Still on the fence with that, but you're growing on me."

I barked a laugh. "I see your point."

He wasn't wrong. I liked Adrian. Not being able to read Niall made it difficult for me to judge his character, but Adrian trusted him. Who you kept at your side said a lot about you as a person, and I knew that well. If Adrian said he was worthy, I actually believed him.

"We have it pretty good if it's the three of us. She could be mated to Ty. That happens sometimes; the fates mating siblings—which sounds awful in general." He shuddered. "Can you imagine being stuck sharing your mate with someone like Ty?" He made a face showing his complete disgust. "There isn't a redeeming bone in his body, and I'd love nothing more than to watch him burn."

He had no idea how much I agreed. The problem was I didn't know if Nikki would ever see it.

"To our new blended family?" I said, holding up the last of my drink in a cheers. He clinked his glass against mine.

"To a family of fae, demon, and shifters." He tossed his drink back and I did the same, swallowing the burn. "And whatever hybrid rugrats the fates have decided for us."

"What?" I coughed, and he laughed, knocking me on the back as whiskey tingled near my windpipe. I hadn't even considered kids . . .

"Relax, Romeo. Grovel and forgiveness first, then fucking."

CHAPTER 27
NIKKI

EVERYTHING HURT.

Was it possible you could die from sex?

I felt like you could.

Tucked into the crook of Niall's arm, I snuggled against his body. His scent was soothing, and his steady breathing lulled me to the edge of sleep. While my entire being now acknowledged that we were mates and the pull to be near him was strong, the feral desire for a marathon fuckfest had finally waned.

Mating frenzies were weird.

My head pulsed painfully to the beat of my heart, trying to recover from twenty-four hours of non-stop sex. I'm sure dehydration played a part as well. Everything between my legs throbbed from overstimulation and being pounded relentlessly. My nipples were sore and sensitive. Even my hair felt bruised.

And it was all amazing.

I didn't have a single regret.

But I could not for one second even begin to imagine what it was like being in heat. I was eternally grateful that

that had never happened, especially considering I'd found Malachi as my mate so young. I think the heat would have killed me.

I couldn't help but think about what an unusual situation I'd found myself in.

Malachi returning wasn't something I'd ever expected. Hoped, yes. Believed? No.

Running into Adrian and discovering that I had a second mate had definitely thrown a curveball. Learning that Niall had actually been my second mate and had been torn away from me was beyond unexpected.

Oftentimes I'd felt like a piece of me was missing, and I'd always attributed that to losing my twin sister and having Malachi reject me.

It was like my life was a book, but having a chapter ripped out so my story never made sense.

Finding Niall was finding those missing pages. Gaps were filled and I had a better understanding of my past—a truer version of it.

It wasn't easy to believe a complete stranger—or at least someone who felt like a stranger—when they tell you that they know you, and that you know them. Insisting that you've had experiences together and that you were meant to be.

I was always a bit impulsive and spontaneous. It worked for me. Marissa was so thoughtful and careful and was good at planning. I didn't want to take the risk of being so methodical. The fractured and grieving part of me wondered if maybe because she was so careful, we'd missed the opportunity to escape safely.

It's hard for someone to intercept your plans when you really don't have plans yourself.

That was my logic. When Niall claimed to be my mate, I

didn't feel it, but he knew parts of my story that no one else did. So if he was my mate, well, there was one way to find out.

And find out we did.

It all came rushing back to me. As scary and traumatizing as it sounded, there was still a level of comfort in having him present in what I'd thought were simply nightmares based on experience. Turns out they were flashbacks. It was all real.

He had been with me. As I was held captive, so was he. It was no longer choppy and distorted images. It wasn't simply my recollection of the entire event being unlocked, but also my memories of *him* that had returned. While devastating in some ways, a part of me was relieved. He had been by my side comforting me and my sister.

He heard my cries in anguish at her loss.

He watched me lose my other half.

He watched me damn near destroy myself and everyone else for it.

He didn't leave me even as the world burned and crashed around us.

No matter what I'd thought all these years—no matter how I'd felt every day since—I wasn't alone.

I never had been, and looking forward, I never would be.

I had three mates, and I'd only bonded with one, but it was the beginning of something new. Something completely different from what I'd been told to expect from life.

Having done it once, I now knew that I needed twenty-four hours to spare when I completed the bond with Malachi and Adrian, so you know, pencil that on the calendar between completing trials for Earth and Emerald,

273

trying to stay away from my overbearing brother, dodging any messages from my father, and then running for chancellor of this House.

"We have an hour before we have to appear in front of the council," Niall said, curling his arm around me tighter and pulling me against his body.

His chest rumbled against my cheek as he spoke. Visions of waking up in a similar position with Adrian only days before flashed in my mind.

Niall growled softly. "I can smell you."

"You can smell what exactly?"

"I can smell your desire," he said, his voice deepening.

"Oh . . . *that* . . ." I said, somewhat surprised. My cheeks warmed.

"Something tells me it's not for me."

Well, this was awkward.

Yeah, we were mates, but I didn't know how to have a conversation that said, *Yes, I just got done fucking you, and now I'm thinking about fucking your best friend. My mate. It's not weird. Don't be jealous.*

I opened my mouth to respond, but nothing came out. Just as I tried to say something to make the silence less awkward, the door burst open, and Sam came in.

"Sorry, Nikki, but I had to—"

"Get the fuck out," Niall said, his muscles tightening.

"No really, it's fine," I said quickly, sitting up in bed and covering my chest with a thin sheet. "What's up?"

Sam opened a drawer and grabbed a T-shirt, then threw it at me. I let go of the sheet to catch it, and the fabric as it pooled around my waist, exposing my breasts.

"Get dressed," Sam said, the tone in her voice indicating she was worried about something. She continued to dig into another drawer for what looked like underwear and pants.

Adrian came in right behind her, with Malachi and Tylea just behind him.

"What the hell?" Niall growled.

"Put it in check," Adrian said, leveling Niall with a stare as though they were speaking to each other telepathically. I was pretty sure neither of them had that power, but when I really thought about it, I didn't know them well enough to actually know the extent of their magic. "We have a situation."

"What do you mean?" I interjected.

"I . . ." Malachi was staring at my chest, having trouble answering.

"Really, Malachi?" I muttered.

Tylea elbowed him. "Smooth, Romeo."

He shook his head and averted his eyes. "Shit. Sorry."

"Is someone going to answer her? What kind of situation?" Niall said getting more irritated with each passing second.

After I pulled the shirt on, I placed a hand on his thigh, trying to send comfort and calmness through our bond.

The muscle beneath my hand loosened and that made me smile. Who knew I would have that kind of an effect on anyone? Usually, my antics were the cause of someone being tense.

"Hey lovebirds," Sam said, breaking me from my trance. As I turned my head, I was hit in the face with my own pants.

"The fuck, Sam?" I chided, feeling annoyed.

"I'm serious, Nikki."

In the same way that Adrian had given Niall a particular look, Sam glared at me her eyes tense, and her jaw set. We'd been on so many missions before that I knew she was serious, but I'd still been coming out of my lust cloud so I hadn't been paying full attention.

As I came to that understanding, Adrian had grabbed clothes for Niall and tossed it his way.

"You both need to come see this," he said.

Niall and I exchanged glances, quickly understanding that the vibe in the room wasn't about jealous mates. This wasn't about us, and judging by everyone's demeanor, it had nothing to do with the council meeting in less than an hour.

After we finished getting dressed, we followed everyone down the hall. Sam looped her arm through mine.

Something was very wrong.

"What's happening?" I whispered.

She shook her head, not meeting my eyes, but her arm around me tightened.

Coming out the front door, I saw exactly what the problem was, and I came to an abrupt halt. We all did.

At the base of the porch stairs, someone had left us a message.

Someone had left *me* a message.

A pungent odor filled the air. It smelled like death.

A body had been torn to shreds. Mutilated. Ripped apart.

Limbs and scraps of flesh spelled out two words: *go home.*

"Whose bod . . . who was that?" I asked, my voice barely above a whisper.

"We don't know," Tylea said. "I called to check in with Jackie since she was left in our cabin alone, but she's fine."

I scrunched my nose, not realizing that Tylea was friendly with Jackie.

"Not the time," Sam muttered.

Tylea caught on. "She's not as bad as you think she is. I have a sense about people. Trust me."

It was hard to talk about trust while I was standing in front of a bloody pile of bones.

"I can only assume this message is for me," I said, swallowing a thick lump in my throat. "I'm the only one who wasn't supposed to be here."

When no one spoke, it was clear that everybody else had come to the same conclusion. Not going to lie; a part of me wished somebody would argue with me and tell me I was wrong.

I liked being right. Who didn't? But I would have been okay being wrong about this one.

The body appeared to be feminine, though there was no head to identify who it could have been. A thought occurred to me, and it made me freeze. If the message was for me, was this the body of someone I knew? My thoughts instantly went to Lindsey, and I inhaled a sharp gasp and began to move toward the limbs.

"It's not her," Sam said. "There's no tattoo. I already checked."

I breathed a sigh of relief, and Sam pressed her lips together in a firm and forced smile. She had panicked the same way, but for her, it would have been worse. Lindsey was her mate. The loss would have been devastating.

"She was someone, though. . ." I sighed. "Someone's loved one. A sister or a wife or a mate. Maybe all of those. I doubt she deserved this."

"Tylea and I will go get something to cover this up," Malachi said before resting his hand on my shoulder gently. "Give her some decency in death."

"Thank you, Mal," I said, nodding absent-mindedly.

When I looked at him, he paused, his lips parted. I realized I'd called him by his childhood nickname. The one I'd given him. Shaking himself out of surprise, he respectfully dipped his chin before heading into the house with his second.

Malachi knew me well enough to know how I felt about death and what I would want for this poor soul. Death was a part of life, and even more so in the world of the supernatural syndicates.

Growing up that way made me more empathetic to saving whatever I could. A baby bird here. A rat kit. A starving kitten.

I'd always nursed them back to health, but if they were too sick, I made sure they died peacefully. It was a kindness we didn't often give to people. Then I would bury them, returning them to the earth so nature could run its course.

It wasn't death that had me feeling depleted now. Part of it was the threat, sure. The other part was that this person suffered. Whoever mutilated a woman to use her body parts to spell out this message didn't value life. They were cruel. They didn't care, which means they didn't give her a quick death.

She'd spent her last minutes in this life in excruciating pain. And to what purpose?

"We need to let Earth and Emerald know so they can contact her family . . . and do whatever else they need to do. Does anybody have a way to contact Courtney?"

"I do."

I closed my eyes exhaling harshly through my nose. It was not the voice of my mates, and our last exchange had left me on edge. Of all the times . . .

"What do you want, Ty?"

CHAPTER 28

ADRIAN

THE DEAD BODY DIDN'T BOTHER ME, NOR THE FACT THAT IT WAS mutilated.

I was syndicate. We all were.

We'd seen bodies like this and worse.

What did bother me was this appeared to be meant for Nikki. Someone was out to scare my mate. To threaten her.

That was a mistake.

She may not have bonded with me or with Malachi, but that didn't stop the intensity in which we felt a connection with her.

We would do anything for our mate. I didn't know Malachi well, but I didn't need to. If he felt a modicum of what I did, then we'd burn the world if she'd asked.

And I wanted to start with her fuckwit brother, if only she'd give me permission.

Nikki's body tensed upon hearing Ty speak.

"What do you want, Ty?"

"Well, I came here to talk to you. I was hoping we could have a more civilized conversation compared to last time."

"We don't have anything to talk about," she said through clenched teeth.

Ty scanned the bloody chunks of remains littered on the ground. "Really? You wouldn't consider this a topic of conversation?"

"You came here to talk about a dead body we just discovered?" she asked, tilting her head.

"Of course not. I came here to talk to you about coming to stay with me. I'm impressed that you remained safe, and that you aren't the body lying on the forest floor—thank the gods. Your housemates weren't able to protect you for the first trial, so I'm eternally grateful you weren't taken and ripped apart to leave some sort of message," he said, loosely waving his hand at the limbs without care.

"Well it looks like a message meant *for* me, so I guess that would be a hard point to make if they'd used me instead."

He turned his body slightly and angled his head as he read it. "So it is. Would you look at that?"

"So is that what you came to talk about? You want me to go home? Are *you* trying to send me a message?"

He tutted. "Nikki, you know I'm a bit more direct when I intend for someone to learn a hard lesson."

I heard her breath stutter, and it sent rage through my veins. He was very careful with choosing his words, but they were a threat, and she knew it.

Niall stepped forward, wrapping his arm around her waist protectively and pulling her to him.

Now that she had completed the bond with him, I had hopes that her animal would help ground his dragon and the fire he had inside. The other part of me worried it could have the opposite reaction, and he could be more explosive in an effort to protect her.

Guess we were about to find out.

"What's this?" he asked, narrowing his eyes

Rather than force Nikki to have any further interaction with Ty, I casually stepped forward. "Lovely morning, isn't it?" I said lightly. "Minus the dead body."

"The last time I was here, you made it clear that she was your mate. Now you're sharing my sister with a hybrid?"

Nikki and Niall growled, but I held my hand up to stop them from moving forward.

"I thought the last time you were here, I told you to get the fuck off our porch, yet here you are. Unwanted. Uninvited. Just overall unwelcomed."

Ty's jaw set, and he looked me up and down.

"I'd back off, Rose. Whatever little faery powers you think you have don't hold a candle to mine."

"It's only weak ass supernaturals that go around boasting about how strong they are. Sure, if you want to put on a display for us, go ahead. I don't mind." I crossed my arm, then shifted my weight while I looked at him expectantly.

Most of the time what I'd said was true. In this case, Ty was immensely powerful. There was nothing weak about him. He just had no idea what I was capable of, so he thought he had the upper hand.

Jackie came out of the woods using her elemental magic to control the air. Wind blasted us on one side; not to knock us over, but it was her way of getting our attention.

"That wasn't very nice, Ty. You underestimate the fae."

I smirked, never taking my eyes off of him. I wasn't going to back down, and neither was he.

"Stop it. Both of you," Nikki interjected. She stepped out of Niall's embrace and lifted her chin in defiance. "Ty, I'm not going home."

" I wasn't asking you to, Nikki—

"And I'm not going back to your cabin. I'm staying here. With my *mates*." She emphasized the plural and there was no mistaking when he caught it.

"Mates?" he repeated. "Isn't that an interesting development?"

"There are a lot of interesting developments as of late," Niall said.

"What's that supposed to mean?"

I pointed to the body parts that were strewn across the ground. "I guess we could start there. That's an interesting development. Kind of like a butcher's work, don't you think?"

Before Ty could respond to my underhanded accusation, Nikki kept going.

"It's *interesting* that you don't want me here, but you also don't want me to go home. I can't figure you out."

She wasn't the only one. It would have been more obvious that Ty was the artist here, *if* he'd come here and been insistent that she left for her own safety. But that wasn't what was happening. It sure looked like his handiwork, but he wasn't encouraging her to *go home*, as the message suggested. Just come with him.

"It's not safe for you here," he said.

"It's not safe for me anywhere."

"Your family has always been able to protect you."

She barked a humorless laugh before glaring daggers at him. "I was with my family when Marissa and I were taken," she said, shaking. "Where was my protective family then?"

The bond inside me pulled hard, and I had to suppress the urge to comfort her. I had to suppress the urge to kill Ty in her defense.

"And I don't want that to happen again!" he shot back.

"No." The single word was firm, and she stood her ground

"That looks like your cue to leave, champ," I said, seeing several council members approaching through the trees.

Ty stepped forward, and I held a hand out, just waiting to touch his chest.

"*Do it*," I whispered menacingly. "Please. See what happens. Come after her and let me show you what a fae is capable of."

Ty considered me, then began to laugh. He looked at Nikki. "This is what you want?" he asked, gesturing to me, then to Niall. "That shit orphan, this useless hybrid nobody, and a fucking fae? You want to stay here and be their whore?"

Nikki shot forward and I caught her with my arm before she attacked her brother in the presence of the approaching council, but I'd misjudged her. She was seething, but she lowered her voice and never raised her hands to him.

"Why is it that fragile male egos think the worst thing a woman can be called is a whore? Hmm? What does it matter to men who I choose to let into my bed? If my choices are between living with a group of guys or going with you, I guess you can just fuck off and call me Snow White."

I snorted. She did like her movies. I was glad I had a younger sister who'd schooled me in the ways of animated films. It helped me know most of Nikki's references and quotes. Niall would have some catching up to do.

"I suggest you rethink this."

She waited a moment, then said, "I've taken your suggestion into consideration." And then she flipped him off.

"You're going to regret this, dear sister," he sneered. His ire wasn't aimed at me or Niall. Just her.

"Shove it up your ass," Nikki said, taking Niall's hand and holding it. They *were* grounding each other.

Thank fuck.

Jackie stepped closer to Ty. She watched my hands carefully, making no moves of aggression.

A group of council representatives arrived, led by Courtney.

"Jackie, we received your mess—" She placed her hand over her mouth in shock. "What happened here?"

"Exactly what it looks like," Niall said. "Someone was torn to pieces and left as a message."

"Why? To what purpose?" she said through her gasp.

"We don't know," Nikki said softly.

"We will need to investigate. This has never happened in all the years Earth and Emerald has held pre-election trials," she said, scanning the scene before her.

"Syndicate." One member scoffed.

Courtney turned to him. "That is uncalled for!"

"He's not wrong," I said, interrupting her.

She snapped her attention to me. "Do you know something about this?"

"No, I don't, but I don't find it surprising." I looked at Ty. "Were Ayla and the vampire still present at your cabin before you graced us with your presence?"

His attitude had shifted in front of the council, but his anger still radiated, and the Earth and Emerald reps could feel it. "They were."

"So I guess we're down to five candidates from your House and seven syndicate. Convenient." Crossing my arms, I returned my attention to Courtney. "You have The Roses' full cooperation during your investigation."

284

She looked surprised. "Do you have that authority?" I nodded. "Why offer this?"

"So you know we were not involved." I glanced at Ty, cocking an eyebrow. "What about you, *Ward*? Do you need to check with daddy first, or do you hold any authority in your family?"

Jackie placed a hand on Ty when his whole body tensed.

"Gentlemen, this is not the time," a member said. "The trials and the competition will continue. Hold that fighting spirit until later."

"My apologies, counselor. I just assumed Ty would offer the same on behalf of the Wards." I looked him dead in the eyes. "You know, to prove he—*they*—have nothing to hide."

I swear, his eyeballs started shaking with pure hatred. "Of course," he said through a clenched jaw.

He was barely containing himself, and knowing what a painful struggle it was for him brought me immense joy.

Courtney forced a small smile. "Hekate thanks you." She looked around at the remains. "In the meantime, we ask that you stay in your cabins until further notice. We will have witches here shortly for strengthening the boundaries, and a team will need to sweep the grounds and collect evidence."

She began to instruct her team on what to do. Her voice and their movement became background noise.

Nikki, without another word, turned on her heel and walked away from her brother, and Niall followed in right behind her.

"You heard the chancellor's assistant," I said to Ty with a wry smirk, then mouthed, "now, I tell you again, get the fuck off our porch."

CHAPTER 29
NIKKI

F*IRE RAGED AROUND ME, STEALING THE OXYGEN TO FEED ITS* hunger. *I began to suffocate, feeling my chest constrict as I struggled to breathe.*

Pain like I'd never known tore at my heart. A piece of me had been ripped from this world, never to return.

They took her.

Now it was my turn to die too.

The heat of the inferno amplified, growing in size and power as my grief spread.

I waited for it to consume me. To burn my flesh and destroy me.

But that would never happen.

Hues of orange and yellow and red swirled beneath my skin.

The flames were within.

I was the fire.

With a startled gasp, my eyes shot open, jolting me back to reality. I wasn't in that place anymore. This was real. The dark room. The crisp temperature. The soft sheets. My mate sleeping next to me.

Still, my nerves were shot. My skin felt like it was burning. Itching.

Like I was still caged.

Niall's steady breathing and soft snores indicated that he was sound asleep. I grabbed a pillow from behind me and tucked it where I had been. Slipping from beneath the covers and off the side of the bed, I searched for a T-shirt and boy shorts I knew to be tossed on the floor and put them on. Then I tiptoed to the door and looked over my shoulder to check that he hadn't moved as I left the room.

The house was silent.

I considered going to the library and sitting for a while, but what I really needed was fresh air. I didn't want to be cooped up any longer.

I cracked open a window, wincing when it made a slight creaking sound then stepped onto the awning beneath it. I sat quietly, feeling the shingles press into my exposed skin. These boy shorts were *short.* Closing my eyes and tilting my head back, I took a deep breath.

"Rapunzel, Rapunzel, let down your hair."

Malachi's voice startled me, and I peered over the edge of the roof.

He stood on the ground below, looking up.

"What are you doing out here?" I asked.

"I could ask you the same question."

"You could, but I asked you first," I said, cocking an eyebrow.

"I couldn't sleep. Needed some fresh air. You?"

I sighed. "Same."

"Would you like some company?"

I twisted my lips into a reluctant smile, then nodded.

Malachi jumped, grabbing on to the edge of the roof , then swung his leg up and landed next to me.

"Impressive. Both agile and graceful."

"Well, you weren't willing to let your hair down, so I had to come up here somehow," he said, settling himself into a seated position by my side. "Do you remember when we were kids, and we'd sit on rooftops after sneaking out?"

"Of course," I said, grinning. "I actually think about those nights all the time."

"Me too." He gave me a tight-lipped smile. "Why couldn't you sleep?"

"Bad dreams."

"Nightmares?" He gave me a knowing look.

"Not really? Just flashbacks of my past. Being taken." I swallowed thickly. "The crushing weight of grief . . ."

"That kind of sounds like nightmares," he said, wincing.

"Yeah," I laughed softly, "I guess it kind of is. There's just still so much I don't understand."

"I heard." I looked at him puzzled. "You knew about this too?" I said accusingly.

"No," he answered quickly. "I didn't know. Adrian filled me in when you and Niall were . . . talking."

I grimaced. I knew what he meant, and I also felt bad for immediately getting defensive with him.

"Sorry," I mumbled, then cleared my throat. "Why did he tell you?"

"He was helping me understand how to be a better mate," he said after a suspended moment. "If you accept me, I mean." He pinched the bridge of his nose.

"Adrian was helping you learn how to be a better mate?"

"Essentially, yes."

"I don't understand how telling you helps that."

"I was your mate Nikki, the first. I was there before the

others came along. I thought it would be me making all your dreams come true. You and me. Together forever."

I smacked his arm. "Okay, now you're just quoting *The Little Mermaid*."

He grinned. "Maybe I am." Then his face fell. "Still, the sentiment is the same. I thought I would be your only mate. So coming back and finding out that you had not just two mates, but three? It was a lot harder to handle than I thought it would be. Logically I knew we needed to do it for you, and I came to the guys stating as such when I confronted them originally and told them I was your mate as well. But when it came down to it, my heart was . . . I was confused and it was just hard to follow through with the strength of my convictions. When you were in there with Niall, and I could hear you, it hurt on a level so deep I can't possibly explain it. I wanted to break down the door and take you myself. But I would never do that. I would never force you into anything and I would never force you to accept me as your mate."

I sat silently letting him finish. I wasn't sure what to say anyway.

"Adrian helped me understand how he controls his desire to be with you, and how he's willing to share you. I want to be that mate for you. If that's what's best, and if that's what makes you happy and complete, then that's all I care about."

I loved hearing those words from his mouth. It filled a part of me with warmth and happiness to think of them working together to be with me. But one thing tainted the possibility of a future, and I couldn't hold back.

"Then why did you leave? Why did you reject me?"

Malachi jerked at the sudden forcefulness of my question. "I don't know if this is the time, Nikki. I've wanted my chance to tell you my side, but with everything that you just learned with Niall, and Ty showing up to rip you a new one—"

"Don't you dare say it's complicated."

"I wasn't going to. I was just going to say if you wanted more time to deal with it all before I add to it, I understand."

"You owe this to me, Malachi. You broke my heart when you left. If you want me to accept you as my mate, you have to be honest with me. No more lies. No more half-truths."

"That's fair," he said softly, then took a deep breath. "By the time the mate bond clicked, I'd already been in love with you for years. I was eighteen when it snapped into place—and you were sixteen and nothing happened to you yet. You were my best friend, and I didn't want to mar that relationship so that it felt like a betrothal you had no say in, you know? So I waited. I didn't have family—I didn't have anything—but I always had you. You were my family. You were my everything."

His voice started to shake, so I reached over and put my hand on top of his, squeezing it to give him the courage to go on.

"It's hard to describe how you can be in love with your mate before you even find out they're your mate. I'd already felt like you were made for me, and then the fates *agreed*. So I waited until you felt the bond. I wanted you to feel the same thing for me. When I felt it strengthen, I knew it'd shown itself to you too. I went to your father, and he told me if I got near you, he'd kill me. That he wouldn't let "a no one" be with his daughter." He scoffed. "I knew they could make me disappear, and he said he didn't care that it would tear you apart."

Malachi had a hard time looking at me as he spoke. He fidgeted, clearly concerned with how I would react to his confession.

"I argued, Nikki. I did. I pushed back. It was fate! How could he make that decision? I was so naïve, I thought that he would respect it. I thought that he would be happy for you, at least—even if he wasn't happy it was me. Turns out he didn't care for your feelings either."

"That's why you left?"

He nodded.

"But you rejected me."

"I was a kid. I was scared. I wasn't even scared about the threats to kill me so much as I was scared it would happen and you would be forever suffering, tethered to a lost mate. That wouldn't happen if we'd rejected the bond. You'd be free." He craned his neck back, looking at the stars. "And the more I thought about it, I was afraid they were right."

"Right about what?" I asked, not taking my eyes off him.

He returned his gaze to me. "That you would be better off without me. That I wasn't good enough for you anyway."

"How could you even say that?"

"Like I said, I was a kid. Impressionable. And seriously lacking self-confidence."

"You're a dumbass, you know that?"

"I told myself that every day, actually. And every day I prayed to any god or goddess in the realms that could have been listening that you'd never accept my rejection."

"How did you know I didn't?" I asked, raising a brow.

"I would have felt the loss, but I never did." He sighed, swallowing thickly. "I just felt . . . *you*. Every day."

"I felt you every day too." I grabbed his hand and laced my fingers through his. My thumb grazed his skin back and forth in a soothing motion as my eyes got blurry with tears. "But it was so far away, it felt broken, Malachi. *I* felt broken. It felt like the distance had to span the ocean. Realms. It hurt to feel you but not be with you. And then I found out you'd been in Queens the whole time…" My voice cracked, and he squeezed my hand.

"I didn't have anywhere else to go. I'm half demon and half fae. The Roses turned me down when I came to them. The Divine took me in, accepting my demon lineage. It helped that I was fairly powerful—I was just inexperienced. They aren't ones to turn down a weapon. They trained me. Built me up. When I realized I wasn't what your father made me out to be, I thought maybe I could prove myself to him, so I worked up the ranks."

"Is that what you've been doing the whole time?"

He nodded. "When the opportunity came for the election and the deals were being made, I jumped on it. I jumped on the chance to see you again."

"Okay, but you also jumped on the chance to win a *person*."

"Yes I did, and I'm not proud of it, but I'm not going to apologize for it either. I just wanted the chance to see you again. I wanted to prove to you that I was better than what I'd been made out to be. I wanted to tell you the truth. I'd never force you to marry me if I won—alliance or not. But I did think if I won, your father would finally approve of me."

"Did you know he was making the same deal with the Roses too? Or that he had tried to make the deal with the Clan Tepes and the Outcast Coven?"

"No, I learned that after the fact. That was when I realized Phaon was going to stab everybody in the back."

"My family's pretty good at that," I muttered.

"We were all raised around the syndicate if we weren't raised in it. Should have known better," he said, shrugging. "I'm here now. This was my only goal." He raised my hand, pressing his lips onto my skin in a firm kiss while he locked eyes with me.

I hummed. "So what's your game plan now, Prince Charming?"

"Well, I thought groveling was a good start." He chuckled, and so did I.

"You have been doing a good bit of that," I said, bumping my shoulder into his.

"Is it working?"

"Telling the truth helped." I leaned my head onto his shoulder, finding comfort in him the way I used to. Gods, I'd missed this. Talking to him. Touching him. Just being with him.

He kissed the top of my head, breathing in my scent. "It was never about keeping the truth from you, Nikki. I just never wanted to come between you and your family. I thought I was doing the right thing."

"Focus on me from now on, not my family. Okay?" I said, looking up at him. He smiled in response.

"Yes ma'am." I nodded, then tucked my head back where it had been. "What does that mean for us?" he asked, not trying to hide the hesitation in his voice.

"I never stopped loving you, Malachi. Don't get me wrong. I role-played how it would go one day if I saw you and I got to accept your rejection, but deep down, I knew I couldn't speak those words. Even when I was mad at you, I never accepted your rejection because I couldn't convince myself to accept that you weren't my mate. Once my phoenix emerged, the demand to find you was stronger. It was going to drive me insane."

"When did that happen? Your phoenix?"

"When I was taken. Four years ago . . ."

He hummed in understanding. "That explains it."

"Explains what?"

"A little over four years ago, I had this overwhelming invisible pull. It was gut-wrenching. Painful. I needed to come to you. While I'd always felt your presence, I'd never felt such intense distress. So I reached out to Alexander to check on you. That's when I found out that you'd been taken. The strength of the pull never really dissipated once you'd been rescued. I figured it was the trauma of losing your twin. Turns out it was your phoenix calling to me."

"I miss her," I whispered. "Every day."

"I'm sorry I wasn't there for you. I'm sorry I wasn't there for Marissa."

"It's not your fault she's gone."

"I know, but that doesn't mean I don't have regrets."

I shook my head. "Don't do that. Don't spend your life with regrets, Mal. It leaves you stuck in the past, and that's not a place either of us should be," I said, trying to stifle a yawn.

"Hey," he muttered, moving his shoulder lightly so I'd look at him. "You need some rest. It's been a rough day. C'mon. I'll walk you back to Niall's room."

"Can I stay in yours?" I asked as he started to move, and then he froze. Malachi stared at me blankly for a moment trying to process if I was being serious.

"Yeah," he said finally, his voice cracking a bit. "I'd love nothing more."

We went back in the window I'd crawled out of, and

then silently went to his room. I hadn't even noticed earlier that the door was cracked.

When we were tucked away in his room, he gathered a pillow and a throw blanket, but stopped when I asked him what he was doing.

"Did you want me to sleep on the couch?"

"No," I said, glancing at the bed and then back to him. "I'm not ready to complete the mate bond, though."

He shook his head quickly. "I didn't expect that you would."

I crawled onto the bed, but I could tell he was hesitant. Maybe just fearing that he might make a wrong move.

"Come here and hold me, you idiot," I said, patting the bed. When he laid next to me, I took his arm and wrapped it around me. Then I placed my head on his chest, listening to his heartbeat.

Peace consumed me as he released a tight breath and his body relaxed beneath my touch.

"I've missed this," he confessed, while he stroked my hip with his thumb.

"Me too," I said, tapping his chest with my fingers. Tilting my head up, I studied his features. The way his eyelashes framed his eyes. The smoothness of his brown skin. "It was my favorite part of each day, just being with you."

Malachi stared at me, but he didn't react. His muscles tensed, but then he said nothing.

I sighed and gave him a crooked smile. "Now is when you're supposed to kiss me."

He didn't hesitate, pulling me up towards him, his strong arm holding me against his chest as our lips crashed together. Hunger and passion fueled a kiss that was long overdue, and I melted into him.

His tongue massaged against mine, and I moaned into his mouth, nipping at his bottom lip. He growled against me, his fists tightening in my shirt when he suddenly pulled back.

"What?" I asked, breathlessly, my brows furrowing.

He pressed his forehead to mine and exhaled. "I can't . . . I don't want—" he took a deep breath and cleared his throat. "I want to taste you. I want to make you come. But I also don't want to cross a line. I don't know where that line is."

"No sex," I murmured and nodded, our foreheads still touching. "No bonding yet. Whatever else goes. That's the line." I leaned in to kiss him, reaching between us to press my hand against his impressively hard cock.

He was massive, and wetness flooded me at the possibilities.

He hummed a "no" against the kiss, taking my hand and moving it away. "That's my line," he said in a rough voice. "I want you to—gods, I want you to—but if you keep touching me, the mate bond will get louder and harder to control. Let me taste you. Let me pleasure you. I can wait."

"Okay." I barely got the word out before he'd moved away from me, hooking his thumbs into my tiny boyshorts and ripping them down my legs.

I inhaled sharply at the sudden exposure, and he slid two fingers inside me, pumping in and out while he came back up and covered my moans with his mouth.

It was bliss feeling him inside me. I cupped his face in my hands and drowned in his kiss while he fingered me at a steady pace. When he took his thumb and started rubbing circles over my clit, my leg began to shake as I felt pressure building in my cunt.

He leaned back, gazing at me with dark, lust-filled eyes.

I nodded, biting my lip, giving him the go-ahead while I spread my legs for wider access. Doing so allowed his fingers to go deeper, and he curved them, rubbing over that sweet spot. Malachi took his other hand and pressed it on my lower belly, putting tight pressure against his fingers, increasing the sensation of my G-spot tenfold. I gasped, propping myself up on my elbows.

Holy hell.

He picked up speed, fucking me with his hand as it pounded hard against my pussy.

My mouth fell open and we locked eyes. As my inner walls began to spasm around him, he grinned, pleased that he was making me come.

I shattered, my orgasm pulling his fingers in, tightening and fluttering around them as he slid in and out of me.

Without giving me a chance to recover, he ducked down and buried his face between my legs. He pressed a hand on each thigh, spreading me wider. With his tongue pressed against me, he licked me from ass to clit, then growled against me, sending the vibrations down to my toes. "You're so fucking wet."

"Coming will do that." My voice was dry and scratchy from all the heavy breathing.

"Then I should make you come again," he said before he wrapped his lips around my clit and flicked it with his tongue.

Whatever words I had were lost in an incoherent grumble as he repeated the action. He scraped his teeth against the sensitive flesh ever so lightly. That action mingled with his hot breath over my flushed skin sent electricity over all the nerve endings in my entire body.

I clawed at his broad back, digging at the muscles

beneath my fingertips, desperate to pull him impossibly closer.

Altering between rolling his talented tongue in delectable waves over my pussy and sucking my swollen and sensitive clit, he took me higher until I was ready to fall over the edge once more.

And fall I did. With a guttural and completely undignified feral moan, I came. He growled against my orgasm, sucking and flicking my clit at a rapid speed while my inner walls spasmed.

Malachi gently kissed the side of each thigh and brought himself up to hold me again. Scooping me in his arms, he curved his body around mine so we were spooning. His heart beat against my back, falling into a rhythm with mine.

"If that was part of your groveling, it certainly got my attention," I said softly.

"I'll spend eternity groveling if you let me."

"I'm afraid to fall asleep," I admitted, even though the sandman was sure to take me at any moment. I couldn't keep my eyes open, but my mind hadn't shut down. "That I'll wake up and you won't be here."

"I'm not going anywhere ever again; I swear it," he murmured, curling his pinky around mine like we had when we were kids. "Sleep, Nikki."

As I hummed in contentment, I intertwined my fingers in his and held his hand close, drifting into sleep. As I was almost completely lost in the darkness, a whispered declaration reached me.

"I love you, princess."

I smiled and let sleep take me into a world of dreams, and there was security in his warmth. He would guard me from the nightmares that had plagued me.

Six years of tension and longing for each other had come to a close, and it lit a fire inside me I never thought I'd feel again.

He was my first love. My safety. My mate.

He was mine.

He'd always been mine.

CHAPTER 30
NIKKI

I WAS NEVER REALLY VERY GOOD AT STAYING IN ONE PLACE FOR TOO long.

I'd spent so many years sneaking out of windows, gallivanting through the boroughs, running reconnaissance for the militia, bartering for passage with pixies, all while pretending to be the complacent daughter of a syndicate leader. So when we'd been instructed to sit around for a few days while Earth and Emerald collected evidence, conducted interviews, and swept the grounds, I thought I was going to lose my mind.

The woman's relatives were notified once they identified who was missing. A candidate for Earth and Emerald, she was a shifter witch hybrid, and whatever got her, she didn't stand a chance. She'd never had the opportunity to use any of her powers against her attacker.

Though they'd not found the culprit, they'd investigated thoroughly and there was nothing more they could do. Today, the trials would recommence.

I'd slept in Niall's room the previous night, and spent

half of it rolling in the sheets. Apparently I needed more sleep than him because I woke up alone.

After getting dressed, I went down the hall and found all my mates in the kitchen.

I stopped at the entryway before they noticed me, and then took a moment to enjoy the view.

What I saw made me smile. They were getting along. Existing in each other's space without argument or dirty looks. There was no growling or alpha vibes being thrown about.

Niall was standing in front of the stove, stirring something in a frying pan. A stack of pancakes had been placed on the bar top where Malachi and Adrian were sitting.

"Are you starting on hers now?" Malachi asked, while reaching into his pocket.

"Yeah, toss me the . . . What is it you used? Reaper somethings?" Niall asked, looking to Malachi for the answer.

"Those were Reaper chips. This," he said, holding up a sealed clear bag, "is ground dragon's breath. A chili pepper."

"Dragon's breath," Niall repeated thoughtfully, and I swore he smiled. "Pretty sure I won't forget that one."

Malachi gently threw it across the kitchen and Niall caught it with one hand.

"How much should I use?"

"At least a tablespoon. You can be pretty generous with it. She won't mind."

I couldn't believe it. Malachi was helping him make the kind of food that I loved. The kind of food nobody wanted to eat.

I knew that I could have a mate bond with all three of them, but it was always a question how the three of them

301

would do with each other. Adrian and Niall would be fine, and Malachi and Adrian would be fine, but I had to wonder how Niall and Malachi would get along. Malachi was my first mate, but Niall felt like he was first, especially now since we'd completed the bond.

Something as trivial as spice made me feel hope for our future together.

I wanted to take a picture of this moment and frame it forever.

It was perfect.

"Morning, sunshine," Adrian said when he saw me standing in the doorway.

My mouth twisted into a smile, and I walked over to him. Deciding to test the waters a little bit, I leaned toward him, and when he turned to face me, I kissed him.

He held me there for a moment, I think partially in shock but also partially in lust. I certainly felt the latter. The feel of his lips pressed against mine made me realize the need to press my thighs together. A sudden and intense craving sent a pulse of desire straight to my core. I pulled away before it was too late.

"Morning," I said in response before going over to Malachi and kissing him as well.

Another pulse between my legs. *Fuck.*

"Good morning to you too," Malachi said, licking his lips afterward.

I smiled, walking over to Niall by the stove. He'd been watching the exchange with his head tilted. I pushed myself up on my tip toes and whispered good morning, and he leaned down to give me a lingering kiss. Then he leaned against my ear and whispered, "I can smell that you're turned on."

"Can they?" I asked softly.

He shrugged, glanced up at my mates, and when he looked at me again there was a smirk on his face.

Test complete.

I kissed all three of them in front of each other, and not one of them reacted. Well, maybe they reacted a *little* bit. Both Adrian and Malachi had to adjust themselves slightly. Never really thought I could make a guy hard just by kissing him. I kind of enjoyed having that power. It made me feel sexy.

Again it was another step toward making me feel like we had hope as a foursome.

"Had no idea you were such a chef, Niall." My mouth watered as the scent of chili peppers reached my nose.

"I had a lot to figure out once I was free. I needed to learn how to function on my own. Cooking felt like one of those things that grounded me."

"I can see that. Did you cook for Adrian?"

"No, he did not, the selfish bastard," Adrian huffed.

I chuckled and sat at the bar, and then Niall placed a plate of intensely spicy corned beef hash in front of me. My stomach growled the moment I picked up my fork.

Malachi laughed. "Your stomach always did give you away."

"No joke. You have no idea how difficult that actually became once I was running missions with Sam." I shook my head at some of the funny memories that replayed in my mind before I scooped up a big spoonful and eating it. The guys dove into their pancakes.

"You'll have to tell me more about how you became a vigilante. I never pictured you as Batgirl, swinging between buildings," Malachi said lightly.

"Robin Hood," Adrian corrected. "And it was the Brooklyn Bridge."

I gave a half-smile and leaned my elbow into him. "Nice. Two points to the Rose."

"We are on a point system now, are we?" Adrian asked.

"It could be fun." I was feeling flirtatious, and I enjoyed the light banter.

"But what do our points get us?" Malachi raised his eyebrows in question like this was a serious conversation, and then he raised his mug to his lips to take a drink.

"Well, I've got three holes . . ."

Caramel macchiato spewed across the table as Malachi inhaled the liquid down the wrong pipe. Adrian hit his chest with his fist, coughing trying not to choke on the pancake.

"Are you feeling okay, Nikki?" Niall looked at the guys before returning his attention to me.

"I'm fine," I said with a shrug and took another bite. After swallowing it down, I reached for a water pitcher. "Going a little stir crazy maybe."

"You don't want anything with caffeine?" Malachi asked, his voice hoarse.

"I'm good." After drinking a glass full, I asked, "Did Courtney say what time we need to be ready today?"

Adrian looked at the clock. "In an hour."

I sat up straight, shoving another bite into my mouth quickly. "Why didn't you wake me up?"

"We were going to wake you up as soon as I finished making breakfast. You got here just in time." Niall watched me shovel in more food, barely chewing before I swallowed.

"But I still need to pack."

"I already did that for you," Adrian said, tilting his head toward the living room.

. . .

"Oh." I supposed this was what it was like to have someone take care of you. I'd been coddled and overprotected my entire life. This was different. They did all of this for me not because they thought I was incapable—but because they wanted to do it *for* me. "Thank you," I said, slowing myself down as I finished my breakfast.

A knock at the front door sounded, and Niall frowned. "She's early."

"It's probably just Tylea and Sam," Malachi suggested as he stood up. "I'll get it."

"I can't believe we leave for Portland right when the weather started to warm up here," I commented while Malachi answered the door, but Adrian and Niall exchanging glances caught my attention. "What was that look for?"

"You think it's warm?" Adrian asked as though it was an absurd statement to have made.

"What? You don't?" I countered, reaching for the knob, and opening the door.

Sam and Tylea came into the kitchen, their backpacks slung over their shoulders.

"Sorry, I slept in," I began, then picked up my plate, "but it'll only take me twenty minutes to—"

"We're being sent home," Sam said, instantly cutting me off.

"Wait, what?" I stopped, no longer concerned with cleaning up. "Why are you being sent home? Both of you?"

"You haven't heard, have you?" Tylea said, looking at Malachi. He shook his head.

"Heard what?" Adrian asked.

Sam and Tylea looked at each other briefly before Sam spoke.

"They're sending all the seconds home for safety. There was another body."

"Who?" I dreaded asking, but we needed to know.

"An Earth and Emerald candidate," Tylea said.

"Was she . . . he... killed the same way?" I swallowed thickly, the graphic detail of the last situation coming back to my thoughts.

Sam pressed her lips together and shook her head. "No, his throat was slit." As I started to exhale in relief, she added, "But there was another message."

I closed my eyes. "What kind of message?"

"The kind of message that was left for you, and this time I have no doubts."

"How do you know?" Niall asked, his voice deepening.

"It said, *we will find you,* and there was a bloody bird drawn next to it." I sighed, prepared for what she was going to say next. "A phoenix."

"Yep," I said, releasing a harsh breath and feeling my nerves tighten. "That was left for me."

"How many people know you're a phoenix?" Adrian asked.

I huffed. "The people in this room, my family, and . . . the ones that took me."

Niall growled in a protective anger, and I felt the vibration in my very bones. I reached through our bond in an effort to soothe him. I wanted to convey without words that I knew it would be okay.

I'm right here.

I'm safe with you.

I'm not going anywhere.

You will protect me. You all will.

"Easy," Adrian said to his best friend gently. "We won't let anything happen to her."

"Not a fucking chance," Malachi said, his tail flicking behind him in irritation.

"Wow, the alpha testosterone in this room is stifling," Tylea muttered, and Malachi shot her a glare. She gave me an apologetic look and whispered, "Sorry, bad timing."

I shook my head. "It's okay. Can you do me a favor, Tylea?"

She stood up straighter, clearly not expecting me to ask for something. "Of course. Anything for Malachi's mate."

"You've been a good friend to him. I trust you." I nodded at Sam. "This is *my* best friend. She's more than capable of taking care of herself, but I need to know that she's safe too."

"You're talking about me like I'm not even here," Sam grumbled, rolling her eyes.

"I was getting to you, you impatient shit. I need you to stay the fuck out of shifter territory. Your family is out of Manhattan. There's nothing for you there except danger."

"Where's your family?" Tylea asked her.

"I don't know," Sam whispered. "We had someone on the inside get Lindsey and the kids into hiding."

"Contact Gavriel and find out where they are. He'll help you get them." She nodded. "I'll come for you when this is all over, okay?"

"How are you going to find me? I don't even know where I'm going yet."

I shrugged, knowing she was going to be annoyed. "I'll use the twilight bark."

Sam groaned and smacked her forehead with her palm. "Be serious, Nikki."

"I *am* being serious. You're the one that never wanted to use that plan."

"What plan is this?" Adrian asked tentatively.

"It's where animals howl and communicate on the rooftops of London, but they can pass a message all the way to the countryside. I saw it in a movie once."

"What kind of movie?" Tylea asked, while Malachi rubbed his temples.

"The kind of movie that's animated and has talking dogs," Sam said, shaking her head at me. "And it will draw attention to us in the *real world*."

"Don't be such a naysayer. We have shifters hiding all over the five boroughs. We can do this." I smiled, encouraging her to go along with it, but instead, her eyes softened, and she looked at me like I was crazy.

"How about we contact Tylea?" Malachi interjected, looking at his second. "Channel three?"

She dipped her chin in agreement. "Channel three. I'll keep it turned on."

I rolled my eyes. "Fine. That also makes sense."

I reached over and gave Sam a big hug while she chuckled. "I hope you never change, even though you are weird with your movie references and your hairbrained schemes."

"Yeah, yeah." I squeezed her tight, knowing how much I was going to miss her.

When she released me, she scrunched her brows and looked me up and down. "Are you okay? You're burning up."

"I am?"

In true mom fashion, she went to do her usual check: cupping my cheek and then putting a wrist to my forehead to gauge my temperature. I was going to tease her for it, but she never even made it past my cheek. She stared at her open palm, and I looked down to see red blistering skin.

"What the hell?" That had never happened before.

"You burned me . . ." she whispered.

308

"I'm s-sorry," I stuttered." I don't know . . .

She looked at all three of my mates, one after the other, her eyes finally landing on me again.

"You're in heat," she stated.

I laughed. "No, I'm not. That's absurd!" Then I turned to the guys, expecting to see them finding the humor as well.

"I think she's right," Adrian said, and my two other mates nodded in agreement.

"I can't be in heat. I never went into heat. I think phoenixes are different. Not even six years ago when I realized Malachi was my mate," I said, trying to rationalize the situation.

"Maybe three is your lucky number," Sam said.

"No. It can't be. This is the worst possible timing," I muttered.

"Yeah, well, you never were good for timing. If it wasn't your stomach growling and giving away our position, it was getting into a fight with a pixie, or going into a sneezing fit when we needed absolute silence."

"The fight with the pixie happened *one* time, and it wasn't my fault," I argued. "But at least I wasn't *in heat*. Ugh. How long before it kicks in, you think?"

Sam shrugged. "I have no idea. Anyone here know anything about mythical birds?"

Everyone collectively shook their heads "no."

I sighed.

Awesome. We had about forty minutes before a portal to Portland was about to open so we could get to the next trial, and I had to steal the show by being horny.

The halls of the Earth and Emerald embassy were painted in muted earth tones, creating a gentle, calm, and inviting feel.

I felt anything but.

The experience would probably be great if my hormones weren't giving me hot flashes.

I didn't mind the heat. Hello, mythical fire bird. But somehow this was different, especially when it was accompanied by the desire to strip my clothes off and have sex right here on the floor.

Public display and exhibitionism weren't exactly my thing, and I would never yuck on someone's yum. There were plenty of hook-ups in alleyways all over the city. To each their own. I was more of a voyeur, if I were going to be honest, so I liked to watch the show. I didn't want to *be* the show, and that left me fighting whatever strange instincts I was now experiencing.

As I had my inner monologue, I realized those were details I should probably share with the guys in case we clashed in that department.

No. That didn't make sense. Niall and Malachi would rip out someone's throat for watching me, and while Adrian was more mellow—he was still possessive.

Just as I refocused my eyes and came out of my haze, several people came walking down a wide corridor in the atrium. Their matching robes indicated they were council, with a few assistants here and there.

Courtney inclined her head politely. "Good afternoon."

Several mumbled the same greeting in return, but my eyes landed on a young woman that walked next to a councilman. Her ears were rounded and didn't mark her as fae, and her eyes and skin didn't have any supernatural quality to them. She was strikingly beautiful for a human, but what threw me off were the dark circles that framed her eyes. As we passed, she briefly looked up from the ground, making eye contact with me before directing her gaze to the floor again quickly and letting her brown hair drape a curtain around her features.

When I faced forward again, I tapped Courtney on the shoulder. "Who was that?"

"Who was who?" she asked as she continued walking.

"The woman with—" When I turned around, they were gone, and Courtney had just turned around to see who I'd been talking about, only to find an empty hallway.

"I'm afraid I don't know. Embassies have council members from territories all over the world at any given time. I don't know each of them personally, even as Hekate's assistant." She leaned in to speak in a softer voice, showing me a large binder she was carrying. "Between you and me, sometimes I need this to help with their names and where they are from, and who their assistants are, just to keep track of all of them."

I smiled in acknowledgment, but turned my head once more, wondering if I'd see the young woman again.

"Courtney, where are the others?" Since I had her attention, I figured she was willing to give us information.

"The other candidates?" she asked for clarification.

"Yes, I assumed we would all be together." And seeing that my brother wasn't there, I was thankful we weren't. Would he be able to see I was in heat? I shuddered. That was at the top of the list of things I didn't want to deal with.

"I personally volunteered to bring you here in separate groups. The intention was for you all to stay here at the embassy, though we'd had different sleeping arrangements in mind. You'll be moved to a larger suite. I've been told you're all mates, so I'm assuming the change won't be a problem."

As long as it had a shower with cold water, I was happy. "Where are the other syndicate candidates?"

She turned around and shushed me. "We don't use that word here."

"Sorry, I didn't mean to be disrespectful," I whispered, wiping some sweat that formed at my hairline.

"The other three candidates from the *boroughs*," she emphasized while giving me a tight smile, "are rooming together. For safety purposes, and since we have lost two Earth and Emerald candidates, we have placed the remaining four together on a secure floor.

"Tonight you'll have your first council meeting, so I suggest you get cleaned up and be ready to answer questions."

We came to a stop in front of large, wooden double doors marked 531.

"Here's your room. There's a restaurant in the atrium, and a concierge on the third floor to help you find anything you might need in the building." She opened the door for us, revealing a spacious, luxury suite. "Remember, candidates, like all embassies, we're in No Man's Land. Do not leave the safety of the building. We have no jurisdiction outside these walls."

After she left, I looked at Adrian. "She does remember we're syndicate, right? That we literally live in a No Man's Land?"

He shrugged, plopping himself on the couch. "Maybe she forgot to write that in her binder."

CHAPTER 31
NIALL

IT WAS PUSHING MIDNIGHT. WE'D BEEN LOCKED IN A COUNCIL room for five hours, and while I knew it was important, all I could think about was my mate.

She answered questions beautifully. I didn't know if she knew it or not, but she was a born leader. Watching her speak with authority made me realize that she should win the election; not because she was my mate, and not because I wanted Phaon to eat a bag of dicks, but simply because she deserved it. On the flip side, I also watched her struggle for hours, fidgeting in discomfort. Every now and then, little beads of sweat began to bead on her skin, trickling down her forehead.

The heat was coming on whether she liked it or not. None of us knew what to expect. None of us had ever been around a phoenix in heat. Hell, none of us had ever been around a phoenix.

During my years with the Roses, I'd been around several females, none of which I'd cared for because they weren't my mate. I knew she was out there waiting for me, and I knew one day I'd be reunited with her.

What I *did* know about shifters and heat—at least with wolves—was that I'd seen them agitated. Frustrated. She was none of those things. Instead, she seemed more affectionate. Suggestive innuendos. A touch here, and a graze there. This morning when she kissed each of us in front of each other, it was no light peck on the lips. It was harder on me than it was for the others. At least that's how it seemed. I could sense the happiness and contentment that filled her when all of us had a good response. That gave her hope.

I glanced over to my right and saw Nikki drinking from her glass of water. Sweat sparkled above her brow. Malachi was talking to one of the councilmen, giving her a break from responding. Beneath the table, I reached over and put my hand just above her knee, giving a gentle squeeze. She placed her hand on top of mine and I could sense her appreciation.

The council sat on a dais elevated above us. Twelve of them. All of the candidates sat below, the long rows of tables facing them.

When Malachi finished a particularly long answer with two council members that had been grilling him relentlessly, Courtney used a gavel to gain everyone's attention and announce that we were finished.

"Oh thank fuck," Nikki mumbled under her breath.

Ty stood up next to the vampire from the Tepes clan. He looked directly at us, clearly pissed off—not that he knew any other way to be. I was not in the mood to deal with him. I was never in the mood to deal with him, but especially not right now. I had my suspicions about Ty, and I didn't like the way that he looked at Nikki.

I looped my arm around her waist and pulled her to me just as two councilmen approached Ty and began to speak with him privately.

I made a mental note to keep an eye on those two. If they were chatting with a syndicate heir in a friendly way, no good could come from it. I knew the council was dirty. It was why so many syndicate were here in the trials.

We filtered out into the hallway, with Malachi, Adrian and I forming a protective cocoon around Nikki.

"I'm so glad that's over." She wiped the perspiration from her forehead. "Does anyone else think that Robert guy was a complete knob?"

"He wasn't exactly my favorite to speak with," Adrian said.

"Courtney," I said politely, dipping my head in greeting.

"Niall," she said in return, cradling her binder in her arm and holding it against her chest. "You all did well this evening"

"Do meetings normally go on that long?" Nikki asked.

"Sometimes yes, but not generally. Today went so long primarily because it was more of an interview process to see how you would respond in public with the council. The topics brought up are often real concerns and issues that our citizens have, and we take great care to handle things as diplomatically as possible."

"Have there been any more findings in the investiga-tion?" Nikki asked, wobbling slightly and grabbing my arm to steady herself.

She hummed. "We're still working on it," she said, her brows furrowing as she looked at Nikki. "Are you all right?"

Courtney casually touched Nikki's arm in a concerned gesture, and Malachi jumped forward, but he was too late. "Wait—"

Courtney jerked back, holding her hand to her chest and then shaking it out. "Oh my! Did I do something...?" She looked at her hand in confusion.

"No, it's me. I'm sorry," Nikki said, her voice wavering. "I just haven't been feeling myself."

"We have healers here at the embassy. Doctors as well. I'll have one sent to your room immediately," she began.

"Please don't," Nikki said, with a slight forcefulness in her voice.

"I don't understand," Courtney said, glancing at me in question.

"I, um, well," Nikki paused, looking between the three of us for help. We weren't going to out her. It had to be her choice.

"Nikki?" Courtney prompted, then lowered her voice and narrowed her eyes. "Are you safe?"

"Oh my god, yeah! No, that's not it." She swallowed, then smacked her tongue in her mouth and coughed. "Ugh, my mouth is so dry."

"I'm fetching the healers."

"I'm going into heat!" she blurted out.

"Oh . . . *oooh,*" Courtney said, a slight blush tinging her cheeks. "Why didn't you say so?"

"Really?" Nikki responded dryly. "I didn't think going around and telling people that you were in heat and horny and on the verge of humping your mates anytime they looked at you was something that you went around and advertised."

"Well no not when you put it that way."

Adrian pressed his lips together trying not to laugh. Malachi didn't succeed, and I did what I was good at. I stood there and remained still.

"The next trial is supposed to be tomorrow," Courtney began while watching sweat drip down Nikki's face and onto her neck. "Clearly, you're not in good shape for the next assignment."

Nikki shook her head. "I'm not missing it."

"You're not going to," Courtney said. "I'll take care of it. We can postpone until the heat has passed. Do you know how long your heat goes for?"

"Um . . . no. I don't," she muttered.

"No matter." She smiled, then looked at me. "If you'd be so kind as to check in with me, that would be useful, just so I know when to have the trials begin."

"You're going to postpone because I'm in heat?"

"Of course. We would do it for anyone. Almost a fourth of the Earth and Emerald population are shifters, Nikki. We're not savages. When accommodations can be made, we will absolutely do that. Trust me. Everyone—the council included—will understand."

She gently pushed Nikki toward us, using the edge of her binder so as to not burn her hand again.

"Go . . . have fun." She looked at Malachi, Adrian, and me, then said, "Take care of her. I'll be in touch."

"Thank you," Nikki whispered. The relief was written all over her face, and I didn't need to be bonded with her to know it.

She wobbled again and her skin began to flush a shade of light red.

"I don't know how much longer she has," Adrian said.

"It's getting worse, but it's not there yet; that much I know. But I would feel better if we were in our room, just in case it comes on and I start mewling like a cat, sticking my ass in the air."

"I'm not saying I'm opposed to seeing that," Adrian commented, and she smacked him on the arm while we took the steps up to our floor.

Malachi saw how much her clothes were starting to

soak with sweat, and he said, "I'll go start you a bath. Maybe a cold one."

"You go on ahead," she said. "I'll be right there."

She grabbed my arm holding me back to talk to me privately.

"I'm worried," she admitted.

"You don't need to be."

"Once I go fully into heat, I'm really not going to be present and alert. That's at least my understanding of how it works. I don't know? Maybe mine is different, but if the mating frenzy took twenty-four hours, I don't know what being in heat is going to look like for me time wise."

"What do you need me to do?"

"If Courtney is going to postpone the trials, that means she's telling the council and the candidates that I'm in heat. Everyone is going to know. There's no guarantee that the murderer isn't still here. I'm not saying it was one of the candidates, but whoever it is knows I'm a phoenix and has been leaving messages for me. I doubt they stayed back wherever we were at that compound and didn't come here to Portland too. They're trying to make a point, and I think eventually they're going to make themselves known when they try to take me out. If I'm in the throes of the heat, we're all preoccupied. I'm a wide-open target."

I bristled, feeling my jaw tense and my fists clench as my knuckles cracked.

"Hey," she said, rubbing my arm. I could feel her warmth soothing me. "If I have the three of you, I'll be fine."

"You know what needs to happen, right? To keep you safe," I said after thinking through what she'd said.

"I do. Are you okay with it?"

I nodded. "Anything for you."

CHAPTER 32
NIKKI

D<small>ID SHIFTERS GO INTO MENOPAUSE?</small>

I had to wonder, because if they did, perhaps this was what it felt like. Uncontrollable sweating, sudden flashes of heat crawling up my skin, my hormones telling me what to do instead of my rational brain.

Portland was chilly and rainy, and I was walking around in underwear and a thin tank top because I was sweating through everything else.

Malachi had run me a cool bath, and I was pretty sure all I did was practically make the water boil.

I stripped out of my clothes again and put on a dry tank top.

Niall and I had discussed how this was going to go, but I hadn't yet discussed it with Malachi and Adrian. It was a conversation that I didn't exactly know how to have, but I figured just saying it was maybe the best approach. It's not like they were going to reject me, right?

I walked into the common area of our suite to find Malachi on the couch, while Adrian sat in an armchair. I fell back into a chair, slouching and crossing my legs. Nope, bad idea. I uncrossed them and sat spread eagle.

Adrian appraised me, then asked, "Are you doing okay? Anything I can get you?"

"I'm sweating like some sort of farm animal," I grumbled, then bit the inside of my cheek.

That was awesome. That was exactly how you told someone you wanted to have a threesome. Compare yourself to a cow. It was a brilliant technique. The guys exchanged a look. "Ignore that I just said that."

"Hmm." Malachi pursed his lips. "I'm afraid that's solidly burned into my memory."

"Well, don't remind me of it. Ever." I pinched the bridge of my nose. This was not going according to plan. "I'm getting closer," I said, finally. "I can't walk or cross my legs without my clit feeling like it's on fire and screaming at me for more friction."

Malachi reached over and grabbed a pillow, placing it on his lap. He chewed on his bottom lip, then nodded.

"I wanted to talk to you both about something important." I looked between them, and they waited for me to continue. "I want to complete the bond."

They looked at each other, then back to me. "Right now?"

"Yeah, right now. I'm going into heat, Malachi. Whether I like it or not, it's happening."

He looked hesitant. "I wanted you to make this choice because it's what you wanted, and not because you were in heat."

"Well, I am making the choice. I still have a measure of control, albeit not much. I'll be the first to admit that. I've already completed the bond with Niall, and I've already talked to him. We're stronger together, right? We're stronger as mates. It makes sense to go ahead and complete it now."

"You want to complete it because it's the practical thing to do?" he asked, the inflection in his tone suggesting he thought this was a questionable idea. I had no idea what was happening. Maybe the heat was clouding my judgment and the ability to speak coherent thoughts.

"I really thought this was going to go a little bit differently," I said and started to stand up. Malachi jumped up and grabbed my hand.

"Wait, sit back down. I think you're misunderstanding." When I sat, he did too. "I think I can speak for myself and for Adrian by saying, yes, of course we want to complete the bond with you."

Adrian nodded. "No argument here, but I think we both imagined that you would be making the choice in a different situation. Not when it sort of seems like you're under duress."

"Would you rather that I fucked Niall the entire time?"

"No," Adrian and Malachi said in unison very quickly.

"All right, then. I'm making this decision for myself, and I'm doing it before the heat makes any decisions for me." I sat up straight, adjusting myself in the chair. Not that it mattered. The discomfort was rising. "So, do you accept me as your mate?"

"Without question," Adrian answered.

"I always have," Malachi said at the same time.

Standing up, I began to fan myself. My temperature was spiking, and my breath stuttered as I began to pant. "Give me just a second. It'll pass."

"I'll go get you some water," Adrian said.

"Is this really what you want?" Malachi asked after Adrian left the room.

"Why do you keep asking that?"

He stood before me, looking down. He cupped my cheek, caressing it gently with his thumb. "I don't know. Maybe I feel like I haven't truly earned your forgiveness."

"You have. I might never forget the way it felt when you walked away, but I'll also never forget the way it felt when you returned. And that's the moment that sticks out the most for me."

Reaching up, I grabbed the back of Malachi's neck and pulled his face toward mine.

Bouncing on my tiptoes, I pushed myself up and wrapped my legs around his waist pressing my heated core against him.

I sensed the moment that Adrian returned. There was something *incredibly* hot about it. I may not have been an exhibitionist, but having one of my mates watch me was a different experience.

Malachi's lips left mine trailing down the column of my throat. As I turned my head to give him access, I met Adrian's eyes and held his heated gaze. He looked down at the coffee table and sat the water down. The seconds ticked by while we watched each other. One of Malachi's hands roamed up my back, the fingertips of his other pressed into my ass as he pulled me closer to him.

Adrian inclined his head and turned to walk away, I pulled away from Malachi briefly and grabbed Adrian's hand pulling him back toward me.

"I think you misunderstood. I want both of you. *Together.*"

Malachi and Adrian looked at each other silently, their movements so subtle, but it was clear they were checking in. Somehow, the fact that they got along well enough to get each other's permission turned me on even more. It meant that there was more to our foursome than just sex, but right now sex was at the forefront of my mind.

Adrian smiled a devilish grin and pulled his shirt over his head.

Finally.

CHAPTER 33
NIKKI

MALACHI BROUGHT HIS MOUTH BACK TO MINE, CRUSHING ME IN A kiss with his soft lips. His fingers pressed into me as his grip on my ass tightened. My nipples hardened, and his length twitched beneath me, pressing into my heat. I moaned in pleasure, rocking my hips against him with force.

I pulled away from Malachi, giving him access to kiss and nibble my throat. Glancing at Adrian, with my lips red and cheeks flushed, I beckoned him. Standing behind me, he cupped my breasts, kissing my shoulder as he massaged each one.

"Get undressed," Malachi murmured, dropping his hands from my legs and slowly releasing me so I could stand.

I stood before him, never having heard the bossy side of him like this. He sounded growly and curt, but Malachi's face was the picture of desire. He didn't want it to stop. He wanted more.

My heart thundered in my chest as I stood up on trembling legs. I wanted this. Oh my god, I wanted it, but that didn't keep me from being nervous. I'd never done anything

324

like this in my life. I didn't know how it worked. I didn't know how I *wanted* it to work, but I knew one thing for absolute certain: I wanted it to happen.

I pulled my tank top over my head and cast it aside.

"That's my girl," Malachi said in praise, and I found I quite liked hearing it. "Take off her shorts, Adrian. Slowly."

Without hesitating, Adrian traced his fingers down the curve of my waist, and hooked his thumbs in the elastic waistband of my tiny shorts and pulled them down in an achingly long motion until they reached the floor, trailing his lips over my leg the entire way. Like a gentleman, Adrian took my hand in his as I stepped out of the shorts and kicked them off to the side.

I'd been changing clothes so often that I hadn't even bothered wearing panties. I stood in front of both of them, stark naked and ready and willing for anything.

Malachi made a pleasurable sound as he held my gaze. His hand moved to his bulge, and he began to stroke it through his pants. I knew I had power over him. I knew he wanted me. But watching him rub his cock because he loved the look of me? That feeling made my insides clench.

"Put your foot on the chair," he told me, his voice dropping low. "Show us your pussy."

Slightly shaking, I lifted my leg and placed my foot on the chair. I angled my body away from it, displaying myself for both of them to see. I hadn't ever felt this vulnerable before.

They both admired me, humming in agreement as they stood side by side.

"You should taste her," Malachi suggested. "She's so fucking sweet."

I brought my gaze back to Adrian. His eyes probed

mine, almost as if he were asking permission. I gave him a slight nod and bit my lip for what was to come.

With a labored breath, he sank to his knees in front of me. My legs already open, he wrapped an arm under my hoisted leg and gripped my hip, pulling me toward him. I twined my fingers in his hair and I shivered with anticipation as Adrian's tongue lapped at my soaking wet slit.

"She's so fucking wet," he told Malachi breathlessly between licks, and he grunted in response.

Adrian dragged a hand up the back of my thigh to hold me close while he took my clit in his mouth. My legs shook. My need for release grew and grew and Adrian seemed dead set on getting me there. He lapped at my clit with consistent pressure and a consistent pace.

"That feels so good," I mumbled.

Adrian moaned against me. The vibration sent new ripples of pleasure through my core.

I made eye contact with Malachi, wondering who this voyeur was. My best friend—my mate—was watching another man drive me wild. He was watching another man taste me. He was going to watch another man make me come. I didn't understand it, but I didn't have to. I just knew I loved it.

"I think that's enough," he said, and Adrian fucking *stopped*.

"No," I panted. "I was so close." I grabbed a fistful of Adrian's hair and pulled his face back between my legs.

For some unknown reason, he listened to Malachi. They got along better than I expected.

Normally, I'd be up for a little wait and a little tease, but I was in heat. My body screamed for release. It screamed for their touch. Every facet of our relationship was new, and I didn't mind taking things slowly, but I was eager to come.

Eager to explore them together. And eager to complete the bond with my mates. I'd been fantasizing about having both of them, and I wanted each and every scenario to come to light.

"I need to come," I ground out, wanting so badly to be touched again.

With Adrian nibbling at my thigh, Malachi cupped my chin in his hand and roughly turned my face to his. He owned my mouth with his kiss. I was so distracted by him and my want that I didn't realize where his other hand was until I felt it on my clit, rubbing gently. I whimpered into his mouth, and my knees buckled, but Malachi was there to hold me up.

When I looked to Adrian, he'd stood up. His face glistened with my juices and at some point, he must've undone his pants. They hung from his hips and all that stood between me and his thick cock was the thin material of his baby blue boxers. He slid them off and I licked my lips, so badly wanting to taste him.

"Let's move this to the bedroom," Malachi said roughly, his lips grazing the shell of my ear. His breath was hot on my skin, but goosebumps erupted all over my arms.

Before I could react further, Adrian had ducked down, wrapping his arm around my legs and putting his shoulder into my abdomen, lifting me up and holding me over him, my ass in the air. I yelped in surprise and felt a surge of heat rush to my face at the new way my body was exposed.

I couldn't have been more turned on.

Malachi led us to the bedroom he'd been staying in. Adrian reached up and smacked my ass hard, grabbing it roughly before he set me down on wobbly feet. I was sandwiched between them, and practically dripping with excitement. I reached for Malachi's shirt and undid one button. I wanted him naked too. I wanted to touch and kiss him and see exactly how excited seeing me with Adrian had made him.

"What do you want?" he whispered, holding my hands, and stopping me from undressing him.

"I thought that was pretty obvious," I answered between heavy breaths.

"Tell me what you like. I don't know this part of you, and I want to," he continued. "Adrian, do you know what she likes?"

"You know, I don't," he said, his hands roaming over the curve of my breasts while he kissed my neck.

"I want to give you everything, Nikki," Malachi murmured against my lips, licking the inside of his mouth as we kissed. "I can't—we can't—give you everything until you tell us what it is you like."

"I like . . . goddesses help me"—I swallowed thickly. "I like doggy style. I like sucking . . ."

"Say it," Adrian prompted, nipping at my earlobe.

I groaned. "I like sucking cock. I like orgasming, for fuck's sake. I like being worshipped and coming until I can't see straight."

"Anything else?" Malachi asked while Adrian chuckled.

"I, uh, I like watching." Both mates growled, and I knew it was at the prospect of me watching others fuck.

"Who did you like watching?" Malachi asked, possession leaking into his voice. Adrian's grip on me tightened, likely in the same response.

"Strangers. I never watched without permission. I wanted to, but if I ran into someone in an alley, I did turn away. But . . . others. Militia. Sometimes members fucked in public. They didn't care. So I watched," I breathed out, admitting that out loud for the first time.

"Why?" Adrian asked, reaching to grab and twist a nipple.

My clit ached, and I was getting desperate.

"I don't know. It just turns me on."

Malachi looked genuinely surprised. "We have that in common, princess."

"Oooh," I said on a long exhale, understanding the connection.

My phoenix called to Malachi. My demon fire fae. My mate. My first love. The one who'd left . . . but the one who'd fought fiercely to make his way back to me.

She practically purred—if a bird could do that—filling me with gratification that we were so alike.

"I want to watch you play with yourself," he breathed.

Adrian hummed in approval. "I would very much enjoy that."

That grabbed my attention, and my body reacted in many ways.

For as eager as I was, and as deeply as the heat was pushing me to keep going forward, I paused at the suggestion. My skin flushed. It was one thing to be spread out in front of them. But to have them watch me in that way . . . as silly as it sounded, I felt embarrassed. No one had ever sat back and just *watched* me, offering no assistance.

The entire idea—while new and terrifying—also made me flood with anticipation.

"I . . ." Taking a shaky breath, I steadied myself. "I've never done that."

"Good," Malachi growled. "I've never watched the one woman I wanted most in the world."

"What do I get if I put on a show for you," I asked. My voice was husky and there was nothing I could do to stop it. I was totally going to play with myself. I liked this game.

The look on their faces. The way they were so attentive to my body and touching some part of me.

I craved it.

I loved the devotion.

And I wanted more.

"Everything you want," Adrian said, sliding his hand down over my stomach and cupping me and sliding a finger between my folds.

My breath caught and began to step back, moving back onto the bed. I propped my head up on the firm pillows. Slowly, teasingly, I let my legs fall open. Malachi and Adrian both took a step closer to the bed, flanking it, Malachi to my left, Adrian to my right.

Adrian sat on the edge of the bed on his side and Malachi did the same on his side. I had their full attention. I started out slowly, moving my hands down my body to cup my breasts. I didn't need any foreplay, I could've jumped right in and fingered my clit, but I didn't want to do it that way.

Once my nipples were taut, I slid my hands over my stomach and then down my hips. I dragged my fingernails up and down my inner thighs then palmed myself with my right hand. It felt good, but knowing they were watching me made it even better.

I took my middle finger and slid it inside myself, pumping in and out a few times. But that wasn't enough. I added my ring finger so I could stretch myself out. My head fell back, and I moaned.

"God," I cried, the mating bond and heat sent my temperature skyrocketing. "This feels so good."

I used my other hand to pinch my nipple and it gave me just a hint of the pleasurable pain I loved. My eyes fluttered closed at the sensation, but that wasn't quite enough for me to come.

I took my soaked fingers and rubbed my throbbing clit back and forth over and over and over. When the bed squeaked with movement, I opened my eyes. Malachi and Adrian had taken all their clothes off. They sat on the edge of the bed, their backs to each other and faces turned to see me, while they stroked their cocks.

I nearly lost it at the incredibly sexy sight of my mates fisting themselves as they watched me. Fingering myself to the brink of orgasm, had gotten them so worked up they had to touch themselves too. Malachi loosely stroked himself from root to tip while Adrian did nearly the same thing at the same time.

"I'm so close," I panted, and my hips turned in motion with the movement of my fingers.

"I want to watch you come, Nikki," Adrian growled. "Show us."

So I did. The world tilted and I rubbed faster, and I came hard with a long moan as my channel clenched and I felt tingles all the way to my toes. But I didn't stop. I arched my back off the bed and fought to keep my legs spread as I kept rubbing even though my clit was almost too sensitive to touch.

Malachi grabbed my wrist to stop me, and I groaned, grabbing the sheets around me in frustration. Adrian crawled toward me on the bed and positioned himself between my legs. He stuck two thick fingers in me without any warning and pumped hard, reaching that sweet spot and pressing against it.

"Oh my--*yes*," I cried out in a guttural moan. My legs shook as Adrian brought me right to the edge, but I kept my eyes on Malachi. I wanted him to join in too.

Adrian followed my gaze and gave me a wicked smile.

"Are you just going to sit there, Mal? This beautiful woman is laid out for you and you're not going to do anything to help her come?"

Malachi's eyes blazed. He got up from the bed, still stroking his cock, and laid beside me. His mouth covered my breast and he sucked and flicked at the taut peak with his tongue. He moved his hand over the other, pinching and twisting lightly to tease. He left a final pinch before releasing the nipple and trailing his lips up my neck and around my jaw.

I turned my head toward him as he covered my mouth with his, kissing me deeply while he fondled my breasts, all while Adrian fingered me. My head was spinning. I wanted this so badly and now that it was happening, it was almost too much to bear.

I reached between us and pressed my palm against Malachi's length, stroking him up and down. He moaned into my mouth and pushed himself against me. Adrian must've noticed what we were doing. He worked his fingers into me quickly, leaning forward and flicking his tongue over my clit.

"Come again, beautiful," he said, his face buried between my legs.

He nipped at my clit, and I shattered around them while still kissing and pumping Malachi's cock in my hand. My orgasm coated his face, and Adrian worked my body as I rode out my pleasure and didn't stop until my legs went limp.

"She's so responsive," Adrian said to Malachi as he pulled away.

I was exhausted, and yet my body demanded more. We hadn't completed the bond yet. This was all just foreplay.

I knew they were talking about me, and I didn't care, but I did note how casual and easy their conversation was all while the three of us were naked . . .

"What do you want next, princess?"

"Everything," I ground out. "I want you inside me, Malachi. I want you to fuck me from behind, *now*."

"On your hands and knees," Malachi said with a placating grin. "And what was it you said you liked? Sucking cock? I think while I fuck this sweet pussy, Adrian can fuck your mouth."

I hummed in excitement.

My clit throbbed again as I got into position. Arching my back, I pushed my ass in the air, spread my knees wide, and rested my hands against the firm mattress. The bed was the perfect level of firm because I didn't sink into it, leaving me perfectly presented for Malachi, and easily balanced for Adrian.

I had never done this at the same time, and the anticipation had me almost trembling.

He moved behind me, used his fingers to spread my folds, and then he thrust into me, my wetness guiding him in with ease. I gasped in sheer bliss and pushed back into him.

"So. Tight." Malachi bit out the words as his cock swelled inside me. "Fuuuck."

Adrian held his cock in front of my face, slowly pumping the shaft, the tip glistening in eagerness. I met his lust-filled gaze with one of my own. I didn't say a word. I just opened my mouth wide in invitation and he grinned.

He placed one hand on my head, moving himself in and out slowly as I coated him in spit. I moaned around him, humming in permission to give me more. The way he twitched in my mouth almost made me smile. He pushed forward with one thrust and held for a second. I gagged as he pulled out, the saliva flowing and coating my throat for more. He grunted, and I opened my throat, letting him fuck my face and he did it, again and again, all while Malachi fucked me from behind.

After a few moments, they fell into a rhythm where they were pumping into me at the same time.

Full.

Empty.

Full.

Empty.

It was maddening. It felt dirty and wrong and so hot and so right all at the same time.

"You look so beautiful with my cock in your mouth," Adrian said, twining his fingers in my hair as he pushed into me and held my head, my mouth and throat filled with him. I could hardly breathe, and I didn't care.

"When you choke her, her cunt squeezes. It feels fantastic," Malachi grunted.

"Then I'll keep doing it."

He shoved into my throat again, holding me there while my gag reflex tried to gain me air. I felt my pussy clench around Malachi as he pounded into me, tightening around his impressive length. They worked me from both ends until the edges of my vision blurred.

"I'm . . ." I mumbled around Adrian's cock. He pulled away, allowing me to speak. "I'm going to come again," I said quickly.

"Then come for us," Malachi said, pumping into me deeper. I felt the heat and the mate bond tightening between us. It was fire raging inside me, screaming to *own* my demon mate.

I twisted to the side slightly, reaching my heated palm

up, and I slapped my hand onto his chest, searing my mark into his skin. He groaned deeply, our skin slapping as he never let up.

Malachi scooped an arm around my waist and pulled me up, keeping himself inside me, keeping rhythm.

With my body curved in front of him, he bit into my neck, his demon fangs piercing the skin. Fire raged in my veins, a mixture of our two flames mingling as one. A smoky scent exploded in my senses and my phoenix smiled, pleased that we'd claimed our second mate—and been claimed in return.

I fell flat on my stomach and panted to catch my breath. My skin held a sheen of hard-earned sweat, and I felt an ache between my thighs from all the attention.

"I want to be inside her," Adrian told Malachi.

As worn out as I was, my body reacted at hearing those words. I wanted Adrian inside me too. Now. I felt a new wave of desire course through me, and I smiled at them, biting my lip, and cocking an eyebrow.

"Lie down and let her ride you. I want to take her ass," he said, slapping it hard. I winced at the sting, feeling the heat of it travel across my skin.

Adrian laid on the bed. His thick cock stood at full attention and would soon be deep inside me. I pushed up on the bed, my muscles still loose from coming twice before. As he placed his hands on my waist, I straddled his body, reaching to grasp him and position his length. I lowered myself and sheathed him completely in one easy movement.

Adrian groaned and bucked his hips up to meet me, instantly rubbing against that sweet spot.

"Oh, god," I breathed, my hands landing on his chest to hold steady. I could feel my palm beginning to burn.

I rocked my hips, meeting his thrusts as I rode him. He touched everywhere he could reach—cupping my breasts, pinching my nipples, grazing my stomach, pressing into my clit—as we ground against each other in fevered motion.

Malachi watched. He walked around the bed, taking in every angle of Adrian fucking me, all while stroking his cock.

"Is this what you wanted, princess?" he asked.

"Fuck yes," I breathed, pushing up and down on Adrian again. "It feels so fucking good."

Adrian reached down between us and then took his thumb and pressed it against my clit. It was too sensitive. I wanted to pull away, but Malachi came up behind me, placing his hand on my back and gently pushed me down toward Adrian.

Adrian moved his hands to grasp my hips, and I leaned forward, placing my hands near Adrian's head as I dipped down to kiss him.

Malachi traced a lubed finger around my rim, gently probing and pushing it inside. "Do you want me to fuck you here?" he asked, pumping his finger in and out as I moaned into Adrian's mouth.

"Yes," I breathed huskily.

Malachi added another finger, the lube allowing him easier access to my tight entrance. He pumped again and twisted, stretching me out, pushing me against Adrian as I rocked over his cock.

"I couldn't hear you. Did you want me to fuck you here?" he said, shoving in deeper.

"Yes, *please* fuck me. I want you both inside me." My temperature was rising again. The bond was coiling tighter. The heat was pushing me over the edge. I was already more than halfway to my next orgasm and the words came out in a begging tone I couldn't have prevented if I tried.

"Where do you want it, Nikki? Tell us." Adrian ground the words out as his fingertips dug into my hips.

"I want you in my pussy, and I want Malachi to fuck my ass," I moaned, moving down to my elbows, and nuzzling my face into his neck.

Adrian growled, sucking on my earlobe as he pulled my cheeks apart. Malachi removed his fingers, and a cold slickness was rubbed over me before I felt his tip press against my rim.

He pushed into me slowly, filling me up as I gasped and cried out. As if they'd rehearsed it, they both stilled and gave me one long moment to accommodate my body to being so completely full and stretched out.

Malachi gently rubbed his hand over my back, tracing the curve of my ass, caressing my skin to help me focus on something else.

So full.

I took deep breaths as I tried to concentrate on the intensity of the pleasure and pain.

"Are you okay?" Adrian whispered in my ear.

"Yes," I panted. "Yes. I want it all."

Adrian covered my mouth with his, and I drank in his kiss.

They worked my holes at different paces; Adrian slow and deep, Malachi quick and rough. I couldn't focus on any single thing for more than a few seconds at a time. I kept one arm to the side of Adrian's head, and another braced on his chest, smushed between us.

I was a bundle of nerve endings and sensations I didn't think were humanly possible. The tension in my core grew tighter and tighter until I didn't think I'd ever be able to come down from the high of finally having Malachi and Adrian inside me.

"How does it feel, princess?" Malachi asked.

"So full, so good," I moaned. "It feels so good to have you inside me, stretching me out."

"Every part of you is beautiful," Adrian said, rocking into me. The movement pressed me against Malachi as he pumped into me in return. "The way you come. The sound of your moans. The way your pussy clenches my cock when you hear my voice."

An instinctual part of me took over, insisting I mark him. Forever brand him as *mine*. Something inside began calling to him silently.

As though he'd heard my thoughts, he growled in agreement.

"Come inside me, Adrian. Make me yours," I demanded, shifting to gain friction where I couldn't rub myself, then tension began to rush through my body.

The hand wedged between us began to flare, reaching an impossible heat. Anyone else would scream in pain—but not my mates. They burned for me, and I for them.

My handprint seared into his chest, my phoenix and I claiming my beautiful earth fae as ours.

He growled deeply and rammed into me at a rapid pace as his cock swelled. I screamed out in pleasure as he wrapped his arms around me and held me down on him with all his might, trapping the hand that branded him between us even tighter. Small fangs pierced my shoulder where it meets the neck, and I saw stars.

A wave of pleasure rode my body, and I felt as though I was floating with the stars. The scent of spring rain descended upon me, and a piece of my soul snapped into place, calling out for what he was meant to be. That fate had always known we would be made for each other.

Like maybe I'd always known him, just in another life.

Adrian came, filling me as I started to come too, grinding down onto him, my knees shaking on the bed. I couldn't help but scream out in pure joy.

"You're mine, love," he whispered as he pushed hair out of my eyes.

Malachi rammed into me hard as if he was reminding me he was still there.

"Put your hand between you two. On her clit. She's going to come again." Every part of me ached, simultaneously wanting to stop but also wanting so much more.

"Malachi," I breathed, feeling the rise again. "Don't stop …"

"I won't stop, princess. I'm going to fuck your ass, and while I do, your swollen, tender clit is going to grind over his hand every … fucking … time until you come again" he said, accentuating his words with powerful thrusts.

Adrian was better at following through than I was. I'd already forgotten what he'd said, so Adrian reached between our sweaty bodies, twisting his hand into position as he found my very swollen clit, so sensitive to the touch that I bucked away as soon as he touched it.

Malachi grunted, pressing me down against it as I whimpered. Adrian found it again, readying himself and he nodded to Malachi.

He pumped into my ass hard, slamming into me and forcing me to rub over Adrian's fingers every time. My fingers clawed into the bed and my thighs burned as they quaked.

I cried out, the shocks of pleasure screaming through my system. My core tightened and spasmed and he kept fucking me, my walls clenching around both of them as they filled me. Malachi deepened his thrusts and quickened his pace as I started to come, pressing his body against mine, pushing my clit into Adrian's eager hands.

I sunk my teeth into Adrian's shoulder muscle as my orgasm poured from me, peaking with a guttural moan escaping my throat.

Malachi shuddered with a grunt, his fingers digging into my flesh as he guided himself in his final thrusts, filling me.

Finally, my body gave out. After Malachi pulled out, I rolled off Adrian unceremoniously, flopping onto the bed, half falling off. Malachi returned with towels, wiping me down with a wet washcloth and tossing a towel to Adrian.

The three of us moved to the center of the bed, a tangled mess of limbs, sweat, and beating hearts. I wanted to clean up more, but in that moment, it was the only aftercare I needed. The newly formed connection between us flared to life in the recesses of my mind.

I had my mates: Niall, Malachi, and Adrian.

They had me.

They were mine and mine alone.

I felt utterly and totally satisfied for the first time in my life.

My eyes grew heavy as I came down from the rush, but I knew after a quick nap, my body would be ready to go in no time. The heat was just getting started.

"You're *ours*, princess," Malachi whispered in my ear.

"Forever," Adrian added, tucking a strand of hair behind my ear.

I felt a faint smile on my face as sleep claimed me.

CHAPTER 34
NIKKI

I JOLTED AWAKE. VISIONS OF FIRE AND THE WHISPERS OF PHANTOM voices had filled my dreams again.

The sticky remnants of sweat coated my body, making the sheets damp. The cool air was welcomed on my skin.

"Finally," I muttered, scrubbing my hands down my face. Something we'd noticed and come to realize was that as a phoenix, my heat waxed and waned. I was incredibly thankful for that, considering I was using my heat to bond. In doing so, it also triggered a mating frenzy. Somehow the heat trumped it, and it gave me breaks.

My temperature would drop slightly. My mind would clear for short periods of time. The ache between my legs was only due to what had been done, and not what it wanted to do.

My phoenix was a hussy.

I wondered if this was it. If it was finished. It felt like a down cycle, and my stomach growled.

"You're awake," Adrian said.

"How long was I asleep? I don't even know what century it is any more ."

Adrian sat on the edge of the bed and brushed the hair off of my face as I laid there and admired him. "You slept for about nine hours."

My stomach grumbled again. "I don't know if the heat is over, but I know if I don't eat something, I get hangry, and then I become someone I'm not proud of."

"Well your stomach has excellent timing."

"That'd be a first." Then I tilted my head. "Wait, why is it good timing?"

"Your personal chef just finished making you dinner, and Malachi picked up a special surprise for you."

My interest was piqued. "What is it?"

"Get dressed and come find out," he said, tossing me an oversized T-shirt. I sat up and caught it, pulling it over my head. As I flung my legs over the edge of the bed, he slid one arm beneath my knees and scooped me into his arms.

"This is silly," I chided. "I can walk."

"I know you can." He leaned in and kissed me. "And I want to carry you."

As we entered the common space, the smell of spicy roasted meat filled my nostrils. "That smells *amazing*."

"I'm glad you think so, because every time any of us gets near it, our eyes start to water."

"That's putting it lightly. I think my eyes are going to start bleeding," Malachi said, as he leaned down to give me a kiss when Adrian set me on my feet.

His lips lingered longer than I expected, and the taste of him teased at my libido. Another demanding yell from my stomach made him pull back.

"Apparently my body had spoken. No more sex until food."

"I have a surprise for you." He grinned and held up a

remote, turning on a television that had been placed on the wall. *Moana* appeared on the screen.

Old technology had been made new with magic, but how we watched movies had remained the same for the most part. I appreciated human entertainment so much, and honestly, I didn't get to live in a time where it existed, but I dreamed of it. That was one thing I wished was still around, but our world didn't have a use for that industry.

"You didn't!" I squealed.

"What can I say?" He sang the line from the famous song, finishing the rest with a hum.

"This one is my favorite," I said.

He side-eyed me. "They're *all* your favorites."

"True, but this one resonates with me."

"Why is that?" Adrian asked.

My stomach released another loud grumble.

"Because she turns into a raging lava monster if she isn't fed," Malachi answered.

No, only when my heart is broken, I thought to myself. I instantly wished my mind hadn't taken such a dark turn with one comment.

Niall came in, carrying plates, saving me from myself without realizing it. He leaned over me, setting it down and kissing me as I murmured my thanks.

"What just happened there in your thoughts?" Adrian asked.

"Hmm?" I asked, shoveling in a mouthful, moaning around the intensity of the flavor.

"I felt it too," Malachi said, looking at Niall and he nodded in agreement.

It clicked.

The bond. As soon as a touch of melancholy had hit me, they would have felt it too. That was going to take some getting used to. Some of those painful thoughts—the ones that made me feel like a Debbie downer—those were private. I'd never shared them out loud with anyone.

When I stayed silent, Adrian spoke up again. "You don't have to answer something if you don't want to, Nikki. Being your mate doesn't entitle us to your every thought, but you have to understand that we *do* feel your emotions change. We feel the fluctuations, just as you'll feel it in us."

I hadn't realized it, but he was right. Somehow I felt like I had the short end of the stick. If they felt through the bond, they knew it was me. If I felt through the bond, I wondered if I would know which one it was, or would I have to play the guessing game.

"It doesn't bother you that I don't want to share it?"

"No, but we can't help it if we worry, especially if the emotion feels akin to distress, sadness, or anger."

"Okaaay," I said, dragging out the vowels. "So I'm sensing that's basically any emotion that isn't in the realm of happiness."

"Pretty much," Niall said.

There was a lot we'd have to get used to, it would seem. In the meantime, I was content finishing my dinner and enjoying a night with my mates.

With Niall on one side and Adrian on the other, I cuddled between them on the couch. Malachi sat on the floor in front of me with my leg draped over his shoulder and resting on his chest. He absentmindedly and gently stroked my skin, savoring the connection between us.

We ate in silence until the end of the movie, but I noticed for the most part that I could sense when they watched me whenever I laughed. And when a movie had a singing, villainous crab, a screaming rooster and an anthropomorphic ocean, I spent most of my time doing just that.

I sat up and scooted around Malachi, then started to collect the dishes off the coffee table when Malachi stopped me, placing his hand on my wrist lightly. "I'll get it."

"You know I can take care of this, right?"

"Of course I do. But there's three of us. We can also take care of you, so let us."

As he cleaned up and took everything to the kitchen, I sat quietly with my thoughts. I'd be the first to admit, I had no idea what having a single mate would be like, much less three. One thing I certainly didn't expect was to have a personal chef, or spending evenings cuddled between them while we watched my favorite movies. I didn't expect to be taken care of on an emotional level.

My temperature had remained steady, and my belly was full. It had been a few hours and my body hadn't reacted to their presence beyond feeling love. I wondered if my heat was over completely. If it was, we needed to contact Courtney.

"Do you think . . ." I started, then trailed off.

"That your heat is over?" Niall said, finishing the sentence for me, and I nodded. "No. I sense something below the surface."

"Like what?" I looked down at my body, seeing that everything looked normal to me.

"You're still in heat. It's like your phoenix is resting for the next round."

"Really?" I asked, glancing at Adrian, and he nodded in agreement.

"Guess you're ours for a little bit longer," Malachi said, winking at me as he entered the room. Sitting back on the floor, he draped my leg over him the same way it had been before. Reaching back over his shoulder, he lifted the remote and handed it to Adrian. "Dealer's choice."

"Why does Adrian get to pick?" I asked.

"Because he won rock, paper, scissors," Malachi answered.

Niall moaned. "Here we go."

Adrian grinned and turned on . . . *Love Actually?*

"What?" I busted out laughing. "A rom-com? Consider me shocked."

"I'm a man of many tastes," he replied.

Niall scoffed and Adrian shot him a glare. "Look here, Rambo, at least I have range."

"Why is he Rambo?" I couldn't wait to hear more.

"Because he only likes action movies—which I have watched with you without complaints, by the way," he said, addressing Niall.

I chuckled. "That's okay. Malachi likes really bad disaster movies."

"They are not *bad*," Malachi said defensively.

"I'm not saying they're not entertaining. I'm just saying they're bad movies." We'd had the conversation so many times in our teens, but I would never change my mind.

"They are shittastic, thank you very much," he muttered.

I held my hands up in surrender. "You won't hear an argument from me. But personally I feel like it's refreshing to have a rom-com. I love vignette movies."

Adrian put his arm on the back of his couch, and I took that as my invitation to lean against him and put my head near his shoulder. He bent his arm and played with my hair. With one leg draped over Malachi's chest as he sat in front of the couch, my other leg was sprawled on Niall's lap. He kept his hand resting on my thigh just above my knee as he stroked my skin with his fingertips.

When one of the character's stumbled through their

words as they tried to explain themselves and their affections, Malachi gave me a little leg squeeze.

That simple flirtatious touch traveled, setting my nerve endings on fire. The heat returned with a powerful wave, and each mate felt the change instantly. Malachi turned around, and with my legs over his shoulder, the motion resulted in spreading my legs wider. His hungry eyes met mine. My skin flushed, and the touch of Niall's hand had turned from a gentle caress to a possessive grip, moving up my thigh. Adrian's fingers tightened in my hair, and he turned my head towards him, covering my mouth with his.

My phoenix had awakened for a final round, and this time she was demanding all three of them.

While I had no complaints, it didn't escape me that she really was a domineering hussy.

CHAPTER 35
ADRIAN

Nikki had been asleep for hours. She'd finally come out of the heat, and her body went into a rest and recovery mode.

A heat coupled with a mating frenzy with two mates was . . . intense.

While Malachi and I had been with Nikki, Niall had spent the time basically on guard duty. But when her phoenix wanted the three of us, we could hardly tell her no.

We had no idea if anything had changed in regard to the trials or the election. Malachi had volunteered to take a walk around the embassy to see if there was anything that he could learn, or if there were any conversations he could listen in on.

Niall sat in a wingback chair with his head tilted back and his eyes closed. I considered doing the same. A nap didn't sound too bad.

Just as I started to follow suit, the door opened, and Malachi came in, closing it behind him quickly. I would have asked him casually if there was anything that he'd heard, but judging by the look on his face, the answer was yes—and it was big.

"What?" I asked, not bothering to drag out the inquiry.

"Another murder," he answered, sitting down in chair and scrubbing his hand down his face.

"Who told you?"

"No one. I overheard a group of council members talking about it before coming around the corner."

"They were just casually talking about this and didn't realize you were there?"

"Of course not. I just have remarkable hearing and I'm good at sneaking around. Comes from years of being an orphan in Manhattan."

"Shit," Niall muttered. "Another Earth and Emerald candidate?"

"No." Malachi shook his head. "This time it was the vampire from the Tepes clan."

I cursed. "How was the body found?"

"The usual way vampires are found dead. Decapitated and burned."

"Was there a message this time?" Nikki asked. We had no idea how long she'd been standing there, but clearly she'd heard enough. She startled us the moment we heard her voice.

Malachi shook his head. "Not this time."

"That means whoever our murderer is followed us," she said, biting her lip as she thought.

"We have no way of knowing who it is, or why they're killing candidates," I said, trying to assuage her concerns.

"Do you think it was one of the council members?" she asked, looking at all of us.

"What do they have against everybody in the election? Two members of their own House have been killed. What purpose would that serve?" I asked.

"I don't know. Why does *anybody* go around murdering

anyone? Self-defense is one thing, but if you're asking me to try to explain the logic of an assassin, that's like trying to reason with crazy. It just isn't possible."

"You think it has something to do with the syndicates and not wanting us in the election?" Malachi suggested.

"Then why kill Earth and Emerald members first?" Niall countered.

"I don't know. To make it look like it was us? To throw us off their scent?"

I shook my head. "There are a lot of possibilities here, but it's all speculation. We have no proof that it was either side. What we have is a pile of dead bodies, and two out of the three left a message—one of which we know for sure was meant for Nikki." I ran my hands through my hair, trying to think if we'd missed something.

A knock on the door sounded, and Nikki jumped, her eyes going wide.

Malachi's pupils tightened, and his claws elongated. Niall was up in a flash, claws extending on his hands as well. I held my hand out to him shaking my head. "Hold that." We were all prepared to protect her, but I needed them to be cautious. A dragon and a demon raging in the hallways of the embassy wouldn't do us any good.

"Announce yourself," I called out as I approached the door.

"It's Courtney. If it's still . . . if you need more time, I can come back." Her voice was hesitant, unsure of how to phrase what she needed to say. What she meant was if Nikki was still in heat and we needed more time to fuck.

I cracked open the door and I was met by Hekate's assistant. Through a grim look, she managed to force a smile.

"I came to check on Nikki," she said softly.

"Come on in." I opened the door to allow her through.

She came inside, dipping her head in my direction and giving me a polite thanks. As soon as she saw Nikki, she caught on very quickly as to what we'd been talking about.

"Ah. I see you've heard."

"I overheard some councilmen talking about it," Malachi said.

"Well, I'm sorry that you had to hear it that way. I intended on coming to check on Nikki before breaking that news to you. It would seem I'm too late."

"That's okay." My mate shifted her weight as she spoke. "I'm not entirely sure there's ever a good time to break news like that. Has Clan Tepes been notified?"

"They have. They are *not* pleased." She shook her head, running a hand over her brow. "I don't think there's *ever* been a more stressful time during our trials. None of this has ever happened before, and now it's threatening to ruin relations, and fingers are being pointed in every direction as to who should be blamed, but so far in the investigation—" She cut herself off, realizing that she was ranting and probably giving up too much information. "Sorry, that's not what I came here to say."

"Will the election continue?" Niall asked.

"As Nikki has completed her heat, yes. The trials will recommence immediately."

"Are we allowed to know what it is this time?" Malachi stepped forward casually. I couldn't tell if he'd heard something or not. We'd not had the opportunity to get that far.

"As a matter of fact, yes. The next trial requires that you negotiate passage for port access to the ocean via the rivers."

"Passage?" Nikki repeated, narrowing her eyes in confusion.

Courtney nodded in confirmation.

"Are you telling me that Earth and Emerald can't negotiate passage with Sea and Serpentine themselves?" I asked, crossing my arms and tilting my head. Something about this didn't make sense to me.

"Not on the west coast, we can't. Asbesta doesn't care for us for much."

"And if we can't succeed where your House has already failed?" I pressed.

"You'll be watched and judged on the merit of your work and negotiation tactics, of course. Diplomacy is key. To be perfectly honest, unless you killed somebody, I'm not entirely sure our relations with the Pacific branch of Sea and Serpentine can get any worse," she muttered.

Seeing that we were syndicate, murdering people to get what we wanted was sort of the way we did things. Not that that would have been part of our plan. A good negotiator knew their audience. Sea and Serpentine controlled all water sources, and in many ways had the upper hand because of it. I kept my smartass comments to myself.

"Are you allowed to answer any questions?" Niall asked and Courtney inclined her head. "What is the passage for?"

"Trade. Earth and Emerald covers the entire East Coast land wise, but Fire and Fluorite cover the west. We already have agreements in place with their House for land trade, and we've worked with Sea and Serpentine to negotiate water access on the East Coast. We're not entirely sure if their distrust of Fire and Fluorite is what's holding us up here on this side, but we still need access. Magic can only solve so much."

It was true. Getting supplies wasn't exactly as easy as an *I Dream of Jeannie* nod of the head. The population was still large, and humans and supernaturals alike needed trade. Portals were expensive and complicated, and access to them wasn't as easy as just creating them constantly for the purpose of transporting goods all over the world.

"You want the remaining candidates to negotiate with Sea and Serpentine for the same thing?" I considered Courtney as she listened, looking for any sign that she was keeping something from me. "Seems like an odd thing to do. That's more of a committee type activity rather than a solo mission."

"Exactly. If there's one thing that I've learned in my time as Hekate's assistant, it's that you might be a great leader and you might be quite intelligent, but working together as a team and using all resources at your disposal is just as important as knowing how to govern people and the land. To achieve a goal, you sometimes have to work with your enemies, and sometimes you work with your friends, and sometimes you work with your competition."

"Strength in numbers," Malachi mumbled, "just on an intellectual level."

"Precisely." She smiled. "I won't tell you how to arrange this yourselves, but I would not suggest an every man for himself approach."

I cleared my throat. "All right. When do we begin?"

"Immediately. I'll let the council know that Nikki is no longer in heat. If you don't have any more questions . . ." she trailed off, waiting for us to speak. When none of us did, she continued, "Okay, then. Good luck to you all. You have one week."

She turned around and left, closing the door behind her.

"I don't know where we'd even start," Nikki said, mostly talking to herself while she walked around the room. After a moment, she looked up with wide eyes. "Does anybody know a witch that can do transfiguration?"

"What for?" Niall scrunched his brows.

"Thinking maybe I could do, like a reverse *Little Mermaid*."

"Oh no," Malachi said, placing his hand over his mouth to hide the smile.

"Instead of a mermaid being turned into a human, maybe I can be turned into a mermaid? And then I can go into the water, and I can negotiate on our behalf." She crossed her arms, and she was dead serious.

Malachi bit his lip, laughing through his nose. "Did you plan on asking a singing crab or a talking fish for directions to Empress Asbesta's palace?"

She rolled her eyes. "No. I figured I'd run into a selkie or a siren somewhere along the way, jackass. You could all join me too. Be merman." She wiggled her eyebrows.

I shrugged. "I can't believe I'm saying this, but I'm actually not opposed to this idea. I'd prefer it was the backup plan, though."

Niall knew me well, and I may have hated syndicate life, but I was good at my job. He tilted his head, considering me. "What are you thinking?"

"Thinking about calling a friend."

"You know people here?" Nikki asked, genuinely intrigued.

"I know a few." I reached into my pocket and pulled out my cell phone. My magic signature opened it, and I used voice command. "Call Queen Dannika."

"Of Blood and Beryl?" Her lips parted, forming an 'o'.

I winked at her just as the other line was answered.

"Adrian Rose." The queen's soft voice sounded cheerful.

"Queen Dannika," I said in greeting.

She groaned softly. "It's really okay. You can call me Danni."

"The last time I did, King Elias suggested my head would look lovely on a pike outside your palace."

"Oh, he's full of it. He isn't going to do anything. Besides, the last time we spoke was at the winter solstice. You'd felt . . . your mate was nearby. Did you find her?"

"I'm actually here in Portland right now, and my mate is with me."

"Oh, Adrian." I could hear the smile in her voice. "I'm so happy for you."

Niall cleared his throat, waving his hand in a circular motion for me to continue the rest of that statement.

"Thanks." I shooed him away. "We're all running for the Chancellor of Earth and Emerald."

"All?" she repeated, confused.

"Me, my mate, and her other two mates."

"Oh? Oh, ooooh," she said again, then dropping her voice. "Oh, wow, um . . . I—"

"It's different, I know," I began, thinking about how I was going to present the arrangement. She and the king had publicly backed me, and that connection mattered during the actual election process. Constituents liked knowing their chancellor played nicely with other Houses. Blood and Beryl were great allies to have. "It's not exactly what you, Elias, and I had discussed when we met up earlier this year. One of her mates is Niall, and her other mate is—"

"Adrian, stop explaining yourself," she said softly, cutting me off. "Would you choose them?"

"Choose them?" I asked.

"You chose to accept her, and she chose to accept them. Do *you* accept them?"

"Yes." I didn't have to think about it.

"Then that's all that matters."

A small smile formed. "I appreciate that, Danni. Very much. I value your opinion more than you know." I paused for a moment, then added, "Will King Elias feel the same way?"

"They're your mates too, in a way, so yes. He will. If she's your mate and they're your mate's mates—What I am trying to say is the mate bond is different, and it creates a binding circle of trust, devotion, and loyalty. Usually, anyway. When you both accept it—in this case, the four of you. The point is, if you trust them, we trust you. Which is a lot of trust—I'm going to stop talking and saying the word trust now." She sighed.

I couldn't help but laugh, and Nikki gave me a look. Her eyebrows scrunched together in a frown while she twisted her lips to the side.

"Goddesses help me," she muttered. "Being diplomatic and finding the right words is an absolute mess sometimes."

"I hope I have the opportunity to be in the same position at the end of the election; being diplomatic and finding the right words."

"Well, feel free to call me anytime so you can sound like an idiot, and it can make me feel better," she said. "I'm assuming you're all in Portland for the trials?"

"We are, and I need a favor. Our next trial is negotiating river passage with Sea and Serpentine on behalf of Earth and Emerald."

She groaned. "Of course it is. What can I do?"

"I have zero connections with Sea and Serpentine. Just tell me where to start. Just point me in the direction and I can go from there."

"Now that is something I can help with. I'm assuming you're staying at the embassy?" I hummed in response.

"There's a pub in No Man's Land called The Salty Siren. When you get there, go up to the bar and look for Myra. She's a mermaid."

"She isn't the one I negotiate with, is she? That seems too easy."

Danni laughed. "Most definitely not, but she'll be able to get you in touch with the right people. Sea and Serpentine are notoriously shady, well-hidden, and standoffish. We have to go through hoops to speak with Asbesta as well. Whatever the mermaid says, do it."

"Thank you, Danni. I owe you one."

"I'll hold you to that." Just as I thought our conversation had come to an end, she added, "Oh, one more thing. When you see the mermaid, try to be *charming*."

"I'm always charming."

She hummed in response. "Not syndicate charming."

"Fair enough."

"Is Niall with you?"

"Yes," I said slowly, meeting his gaze. He'd heard his name.

"Tell him not to be a dick."

I barked a laugh as the queen chuckled and said goodbye.

"She has you pegged, brother," I said, looking at Niall. He rolled his eyes.

"I'm not a dick. I just don't have any patience," he grumbled.

I glanced at Nikki. "Did I sense some jealousy?"

"No." The answer was not at all convincing and it came just a little bit too fast. I wrapped my arm around her waist and pulled her to me, planting a kiss on her.

"Get ready," I said, nipping at her lips. "We have a date at The Salty Siren."

CHAPTER 36
NIKKI

THE SALTY SIREN WAS AN INTERESTING NAME, CONSIDERING THE mermaid that owned it.

Niall held the door open for me like a gentleman even though he, Malachi, and Adrian had just fucked me seven ways to Sunday.

Was it Sunday? I shrugged.

That was okay. I liked them better that way.

I stepped into the dimly lit atmosphere, not entirely sure what to expect. I didn't get to hang out in bars much when I was in New York—and I had never left the boroughs.

Dad wouldn't allow it. It would ruin the image of his sweet, innocent little bargaining chip.

When I did sneak out, there were very few who would let the daughter of the don inside. Sam typically had to pay them off so they would turn the other way. At least until my last birthday when my favorite brother gifted me the best damn glamour ring there ever was. He didn't anticipate I'd use it on my missions for the Movement more than I would enjoying my twenties.

To say that I was curious was a bit of an understate-ment. The scents of smoke and saltwater washed over me. It wasn't like tobacco where the smoke was harsh. There was a soft undertone to it. Something that made you want to lean in and breathe deeper. Inhale more. I didn't resist the urge and took a nice lungful. My senses calmed as my skin began to prickle. Not in a bad way, just sensitive.

Malachi brushed a hand over my lower back, and I had to bite down on a groan. I'd literally just come out of heat. And yeah, I healed fast, but my sex drive really needed to get in the backseat for a hot second.

I stopped in my tracks only a few feet in, admiring the atmosphere. Red brick, aged from time. Dark wood was used for the floors, seats, and tables. Metal accents gave it an industrial feel, but not cold. It was a bit rustic too, with all the distressed tabletops and old tin cans serving as napkin holders. My mom would have loved it. We had the same look in our house, minus things my father would consider trash. He never saw the point in repurpos-ing. Our house was more intentional, trying to go for this same vibe, but not quite meeting it. Here, nicks and chips marred every table and chair. The furniture that had fabric was riddled with tears that had been patched with mis-matching material. The metal end tables had small dents, probably from fights that broke out. It was a bar, after all.

There were skylights that showed the night sky above us, not that you could see many of the stars with the faerie lights in here. Hovering over the center of tables and along the bar were candlesticks that burned but didn't melt. In contrast, the faerie lights were like a ball of flame, contained in an invisible sphere the size of my fist. They moved around the ceiling, keeping every corner of the place lit enough that nothing too skeevy would probably go down in a dark corner.

Depending on who was in the corner I probably wouldn't be taking any chances, regardless.

After a single sweep, I turned towards the bar.

"I'm going to go talk to Myra and see what I can learn about our little predicament here."

"I'll go with," Adrian said, stepping up.

"Actually, I think I should go alone."

Slightly flustered by whatever was in the air and feeling a little too warm for being out in public, I tucked a stray hair behind my ear just for it to bounce back out and agitate the hell out of me.

"I just don't want her to think that we're ganging up on her. If we bombard her with questions, she might not be as willing to talk. I don't know if you guys realize this, but you can be intimidating. Even you," I said to Adrian. "I'm a woman. I'm small. I'm inconspicuous. For a shifter, I'm especially tiny, and well, I don't feel like seeing anyone flirt with you guys." Adrian's lips parted before a chuckle escaped him. The guys all seemed to find that hilarious.

"Nikki, you know that we wouldn't flirt with anyone," Malachi said, not so subtly tossing his arm over my shoulder. "Not that I think Niall could flirt if he tried."

My dragon pursed his lips, shaking his head at him, completely unamused.

"I never said you would. I said I don't want to see *her* flirt with you—any of you. It happens everywhere we go and I'm feeling sensitive to it right now after . . . you know." Their grins said they understood perfectly what I meant. "Why don't you do some rounds. Order a few drinks. See what you overhear from the other people while I talk to her. I'll join you after."

"Just don't do anything rash, okay?" Malachi said, squeezing my shoulder.

"Rash?" I repeated. "I would never." I touched my chest, acting mock offended. Okay, maybe it wasn't completely mock. What was it with people calling me rash or impulsive? I was quick on my feet. Decisive in stressful situations. I knew how to pivot. It wasn't a bad thing. It all depended on how you framed it . . . And maybe what kind of movies you watched.

Malachi rolled his eyes, letting his arm drop away from my shoulder. Adrian clapped him on the back, flashing me a wink before pulling him in the opposite direction.

Niall hesitated, torn between following the others and staying with me.

"Don't drink anything even if the bartender offers it." After a suspended moment, he added, "Please."

I could be annoyed and tell him he was being high-handed, but not only had he softened the approach, this wasn't about him being overprotective. It was about safety. My safety.

As Nikki Ward, the syndicate princess, my life was a beautiful cage. Not just to keep me in, but to keep dangers out.

Now I was that and so much more. I was running for a House. I actually stood a shot of winning it too. People had killed for far less.

"I won't. I promise."

"I'm going to go sit with them, but I'll keep you in my line of sight. If you need anything at all—" I cut him off by lifting my hand, a slight smile curling the edge of my lips. "I know." I put that hand on his cheek and kissed him softly.

"I'm just going to talk to the bartender and find out who we need to talk to next, then I'll join you."

He dipped his chin in acknowledgment and took a step closer. Niall wrapped an arm around my waist, pressing his firm lips against mine. His tongue slid into my mouth, making a statement for anyone and everyone to see. I was his—and he was mine. The possessive kiss left my skin tingling and my panties wet.

"One more thing, mate, "he said, murmuring against my mouth. "No flirting with another guy. Not even to be nice. I might just drag him out back and rip his arm off to beat him with it. We wouldn't want that now, would we?"

My lips parted and he flashed me a smirk like the arrogant asshole he was. If I hadn't just pointedly said that I didn't want them flirting with the bartender, I might have tried to be sassy back and give him some song and dance about how I'll flirt with who I want.

But, what's good for the goose is good for the gander.

Niall already had to share me with two other men. I wouldn't tolerate the jealous crap between them, but I wasn't going to further inflame his possessive instincts or disrespect *any* of my mates by coming on to someone else.

Or letting them come on to me.

I turned on my heel and started for the bar.

It wasn't terribly packed, but a motorcycle gang of shifters took up most of it. They wore worn leather jackets with 'The Ark' stitched on the back. Beneath it was a literal Ark, as in Noah's Ark.

Whoever's idea that was, at least they had a sense of humor.

I took the only seat that had another empty one beside it.

To my right, a big, beefy man with dark brown skin and yellow eyes surveyed me.

362

"You're not from around here." He cast me a sideways glance.

"Nope," I agreed, mindful of the three sets of eyes practically drilling a hole in my back. "I'm taken too," I added, pulling down the collar of my shirt enough to let him see my fully healed mate marks.

Niall's in particular was a bit, shall we say, savage.

The biker's mouth curled up in a grin and he chuckled.

"Not hitting on you, darlin'. You're probably my daughter's age or younger. I'm no cradle robber."

My muscles relaxed, feeling a tiny bit more at ease.

Big scary men didn't really scare me.

I grew up around them.

My brothers were big guys. My guards were big guys. Hell, my mates were huge.

Size didn't quantify anything in my eyes.

I was more wary of the kind of man that didn't take no for an answer.

Since he seemed like he was nice enough and wasn't making any moves on me—we were good.

"Those three blokes in the back yours?" I didn't have to follow his gaze when he thrusted his chin in my mate's direction.

"Yup," I said. "Those are mine."

He smiled again; this time fuller.

"You're a good woman," he said. "Making it clear you're taken. Although, I gotta ask, three? Ain't that a crowd?"

I snorted. "Yeah, that's about what I said when I first found out." I picked at my nails without looking at them. The bartender was at the other end helping some of his brothers with their orders still. "I guess the fates decided to throw three of them my way. Must have done something good in a past life. Or not. Some days it's hard to say."

He chuckled again, a deep but genuine laugh. "Well, good for you, little lady."

"How about you?" I asked, finding myself more curious about the stranger I'd struck up a conversation with. "Got a mate?"

His smile dimmed. "You must not know who we are." He motioned to the two dozen or so men that took up most of the bar. My quizzical gaze answered him. "The Ark was built to carry one male and one female from every species. Us here, we're men that lost our mates. A widowed brotherhood. These boys held me together when my Lucia died."

My heart panged with sympathy for him.

I'd heard stories of what losing one's mate could do.

A lot of people died.

And those that didn't, they seemed to just waste away.

Like their will to live was gone.

Or, you know, half their soul was no longer here.

Some of them lost their minds.

A fair portion killed themselves.

I'd been told it wasn't common for someone to lose their mate and move on in life.

I felt a sense of camaraderie with them. Marissa wasn't my mate, but twins were more connected than anyone could possibly understand.

"That's really awesome," I said, feeling kind of lame.

He smiled again, showing pure white against his umber skin.

He wore long locs like Malachi and kept them tied back out of his face.

"Yeah," he agreed. "It is pretty awesome. Ay, Myra!" he called out. The mermaid at the other end of the bar snapped her head up, sending her flowing black hair flying. Piercing blue eyes stared him down.

364

"What do you want, Uriah?"

The biker next to me, Uriah presumably, clicked his tongue. "Now, is that any way to talk to your customers?"

The mermaid huffed. "Please feel free to file an official complaint with our HR department—oh wait, we don't have one because nobody here gives a shit." She practically glided along the back of the bar, coming to a stop in front of us.

"I'll take a lager. Whatever you got on tap." The mermaid's hands moved, reaching to grab a glass without looking away.

"And you?"

She filled a massive beer mug for him and didn't spill a drop. It was unnerving.

"Oh, nothing for me. I'm good."

Her eyebrows came together in a curious expression.

As she slid the beer across the counter, Uriah rolled a tiny vial of blood her way for payment. She pocketed it between her boobs, still watching me.

"If you're not thirsty, then why are you at the bar?"

Well, then. Wasn't she direct?

I could get on board with that.

"Friend of a friend sent me here." I leaned forward in my seat. "I'm looking for information."

Her eyes narrowed and she crossed her arms, jutting out her hip.

"What kind of information?"

I tilted my head, lowering my voice. There was enough background noise that most people wouldn't hear us, but you could never be too careful. "I need an in with someone from Sea and Serpentine. To make a deal."

A second passed, then her eyes widened a tiny fraction.

KEL CARPENTER & AURELIA JANE

"You're a candidate," she said, suddenly more interested.

I pressed my lips together and dipped my chin.

"Well, I'll be damned."

She looked over my shoulder, eyebrows rising. I had a good idea of who she was looking at.

"Can you help me?" I asked, drawing her attention from the three men across the room and back to me. Call me territorial, but I didn't care for other people's eyes on my mates.

I was theirs unequivocally. Irrevocably.

But I was still insecure about our bond.

Who wouldn't be? Security took time. Trust took years. They were making an effort ,we all were, but with the fading aftereffects of my first heat and newly healed mate marks—I wasn't overly keen to test my still budding relationship with three different men.

"I might know a guy." She took a wet rag from beneath the counter and started wiping it down. "What's the trial?"

I bit the inside of my cheek debating how much to tell her. The trials weren't made public until after they were over for good reason. While it wasn't explicitly a rule that we couldn't tell people, you always ran the risk of the public complicating it further.

That said, I needed her help more than I needed secrecy.

"I need to make a deal with Sea and Serpentine."

"What kind of deal?"

"Trade deal. We need access to the Columbia River."

Whatever she thought about my admission wasn't revealed in her features as she slowly continued to clean the already clean bar top.

"The embassy's in the middle of No Man's Land, but Earth and Emerald doesn't have territory that touches us.

366

You gotta cross other House borders to get here, but if you have access to the river—that changes things. Opens up a lot of opportunities." She tilted her head working through the situation with very little to go on. It was impressive in a way. "It's a good idea. Perfect for a trial, if nearly impossible."

I didn't comment. She was direct enough that I got the feeling we were approaching whatever her price for the information was. It seemed better to wait and let her bring it up on her own, instead of being rude and hurrying her along, as Niall certainly would have.

"What's in it for me?"

Without blinking, I answered, "A crisp high five and the afterglow of doing a good deed."

Her hand stopped. The bar seemed quiet for a moment. I could tell Uriah's attention was also on us. The second suspended for too long for my liking, before she threw her head back and laughed raucously without regard.

"Funny," she said, "I like that—but seriously. What's in it for me?"

I lifted my shoulders. "I don't exactly have a lot of bargaining power yet, but I've got a good sense of humor. How's that saying go? Use what your mama gave you."

A deep baritone rumbled from Uriah laughing into his beer, followed by choking as it went down the wrong side.

"True—but that doesn't really help me, does it?" She gave me a wry smile. It was better than the scowl she'd been giving the bikers. Although I got the feeling, the scowl was more of a "you're here whether I'm nice or not so I don't have to give a fuck" versus an actual fuck off.

But admittedly, I wasn't all that familiar with these situations.

So I could have read it wrong.

"Here's the reality of the situation: unless you can convince the sea witch to let me set foot in the water again, there's nothing you have that I want. Given you're here for an 'in' with her, I'm going to take an educated guess and say that's not something you can do."

I pressed my lips together in a silent no. "If by 'sea witch' you mean Asbesta, then probably not. I don't have any more negotiating power with her than I do with you, I'm afraid. But I won't forget this either. Nothing comes free in this world. If you help me, I will find a way to repay it later."

"Or maybe you can now . . ." The mermaid considered my offer, then extended her hand.

"Give Asbesta a message for me and we'll call it even."

"All right, what's the message?"

"Just tell her I'm ready to talk. She'll know what it means."

"Deal." I took her hand, and we shook on it.

"Good, now go to No Man's Circus and ask for the ring-master, D. He'll tell you what to do."

"Thank you, I really appreciate—"

She chuckled. "I wouldn't thank me yet. I may be understanding about some things, but D . . ." She trailed off for a second before finishing. "He doesn't do anything for free. Be prepared to pay."

I swallowed.

Well, that wasn't ominous.

Letting one leg slide from the barstool, I was turning away when Uriah suddenly said, "You'd make a good chancellor." I paused. "Nikki, right?" I nodded. "I was from Earth and Emerald before The Ark. My daughter is still there with her mate. He's a piece of shit. She's taking care of both my grandbabies while she saves up to leave him. I may not be part of the House anymore, but I care about what goes on there. Anyway, I got some friends back home. They'll be voting for you."

My lips parted.

There's the initial awkwardness of not being sure what to say, but then the manners that were instilled in me kicked in, forcing their way between my lips.

"Thank you," I said sincerely. "I really appreciate that."

"You've done good in the trials so far." He paused to take a drink of his beer. "Keep it up. I think you got what you need to win. Just don't let them boys of yours drag you down too much. They may be your mates, but they've got trouble written all over them."

"Looks can be deceiving." I nodded pointedly toward him and his motorcycle club. Uriah smiled.

"Fair enough, little lady. You make a right good point there. Have a good one, and be safe in them trials."

"You too," I said, pausing a second longer before walking away. "Hit me up when the election is over. I can help your daughter."

I didn't stand around awkwardly waiting for thanks. I didn't need it. Whether I won or not, if there's anything I had in this world, it was wealth. If what she needed was the means, that was easy enough for me to provide.

My pants pressed a tad too tight on my stomach from how bad I needed to pee.

I may not have drank anything here, but I practically guzzled a gallon of water before we left.

Not sure if that was the best idea, but hey, heats were a lot of work. A hand painted sign labeled "shitter" sat above the hallway on my left. I turned for it, making eye contact with Niall. Just as he promised, he was watching me with a clear line of sight.

I hooked my thumb toward the bathroom and mouthed, *be right back*.

He nodded once. I turned down the dark hallway. The door at the end opened and closed, letting a cold gust of wind funnel toward me as it bounced off the narrow walls.

I paused outside the door that had "ladies or whatever" written in pink.

I expected it to be one of those disgusting bathrooms where you wished you had paper towels that you could place on the toilet seat just to sit down and pee. You know the places I'm talking about. Where the edges of the toilet have built up grime. The sink has exposed pipes with rust.

The lights flicker and the hand soap is usually out.

I was pleasantly surprised that wasn't the case.

It was simple but clean. A small bathroom with two stalls.

The same rustic wood flooring from the rest of the bar continued. The stall doors had little ship wheels that you turned like knobs to open and close.

I thought that was kind of cool as I sat down to go about my business. As I flushed the toilet, I heard the door open again.

I walked out, heading for the sink, not paying attention. It was rude to stare. Not to mention, it's just weird in a public bathroom. Apparently that was my first mistake.

Someone came up behind me. One gloved hand wrapped around the back of my neck, propelling me forward. He—I was assuming a he unless they had fucking troll hands—slammed my face into the counter vanity. My forehead hit the metal with a bang. Spots danced in my vision, the edges turning black.

I tried to push back, but he was stronger.

When that failed, I turned my head to the side, my

cheek pressing against the cool stone.

Why did bad shit always happen to me at night when I was weakest? Like seriously fate, what the fuck?

If it wasn't midnight yet, it had to be close to it. This wasn't a new moon, so I could still start a fire if I really wanted. Niall's words about the day Marissa died quelled the urge. If I lost control, a lot of people might die.

I may not have killed her, but I had little doubt that I'd kill the rest of them in my phoenix's fiery rage. I had to think.

Even weak, I still healed pretty fast for a shifter. Small blessing that would be since he didn't seem to be doing anything to hurt me just yet, other than slamming me into the counter. Hot breath brushed across my earlobe as he leaned over, pressing his lips to my skin.

Ew. Hotdogs? Is this guy for real?

It was a common courtesy to brush your teeth or use a damn breath mint before assaulting someone. For fuck's sake.

"You should have backed out when you had the chance."

With the hand not holding me down, he reached around to undo the front of my jeans.

"What are you doing?"

"What's it look like, princess?"

Fear touched me with its cold hands, and my stomach roiled when my nickname came out of his disgusting mouth.

I'd been hurt in many, many ways, but not this.

Sure, a few guys got handsy when I was undercover at bars. It only took Sam ripping someone's arm off one time for the word to spread you don't fuck with her or anyone she's with. I'd never had it get this far.

It was a shock that seemed to freeze me in place for too long.

His rancid breath turned my stomach. He dropped the zipper on my jeans.

Thick fingers tried to push inside the rough denim material. Only thin panties and the tight cut of my jeans kept him from doing something more.

Breathe, I told myself, biding my time.

"I wonder what it is about this cunt," Mr. Hotdog Breath said. "Three guys. One girl. Either you're the best fucking lay there is, or that pussy is made of gold."

I waited patiently as he pulled his hand away from my panties. "I'm going to find out which it is."

Mr. Hotdog breath maneuvered his other hand to my backside, giving my ass a tight squeeze before his fingers curled over the edge of my waistband. He wanted my jeans off of me so he could assault me.

That wasn't going to happen.

I may be weaker at the tail end of my heat, probably dehydrated, definitely exhausted, and not at my strongest thanks to it being night . . . but I wasn't *weak*.

And I wasn't going to let anyone hurt me *ever again*.

I was a phoenix.

Fire itself.

If he tried to steal from me, *he would fucking burn.*

I shoved my elbow back into his sternum as hard as I could. He grunted, his hold on me slipping. I tucked the tip of my boot around the back of his ankle and used all my weight to yank my leg the side. My body spun as I pivoted with the momentum, turning so that I was facing him as he stumbled.

I brought my knee up, aiming for his junk. He maneuvered out of the way but still took the hit in the leg. As he

372

fell forward in an attempt to overwhelm me with his size, I threw my right elbow and hit him square in the jaw.

His head whipped to the side. I sidestepped, putting distance between us as I got a good look at my attacker. He was tall, not as tall as Niall, but just as broad. His skin was taupe and scarred. The color of eyes would have been brown, but they were effervescent green with slits like a snake. Scales ran along his neck and disappeared beneath plain nondescript clothing.

I had no doubt he was a hitman for hire and not some rando from the bar. But who hired him?

"Tisk ,Tisk," he said. "You shouldn't have done that." A bruise blossomed across his cheek from where my elbow hit him, coloring an otherwise nasty expression.

"Lemme guess, 'I'll regret it'?" I mocked him, using finger quotations.

His gaze hardened. A snake tongue slid from between his parted lips.

I snorted a laugh despite the fear coursing through my veins. That confirmed what kind of shifter I was dealing with at least.

"Oh, I'm sorry, did I steal your punchline? I was gonna regret you assaulting me, so I figured throwing a few punches was just good manners." I challenged him to say otherwise with a lifted brow. His scowl deepened. If I had to guess, he wasn't a fan of my smartass mouth. Well, get in line, buddy.

Hotdog Breath the snake shifter charged me.

I sidestepped it with the one major advantage I still had. Speed.

I was a bird, for fuck's sake.

He might move fast, but you know what hunted snakes? Birds.

I didn't usually think of myself as a predator, but today I was going to be one. I was over being the victim.

He missed me and caught himself on the edge of the stall.

I rounded to grab the metal hand soap dispenser and swung for his head as I turned back around.

He turned too, taking the blow straight to the temple.

Nikki: two.

Hotdog Breath: zero.

Another bruise instantly formed there, black and blue leeching into his face like poison. It spread from the temple to his eyes, turning the white of his eye red.

"You bitch," he growled.

"Wow," I said blandly. "You're so creative. I've never heard that one before. I'd ask if you also thought you were a nice guy, but I suspect I already know the answer." His brows dipped for a moment, just a little too slow on the uptake.

I threw the soap dispenser at his head and dashed for the door.

A hand fisted the back of my shirt. I didn't even make it three feet.

"NIA—" I started to scream at the top of my lungs.

My back hit a hard chest as he pulled me into him and slapped a hand over my mouth.

"Now you've done it," he hissed. "I was just gonna have a little fun with you after my warning and be on my way." Teeth sank into the joint where my neck met my shoulder. I screamed through his hand and fire rose to the very surface of my skin.

He yelped, releasing me from his fangs but not his hold. Guess he didn't like the burn.

I twisted in his arms. Instead of diving away, I got a

374

good firm hold on his shirt before shoving him backwards into the open bathroom stall.

The back of his knees hit the toilet and he sank to his ass. His hands came up to grab the rail and toilet paper dispenser and he used them to launch himself at me.

Mindful of his longer reach, I stepped back and slammed the stall door on his head.

"Ugh!" he yelled again as it bounced off with a thud.

He grabbed for my face, and I bit him hard, tasting blood as I clamped my jaws down on the muscle between his thumb and index finger.

"Fucking devil woman," he grunted.

He tried to pull away, but I refused to let go. A chunk of his hand ripped off, stuck between my teeth, and I spat it on the floor.

"Says the wannabe rapist." I bared my mouth to him, letting him get a good look. I didn't have to look in a mirror to know that there was blood running down my face. I probably looked like an unhinged vampire in bloodlust.

"You're fucking crazy."

"You don't even know the half of it, Mr. Hotdog Breath."

I chuckled at his shock. Was everything moving slower or was it just me?

His foot snapped out. I tried to back away, but I was slow. He hit me square in the jaw.

My world tilted as my body tipped sideways and smacked into the hard floor.

"Well fuck. That hurt."

Disoriented, I couldn't fight him off when I felt something pull up my hair. His hand, I realized as he dragged me a couple of feet and lifted my head higher. Cool porcelain touched my neck.

OH HELL NO.

I was gonna be sick. He had me bent over the fucking toilet . . . and there was a faint yellow tint inside it.

"Do you know how many people pissed in these?" My voice came out sluggish and woozy.

"That's going to be the least of your worries," he laughed.

It took all my willpower to brace against the edge of the toilet seat. I clutched it hard, using what strength I still had to stop him as he tried to thrust my head forward into the bowl. No more than an inch or two separated me from the water.

I could survive a drowning, but I wasn't sure I wanted to if it was in a public toilet.

This was quite possibly the worst way to die.

My fingers curled around the plastic seat, nails digging into the hard finish.

I didn't want to hurt anyone, but he had me two seconds from throwing caution to the wind. Fire started beneath my fingertips. The toilet heated under my touch.

"Put that shit out or—"

The bathroom door swung open, and my attacker faltered. I smiled despite the extremely close and disgusting proximity to the dirty water.

I let the fire fizzle out as I threw all my weight to the side, ripping the toilet lid off its hinges.

I let my arm swing so hard I flipped my body around as I slammed the toilet seat into his throat.

"You are so fucked, Mr. Hotdog Breath."

I wasn't sure if he could understand me. He didn't really need to. His chest was heaving as he tried to scramble for air after the impact to his airway. His blind desperation to stop me from hitting him again, had him backing up.

Right into the arms of my waiting mates.

CHAPTER 37
MALACHI

THE HANDPRINT ON MY CHEST BURNED.

Nikki's emotions whipped through me, overwhelming my sense of self. When we entered the bathroom to find some fucker attempting to drown her in a toilet, red misted my vision like a wrath-filled lens.

A toilet seat clocked him in the throat. He gasped like a dog in heat, backing away.

Nikki's fear dissipated like ashes in the wind. She knew we were here. That she was safe.

I might have felt good about that under different circumstances.

"Going somewhere?"

The snake shifter let out a hiss when Niall wrapped a hand around the back of his neck. Niall flicked his attention to Adrian and thrust his head toward the stall where Nikki was splayed out, looking dazed.

The front of her pants had been unbuttoned, and the zipper undone.

"I was just gonna scare her, I swear!"

His yellow eyes stared at Niall, who wasn't laughing or

smiling maniacally as I'd expected. He struck me as the type that took enjoyment in hurting bad people. If that was the case, he didn't show it. While he looked every part the monster, he was one you'd never see coming.

Snake Eyes thought to try his luck with me instead, like I would somehow go easier on him.

Whoever this asshole was, he was a fucking idiot.

"F-oo-king Liiiiiiar," Nikki slurred.

I stepped to the side as Adrian moved to get past me. My demon claws popped out, threatening to puncture where I gripped the snake's shoulder.

Adrian crouched down low, making himself smaller as he approached Nikki. Her eyelids drooped; pupils blown. She could be mistaken for being "in the mood" with the way she was staring at us, were it not for the sickly black tendrils crawling up her neck and to the side of her face.

"Nikki," Adrian said softly, but there was a hard under-current to his tone. He was trying to keep himself in check so as not to scare her. She'd already been assaulted, even if the asshole didn't complete the act. The last thing she needed was more aggression, and out of the three of us, he was the most adept at keeping his own emotions under control. Adrian was the best at softening his approach for her. If the last six years didn't happen, that might have been me. But they had, and I wasn't the boy that left her.

I became a man forged by killing.

It created a darkness in me. A rage that was now threat-ening to consume what good was left.

"Whyyyyy you taaaalking like dat?" Nikki mumbled. Her eyelids dipped lower.

Black tendrils spread further across her face, bleeding into the whites of her eyes.

The thin band of color so close to black flashed crimson.

Some might have said it was the color of blood, but that wasn't true. Blood was deep and dark. Murky. Closer to maroon. It didn't glow. No, when she tilted her head back and the fluorescent light touched her eyes it became clear what it really was.

Fire.

"He bit her." The softness Adrian had aimed for bled away as he pulled the collar of her shirt down enough to see a cloying, festering mess where two fang marks had punctured her.

"No shit," I snapped.

"Will she be okay? I don't know—" Adrian was looking at Niall when he asked, but our mate wasn't down and out for the count just yet.

"Mm' fine," she mumbled. "Stupid hotdog . . . shoulda known better." She closed her eyes for a moment. With the nonsense she was spewing, Adrian wasn't the only one starting to worry.

Logically, I knew she was a phoenix. Rumors were nothing could kill them.

She was also my mate, which meant my logical brain wasn't home.

"Get her out of here," Niall said through clenched teeth.

"I'm going to pick you up now." Adrian grabbed her under the arms like a child. "I know this is scary, but you're going to be all right." He pulled her flush to his chest and then adjusted his hold. One arm went under her knees and the other banded around her back.

Nikki's eyelids fluttered. "'Course I am. Dum dum." She grumbled, her hand weakly swatting at his chest. "I'm fire. Phoenix. Badassss."

Adrian's eyebrows drew together.

"Okay, babe, you're a badass."

We didn't know what this asshole did, but something told me it was more than just scaring her "a little bit".

She did call him a liar, after all.

The bathroom door opened. Without looking, Niall said, "Get out."

"Yeah, no can do." The sassy mermaid shook her head. "You got an issue with someone, take it outside."

"Bloodstains are a biiiiitch to clean," Nikki said under her breath. Her words were still slurred, though they came through clearer that time.

"Exactly," the mermaid said motioning to her. "She understands."

Stepping into the bathroom, the mermaid held the door open. Myra waved her hand toward the exit with an impatient, "get a move on it" kind of look.

Our snake shifter got squirrelly. Scales emerged under my hand as he tried to shift into his animal form to get away.

Niall's voice deepened so low that it was hardly intelligible.

"Stop."

I didn't have an ounce of shifter blood in me, but even my spine snapped straight. Shifters talked about how an alpha's call could control them. I had no idea what his animal was, but with a command like that, he could be the alpha of alphas.

Snake Eyes froze, completely unmoving. His scales receded and his chest undulated as the reality of the situation started to set in.

"Come on, boys. Chop. Chop." Myra had an irreverent air that rivaled Nikki. Where my mate's was endearing, hers was *not*. "Don't make me get The Ark to come back here and help you along. Just take him out back and do your business there. I don't give a shit if you kill him, but it can't be in here."

I moved first, dropping my hand from her attacker.

Adrian had Nikki, and Niall had the snake shifter.

I'd make sure there was no one else waiting to join the party as I exited first. The mermaid dipped her chin in acknowledgment as I stepped out of the bathroom, heading straight to the rusted metal door that led outside.

I slammed my hand against the handlebar, and it flew open. The hinges screamed like a banshee before it slapped the exterior wall with a bang.

I held it open for our new friend walking death row.

It was Niall that grabbed my attention as he shoved the sack of shit ahead of him and out into the cold. His eyes glowed red hot like the end of a poker that had been in the fire. Slitted pupils appraised me, silently waiting to see if I'd ask the question.

A few animals had pupils like that, but I instinctively knew it wasn't anything I'd seen before. There were traces in his scent that were familiar, like Nikki's. He had a warmness that was hard to miss, but it was also distinctly different from anything else.

Adrian came through with Nikki, and her eyes were now open again.

The toxin was already making its way out of her system.

"Get her back to the embassy," Niall said as I let the outer door slam shut.

"No," she protested. "I want to be here."

We all shared a look. Adrian took one for the team and tried to talk her out of it.

"Babe, we all know that you're a strong, independent badass, but you were just poisoned—"

"Can it," she groaned. Not in pain, but annoyance. "I'm the one he attacked, and I want to watch."

Adrian pressed his lips together like, *what do you expect me to do now?*

"Firebird," Niall murmured, going to his pet name for her.

"Oh, don't pull that shit."

"I'm not pulling anything. You're not going to want to see this," Niall insisted, any softness in his tone dissipating.

"You of *all* people know what I've been through. Don't tell me what I do or don't want. I'm awake and alive. I get to decide that. He wanted to waterboard me in a fucking toilet. Do you know how unsanitary that is? People shit in that." And here we were again with Nikki logic. Because clearly, the toilet being the instrument in which he drowned her was of the utmost importance. "Now back off and punish the asshole, or do I need to do that too?" The fire in her eyes didn't fade a bit. If anything, it was growing the more that toxin leached out of her system.

Snake Eyes appeared completely shocked beyond words as he took it all in.

"Crazy," he eventually muttered under his breath. Niall squeezed his neck, blood dripped down his throat. I tilted my chin. Apparently I wasn't the only one with claws. One of the perks of my demon heritage was my nails could thicken to a sharp obsidian point. Niall's weren't just similar. . . they were the same.

Most shifters that could manage the partial shift and have claws, the whole tip of their finger changed. Niall's hadn't. They were still fingers, just with wicked sharp nails that we're currently buried in the side of this guy's neck.

"Hey, you." I reached up snapping in front of his face. He blinked, trying to focus on me. "You're not walking out of here alive, but it's up to you if we do this the easy way or the hard way. My mate's cold. I'd like to get her home so she can relax after what you just put her through. As much as I would love to drag this out, and I do mean *love*, if you answer all my questions, it'll be over before you know it. If you don't, this will go very, very slow. Which will make my mate grumpy because she's too stubborn to leave, which will make the rest of us unhappy, and well, let's just say, option two involves a lot more pain. It's your choice, though." He swallowed and fresh blood trickled from where Niall had his neck in a vice.

"Who are you?"

He hesitated, seeming to debate how serious I was being. That or he was wondering if there was still a way out that didn't end in him dying.

There wasn't.

Nikki was right. Stupid snake.

"I'm no one. Just the hired muscle," he said through dry lips.

"I got that, thanks. I mean *who* are you? What's your name?"

"Lucifer," he said begrudgingly.

I lifted both my eyebrows. "Lucifer?" I repeated. "Your mother give you that name? Or are you just full of inflated self-worth?"

Nikki chuckled. "Definitely inflated self-worth."

"It's my alias," he said defensively.

That made a bit more sense. It was still stupid.

"All right, Lucifer, we'll go with that for now. We can always revisit it if you don't want to talk. Who sent you here?"

"I don't know. He's—I don't know."

"Do you just take jobs from anyone without asking questions?"

"Look, I—she—" Niall growled and flexed his hand in impatience and Lucifer hissed in pain.

"He didn't give me his name, all right? He reached out through a broker. Guy was offering a kilo of pixie dust. A kilo, man! I couldn't say no to that. All I had to do was get her alone, rough her up a little, and tell her to go home."

"And that didn't seem odd to you?"

"Not my job to ask questions," he said. "Questions are dangerous. They get you killed."

"Yeah, well, not asking questions first ended with you here, so not the best choice."

His tongue darted out, licking his lips in a nervous tick. I didn't say anything, letting the silence pressure him for me.

"Look, I don't know who it was, but the broker said the guy seemed to have a real issue with her being with all of you. Apparently he was going on about how she'd turned into a slut—"

I couldn't help it. He didn't get to finish what he was saying before I slapped him so hard his head cracked to the side. Normally, I wasn't one for slapping. But it was a show of disrespect that I didn't use my fist and that's what he deserved.

"The fuck?" he spluttered, blood leaking from his split lip. "I'm just telling you what he told me."

"True, but you did try to drown my girl in a toilet."

He had the decency to avert his eyes.

"I'm just telling you what my contact told me," he repeated. "I was supposed to come in here and deliver the message, that's it. Client was *real* specific that he wanted her alive. Not hurt too badly, but . . ." Lucifer looked away.

"But?" I prompted.

384

"You're not gonna like it. I'd rather not get beaten to death if there's an easier way out."

"Noted," I said, cracking my knuckles.

"He said if she's going to be a slut, then I should treat her like one."

Red descended over me, filling the edges of my vision, blotting out all reason.

Without so much as a blink, I snapped my fingers.

Black fire burst to life.

For a split second, the snake looked stricken. His fear didn't last long. All it took was a couple of seconds of staring into the flames for it to evaporate, replaced by another, stronger emotion.

Desire.

His lust for the flame would override the logical part of his brain that told him to fear it. It would entice him like the most delicious meal would a starving man.

He would do anything to have it.

Answer anything, as the trance fell over him.

Lucifer leaned forward, pushing against Niall's firm grip.

Blood gushed from the self-inflicted wounds, spurting out of him and onto the dark concrete.

Much more of that and he would die. Shifters may have accelerated healing but not that accelerated. Not unless you were uber powerful like Niall, or as unkillable as Nikki.

All it took was nicking one major artery and "poof"— you bleed out the same as any human.

"What's your broker's name?"

"John."

"Got a last name?"

"Smith."

Apparently the broker wasn't as stupid as the muscle he worked with. I snorted.

"Do you know who John Smith works for?"

"Only rumors," he murmured. "Word is he's part of the shifter syndicate in New York."

"Shifter Syndicate," I repeated. "Anything else I should know about John?"

"Pays well. Given me a few jobs over the years."

"What kind of jobs?" I asked.

"Couple of hits. Had me find some people." He was completely enraptured by the fire and under its spell. "Had me following you," he added. "When you left Manhattan, I had to track you down. Make sure that you stayed gone. He had me kidnap a couple of girls in a park one time—"

"You followed me?"

"Yeah."

"How long ago was that?"

"Four years back. I had to check in every now and then. Let him know what you were up to. If you'd climbed in rank. After you took over, he stopped asking for reports."

Blood rushed to my head as he confirmed what I'd already suspected. There may be a lot of people in the shifter syndicate, but not many of them would put a tail on me. Even fewer would want updates on how I climbed the ladder. Add in the slut shaming and message for Nikki—it didn't take a genius to figure out who hired this guy. Broker or not.

Phaon couldn't possibly be this stupid. So either he'd gotten sloppy in hiring this guy, or he wanted us to know— wanted Nikki to know.

"Is there anything you won't do for the right price?" I asked, absolutely disgusted with the man before me.

"No." The fire made it impossible for him to feel shame or pretend to be regretful of his actions.

"Let him go."

"What?" Niall growled.

"Let him go," I repeated. "He won't run. Will you, Lucifer?"

"No."

Niall eyed me warily, wanting to fight over this.

We were both slaves to our rage, but for as much shit as I gave him, Niall kept his monster on a far shorter leash.

I couldn't. I didn't know how to when someone applied the right pressure to open the door.

I wasn't born this way. I was made.

Forged so that I could be strong enough to not just live to see Nikki again, but to survive with enough of me intact for her to love.

I kept that part of me buried for six years, guarded by a monster that also loved her.

His love was different than the boy she knew.

It wasn't sweet and innocent. It wasn't kind or compassionate like the love we'd shared as children.

It was dark and obsessive.

It would kill for her.

Niall must have seen that in my face. His finger's snapped open and Lucifer instantly canted forward.

"Give it to me," he said grasping for the fire.

His hands reached into the flame, blackening beneath its lethal touch.

Tears instantly leaked down his face, his muscles bunched in pain, but he couldn't stop himself.

"Give it to me," he repeated more aggressively. "I have to have it. I answered all your questions. Give it to me!"

"What the hell?" Adrian said from behind me. "What's wrong with him?"

"Cupido Flamma."

Nikki's voice was soft but distinct. It surprised me.

"You've heard of it?"

She nodded, her eyes also on the flame. "The lustful flame. Alexander told me it was a myth. Ty didn't think so."

Of course he didn't. Ty, for as much as I couldn't stand the fucker, was not one to make assumptions on rumors.

"When a succubus demon mates with a fire fae—one in fifty thousand will be born with Cupido Flamma. The last hybrid with it was over two thousand years ago. It's the most potent aphrodisiac there is in the world. Rare and deadly because the fire doesn't just kill you. It makes you choose it. Lust for it. You want it even if everything inside you is screaming not to. You'll burn yourself alive just to have it."

Lucifer's grotesque hands were proof. Liquid fat and muscle hung off his bones. What skin he had left was red and angry, bursting with boils and blisters.

"Please," he moaned. Begged. "I want it *inside me*."

"That's nasty," Adrian grimaced. "If the fire makes you want to die for it, why do none of us feel anything?"

I smiled savagely. "Nikki's immune as my mate. I'm guessing that immunity extends to you through her."

"You're guessing?"

I shrugged. "You're not trying to kill yourself, so it seems I was right."

Adrian cursed under his breath, but in all fairness, I never would have let them die. Obviously. The same could not be said for Lucifer here.

I stepped forward and lifted my hand.

"Open up."

His lips parted instantly, tongue sticking out to accept the flame.

I tipped my hand pushing the ball of fire down his throat.

"Holy shit," Nikki whispered. "And I thought I was badass."

I took a step away as the real show started.

He collapsed to his knees and began to claw at his skin.

Cupido Flamma was named the lustful fire because it made its victims need it with the same fervor that mate's experienced when a female went into heat. He had to have it, even when it was inside of him. So he reached. He clawed. He ripped.

The fire ate at him from the inside while he tore himself apart from the outside.

"Is no one going to talk about the fact that he wasn't sure we would be immune?"

"Oh hush," Nikki said. "It's not like he'd let you eat it."

That was my girl.

CHAPTER 38
NIKKI

I WRAPPED MYSELF IN A SILKY BATHROBE AND STEPPED INTO THE bedroom. Adrian sat on the bed, leaned back against the headboard with his ankles crossed and one hand tucked behind his head. The other was playing with a stray fabric on the bedspread.

"How are you?" he asked me, hesitantly. I sighed, barely resisting the urge to roll my eyes.

"I'm fine."

"If you need time—"

"Stop it." I lifted my hand, cutting him off. "What's with the coddling?"

"He tried to . . . I *know* what he tried to do."

I broke him off, my tone sharp. "But he *didn't*." I crossed my arms over my chest. "I hate to break it to you, but this isn't the first time something like this has happened."

Adrian's face went blank. He hid his emotions so well that if it weren't for the bond, I wouldn't have been able to tell that the thought deeply angered him. The idea of me at someone else's mercy sent him to a dark place.

"I've been involved with the Movement for four years,

390

going on five. I've trained with them. I've spied for them. I've even killed a few times, when it was absolutely necessary." I walked past him to grab my hairbrush off the table so I could start working my way through the unruly tangles. "He wanted power, and I didn't give it to him. It's as simple as that for me, Adrian."

He let out a terse breath. The hand behind his head fell to the comforter. He fiddled for a second before letting his fingers smooth over the fabric.

"I know you had a life before us, and that as much as your family tried to keep you inside a cage, you still found your way . . . into trouble." I snorted. "I know that you can handle yourself, Nikki. But it's still hard to see; it's hard to know that something could have happened. If we hadn't been there, if we were too slow, if there was more than one—"

I had to laugh under my breath. "You do realize how self-obsessed that sounds, right?" I said, pulling the brush gently around the knots in my hair. "Something could have happened to me, and *you're* the one freaking out about it. Way to make the situation about you, Adrian." I infused a joking tone, but Adrian's face paled in horror.

"That's not what I meant."

I let out a rough chuckle that had him sputtering to find better words. "I was messing with you to get you to stop worrying over the what if's. Nothing happened other than that *very* unfortunate encounter with a toilet. I think I'm more scarred by that than a man trying to feel me up."

He shook his head. "I don't understand how your mind works. You're flippant about important shit, especially your own safety. If you weren't a phoenix, I'd say you have a death wish."

"I know that you guys worry about me," I said, using a

more serious tone since being dismissive seemed to throw him for a loop in this situation. "You're my mates. That's normal. I would worry about you if the situation were reversed. But I need you to believe me when I tell you that I'm fine. Really. You're all expecting me to snap, which for some people would be the case. That's understandable. I'm not just anyone, though, Adrian. I'm the daughter of the most ruthless syndicate leader and a leading member in the militia. A couple of weeks ago, you saw me withstand torture longer than *anyone*, including you. It peeves me that you think I'm going to break because some asshole wanted to fuck me for a paycheck. Rape is horrible. Assault in general is terrible. Murder is deplorable. For some reason though, it feels like this is a big to-do, and it shouldn't be. Not when I tell you I'm fine."

He opened his mouth, but I continued.

I just needed him to listen.

"I grew up in a household full of men that believed I wasn't capable of much because I lack an appendage between my legs. I was supposed to be auctioned off to you as a commodity in return for power. I've been through worse horrors than anything the trials have or could throw at us, so just trust me, I may be tiny—and I'm not exactly anyone's first choice at dodgeball—but I don't break so easily."

His ocean blue eyes softened, and he dipped his chin.

"Here"—he motioned to the brush—"let me." I happily took a seat on the edge of the bed, and he grabbed me by the waist and seated me between his legs. I crossed my legs and leaned forward to let him comb through my hair.

Some guys were too gentle, doing such tiny bits that they pulled more. Most of them didn't seem to understand that you couldn't just yank it from the root down to make it unravel. That resulted in a bigger knot and a broken hairbrush. Adrian used the perfect pressure and touch, starting at the bottom and then working his way up to get the stubborn knots out of my hair. I loved it when people played with my hair. Sam did when we were little, but when we grew up and she found Lindsey, it became weird. Gavriel still would sometimes, if we were watching a movie. Usually because I pestered him until he would. He hated talking during movies, so I promised to not make a sound if he did. With Adrian it was different. It wasn't just the physical feeling, which was amazing. There was intimacy too. A subtle tension built between us, not dissipating when he finally set the brush aside.

He ran his fingers through it, feeling for any snags.

"Can I braid it?" he asked, his voice dropping in tone. I glanced over my shoulder.

"You want to braid my hair?"

He didn't speak, but lifted a brow as if to say, 'that's what I asked. Isn't it?'

"Okay." I turned, facing forward, and letting his strong fingers carry me away. His nails lightly scratched my scalp, making my skin tingle.

I had to bite back a groan a few times . . . or ten. It was the best kind of slow torture, and he was barely touching me.

When he finished, Adrian gave my hair a little tug. He pressed a sensual kiss on my neck, just beside the hem of the night robe.

"All done."

I stood on slightly shaky legs and walked to the mirror to admire his work. Not a single strand was out of place. The braid was smooth and sleek, starting from the top of my head and descending to just pass my shoulder blades.

"Where'd you learn to French braid? Sister?" It wasn't unusual for guys to be able to braid, but French braid? Couldn't say I'd met one until now.

Adrian shrugged.

"Some girls I used to hang out with."

"Some girls?" I teased. There was no jealousy to it, but I was incredibly curious. I mean, yeah, if I thought about it too hard, I'd probably be jealous. But whoever they were, it was the past. I was his present, and his future.

Besides. I'd have Sam's sabretooth tiger eat him if he ever acted otherwise.

"My father used to drag me to the brothel when I was young. He and my mom aren't what you'd call happily mated." His slightly bitter smile made my heart clench. "I'm pretty sure he spent more of my childhood there than with his family." I drifted back toward the bed and perched on the edge, taking his hand. "He took me there to 'teach me how to be a man'. In reality, that looked like him dropping me off with the Madam while he took a few women to a back room and didn't reappear for days."

"I'm so sorry," I said softly. He squeezed my hand lightly.

"It wasn't so bad. I was just a boy. Ten or eleven at the time. The girls doted on me. They taught me how to braid hair and paint toenails. That's where I learned to cook and clean. There were other kids there. Mostly young girls that weren't sex workers yet but lived at the brothel. They handled a lot of the errands and upkeep in return for room and board. I learned a lot from them. From all of them."

"They sound like good people."

"The best," he answered, a faraway smile touched his lips with real happiness at the memories he saw. "As I got older, I started going there on my own, without my dad.

My mother was cold and distant. She shoved my younger sister to the nanny and spent most of her time with her own lovers, or with my older brother, since he's next in line to take over for my father when he kicks the bucket. My family thought that I was fucking some of the girls there. Given the desire for powerful fae children, they weren't opposed to it, even if the kids would be bastards. So they let me be." His lips curled in disgust. "I wasn't fucking them. Those women were the family I never got to have, and I paid the nanny off to bring my sister there so we could be together often. We all kept her safe. She didn't even know we were at a brothel. She called it the lady's hotel." He huffed a brief laugh. "The house was built in the early nineteen hundreds, and it needed a lot of upkeep. They hired out where they could, but work is expensive. Especially when you're barely surviving. I spent a lot of weekends fixing up that house. Had to redo the plumbing. All the walls have been torn out and rebuilt at some time or another. Floors too, ever since asbestos was discovered. While most of the girls were at least hybrids, not all of them were immortal. The fae in particular have a low tolerance for asbestos, due to the need for nature many of us have."

"You took care of them," I said, an odd warmth filling my chest that I knew to be pride. My mate was a good man, even if he did bad things.

"We took care of each other," he corrected. "When I was a teenager, they used to tell me all the things that I should never do because women *hated* it. Like leaving the toilet seat up or trying to go ass to mouth without washing first." He chuckled at my grimace. "Yeah. Unsanitary as fuck, but they had clients try that shit all the time."

I wish I could say I was shocked, but after living in a

house full of men that were mostly self-entitled assholes, I wasn't.

"They're the only reason I turned out half as decent as I am."

"I'd like to meet them," I said, moving closer. I rose up on my knees and lifted a leg over his lap, straddling him. "And thank them. For taking care of you."

Adrian cupped my face, brushing a thumb over my cheek. "They'd love you. We probably shouldn't bring Niall or Malachi though, because I'm certain Madame Dupont would try to proposition you."

"Oh?"

"Not to fuck. To hire," he clarified. "She collects women, brings them into the fold. Sometimes they're running from a bad situation, and other times they're just lost souls trying to find themselves, but the girls she takes are always strong here." He slid one hand up to tap my temple. "She protects them, treats them like family, and takes care of them—but they also do that for each other."

"I'm not lost or running," I murmured, noticing his lips and how kissable they looked.

"No," he agreed. "You're the third kind of woman. The rarest." His other hand slid down my neck, over my sternum, to rest in between the valley of my breasts, just above where the robe tied. "You shine, not with goodness or some other bullshit. You shine with *you*. No matter what life throws at you, your situation, your circumstances, you are still you—and you radiate this energy that makes others feel it too." My heart stuttered beneath his palm. "It's addictive. Intoxicating. How could she not want you?"

I leaned forward, my lips ghosting his.

"She can't have me," I breathed into him. He seemed to

swallow the oxygen around me. "No one can. I'm already taken."

A rumble worked its way through Adrian's chest. "Damn straight, you are."

He pulled me to him, his mouth covering mine, and Adrian kissed me with abandon. I wrapped my arms around his neck, reciprocating in fevered passion. I could feel his cock, hard and ready, pressed into me. Sitting back, I quickly shrugged out of the robe in a second flat and tossed it aside like I'd never need clothes again. Reaching down, I pulled his shirt over his head and threw it to the floor.

My handprint, the brand I'd left claiming his was forever mine was seared over his pec, near his heart.

He wrapped his arms around my back and buried his face in my breasts, sucking and kissing one, and then the other. He brought a hardened peak to his mouth, sweeping his tongue over it, and sucked deeply as he teased the other nipple. I let my head fall back to focus on the feeling, soft moans escaping my mouth as I did.

I panted, the mark on my neck aching, reminding me of the throes of the mating frenzy-heat sexfest. Need pulsed between my legs.

"Adrian, please. I need you inside me."

He groaned against my chest and stood up, turning us around and laying me down on the bed. My heart hammered so loudly I assumed my two other mates could hear.

I reached between us, feeling his bulge and pulling at his pants to take them off. But he pulled away, using his hands to push my legs apart as he kneeled between them.

"Not yet. I want to taste you."

My brain said to protest. To tell him I didn't need one

second more of foreplay, but then he kissed my inner thighs, and my body told me to drink up every moment he was willing to give, and my head lulled back. He slowly licked around my folds, pushing my legs further apart until he had me exposed and open. Then, with great purpose, he lapped at my clit, pressing against it with his tongue, and sucking it into his mouth.

My orgasm was already building, the feeling causing my legs to shake. He plunged two fingers inside me, curling them up and massaging my G-spot as he flicked at the sensitive flesh he'd taken between his lips.

"Oh my god," I moaned.

I reached down, grabbing his hair and holding him there so he wouldn't stop. He growled and picked up his pace, stroking his fingers in and out of me. Just when he felt me tipping over the edge, he pulled his hand away, fully taking my clit into his mouth and sucking hard.

My legs stiffened and I let go of his hair, my back arching off the bed as I grabbed at the sheets beside me. His hands slid underneath my backside and gripped my tightly as he sucked, keeping me pressed against him. I screamed as I came, the sensation sending shockwaves through my body.

I lay there unwilling to move as ripples and aftershocks from the orgasm moved through me.

The bed dipped with added weight and Adrian hovered over me. I grabbed his face and brought it to mine, opening my mouth for his. He let out a deep moan as I tasted myself on his tongue. I reached between us, unbuttoning his pants and pulling his cock free. Flattening my palm, I rubbed it against his hard length.

He leaned back, pulling me with him to the edge of the

bed. He took his pants off, pushing them away with his foot.

"Turn over," he whispered.

I bit my lower lip and gave him a suggestive smile. "I want to taste you next."

"I want to make you come again first." A wicked grin spread across his face.

I hummed, quite liking that idea. "Promise?"

He growled and flipped me over, guiding my hips toward him. He teased me, rubbing his tip over my opening, moving the slickness of my fluids around. I leaned down on my elbows, sticking my ass in the air more, swaying my hips in eagerness.

He entered me slowly, only pushing himself in a few inches, moving in and out at a gentle, steady rhythm, never fully penetrating me. He reached around and found my clit, rubbing it in smooth, wide circles.

That wasn't at all what I'd expected. Neither was how it made me feel.

"Oh my god . . . what . . . are you doing . . . to me," I whimpered, gripping my hair in my hands. I couldn't understand how something so simple and slow felt so incredibly intense, teasing me and winding me up until I felt like I would burst.

"Shallowing," he answered roughly, keeping the gradual and methodical movements at a steady pace.

Minutes passed as he tortured me slowly, building up what amounted to be something amazing from the way I felt like I was consistently on the verge of release. My core tightened and my inner walls fluttered repeatedly, an orgasm just out of reach with every little thrust.

A guttural moan escaped from deep in my throat as the sensation started to tip me over the brink. Just as I began to come, Adrian grabbed my hips and slammed into me, stretching me fully with his girth. I cried out and fisted the sheets as he fucked me hard and fast, drawing my pleasure out as I came with back-to-back earth-shattering orgasms.

I panted into the sheets, and he slowed his pace. Just when I thought I couldn't take anymore, he reached around and rubbed my clit in tight circles as he pushed himself into me fully. I came again, my pussy clenching tightly around his cock as I poured into his hand.

Letting go, he growled a satisfied "*yes*" and thrust in and out of me as I rode out the waves of pleasure. He grunted as he found his release moments later.

He stilled, my inner walls fluttering against him as he twitched inside me. When he pulled out, I fell forward, rolling over and pushing my sweaty hair from my face, trying to catch my breath.

He disappeared into my bathroom and came back with towels, putting one down on the bed where I'd left a rather large wet spot. He handed me one and I reached out to take it as he laid down beside me, propping himself up on an elbow and stroking my hair while he just gazed at me.

"I, uh . . . I didn't know I could do that," I said, my words coming out jarred and breathless.

"I bet I can make you do it again," he murmured, kissing just beneath my ear.

"Promise?"

CHAPTER 39

NIKKI

No Man's Circus was somehow *other*.

The big top stood out from a sea of concrete. Its disconnectedness almost seemed like an omen. Not necessarily a bad one. Just different.

We approached the grounds, walking as a group. Malachi wanted to stand in front of me like a bodyguard, but a quick glance at Adrian and a small shake of his head made him pause and grit his teeth. Instead he took the spot behind me. His anxiety was palpable; the remnants from the previous day's events still lingering.

A flash of guilt hit me square in the chest. I should have checked on him. I didn't realize that *he* wasn't okay. That yesterday wasn't as normal for him as it was for me. That much like Adrian, he needed reassurance.

Niall wasn't the same in that regard. He didn't express his emotions the same way. Where Adrian and Malachi felt more human emotions, Niall was oftentimes a wall. Anger was his safety. Steeped in trauma and distrust, he buried his anger to stop himself from being a slave to it, and in turn came off as emotionless at times. The truth was that he hurt so deeply, he couldn't feel it. The pain would overwhelm him. So he leaned into an easier emotion. Something that helped ground him.

He and I were alike in that. I felt things just as deeply as they did, as Niall did, but like my surly dragon shifter, I handled my emotions differently.

Niall repressed his by being cold. I handled mine by choosing not to get bent out of shape.

It wasn't something we'd spoken about, but he seemed to "get" me when it came to these things. He understood that I could take care of myself, but that when I couldn't, I trusted them to back me up. That I would lean on them when I needed to, but I would stand on my own when I didn't. He understood that I knew myself and my limits because of our dark past.

Like it or not, incidents like the night before didn't land on my radar the same way because I'd already lived through the worst possible thing imaginable.

I'd lost my twin. I'd been kidnapped and tortured for a week. And I'd had all bodily autonomy stripped when my father decided to auction me off to the highest bidder. So yeah, some handsy fucker wasn't exactly at the top of my worries at the moment.

But Malachi wasn't there for any part of my history, nor was Adrian.

Their mate instincts told them I was theirs to protect, and it clouded their judgment. It told them I was young and breakable, even though I wasn't.

In hindsight, I'd made a mistake in staying with Adrian last night and not checking on Malachi. An error that I would correct the second we were out of here.

The pavement slapped under our feet, or really, my feet.

Despite his hulking size, Niall was absolutely silent when
he walked, unless he wanted to be heard.

Malachi naturally had the grace of a ballerina, despite
never having danced in his life. As for Adrian . . . Well, he
was fae. They practically glided whenever they walked.

The sun was setting, casting long shadows as we closed
in on the tent. Just as we reached the entrance, the folded
cloth whipped to the side.

A man stepped out, his large frame dwarfing the
entrance as he completely blocked it with his body. His
sandy blonde hair was longer on the top and shorter on the
sides. Tattoos covered his throat and forearms; his brow,
nose, and lip pierced. His entire presence was commanding,
yet his hazel eyes told another story that I knew we
shouldn't take lightly. They carried darkness, cunning . . .
and rage.

"Who the fuck are you?"

So, not off to the best start, but we were here during
non-working hours.

"We need to speak to the ringmaster," I said, and he
arched an eyebrow in response.

Sniffing once, his lips twisted in contemplation as he
surveyed each of my mates before his eyes finally landed on
me again.

"Why?" he asked.

Before I could answer, Niall cut in. "That business is
between him and us. So unless you're the man of the hour"
—Niall's cold, unfeeling head to toe appraisal somehow
conveyed that he found him lacking—"which I highly doubt,
our reason isn't your concern. Either bring us to D, or have
him come to us." Niall infused the demand of an alpha in his
voice, just as he had with the snake shifter the night before.

This shifter looked at him in what could only be described as, *Da fuq? Who do you think you are?*

His bewilderment dissipated as he began to laugh in earnest.

"I hate to break it to you, alpha, but that won't work on me."

The slight twitch of Niall's lips was his only tell of surprise. His command—the one that made other shifters bend—had failed.

I could tell our new friend was a strong supernatural, but his exact animal evaded me. He smelled similar, familiar even, to a scent I was well accustomed to. Almost like . . . Sam.

"You're a cat shifter, aren't you?"

"Lion," he said in acknowledgment. I nodded. That made sense. Cat shifters were resistant to any sort of alpha command. The more powerful they were, the better they were at ignoring its call. If he could resist the power of a dragon, something told me that no shifter alive could make this man obey unless he wanted to.

"Myra at The Salty Siren pointed us in your direction," I explained, taking a less aggressive approach than Niall. "We need information. She told us D might have it."

He watched me a moment longer, sniffing again. Scenting.

"I can't quite tell what you are," he replied, avoiding the reason I'd given him for our visit.

My lips curled into a slight, knowing smile.

"If I let you guess, will you bring us to D?"

His expression changed. He was intrigued. The thing that my mate did not realize, that many who were unfamiliar with large, majestic cats did not realize, was they were distrustful to anyone but their own.

And they loved playing games with creatures they considered beneath them. Which was most of the shifter kingdom and supernatural kind . . . because *cats*.

You couldn't make demands. They wouldn't go for it.

He was more likely to turn around and tell us to piss off. The only way to get what we were looking for, *who* we were looking for, was to pique his interest.

"All right," he agreed with a subtle purr. "I'll take you to D, but if I guess correctly, you have to tell the truth."

On my right, Niall stiffened. As another rare breed of shifter, he was incredibly wary of anyone knowing what we were.

While the portal to Arcadia was the newest, it wasn't the only portal that their world had. Shifters had been on Earth for hundreds of years, traveling from their worlds to other realms, then entering through those portals to come here. Shifters also had the easiest time conceiving and giving birth, so our numbers were great. They were the most abundant supernatural on the planet. Witches were the only species that could give us a run for our money.

Much like animals, shifters were often prized for our rarity. Even more so if you were exotic and unique, with powers to match.

What was more powerful than a girl that couldn't die?

An errant wind brushed against my skin, like a warning telling me not to do this.

"Three guesses," I answered, holding my ground.

I made the choice to trust my own instincts over the learned fear and possible warnings that nature was giving me.

His lips curled into a very feline smile.

"Ten," he countered.

My palms began to sweat. We needed this, but I also wasn't going to give him more than absolutely necessary.

While my father had kept me sheltered and locked away from many things, business negotiations were an exception.

I didn't get my hands dirty because "that wasn't befitting of a woman." *Gag*. But like some sort of archaic noble, my father made sure I was well versed in certain things.

I always thought his reasoning was because he expected me to help him one day, as much as I dreaded it. My current reality made me think the archaic noble metaphor was apt. I needed to be pretty and useful—so he could sell me off.

Nonetheless, he taught me many things. To read a person's tells and know when they were lying. To be able to discern one's true intentions by reading between the lines. Because of him, I knew when to push for more, and when to accept the draw.

Or to walk away, if needed.

People could smell desperation, so you never went to the negotiating table without a hard line you refused to cross. It was bad business, and beneath a Ward.

My father taught me to never, ever let another man or woman get the upper hand on me. I might have been a priceless thing that he owned, but I was still his priceless thing; his family, his blood.

There were standards I was meant to uphold.

It would be an insult if I wasn't capable of handling the family business, even though my role was most likely to be sidelined, a trophy meant to host lavish dinners and be another set of keen eyes and ears. To be seen, but not really seen.

I was groomed to be the legs that held up a man's

throne, because clearly that's all the woman was good for.

That was sarcasm, obviously.

"Two."

I followed my gut. The lion blinked in surprise.

"All right. Three."

I smiled politely.

"It's a deal." I extended my hand to shake his. I was a small woman. Only a little over five feet. For a shifter, I was absolutely tiny, but I could give a firm handshake.

After all, what kind of Mafia princess would I be if I couldn't?

His hand wrapped around mine. Warm and calloused, it was the hand of a working man. I had a feeling he'd not just seen things that would make me terrified, but probably done them as well.

I gripped his hand firmly, meeting his strength with my own. Odds were, he went a little easy on me because I was a woman. That was okay. Men often underestimated me for that reason. It'd worked to my advantage before, and it would until the end of time.

I chose my battles wisely so I would win the war.

He swept the curtain aside and motioned with one hand. "Right this way."

I took a step forward and my mates followed.

"Ah, ah," he chided. "You didn't specify *who* I would take to D."

Instead of letting myself appear thrown off, I gave him an unamused smirk. "I said 'us'. That's plural. Nice try, though."

"But you didn't say *all* of us." He was correct, and that irritated me. "You can take one," he added. I didn't even need to see my mates' faces to know that they weren't going to go for that. "Sorry, D's rules. He doesn't like outsiders. He's already going to be less than thrilled that I brought two of you back."

We needed his boss's cooperation. Pissing them off didn't seem like a great idea.

"Fine."

My mates began to protest, and I ignored them. "But you need to guarantee our safety." The lion looked at me like I'd grown a second head.

"Yeah, no can do. If you try something, I will put you the fuck down like it's my hobby." He leaned in. "Which, it is." I dipped my chin in acknowledgment.

"Understood, but we have no intention of harming anyone here. Can you say the same? It would be very regrettable for everyone here if you don't," I continued in a conversational manner. "You see, I have three mates." I lowered the collar of my shirt to show him the three bite marks. "If something happens to me, the other two out here will know."

Unease flickered beneath the mask, but he composed himself carefully, making me question if it were real.

"A fae, a hybrid, and another shifter." He looked at Adrian, then Niall, followed by Malachi. "I can tell you're all strong, but you're no match for the circus as a whole."

I nodded. "Maybe not, but this one"—I inclined my head toward Adrian—"is one of the Roses. As in the supernatural syndicates of New York City." His eyelid twitched. My message was getting home. Good. This would be easier than I thought. "This one"—I tilted my head in the opposite direction, toward Niall—"is also with the Roses."

"They don't accept shifters," the lion said.

I smiled. "And yet they did. Maybe you should think about that. He has many talents." I tapped my index finger against my lips. "One of which is something you seem

408

familiar with. He collects debts, and not in the form of tangible things. One word from him and I wonder how many mercenaries would be snooping around here?" Our lion didn't care for that. Yeah, well, I didn't care for dying. I came back, but it still sucked. My mates didn't have the luxury of coming back, so I wasn't going to risk it. "And the one behind me? He leads The Divine. His second is a friend of mine and would be quite displeased if something were to happen to me. Are you prepared for an entire legion of angels and demons? An army of fae?" He pressed his lips together in a firmer line. "And we're ignoring who *I* am." My legs weren't long, but it only took one step to close enough distance between us to make my point. Adrian grabbed my forearm and Niall let out a growl. Yeah, they weren't fans. Newsflash, I did not care.

"My name is Nikki Ward." The smile I gave him then was sardonic at best. I felt like the cat that caught the canary, ironic given I had more in common with the canary. "I can see you've heard of us, which means you know that my father is not the forgiving sort. So on the off chance that my mates don't respond, which we both know is impossible—or that their people don't come to avenge me—which is highly probable, there is no way in this world or the next that my father will let it go. You seem smart. I don't need to tell you that Typhaon Ward is not someone you want to piss off."

Hook, line, and sinker.

"Fine," he answered, "but I'm only guaranteeing safety provided that none of you assholes attack, attempt to injure, or harm *anyone* that resides in the circus."

"I think that's more than fair."

He grunted, not quite as eager as he'd been earlier.

"Pick which one and come on. He's a busy man."

I turned to my mates, all three of which were eyeing each other.

"Only one way to settle this," Adrian said. He cracked his knuckles, and a whisper of trepidation touched me. They were not seriously going to duel it out for which one got to go into the fucking circus tent with me . . . *were they?*

"Rock, paper, scissors."

"For fuck's sake," the lion muttered. A fit of giggles burst out of me, like I was a naïve schoolgirl and not the woman that just threw her weight around.

Adrian faced Niall. My dragon shifter's expression was blank, but I sensed amusement coming from him. I had a feeling how this was going to go down.

Together they said, "Rock. Paper. Scissors."

Adrian chose scissors. Niall chose rock.

"Best two out of three?" Adrian asked.

"Oh, fuck off," Niall said, echoing the lion. Adrian side-eyed him as Niall faced Malachi.

"Ready, demon boy?"

"Bring it on, old man." Malachi narrowed his eyes. "On three. Rock. Paper. Scissors."

Malachi chose paper. Niall picked scissors.

The weight of his arm settled around my shoulders. He pulled me in tight, practically gluing me to his side.

"You cheated," Malachi muttered.

"That's what I'm saying," Adrian griped.

"We'll be out in fifteen minutes." Niall silently communicated with Adrian and Malachi with his eyes alone.

"I can't imagine this being more than ten," the lion said, dropping the curtain behind us, seeming mildly annoyed. "For people that came here wanting to speak to the ringmaster, you sure are wary of the place." It might have been nonchalant if not for the slight edge to his voice.

410

"You know who we are, where we come from. Are you really surprised?"

The lion seemed to weigh that. "No, can't say I would be in your position." He led us along the edge of the big top, giving us a scenic view of the back of the bleachers. When we came to an actual hallway with real walls, he started talking again.

"You're some kind of bird, but I'm having trouble putting my finger on it. I've smelled most bird shifters and there is a certain lightness to them that you have, but yours is different. Less airy. It's hard to place. I think I've got it, then it slips away."

Most shifters had very adept senses. Mine was sight. My hearing was just all right, not as great as a cat, but definitely could be worse. Taste and scent were where I struggled. I'd figured out over the years that the reason I needed food that was so heavily spiced was because I lacked those senses that everyone took for granted. I could be in a room with something utterly rancid, but never know unless it was truly overpowering. Candles didn't burn strong enough for me. Pheromones I could detect, but not with amazing accuracy. It didn't help that I wasn't as familiar with shifter-kind as I would have liked to be, *thanks dad,* but I could still pinpoint notes that were familiar. Like Sam

We stopped before a black door.

"The more I think about it, the closest thing to your scent that I've encountered was a gryffin, but I don't think that's it." Niall squeezed me a little closer. If my positioning next to him were any different, he would have squeezed the air right out of my lungs. "Are you a hippogriff?"

Clever. My scent was similar enough to a griffin he went with their only known relative. Still wrong, but close enough to the truth that I started to sweat.

"No."

If anything, he seemed keener now that he got it wrong.

The lion rapped the door twice with his knuckles. "I'm coming in. Make sure Liv is clothed."

A faint curse echoed through the door, along with an airy trill of laughter. The lion rolled his eyes, counting to five before walking in.

"Can you hear them?"

Niall shook his head.

One minute passed. Then two.

By the time I counted to one hundred and forty-seven, the door opened, and the lion shifter pulled it wide, revealing a dark room with a single couch, small table, and a large, mahogany desk. The man behind it oozed power. It was a little unnerving. His dark hair was styled similarly to the lion's, but his copper gaze was far more sinister. Then again, it could have had something to do with the strangers in his home, and the very pregnant woman leaning against his desk, a hand on her swollen belly.

"Ah, Nikki Ward." The huge man behind the desk leaned forward an inch. "Are you looking for something, or rather *someone*?"

I stepped into the room but didn't get too close. Niall's nails had turned to talons the moment the door opened, and they were pressing into my hip uncomfortably.

"We need an in with Sea and Serpentine," Niall said. "The mermaid with the bad attitude at The Salty Siren sent us."

"Ah, Myra," D said. "Word gets around. I knew you'd be coming sooner or later."

"From Myra," I asked.

D shook his head. "From your brother."

Shit. Ty had beat me here? That did not bode well.

"You spoke with Ty?"

D dipped his chin in acknowledgment.

"I'm going to take a wild guess that you're after the same thing." His hand wrapped possessively around the woman's thigh. She wore a loosely fitted dress, made of a light, gauzy material. It was pretty. Innocent even, and so at odds with the man next to her.

D didn't seem to care for me watching her, so I could only assume she was his mate. His hand tightened around her, much like Niall did to me, as his eyes hardened.

"You want to negotiate a trade contract with Sea and Serpentine."

"Yes," I answered. D didn't seem like a man of many words, and certainly not someone that was up for casual chitchat.

"I'll tell you what I told him. I want"—he paused, his eyes briefly flaring with power. His steady gaze whipped from me to Niall as his muscles bunched.

"Killian," he said without looking away. "Take Liv back to our apartment."

The woman on the chair, Liv, turned and kissed D's cheek.

"If you get blood on the carpet, I'm not cleaning it."

Great.

D's lips twitched in something akin to amusement. "Noted," he said. "I'll be with you shortly."

Killian went to give her a hand, and she bristled at the gesture. "I'm pregnant, not an invalid."

He chuckled.

"Yes, yes, we know. You're a strong, independent woman who doesn't need a man—"

"Oh, shut up."

He ushered her toward another door, laughing all the

way. It didn't escape my notice he did so carefully, despite her snapping at him. Before he closed the door, Killian looked back at us.

"Fury?" he asked.

I smirked and shook my head. Two down, one to go.

"Dammit. I'll be right back. Don't go anywhere until I get my third guess." He disappeared through the door with Liv, closing it firmly behind them.

"If you're here to challenge me, that would be incredibly unwise," D said quietly, his voice rumbling with authority.

"I have no interest in challenging anyone," my mate replied. Niall narrowed his eyes after a sharp inhale. They flashed red from his dragon, the pupil narrowing to a slit as the creature took a cautious assessment of D, deciding whether he was a threat to us. "I was under the impression I was the last of my kind."

D's mouth twisted. "Not quite. What family do you come from?"

"Family?"

"There are families of dragons, much like the syndicate you're a part of."

"I wasn't aware."

Silence passed for a suspended beat.

"I see." I suppressed the desire to roll my eyes. This had to be the most unhelpful conversation in the history of the world. "Where did you say you're from?"

"I didn't."

"That's not an answer."

"It's the only one you're getting unless you part with some of your own."

"But you have no family?" D continued, pushing the topic.

"You're looking at her," Niall said, making my chest feel

414

warm and fuzzy. He might not be a man of many words, but he knew how to make them count.

"No *biological* family?" D clarified.

Niall tilted his head. "I don't know, and I don't particularly care. Blood means very little to me."

D let out a quiet sigh.

"I haven't seen one of my own kind in a very long time."

Well damn. In the span of a month, I'd gone from thinking dragons were extinct, to mating one, to meeting another. Next I was going to find out pigs could fly, Merida was a real live fae princess, and if I were really lucky—the most magical place on Earth still existed: Disney World.

"You're the first of my kind that I've ever met," Niall replied.

"Your scent is off," he said "Tainted somehow . . ."

"If you have a problem with some of our kind, I'm not them. I don't care if you're a dragon or a gecko. We're here for information on the trials, that's all," Niall said, swiftly cutting him off.

D's lips parted. The stunned expression evaporated within a second.

"The trial," I said, pulling his attention back to me and away from Niall. Call me territorial, but I wasn't overly keen on anyone—not even a mated male—showing too much interest in him. Certainly not one that was also a dragon. It seemed D and I had that in common.

"Yes, the trial. I'll tell you what I told your brother. I want a favor. And in return, I'll put you in contact with who you need to talk to."

"Favor?" I repeated. "What sort of favor?" D lifted a shoulder. "Whatever kind I want. You're running for Earth and Emerald. With my contact, you'll have the greatest odds of winning this trial, which means you'll have great

KEL CARPENTER & AURELIA JANE

odds of becoming the next chancellor. I want a favor. A blank check, if you will. When I call on you to cash it, there'll be no questions asked."

Oh, boy. Favors were hard no. They were too open ended, and it was poor risk management. While it could be as simple as finding something, it could also be murder, kidnapping, treason. He could demand I take the fall for something that would end with me in a supernatural prison, or worse—he could make me commit the very act that would land me there. The Houses wouldn't care about it being a favor. It would be *my* head on the chopping block. Or guillotine. I wasn't sure how Earth and Emerald handled traitors, but my father was a fan of feeding them to his monster.

I shuddered.

"Did Ty accept your offer?"

His lips curled into a smirk. "If you agree, I'll tell you that as a freebie. Consider it a gesture of goodwill."

"No," Niall said, shaking his head. He started to pull me backwards.

"With all of the problems the trials have encountered, and the rumors of a serial killer being amongst the candidates, I suspect this one will be weighed quite heavily in the eyes of the public. If the trials were to be cut short for whatever reason, it would likely be the deciding factor for most of Earth and Emerald."

My father's negotiation for alliance no longer held meaning because the three he'd made a deal with were already my mates.

The idea of Ty potentially ending up in charge of an entire House was beyond horrifying. "I'll do it."

Niall stopped at the edge of the door.

"What?" he hissed.

416

"Don't 'what' me?" I snapped back. "Ty's already been here. We need to succeed with this trial. He can't win." I glared at him, trying to convey with my eyes how serious this truly was for us. Understanding crossed Niall's face, and his jaw clenched.

"I don't like it."

I snorted. "Color me shocked."

"That's not a color."

"It's an expression."

"A stupid expression."

"I'll do it," I said, ignoring him to focus on D. We were past the ten-minute mark and needed to wrap up before Malachi and Adrian stormed the place, with metaphorical guns blazing. "One favor. No questions asked. In return, you'll tell me who to meet with, where to meet with them, and any pertinent information that may help me with getting this contract."

D smiled, but it didn't seem genuine.

More like a predator amused by the demands of someone beneath them.

"Very well," he said. "Tomorrow night you will go to the edge of the river where Burnside Bridge meets the Old Naito Parkway. There will be an older man that looks to be in his sixties, sitting on a bench by the water. Hill. At midnight, approach him and say, 'What did the walrus say to the oyster?' He'll know who you are and why you are there. He'll take you to the final person you need to nego-tiate with—Asbesta. Given that this is something Earth and Emerald has never accomplished, I'd say your odds of succeeding are quite low. On the off chance they aren't, I'll tell you this: Nobody loves themselves more than the Sea Empress loves herself. She's cruel because she can be. Pain amuses her. Much offends her. She believes that men are lesser. I highly suggest not having any of your men talk to her directly. She likes to play games. Amuse her and you won't lose, but there is no way to win."

She sounded like a real winner. She and my dad would make two peas in a pod.

"Seeing as you're not already chancellor, it's going to be even harder to negotiate with her because your words don't hold the same power. She and Hecate don't get on well, so don't bring her up."

"So essentially it's a pointless mission," Niall commented dryly.

D inclined his head. "Pointless in the sense that you're unlikely to negotiate a deal? Yes. But the whole purpose of the trial is diplomacy. To show what sort of leader you could be. If you get far enough to meet with her in person, that's still further than Ty will have gotten. He didn't take the deal."

The knot in my chest loosened. Unless he found another way, we were at least still one step ahead.

The door opened and Killian returned. "Everything good in here?" The question was clearly aimed at D.

D grunted. "Show them their way out—"

"We remember," Niall interjected.

"I don't care," D said, remaining irritated by our presence. "This is my territory and you're outsiders. I won't have you walking around without an escort. So unless you want to make a different sort of deal, Killian will show you out."

I nodded. "Thank you."

"I wouldn't thank me just yet," he replied.

He was right. The unspecified favor had yet to be defined, and I had a feeling I'd be cursing his name rather than thanking him.

The walk back to the entrance was short and silent. The lion didn't ask any questions or attempt to make small talk, but he did lean in and sniff me every few seconds. I could tell that it was grating on Niall's nerves.

"Smoke," Killian said suddenly. "It's prominent. I can tell that you're a flying creature. A mythical one, but it's difficult to pinpoint. Your scent might be light, but it's harsh like smoke. Are you a dragon of some sort?"

Rare as dragons were, they were still more common than I was apparently. "Nope," I answered with a slight smile.

His brows furrowed. "Are you a hybrid?"

"That's a fourth guess, and you only had three."

His lips pinched together in a surly expression. Now that I knew he was a cat shifter, it was easy to see the feline resemblances. "But in a gesture of goodwill," I said, imitating D, "no, I am not a hybrid."

"Interesting." If he had a tail, I could easily see it flicking back and forth in thought. "Well, this is it. Until next time," he said.

"No offense, but with any luck, there won't be a next time. I'd rather never see either of you again."

The lion laughed. "That's what they all say."

Unsure whether that was a warning or simply a statement of fact, I stepped out of the tent with Niall at my side and the curtain fell behind us.

As we were walking away, I spotted someone on the far side. A woman poked her head out from behind one of the heavy flaps. I recognized her, but it took me a second to place where I'd seen her before. By the time it clicked, she was already gone, leaving me to wonder why a human from Earth and Emerald was now a lost soul in No Man's Circus.

CHAPTER 40

MALACHI

"WHAT DID THE WALRUS SAY TO THE OYSTER?"

I had to look utterly ridiculous, speaking poetic nonsense while standing a healthy distance from the old man on the bench.

He stared at nothing in particular. With his jaw hanging open, and hazy, clouded eyes, he looked as though he already had one foot in the grave.

If not for the slight movement of his Adam's apple, I wouldn't have known if he were alive.

He blinked and focused on me with more attentiveness than I thought he'd be capable of.

"The time has come, to talk of many things: of shoes—and ships—and sealing wax—of cabbages—and kings."

He quoted the Lewis Carroll poem in a voice that didn't match his frail form. I stepped back, lifting an eyebrow. The old man looked up with a wide smile spreading across his face, showing off his yellow teeth.

"We're here to see Asbesta," I said, looking over his shoulder and past the bench, where Niall, Adrian, and Nikki stood as a unit.

My heart stuttered when I realized that it wasn't just my mate that I cared for, but also the two other men that were bonded to me through her. I wanted to protect her, but now I wanted to protect all of them.

It was an interesting turn of events.

If I had my way, none of us would be going to meet the sea witch. She might call herself an empress, but a royal title didn't change what you were.

Back in New York City, I ruled Queens, and I'd had the joy of dealing with her highness, more than once. It was never a pleasure, and I despised having to pretend otherwise.

"Right this way."

He slapped his hands down on his knees. And in the second it took him to go from sitting to standing, his appearance changed like an old movie on rewind. The wrinkles of old age disappeared, revealing a youthful, almost juvenile and feminine face.

Fuzzy, white hair transformed into long locs inter-woven with natural bits of sea stone and shells decorated in them. She had strong features and a tall posture, with tipped ears like mine, showing the signs of a fae.

That is where the similarity ended. Gills formed, protruding where the neck and jawline met. Her arms glittered with iridescent scales. Either she was some sort of half-breed like me, or some sort of experiment like Niall.

I couldn't help but stare in awe of the stark contrast to the old man I'd seen only moments before.

Nikki had suggested transfiguration, and I just thought it was a movie joke.

"As pretty as I am to gawk at, the sea queen won't be happy if we're late," she said, both chiding and flirtatious in her tone.

I pressed my lips together and stepped back, turning toward where she'd pointed.

The river floor appeared as the water curved to the side like pictures of the Red Sea when it was parted.

I looked back at her in suspicion.

"I know that Sea and Serpentine can be an eclectic sort, but I'm not quite sure what your intention was by showing us the sandy river bottom."

She laughed; the pitch higher than I expected. "To meet with our empress, we must go below the water."

"Well, I've met the empress a few times and I've never been below the surface." As a demon and a fire fae, the water held no intrigue for me.

"So I'm really digging this," Nikki said. "I love new experiences, and this is about as cool as it gets. But we have a tiny, little problem here." She leaned forward. At the circus, she'd taken a harder approach, but here she slipped into a friendly role.

"What's that?"

"I can't breathe underwater," Nikki whispered in amusement as though it were a secret. "And I rather like being alive."

"Sweetie," she hummed. "Asbesta wouldn't kill four candidates running for chancellor. Not when she could *use* you. You'll be contained in an air bubble until we reach the port city."

Nikki's eyes widened in excitement. "You can do that? That's so cool."

Adrian chuckled while Niall pinched the bridge of his nose. His head dipped forward as he shook it.

"You haven't seen nothing yet," she said, flicking her locs behind her shoulder. "Stick with Princess Kida and I can show you a whole new world."

Princess? I knew Asbesta had multiple children. She kept a harem of concubines and had no shortage of heirs—but most of them were illegitimate in her eyes. That Kida had any title at all was indicative of her lineage. She was either fathered by someone the empress saw befitting, or she was a favorite of her mother's. Considering her disdain for men, it was probably the latter.

"A princess?" Nikki asked. "Can't say I've met another one. Although, I suppose my position is a lot less formal than yours."

"You're a princess?" Kida asked in surprise.

"Sort of. I'm more like Rapunzel, coveted and sheltered by someone that only wants to use me for their gain. My father might as well be Mother Gothel. They're both assholes."

Kida laughed as Nikki looped her arm through hers like she didn't have a care in the world. Like she wasn't a literal bird made of fire who was voluntarily walking toward the muddy shore of a river where we would be pulled under it.

Fire couldn't burn in water. Not for a phoenix, not for a dragon, and not for fire fae.

Even Adrian seemed a bit wary about going below the waves. There was still earth beneath it, but none of us would be in our element.

Of all the trials and all the challenges, this one was the most difficult because there was very little we could control. We would have to surrender a great deal of it to even potentially make a deal.

"Nikki, wait," I said, reaching out to touch her arm. She paused, and Kida looked over her shoulder.

My mate gave me a look I'd not seen before. She knew what she was doing, and we needed to play along. "You

423

heard Kida," she said. "Asbesta doesn't wait for anyone, and the last thing I want to do is offend the empress."

The princess nodded. "The last guest I took down to the sacred city wasn't very respectful. He's lucky that he's a candidate, or he wouldn't even be alive."

Did she mean Ty? Or was it another candidate?

"I wasn't aware that Asbesta allows outsiders into her realm," I said, diplomatically.

The smile Kida gave me was knowing. "Under normal circumstances, she doesn't. It's an honor and a privilege to see one of our cities. She's agreed to grant the candidates access in the hope of a more prosperous future between our Houses."

It didn't take reading between the lines to know that meant she liked the idea of someone she could manipulate. Sneaky she was not, although the sea witch certainly viewed herself as such.

"The Houses have become one giant sausage fest," Nikki declared, and I struggled to maintain my reaction. I glanced at Adrian, and he quickly schooled his features, but I didn't miss the blatant confusion on his face. "I agree. It'd be nice for the female leaders to have an understanding."

Kida smiled. "I'm gonna like you." I couldn't tell if her statement was genuine or not, but it certainly seemed real.

"I couldn't agree more."

The sea princess towered over my mate as they walked hand in hand toward the riverbank, discussing mermaids and whether or not they really wore seashells for bras.

Instead of finding Nikki annoying, the princess was amused by her. A lot of my mate's questions were a lack of knowledge about how the world worked, but it left her open-minded as a result. She truly wanted to know more about Sea and Serpentine, even the things that most

ambassadors or diplomatic representatives would
never ask.

That would either work in her favor, or it would blow
up in her face.

Guess we'd find out soon enough.

"I don't like this," Adrian said, speaking quietly so that
they couldn't hear him.

"Me neither. But what choice do we have?" I said. "She's
going down there whether we go or not. And if we try to
stop her, it's not going to look good."

"We're her mates, not her keepers." Niall shrugged.
"She's made the choice to go down there. I'm following
her." He started walking, leaving Adrian and I in the dust.

"It's two on two now. I'd say our odds of dragging them
away are about equal with Asbesta drowning us all," Adrian
chuckled, and I sighed. He patted me on the arm. "Nikki's
not stupid. She's got a smart sense about things. She's been
running that militia now for years."

"If she thinks it's worth going down there and playing
the game, then that's what we do," I said, dipping my chin
in agreement. As much as I didn't like it, where she went—I
went.

I'd left her behind once and paid for it dearly. I made a
promise to us both that I would never leave her again.
Nothing would stop me from keeping it.

Not even a bit of water.

CHAPTER 41
NIKKI

"So Kida . . ." I strolled with her, arm-in-arm.

Being taken to a secret underwater city in a giant air bubble was equally as terrifying *and* as cool as it sounded.

My mates were nervous and tense. Malachi most of all.

They acted like I couldn't see the looks they were giving me.

It's like they didn't realize that I was terrified too. Nothing was more dangerous to me than water.

I could be trapped down here. I would never be able to escape. Even if I shifted into my phoenix form, these watery depths would be my prison.

A creature of living flame could burn hot enough without burning out.

Oh, I wouldn't stay dead.

Probably. I can't say that for certain, but I did drown myself once in my attempts to figure out my limits after my phoenix emerged. Was it incredibly stupid? For sure. Gavriel had intervened over a dozen times when he found out, but he couldn't stop me. No one could. I was so deep in despair that I felt the need to punish myself for being alive, for being unkillable, when Marissa was dead.

We were all scared, and I felt it more than any of them because I was the primary. All three of their emotions ran through me, along with my own. They only had to contend with me.

No matter how scared I was, that fear wasn't going to control me.

It sounded like a broken record every time I said it, but I'd lived through the worst thing imaginable.

I could do this.

I had to.

It's not that I was so dead set on winning the election and becoming Chancellor of Earth and Emerald. Don't get me wrong. I loved the idea of being able to make a change. I could implement it on a much larger scale compared to what I'd done with the Movement. This would be exactly what we'd worked towards: the power to actually help people.

At the end of the day, I was still just a girl. A woman, and a young one at that.

The world wasn't nearly as sexist as my father, but my lack of experience would be a barrier.

I wasn't as calculating as Niall or as well read as Adrian. I wasn't the leader of a syndicate already, like Malachi.

Yes, I was calculating, well read, and familiar with leading a syndicate—and a covert militia group. I was good with people, and I knew how to keep my head in stressful situations. I could withstand more pain than any of the candidates, though I suspected Niall would outlast me if it really came down to it. I got us this far in this trial, but was it enough? I didn't know. I also didn't really care. I just didn't want Ty to win. My brother was referred to as The Sadist. Nicknames like that were given for a reason.

He'd easily killed more people than I had fingers and toes, and he probably didn't know most of their names or remember their faces.

I'd killed in self-defense.

Was that still murder? Yes. Was it a shade of gray that not everyone would be understanding about? Also, yes. But I didn't live for everyone else or their opinions of me.

I couldn't please everyone, and I wasn't going to try.

My singular goal now was to make sure that Ty wasn't the one who got elected.

"Yes?" the princess prompted.

I'd been quiet too long. My brain had already moved on to the next thing, the next thought, the next plan, that I forgot what I was going to ask her to begin with.

"You know how you have a question and then you get distracted by a thought, so you forget the question?"

She laughed lightly, patting my hand. Her dark brown skin appeared to have blue tones under the dim lights. Orbs of fire—fairy lights—moved throughout the corridor. One followed us, close enough to touch, its turquoise flame casting a soft glow.

Their sacred city, New Kelsland, was more modern than I'd expected. Glass surrounded us from above down the right side as a wall—showcasing the murky depths of the river. The occasional fish swam close enough to get a good look, but what I was really into were the mermaids.

There were literal mermaids down here. In their mermaid form. With their mermaid tails.

What was even better—they didn't wear seashell bras. They wore nothing.

All the mermen and merwomen went around topless.

These people had no idea how lucky they were not to be subjected to a bra. If I weren't a phoenix, I'd consider switching Houses.

"You're different," Kida said.

"Good different or bad different?"

"Informal different. The delegates I meet are often very stiff. Much like those three." She flicked her eyes behind us without turning her cheek.

"They're cautious," I said, curbing the defensive tone.

"Not you?"

I twisted my lips, making a "meh" face. "I wouldn't say that I'm not cautious. I just see this for what it is—a once in a lifetime opportunity. We also have a trial and if we want to win we need to succeed. Yeah. Your mother has a very fierce reputation, but like you said, she can't form an alliance with a dead person. They know that as well. However, knowing it and being comfortable somewhere that's so foreign to you are different things."

Kida smiled. "I know exactly what you mean." Cerulean eyes focused on me, both startling for their intensity and their softness. It was a beguiling combination. "My home is the sea. I've been to so many cities all over the world, but I'm never on land for more than a few hours. I had to beg my mother to let me go. She didn't trust that nothing bad would happen. She knows that bad things can happen anywhere, even under the sea, but on land where she has little power? Where *I* have little power? She was scared, as hard as that might be to believe. My mother, the fierce empress, fears very little. I had to become trained in combat and learn to wield my water magic better than anyone for her to finally agree. I was so excited. I could barely wait, but when we approached the shore for the first time, I got cold. After all that I did to earn it, I couldn't leave the water." She shook her head, glancing up at where the ceiling should have been. Instead it was darkness. "I have legs. I'm far from helpless. I can glamour so effectively, even gods don't see through it—but I'm not immune to fear of the unknown. When you've lived your entire life in the sea, it can still be scary to venture out, even if it's something you really want."

"You really are The Little Mermaid," I murmured.

I guess I had to hope that her mother was more like Triton from the second movie and not Triton from the first where he was very anti-people and all for letting them die.

"I'm not little. I'm quite average for my kind."

I stifled the laugh. "That's not what I meant. *The Little Mermaid* is a Disney movie. I'm going to guess you've never seen it."

She lifted a brow. "What is this "Disney movie" you speak of?"

My eyes went big and round in excitement.

Behind us Malachi muttered, "Oh good lord."

My smile widened. "You've never seen a movie?"

She blinked considering my question. "I don't know if I have. Explain what it is, and I can tell you."

I shook my head in disbelief. Wow. And I thought I'd been sheltered.

"It's a play, kind of, but it's not happening in front of you, live. It's recorded using electricity and technology. They used fancy machines to put them on discs and special metal chips. If you plug them into a TV—which is a magic box that shows you the picture—you can watch the movie."

Kida nodded along seeming to understand my very simplified, not completely accurate, description of movies.

"We have plays here," she said. "They're mostly about my mother. Tales of how she defeated great empires of man. The story of her seceding from her sister, Vermicula, and bringing us freedom when she crossed the portal to this world and starting a new colony."

I nodded slowly, keeping the judgment off my face.

Her being a narcissist definitely checked out.

"Disney movies are love stories. There's usually a boy and a girl and some sort of adventure that they go on. At least the good ones. There's a lot of them where the boy ends up saving the girl and she marries him because he's pretty."

Kida made the face I wanted to when hearing about her mother's choice of entertainment. "That doesn't sound like a very good play."

"Yeah." I scratched the back of my head. "They were still finding their feet. I prefer the later ones they made. *The Little Mermaid* is one about a mermaid who falls in love with a human man she saves. She wants to live on land with him, but she can't because she doesn't have legs."

Kida lifted her eyebrows again. "That doesn't sound very much like a love story."

"She goes to a sea witch named Ursula to get her fins turned into legs, because then she can be on land with the guys she "loves."" I used quotation marks with my one freehand, not sure if she'd understand the meaning. "The problem was, he had to fall in love with her in three days—and she couldn't use her voice because the sea witch took it as payment. If he did and gave her true loves kiss, she'd be a human for the rest of her life and could never return to the water, but if she failed, Ursula took her soul. Essentially. She made the merpeople these weird seaweed things if they didn't hold up their end. There was a whole song about it."

"A song?"

"Oh, yeah. These plays—movies—have a lot of singing."

Kita squinted at me. "But she didn't know him."

"No," I agreed. "He had a really nice statue that fell out of the ship that wrecked at the beginning of the movie, though. The biceps were on point." I made the okay sign with my hand, and she busted out laughing as we walked down the fairly empty hall. Some mannerisms came across at least. That was something.

"So she gave up being a mermaid for a guy."

"Uh huh," I said. "That's not the part I'm comparing though. My point is she was born a mermaid and she always wanted to experience land. She was curious, fascinated. Yeah, she was also kind of stupid to give up being a mermaid princess for a guy—especially one that didn't even know her and low key, would have turned her down if she wasn't hot—but she had a longing for something more."

Wistfulness crossed Kida's face; her white locks swayed as we drifted farther and farther from the airlock that was guarded by other water creatures.

"Yeah, I'd say that's true. I'm not sure the sea witch was in the wrong there if she was willing to make such a dumb deal." I laughed lightly while she grinned. " I think for me, part of it is that I wasn't allowed to go there. It was forbidden for the longest time. In her fear, my mother tried to convince me that the land corrupts people. It makes them want things that they wouldn't normally want and do things they wouldn't normally do." She shook her head. "I don't think that's it. Now that I've seen it, I know better. I wanted to see the world above because it was denied to me. It felt like a secret that I was being excluded from. I have seen much, but there is still more I'd like to see and experience. A few hours above water every month or two hasn't satisfied my curiosity. I'm not sure I could ever live there—and I definitely wouldn't trade my fins for it—no offense."

I waved her off. "None taken. I mean, why would you when you can have this." I motioned all around us. "I've spent all of my life in one city; an island. When it's the only place you can go and you don't have the choice, it still feels like a cage."

"Yes, it does." There was no faking the genuine tone she was using with me now.

"This is the farthest I've ever been from home," I told her. "I'm from Manhattan. So the west coast is the farthest I've been. Now I've seen an underwater city, which is maybe the coolest thing ever. My mates aren't like us, though. They can't see past the uncertainty. Would you have been able to if you didn't really want to see what was on land for yourself?"

She tilted her head, thoughtful. "I'd never considered that point, but I don't believe I would have." Guards standing post at a set of double doors came into view as we turned the corner of the circular hallway. The doors were large, made of stone and seashells, and held together but some sort of glowing green mortar. They were pretty in a crude sort of way.

"You are wise, Nikki. Despite your informalities, the eagerness you show to learn has impressed me. I like you, so I'm going to give you some advice." Her declaration was unexpected but not unwanted. I needed all the help I could get with Asbesta. "My mother can be cruel. I know she is. I probably know better than anyone. You'd never guess how old I am, or how much longer I had to work because I made the mistake of begging for this position." I nibbled the edge of my bottom lip with my teeth. Neither agreeing nor denying her. "Do not beg," she whispered. "Don't grovel or lower yourself. My mother won't respect you. She controls every water source on this planet. There is no shortage of sea and land dwellers that yearn for her approval and will do anything to get it. What she respects is strength when you wield it the correct way."

I might have asked her more if we hadn't stopped before the doors at that very moment. Kida stepped away, putting more distance between us again, even though she kept our elbows looped through one another's.

The stone doors swung open. How? I had no idea. It's not like there were door handles.

We stepped into the throne room. I'm not sure I would have realized what room it was with the orgy going on, if not for the singular chair made out of bones directly across the room.

Her throne stood alone on a dais constructed of more bones. This was going to be interesting.

Kida announced, "The last Earth and Emerald candidates are here."

In her shoes, I would have been cringing and running away with disgust. No kid wanted to see their parent fucking, but Kida stood straight and spoke clearly. She didn't portray any level of discomfort at seeing her mother's naked body being impaled. She'd just become my hero. Any chick that could do that deserved some applause.

Asbesta's orgy was taking place on a chaise that didn't look comfortable. It was all white stone, like some sort of ancient Greek memento. The type only those who were true royalty had the luxury of owning.

Behind the Sea Empress was a man with two octopus arms. He had them wrapped around her legs, pulling them apart. His muscles shined under the fairy lights while he

434

pushed forward into Asbesta's ass. She'd straddled a man lying beneath her as he reclined backwards on the chaise, head hanging off the end. He rolled his hips upward, thrusting his cock inside her. I couldn't see well from this angle, so I had no idea if he had a cock or if he was using the sea creature appendage equivalent.

A third man sat on the second's chest, facing the sea goddess. Man was a stretch. He was either merman with a crazy long tail, or he was part snake. His bottom half dropped down onto the floor and snaked around the chaise. His upper half might as well have been a Greek god modeled from a statue. He was beautiful, as you would expect a concubine of a sea goddess to be.

While it was dickish to subject her own daughter to this porno, I could see the appeal to fucking three strong, beautiful men at the same time.

"Do you like that?" Malachi whispered.

"What?" I asked without taking my eyes off them. It wasn't that I *couldn't*, but that I didn't want to. Her reputation may be horrid. For all I knew, she was the worst person alive. No one could deny that Asbesta was the most beautiful creature that likely ever existed.

Turquoise hair cascaded around the pile of writhing bodies. Her silver skin was otherworldly. Along her arms and outer legs, iridescent scales dotted her features. I wanted to see more, but the man fucking her prevented it. She gripped the half serpent thrusting into her with slender hands that had incredible strength. Her nails were longer than the first joint between my hand and my knuckle. He moaned as she made him bleed, pumping harder.

She tipped her head back, making the most beautiful sound as her body trembled. Around us, the river's tide made the city shudder.

"Us sharing you like that," Malachi said.

My cheeks warmed. He knew me so well.

"I've already taken two of you at once while a third watched. What's one more in on the action?"

"I'd be game," Adrian said, pressing himself into my back. "If our mate wants to take us in every hole, who am I to deny her that?"

My core tightened at his whispered words. Fuck, I liked the sound of that. It was all too easy to imagine Malachi in my pussy, Adrian taking my ass, and Niall fucking my throat.

Niall growled under his breath in agitation at the lust he had to be feeling through our bond.

Asbesta stood, stepping away from the three heaving males. A thick cock nearly as wide as my wrist and long as my forearm unsheathed from her, attached to the merman-snake-dude. Semen ran down her legs, along with her own release, but the empress didn't seem to care.

If I were any less confident in myself, I would have felt self-conscious standing in the same room as this woman. Jealous even that my mates could want her instead. I wasn't as pretty as Asbesta, but I was certain that no one was, and beauty had nothing to do with why they wanted me.

Malachi took my hand as he stepped up beside me, but not quite equal. He stayed half of that step back, showing the difference. Niall came to my other side, between Kida and me. He didn't touch me, but he didn't need to. His strong presence said it all.

Asbesta didn't spare them a single glance in her appraisal. To be fair, she was just thoroughly fucked by her own men. One of which had a cock that I was pretty sure would break me in two. Unlike me, Asbesta wasn't a small

woman. It was hard to tell when she was sandwiched in the
fish pile, but as the goddess approached me, naked and
glowing, I had to crane my head all the way back to
watch her.

"Which one is this?"

Her voice held scorn, and yet it was so beautiful and
ethereal that her derision didn't land the same. Instead of
feeling anger, I wanted to please her. To gain her approval.

Somewhere deep inside my chest, coldness was spreading. A keen sense that this was not right. Not normal.

Everyone knew that sirens were mermaids that sold
their souls for power. Asbesta was the Queen of Sirens, of
Mermaids, of the Oceans—but she wasn't just a siren. She
was *more*.

I'd never met one of their kind before, but the rumors
said their voice was so dangerous that it could lull someone
into a state that they would do anything the siren said.

Become a slave. Kill someone. Drown themselves.

Asbesta had barely spoken and yet I could feel myself
falling under her spell.

"Typhaon Ward's daughter," Kida said. She didn't
sound terrified, but her tone wasn't as easygoing as before.
There was an undercurrent of unease, similar to what was
spreading through me.

"Ah, Typhaon," Asbesta said, her lovely mouth wrapping around my father's name with fondness. It made me
want to puke. "Now there is a male that I could have under
me again. Or over me." She spun her turquoise hair on a
silver finger as she contemplated how she would fuck my
father while covered in the release of three other men. I'd
assumed the beautiful, monstrous males were her concubines. Maybe not. They silently listened to her talk about a
married man whom she implied she'd had some sort of

437

carnal relationship with. One that she wanted again. Acid burned in my throat, and my stomach roiled.

I'd heard the judgmental whispers at the compound and at the embassy when they realized I was with three men.

People loved to make assumptions. Men. Women. Supernatural or not. They all sneered vile insults, much like Lucifer who met his well-earned demise.

The reality was there was nothing wrong with fucking two or three or ten people, as long as they were all consenting adults.

I was the last person to judge that.

My issue with Asbesta was the objectification and disregard for the men that were right there.

D said Asbesta only cared about herself. He was right.

"It's a shame that your brother didn't inherit your father's mind," she continued.

"Ty?"

"Yes, that's the one." Deep gray eyes the color of stormy, churning waves stared at me. "He was here yesterday, for the same reason you are."

"Did you make a deal with him?" I asked, trying not to let my face or voice show my own frustration. The last thing anyone needed was those two working together.

Asbesta smiled, her teeth were like newly shined pearls. When she looked at me, it was as if Aphrodite herself was smiling at me with her favor. Some part of me was desperate for her love. She made me yearn for her approval.

But it wasn't real.

"What would you say, if I did?"

It was on the tip of my tongue to tell her that this was a waste of time and we'd endangered ourselves for no reason.

Something D had said floated back to me, that it was about the *how* not the *what*.

No one thought we could negotiate a real contract with her. Giving up and not bothering because she might have already done so wouldn't look good.

That wasn't the answer that a chancellor would give.

I thought about Kida's advice. The goddess respected strength when applied right.

"I would say that you'd bet on the wrong candidate," I declared in a clear voice.

Asbesta blinked slowly, her eyes sharpening with new interest.

"Oh?" she asked. "Is that so?" Her tongue traced the bottom of her sharp teeth. I didn't notice the points at first. I wondered how many others hadn't either. "And are *you* the right candidate?" Before I could answer, she glanced at each of my mates. "Or is the half-breed demon king? Or did you mean the rakish fae prince that has no interest in anything or anyone unless it has to do with this cock?" Niall was last, and by the time she reached him, there was no smile on her face.

Instead it was only beautiful scorn.

She sneered, and yet I couldn't help finding it to be the loveliest action.

"You certainly can't mean *Subject Twenty-Three*?" My lips parted as she continued to rip into him with secrets she shouldn't know. "He's as damaged as they come. His brain was broken and scrambled like an egg. Have you any idea how many women *he's* broken?" she said, turning her cheeks to focus on me again. "How many girls didn't survive a night in his cell, let alone a week when he was in the rut?" Niall's eyes flared, turning a red so deep it was no longer crimson. His pupils turned to slits as his dragon moved to the surface, but it wasn't anger that drove it.

Pain did. Pain that he needed protecting from.

I still hadn't met the creature that I'd bonded myself to irrevocably. She was right that he was broken. Shattered. Hurt.

But she was also so wrong.

"Look at him." She motioned, stepping closer to me. Adrian stiffened at my back. "Words are sending him into a rage. He's not fit to rule a House. If you had taken him as a consort, I would have understood, but he can't even do that. The beast is sterile. He's not even a proper stud. This creature is incapable of the most basic functions."

Asbesta walked around me in a circle. Niall's head swiveled, his dragon not letting her out of his sight. Given that Niall the man was no longer home, it was only the understanding that billions of gallons of water surrounded us that kept the dragon subdued. He had tried to close the bond between us when she focused on him. To shut it down, to shut it out, to shut me out—so that I didn't feel his pain at what she had said.

Asbesta may be beautiful, but perfection often hid the ugliest of traits.

Beneath whatever hold she'd cast by merely existing, something else was forming. Something dangerous. Something new.

Or maybe it had always been there. Hidden by the chains my father put me in. Shrouded by the insecurities and invisible bindings I'd let hold me back.

Something angry.

"Let me get this straight, you want a leader that has never been through anything, never suffered hardship of any sort, and is essentially perfect in every way?" My open and friendly tone I'd shared with Kida had gone cold. Unfeeling.

Asbesta lifted her brows, coming to a stop in front of me. "You're not going to defend him? He is your mate, is he not? Degenerate, though he may be."

I took a step forward despite Malachi's squeezing my hand and Adrian's arm trying to hold me back. I closed the distance between me and the sea goddess and lifted my chin.

"I agree that he's not perfect. He's surly and sleeps way too hot at night. Probably thinks I talk too much. He has no interest in being around people and can be overprotective, even overbearing at times. I've only been with him for a month now and I'll be the first to admit that I don't know him as well as I wish I did. Thanks to my father, whom you hold in very high regard. Phaon doesn't believe women should get a choice in their own lives or who they mate, so I was kept apart from him—for years. Here's the truth, Your Highness, Niall Thorn is mine. He's not perfect, far from it, but he'd probably drive me insane if he were. I don't need or want perfect because I'm not either. No one is. Perfection doesn't exist. It's an impossible goal that you can't reach even if you get close. Niall was loyal to me those four years. He's honest, occasionally to a fault, but I'd much prefer honesty over shallow flattery." I lifted my own eyebrow to silently show her the middle finger. "I'm not correcting you because I can't change your opinion of him. I can't make you believe something you don't. You think he's worth nothing. That's your opinion. It's subjective and inconsequential at the end of the day because to me he's worth everything."

I stepped back then, not in fear or retreat, but to make a

point. I stepped into Adrian's waiting arms and took Niall's hand in mine, intertwining our fingers.

"I don't have to agree with you to work with you, which is why *I* am the right candidate."

The Sea Empress hummed in contemplation. "You're not what I expected for Typhaon's daughter. Ty is much like his father, but you are right about one thing. They are both men and prone to emotion. They allow it to rule them, whether it be by anger or lust. But you," she paused stepping back and looking at me with sharper eyes. "You'll do."

I'll do? That wasn't exactly a ringing endorsement.

Asbesta turned and started for her throne.

"I'll agree to a trade agreement that will allow Earth and Emerald uninhibited access to the river's surface on two conditions," she said without turning. "The first, is that you owe me, Nikki Ward. Chancellor or not, the princess of Manhattan is a rare breed of land dweller. I want a favor from you, regardless of whether or not you win this election."

What was it with these west coast supernaturals wanting favors? For pete's sake.

"Within reason," I replied. Asbesta paused partway up the stairs. "I won't commit treason or unjustified murder. It cannot involve my mates in any way, nor can it involve my brother, Gavriel. It cannot hurt the people of New York nor the people of Earth and Emerald."

"My my," she purred. "Phaon has done his work with you. Agreed, since now that you've said it, the people won't vote for you if they believe their lives to be in danger."

My heart thundered. I was *this* close to doing what everyone else had deemed impossible.

"Your second condition?" I prompted when Asbesta reached her throne.

"The trade agreement will only happen if you are elected chancellor." She smiled like the cat that caught the canary. "You have my word I will uphold this. We can discuss the specifics when you are sworn in."

Stunned didn't even begin to describe me. She just—I just—holy mackerel.

I locked my jaw to keep it from hanging open as I struggled to process her demand.

What she was offering might very well have just given me the election.

She had her reasons. I wasn't naïve enough to believe that her favor would be for something benign or easy.

Victory was actually in my grasp. I wouldn't just stop Ty from winning. I could be the next chancellor.

That realization hadn't actually hit me until now.

"You've got a deal."

She smiled placatingly like I were a child. "Of course I do," she said. "You'd be a fool not to accept. Now go, Nikki Ward and company. Kidakoshara will take you back to the surface. I'll have to miss your inauguration, but we will meet shortly after. My people will be in touch."

The dismissal was clear, and we were all happy to be leaving.

Just before I stepped out of the throne room, I remembered another deal I'd made.

It was time to pay my dues.

"One more thing, Your Highness. Myra wanted me to tell you that she's ready to talk. She said you would know what that means."

Not wanting to stick around for another interrogation, I quickly caught up with Kida and my men, only glancing back over my shoulder when we were clear.

The doors were closing, but for the briefest second, I

saw the empress in the crack between them, wearing an expression I doubted I would ever see on her again.

Despair.

It was still dark out when we got back to the embassy. I was more than ready to crash. If beds could talk, mine would be calling my name. We entered the lobby shortly before dawn, expecting it to be fairly empty. There was always someone up; it was an embassy. The crowd we ran into just past the door burst the bubble of happiness surrounding me since we'd left Kida on the riverside.

"What's going on?" I asked the nearest person, a girl that appeared in her younger twenties with tipped ears that marked her as fae.

Both dazed and terrified she answered, "There's been a murder."

No.

Dread coiled in my gut. "Who?"

I jumped from one thought to the next. There weren't many contestants left outside the four of us and Ty. I wasn't scared for my brother, not when I suspected he was the culprit, but everyone else . . . They didn't deserve to die. Syndicate or not. Candidates or not. "Which candidate died?" I asked when she didn't immediately answer.

Her features paled further. "Not a candidate. Hekate's assistant. Courtney Renee."

I lost feeling as my lips trembled. "She's . . ." No. No. They were attacking candidates, not the staff. Not Courtney.

I pushed forward, not caring who was there. It's not

444

that I was close with the woman. We weren't friends, but we did know her. She'd been nice to us when I was in heat. Understanding.

All these murders led back to me. Every crime scene had a message, and I needed to see what the killer had left this time.

Malachi cursed. I heard him and the other two trying to follow, but they couldn't squeeze between the crowd the same way I could.

I broke through the wall of bodies coming to a sudden stop.

Blood pooled around an upside-down body. A knife stuck out of the side of her throat where her attacker had attempted to behead her.

Her face was turned to the side, showing vacant, unseeing eyes, and bile rose in my throat.

I searched over every inch of her and the visible floor, stopping only when a face that shouldn't be here caught my attention.

"Lindsey?" I gasped.

She stood on the other side of the circle, talking with some of the council members that I recognized from my interrogation. One side of her mouth quirked up in a sly hello.

I almost bolted over the dead body, forgetting that was generally uncouth. With enough pushing and a few well-placed elbow jabs, I made it around the circle without contaminating the crime scene.

"Nikki—"

I threw my arms around her, pulling her tight. Lindsey laughed, hugging me back and tears welled in my eyes.

"I've been so worried about you. Where's Sam? Did she find you? What about—"

"Shhhhhh," Lindsey whispered, rubbing my back in rhythmic circles. She was such a maternal person. "Not here."

After a few more seconds, she pulled back to excuse herself from the council members. As I went to follow her, several of them dipped their heads in my direction in acknowledgment and respect.

"Well done," a woman said. Nikita Chen. I started to ask what she meant, when I realized in my surprise at seeing Lindsey, I'd forgotten the deal. "I expect I'm looking at our next chancellor from what Empress Asbesta had to say."

I gave her a slight smile and dipped my head in return. "The trials aren't over," I said, not wanting to sound too cocky.

Councilwoman Chen unexpectedly snorted. "Not officially, but after this?" She shook her head, not a single black hair out of place despite the early hour.

"You're planning to cut the trials short?"

"The decision hasn't been made yet." She left it there with a pointed look at the nearly headless body. "Check with Lindsey for when your group will be leaving."

Check with Lindsey?

I didn't even know what she was doing here. With a polite smile, I went to do just that.

A hand grabbed my arm and fire shot to my fingertips as I jumped in surprise.

"Just me, firebird," Niall said, stepping close. I relaxed instantly. Between the murders, attempted assault, and everything else—I was getting kind of jumpy.

"Jesus Christ," Malachi said as I walked toward us, followed by Adrian. "That wasn't a clean cut. Whoever killed her practically sawed her neck open with a damn butterknife."

446

"Most supernaturals could," Niall said in a matter-o-fact tone. "What I find curious is they didn't leave a message this time."

"Maybe they didn't have enough time?" Malachi suggested.

"Or we've got another murderer running about," Adrian said. I really didn't like that possibility.

"Okay this is bad—really bad—but Lindsey is here and I need to see what's going on before trying to play Clue with you guys." I hitched my thumb over my shoulder toward the hallway where I'd seen her go down.

"Lindsey?" Malachi asked. "Like, Sam's Lindsey?"

"The very one, so—" I started walking that way when they all followed. I held up a hand to Niall and Adrian. "Lindsey . . . she was the duck shifter that night. On the boat." Understanding crossed Adrian's face first.

"Oh."

"Yeah." I scratched the back of my neck. "I need to talk to her without you two. Explain things first. Find out why she's here. You two should stick around, though and see what you can find out from the gossipers. Maybe one of them saw something."

"Unlikely," Niall said, not getting that it was an excuse for them to do something because I simply could not bring over two of the guys that terrorized her on our last mission together.

Adrian shook his head at Niall's obliviousness. He threw an arm over his shoulder and shot me a wink. "I got this, babe. You go do your thing with Mal."

Mal? I wanted to ask when he got cozy enough to call him by his nickname, but I wanted to talk to Lindsey more.

Hightailing it out of the lobby, I all but ran into her as I rounded the corner.

I jumped again and she laughed, then covered her mouth with a quick peek around the corner.

"Why are they leaving?" she asked.

"You don't recognize them ?" I tried to hedge around her question.

Her brown eyes filled with warmth. "I know they were on the boat that night. I remember them, but Sam and I talked. I know the abbreviated story. I won't say I'd want to be in a room alone with them, but I was hoping to meet your mates officially—"

Malachi came around the corner and engulfed her in a hug. She squealed, patting his shoulder.

"Help. Me. Can't. Breath."

Malachi dropped her on her feet with a roll of his eyes. "Good seeing you too, Linz."

She punched his shoulder hard, dropping the act.

"Ooof," Malachi grunted. "What the hell?"

"That was for leaving Nikki heartbroken."

I put my face in my hand. I appreciated the solidarity, but we had moved past that.

"We're bonded now," he argued.

"That's why you're breathing, devil spawn," she sassed back. I could see her in duck form, practically shaking her tail feathers.

"Girl, I am so happy to see you, but what are you doing here?"

She turned to me and grabbed my forearms softly. "Gavriel negotiated with the pixies to get us out safely through the tunnels."

My jaw slipped. "No way. The pixies never do that. We're lucky to come out unscathed with Pixlaria."

"It's true," she squeezed gently. "Remember that pixie you met—"

"The one that kicked my ass?" I asked suspiciously. I highly doubted they helped her out because they got to whoop some syndicate ass. That wasn't exactly abnormal for them.

Lindsey laughed. "No, the one whose kid you saved from being eaten by a vampire last April."

"Oh yeah . . ." It was a vague recollection. Rouge vampires tried to eat a lot of people.

"The favor's been repaid. She smuggled me and the kids out. Took us to the border of Earth and Emerald."

"Good," I breathed. "I'd never forgive myself if something happened to my nephews and niece. That doesn't explain what you're doing here, though, or why Nikita Chen told me to come check with you for when my group would be leaving."

"Oh that? Psssh. I'm Hekate's assistant. Her other assistant. Well, one of. There's a few dozen of us. They've even got an assistant program for her. Apparently my people skills impressed the resource agent who was assigned to help us relocate. They offered me the job about, oh"—she glanced at her watch—"six hours ago now."

"Got the bloody end of the stick?" Malachi chuckled and I shot him a glare.

"Too soon," I said pointedly. He looked away, properly embarrassed. Lindsey made a bunch of cooing noises.

"You two are just *adorable*. Anyway, I'm your new liaison since Courtney bit it."

I swerved my glare from him to her. Was I the only one who thought we needed to show just a tiny bit of respect for the dead even if we didn't know them well?

Like damn, I know we're all syndicate, but she was hardly in the afterlife.

"It's cute you think that'll work on me," Lindsey said,

449

patting my cheek. "Sam's glare is way better, and it doesn't either."

"It's just that you seem . . . indifferent. It's not like you, *at all*."

"Look, I need humor and detachment to deflect from this very terrifying situation. I got a job because Courtney was murdered. Now I'm in her shoes. Not the most secure feeling. But if I make light of it, it seems less real."

That made more sense. If I looked at her, and I mean really looked at her, I could see the fear she was pushing beneath the surface. If this was what made her feel more secure, then I would go along with it.

"I actually understand that feeling." I pressed my lips into a smile. "How's Sam doing? Did she find you?"

Lindsey nodded. "She was brought straight to me. I talked to my supervisor, the senior assistant. She made sure they knew not to send her back to the syndicate since we're mated and all. She's at home with the kids, getting all the snuggles and going stir crazy from not working. She texted me a bit ago with a picture of James. He shit in his sister's bed." I widened my eyes.

"Kids do that?" I asked.

She shrugged. "Kids do a lot of weird and gross things. If you have them, maybe you'll be lucky enough to find teeth in their pockets." Lindsey shuddered, then added, "She did hear about how you did with the sea queen, and she told me to tell you "fabulous job and to keep being a boss.""

I chuckled, rolling my eyes. "I'm glad she's safe. That you're now in this shitfest? Not so much. Why isn't Hekate here if people are dying?"

"The official answer is that it's too dangerous for her." She leaned closer and used her hand to block her mouth as she whispered, "Between you and me? The best that I can tell is that she's out of fucks to give. Apparently Blood and Beryl offered her a swanky set up with a dozen peons to use however she sees fit if she'll be their witch."

Ummm . . . "Isn't she a goddess?"

Lindsey shrugged again. "Goddesses want tenure too. Apparently she goes through cycles. Running Earth and Emerald was her 'give a shit phase'. This gig with Blood and Beryl is like retirement, but not. Apparently she can't stay in retirement because she gets bored. So Blood and Beryl are setting her up."

"Hope she doesn't leave before the election," I muttered. If she was one foot out the door, I worried what would happen. "Just a bit ago, Councilwoman Chen said something about leaving?"

"Oh that!" Lindsey snapped her fingers. "Once they found Courtney, they called the remaining candidates to be escorted back. You're the only ones left. Once you grab your things, we're heading back to the compound."

"Are there more trials?" Malachi asked.

"Undecided at the moment. The main thing is getting the candidates cleared out of the embassy."

"It's not like the compound was any safer, Linz," he argued. "There were two murders there. Does Earth and Emerald even have a plan?"

"You're asking the wrong person. I'm not allowed in those meetings—I don't think—and I don't have any access to guard personnel yet. I'm just a professional mouthpiece with a nice customer service voice who's been in this job for six hours. When I know, you'll know," she said in a flat and exhausted tone.

"Was it your charm that got you hired?" he said in jest.

"Of course it was. I'm a duck shifter. Everyone likes

ducks. We're cute and unassuming." She turned, then looked at him over her shoulder. "No one expects that I can lay the smackdown on a bitch if they give me any shit," Lindsey added with a plastered smile and a wink.

Malachi blinked but said nothing.

I laughed, throwing an arm around her. "I've missed you."

CHAPTER 42
NIKKI

I DIDN'T KNOW WHY THEY BOTHERED SENDING US BACK TO THE compound. We were no safer there than when we were at the embassy. Oddly enough, growing up in No Man's Land felt safer than what we had been experiencing over the course of the trials.

I didn't know the people from Earth and Emerald that died, and I didn't have any interactions with the vampire from the Tepes clan, but I'd had a lot of interaction with Courtney. Not that anyone deserved what happened, but Hekate's assistant being the most recent victim struck a chord for everyone.

We all stood quietly by the lake while members of Earth and Emerald silently shed tears during her memorial. A wreath of flowers floated on the water in her honor, and it drifted away.

What should have been a solemn and peaceful event was made even more uncomfortable by the presence of multiple guards. Hekate had sent a message on a holographic device where she gave a eulogy for her assistant.

"I figured she would at least be here to say goodbye to Courtney," I said quietly.

"They're not willing to risk it," Adrian whispered in return.

"Do you think anybody would really be stupid enough to attempt an assassination on the chancellor in front of this many people?" I asked.

Malachi shrugged. "There's no shortage of stupid in this world."

"No, I can't really argue that. I guess if they're willing to go after her assistant, they're willing to do anything."

I glanced around, taking note of the people that were holding hands or huddled together. Most of them were dressed in all black, many of them were dabbing at tears with a handkerchief or cloth of some sort.

They were all open with their grief and they were clearly shaken by the loss.

Not that I wanted to downplay Courtney's death—or the death of anyone else—it was just unusual to see the difference in how a syndicate family dealt with death compared to how House supernaturals reacted. Maybe all Houses weren't the same. I had no way of knowing. I had nothing to compare it to except for my own experiences.

Niall must have seen the way that I was looking at others as he leaned down and quietly hovered near my ear. "Earth and Emerald aren't used to death the way that we are," Niall said softly.

"That's not such a bad thing."

Lindsey and I wrapped our arms around each other in a hug. It terrified me that she had taken Courtney's position, but now even assistants had assistants, and all people were traveling in pairs. Her traveling partner was nearby with their family, but out of earshot.

"Anything new?" I asked.

"No, nothing." She shook her head. "Investigators and witches are scrambling, but those that were murdered weren't connected in any way. It's not a coincidence that it's during the trial, and someone's trying to make a point, but nobody can figure out what point the perpetrator is trying to make, or what message they're trying to send. Apart from the literal words that they've left and a picture of a bird that might as well have had your name on it." She paused, her eyes flickering to the guys beside me and then widening in concern.

"It's okay. They're my mates. They all know what I am."

Lindsey gave me a tight-lipped smile. "I know, but I've never acknowledged out loud what . . . you know what I mean. It's been a closely guarded secret for so long. Feel like I've done something wrong by almost saying it."

"You've said nothing." I winked. "Has Earth and Emerald said what they plan on doing?"

"Right now the council is debating ending the trials early."

"Really?" Adrian asked.

She hummed. "They won't cancel the election; they'll just move it up. It seems like the longer the trials go on, the more likely we are to lose additional candidates. Or other people." Her mouth turned down.

"What would that look like if they ended the trials early?"

"I don't know yet. It's a democratic House, so right now they're discussing options and voting on it. There's a possibility that they'll do one more trial and those people will push to the election, and then another possibility is that they don't do anymore trials and all remaining candidates are on the ballot for the election but having that many people in the running presents issues as well."

I groaned. "Each one of the trials is supposed to determine what kind of people we are and what kind of leaders we could be. Cutting the trials short could potentially shift to a popularity contest and we end up with a twatwaffle as chancellor."

"Or the culprit," Niall added, and I pointed at him in agreement.

"Or Ayla," Malachi said thoughtfully. "The witch from the Outcast Coven. I've had a few interactions with her before. She's not the kind of person I would turn my back on for fear of ending up with a knife in it."

"See, I didn't know that, but that's exactly what I'm talking about." I wanted to throw my hands up in exasperation, but we were still in public.

"Are you sure she didn't just want to put a knife in *your* back?" Adrian asked, elbowing him. "She's always been fine with me."

Lindsey shook her head, but suppressed a smile at their antics. "Look, I'll be honest, the chatter I've overheard isn't favored to anyone in the syndicate. I can't imagine any of you will win. I know that some shady deals went down for syndicate to even be a part of the trials, but the powers that be in Earth and Emerald do *not* want any of you to win. That much I know."

"If they don't want us here, why would they invite us? Why make the deal?" I asked.

"It's good business," Adrian said. "That's all this is; that's all it's ever been. Bring us in and make it look like they're doing a deal with the syndicate families, but they wouldn't want someone from the syndicate to actually rule. Why would they?"

"But it's not ruling," I argued. "It's governing. It's a council. It's not a dictator. It's not a king. Or queen. Anyone can be a tyrant. That's not a quality unique to the syndicates. Look at Empress Asbesta."

"The sentiment is still the same, whether the leader is elected or not."

"To be honest, I don't think anybody thought that you guys would get this far," Lindsey admitted.

"How are they trusting you with this information? They know you came from Manhattan."

"Yes, they do. It was a topic of great discussion, believe me." She huffed a laugh. "But it's different. I'm not in a family syndicate. I'm just an unfortunate occupant in No Man's Land and I came here seeking asylum. That resonated with Hekate. I'm on a trial period, of course. There are a couple of council members that don't trust me at all, and then I keep my distance from anyone I know that has a connection to the syndicate. But a lot of the information I have is honestly what I overhear. These people talk an awful lot, and it's impressive the amount of people that are chattering and not considering the supernatural hearing around us."

"They're too comfortable," Niall said. "That's dangerous."

The guys nodded in agreement, and Lindsey and I knew very well how true that was.

"If the council does have another trial before the election, did they say what it would be?" I wanted to prepare myself however I could.

"They were mum on that. They were trying to figure out a trial that would be the most efficient in a short period of time in determining the quality of a leader. That's all I was told."

Turning to look at the guys, anxiety rode me at the sudden realization that this would be over soon. "I don't know what to do if we don't win. If one of us doesn't win."

"What do you mean?" Malachi asked.

"I mean I'm not going back to my family. I'm staying with my mates. My father was not going to honor the deal with any one of you. My plan was always to escape Manhattan. I never intended on staying long-term. I want to stay in Earth and Emerald, even if we don't win, but I don't think they're extending asylum to members of the syndicate—especially not those of us that are blood relatives to leaders."

Just then, Lindsey's phone buzzed in her pocket. She picked it up and checked her message. "It looks like you're being summoned."

"All of us?"

She nodded. "I guess the council came to an agreement and there will be one more trial before the election."

We had one more opportunity to show them who we truly were, and I wasn't going to fail. I didn't care what it took. Even if Earth and Emerald didn't want to let one of us into the elections, I would show them they were wrong.

I was not going back to Manhattan.

I was going to stay in this House, no matter what it took. I would show them what I was capable of, and I'd do anything to prove myself.

Anything.

CHAPTER 43

NIKKI

WE ENTERED A LARGE OPEN ROOM WITH THE COUNCIL STAGED IN front of us on a dais. A hologram of Hekate filled the center seat, and Lindsey stood nearby.

There were a few remaining candidates from Earth and Emerald, Ty, Ayla, my mates and me.

An equal number of small tables were placed in the room. Atop each table was what appeared to be a square box with a black cloth draped over it.

"Candidates," Hekate began, her hologram form standing up. "This year's trials are very unusual. We've lost valued members of our House, and the boroughs have lost one of their own. Never in the history of Earth and Emerald have we had election candidates murdered during any stage of the process.

"The council and I have agreed to change the timeline and move the election forward. In one week's time, the citizens of Earth and Emerald will cast a vote alongside our council, and we will determine our next chancellor. With this final trial, we can see you for the type of leader you are. How you are able to weigh an important decision when considering the lives of the people you are charged with protecting.

"A House leader has great responsibility, but they also carry a heavy burden. Millions of lives are in their care and each of them are affected by the decisions the chancellor makes. It is a noble and humbling position."

As Hekate spoke, a door opened, and a number of people were escorted in by guards. The other seconds were unknown to me, but Sam, Tylea, and Jackie were amongst them.

My heart jumped in excitement at seeing my best friend. I wanted to hug her and tell her how much I'd missed her. I wanted to tell her I'd completed the bond with Adrian and Malachi. I wanted to hear her tease me about having three mates. The gods knew I'd given her my fair share of mock-disgust when she and Lindsey were all sappy with each other.

Though she'd entered the room with a look of concern, relief filled her features as she saw me and Lindsey. She smiled at her wife and came to me as instructed. I wrapped my arms around her and pulled her in for a hug.

"I'm so glad you're safe," I whispered. "I have so much to tell you."

The remaining seconds went to their candidates, Jackie and Tylea went to Ty and Malachi respectively. While Jackie walked to my brother and didn't show a sign of emotion beyond her haughty smirk, Tylea gave my mate a sisterly hug.

"Candidates, for this trial, you will not work together as a team—not even as mates," Hekate said, pinning me with a stare. My cheeks heated under her intense gaze, and I could feel my brother glaring at me. "You will only have your second. Niall and Adrian, as you have chosen to not bring a second, you will rely on each other."

I looked at Sam with furrowed brows, wondering what kind of trial would benefit from two opponents working together. This was supposed to be the final determining factor to see which one of us stood out. It seemed like a setup if Adrian and Niall couldn't outshine each other.

"That isn't fair," I blurted out, not thinking.

"I beg your pardon?" Hekate said, surprise coloring her tone.

I cleared my throat. "Sorry, ma'am, I just mean, why are you putting them together? This is supposed to be a fair trial, meant to judge our individual qualities. Adrian and Niall are opponents."

"They are also best friends," Hekate said, glancing at the two of them to consider them. When Adrian tilted his head in question, she added, "Don't act so surprised. We know more than you think."

"Okay," I trailed off, not sure how that was meant to make it any better. When she fixed her eyes on me, I felt the weight of her judgment.

"You have chosen your seconds because they're important people to you. You trust them. You value them. As they didn't choose seconds, we looked into it and we know they find that in each other. For the purpose of this trial, that is exactly the relationship we are looking for."

I pressed my lips together tightly and gave her a single nod. I should have kept my mouth shut.

"Approach a table with your second."

We each did as we were told, and we waited silently for our next order.

I realized that whatever the trial task would be, it was

happening here. This meeting was beyond just getting instructions.

An attendant came to each table and removed the black cloth from the box, showing us the contents and removing a gun to place in each candidate's hand including mine.

A collective gasp filled the room.

"What is the meaning of this?" Malachi asked, staring at the Chancellor's hologram in disdain.

"When we give you the instruction, you will pick up your weapon, you will aim it, and on the count of three, you will shoot your second in the head." Hekate said it so coolly, it made me feel sick.

Lindsey's hand shot to her mouth to cover the sob I knew was about to escape, and two guards hovered near her, preparing to stop her from going to her mate.

I looked between her and Sam. My mouth fell open.

"Are you fucking serious?" I shouted.

"Absolutely," the Chancellor said. "We would never joke about something as important as the trials."

Niall and Adrian remained quiet and unmoving.

"This is absurd," I said, choking out a disgusted laugh and refusing to believe the truth. "You go on about nobility, the loss of candidates and the importance of life—then you turn this around and you want us to *kill* our second? Someone you just said we valued and trusted as a best friend?"

"And what if you had to choose between the life of your second and the life of your people?

"Wha-what?" I stammered.

"As chancellor, you often have to make very difficult decisions. What if you were forced to choose between the life of someone you care for, or choosing the lives and safety of the people you are sworn to protect?"

The silence in the room was violent.

I looked at Tylea and Malachi. She stood proud, her one wing on display. Jutting her chin out, she appeared strong, but I could see the pain on each of their faces.

Adrian and Niall didn't speak but regarded each other solemnly.

An edge of anger had taken over Jackie's face, but Ty's stoic features gave away nothing. They'd been lovers on and off for a long time. He'd trusted her without a second thought when he'd made the last-minute decision to join the trials, and now he was being asked to kill her.

Then I looked at Sam. Tears shimmered on the brim of her eyelids; her chin quivered, but she held her head up high.

The temperature of the room was absolutely frigid. I could taste the bitterness of fear that saturated the room, and it was overriding my senses.

"You will not go back to the syndicate," Sam said through gritted teeth, bringing me back to reality.

"Are you out of your fucking mind?" I hissed. "No!"

"I swore to protect you with my life, Nikki. That's what I am doing. You *cannot* return there. So do it."

"You are. You're out of your fucking mind," I said, mostly to myself and shaking my head in disbelief. I'd always said that I would do anything to get out of the boroughs, and now I was being faced with the decision to do anything to prevent me from going back.

"Candidates, aim your weapons."

"Wait," I said rapidly. "We need to talk about this more. This is barbaric."

"If you refuse to aim your weapon, you are no longer in the trial and you will forfeit the election," she said with

more authority. "You will be sent back to Manhattan immediately—"

"Raise it, Nikki," Sam ground out.

"Are you on fucking drugs, Sam?" I screamed. "This is
insane!"

"Now, Nikki. Don't make all those of years of sacrifice
worth nothing."

My mouth dropped open. This wasn't real. Couldn't be.

As each candidate slowly lifted the gun to their second,
I followed suit while Niall and Adrian each held a gun to the
other's head.

"On the count of three, pull the trigger," Hekate said
with cold indifference.

"One."

Sam looked at her mate and mouthed "I love you." With
her jaw clenched, she closed her eyes as tears streamed
down her face. Lindsey could no longer contain herself, and
she fell to the floor crying while two guards held her back. A
strangled sob escaped me.

"Two."

I'd always figured I'd make it out of New York. The only
way I was ever able to get this far was because of my best
friend. Because she loved me. Because she protected me.
Because she believed in me.

Courtney was wrong. She had said that Earth and
Emerald weren't savages, but they were no better than the
syndicate.

Fuck them.

"Three."

Moving quickly, I pointed the gun in the air and took
my finger off the trigger, holding the weapon in a non-
threatening stance.

As I did, I heard the deafening crack of a gun firing.

Ty hadn't wasted a moment and had instantly fired, shooting Jackie. Except it didn't work. Jackie let out a strangled scream and bloodred rage filled her eyes. It took a second for Ty to register that we had blanks and not live rounds. She spit in his face while she took three steps back from him, appraising him in disgust.

Malachi had refused to shoot Tylea, and Adrian and Niall had both dropped their guns to the side. The witch hadn't shot her second, but one member from Earth and Emerald had.

The guards had released Lindsey, and she'd rushed over to Sam crying pulling her in her arms and holding on to her tightly.

Guess that showed them it wasn't syndicate that made you a shitty person.

"Congratulations, candidates," Hekate said. "All but two of you chose to protect the life of your second. Those of you who didn't shoot have passed the test."

"Why would you do that?" I said, my throat thick with emotion. "Why would you put us through that? Why would you put *them* through that? My best friend just lost her damn marbles and *told me to kill her*," I said through my tears, but the Earth and Emerald candidate's shouting drowned out my questions.

"You said it was us choosing between a second and the entire population. You said that is why we had to shoot them," he barked at the chancellor, trying to understand where he'd gone wrong.

"What are the chances of that actually happening?" Hekate said, unbothered by his demeanor. "Anything is possible, sure, but that scenario is so highly unlikely, it's absurd. Answer me this, candidate: why is one life more valuable than the other? You have made your decision and you were willing to take the life of a trusted friend in exchange for an election. *That* was the measure of this trial. The hypothetical scenario I proposed is inconsequential, for each one of you *knew* that it was this trial that would determine if you made it into the election. It didn't matter what story I fed you, or if I simply said shoot them and gave no further commentary. Would you or would you not kill someone in cold blood simply for your own gain?"

I saw her reasoning. I truly did, but it did nothing for my emotions.

"But what about them?" I asked, pointing my finger at Sam. "Why would you put them through that?"

"There's a measure of cruelty to it, yes, and for that I do apologize. However," she said glancing at Jackie and the other second, both of whom had stepped far away from their candidate, "it would seem that all of you now know the true measure of your friend."

I let out a stuttered breath, unable to say anything further as I pressed my lips together with my nostrils flared. Sam and Tylea were comforting Lindsey, even through their own traumatic experience.

I kneeled down and hugged Sam, whispering in her ear while I held back my tears. "You are stupid and crazy and just—what the hell is the matter with you? I would *never* have done it. Not for anything. I didn't even consider it."

Sam sniffled. "I have always told you that no matter what, you had to get away from New York. I've always told you to do whatever it takes and don't look back. But this? I knew you wouldn't."

My mouth fell open. I was so confused. "Then why did you say that, you twit?"

With her back to the council, she faced me and winked.

In a barely audible whisper, she said, "I wondered, 'what would Nikki do?' And then I thought about *Big Hero 6*—"

"I . . . you what?"

She grinned. "That end scene when Baymax tells Hiro to sacrifice him? It was *emotional*. Totally made me cry."

"You cried? I didn't see you cry," I argued, totally distracted from the point.

"I knew you wouldn't do it—which, thank you, by the way—but I figured I could give the performance that no one was expecting, and I bet it looked really good from the audience's perspective."

"Holy crap, that was brilliant," I muttered, then snapped back to my mock outrage. "And so out of character for you. Is this how I make you feel when I wing it? Good lord, how do you handle it?"

"When I shift, you can see I have some gray hairs behind my ears." She wrapped me in a hug, then turned back to tend to Lindsey.

My mates came and stood beside me, and I felt their comforting presence without even turning around.

"Now that *that* shitshow is out of the way, we're almost there," I said as I looked at Adrian.

Malachi stroked my hair, and it sent tingles throughout my body. "Almost. Now it's just the election."

I needed them. I needed to be alone with them where it felt safe.

As I turned my head and placed it on Adrian's chest, I now had a direct line of sight to my brother. He had been escorted to the side of the room with the other disqualified candidate. With his arms crossed, and a deep crease in his forehead, his body tensed in anger.

"Candidates, as a reminder, the election will be held in one week's time. All of your trial results will be available immediately to the members of Earth and Emerald for consideration before they cast a vote. As there are no more trials until that time, Carlton will see to it that you and your second's return home to your family during that break." Hekate's hologram disappeared and only the council members were left.

Like hell I was returning home to my family. I had a bone to pick with my father and I didn't have the energy for it. I could only imagine how that conversation was going to go. Not that I had to bother with it. I wouldn't leave my mates, and they wouldn't leave me.

"Come on. Let's go get our things and get out of here," Malachi said, intertwining his fingers through mine as he brought my hand up to kiss the top of it. Looking at my mates, he asked, "How about Queens? No Roses or Wards to deal with there."

"That you know of," Adrian quipped, but he and Niall both agreed that was the best place for all of us to go.

The four of us turned with the intention of walking out the door. Malachi was on my right, Niall on my left, and Adrian followed behind me.

"How do we get home? We don't even know where we are," the witch said, and we paused. It was a good question. "We were all brought to the portal field through your system."

One of the council members stood up and inclined his head. "We'll send you back the same way we brought you here, just in reverse. You'll return to the place you were at the day the trial's commenced; before the portal field."

Before the portal field?

"Wait, hold on," I said, but I didn't know that anyone heard me.

As though it were in slow motion, the warlock lifted his

hand, his middle finger pressing to his thumb and then . . .
SNAP.

I shouted, grasping for Niall as I felt Malachi's hand
disappear from mine.

My mates disappeared and I found myself in the one
place I never expected to return to.

CHAPTER 44
NIKKI

My father stood slowly from behind his monstrous desk. The way he was looking at me, the power wafting off him in a not-so-subtle warning sickened me.

You'd never know that I used to go under that desk when Marissa and I played hide and seek as little girls, or that it was my go-to place when I wanted to be left alone. There were many times my father let me stay there while he handled a business transaction. I used to sit on his lap and listen attentively when he taught me how to read people.

That was when he'd explained to me that if someone doesn't give you what you want, then you take it.

You'd never know that man in my past was the same man before me.

The way he looked at me was nothing short of furious.

"Nikki." My name sounded like a threat. "Ty."

I stiffened, straightening my shoulders.

"I take it the trials have concluded."

I glanced at my brother, and he gave me a faint head-shake, clearly not wanting to divulge his disqualification just yet. Couldn't say I blamed him.

470

"They have. Ended early," he said, appraising our father's office and the fact he was in it, waiting for us. "But you knew that already."

"I did. So unfortunate, though necessary given the circumstances." He picked at a nail in complete disinterest.

So many people had died because of him. Not just the trials, but all over the boroughs. He had no regard for life.

"They didn't see another choice given the number of candidates that were dying off," I said, finding my voice even though it trembled. "I have to ask, was it Ty? Or did you have others in your pocket, murdering innocent people because you were pissed off that I didn't ask 'how high' when you told me to jump?" I suspected my father would think my reaction was based on fear. He was used to that; intimidating anyone—his wife, his kids, his syndicate—to get what he wanted.

The actual reason couldn't be further from it.

"Watch your tone, Nikki."

"You watch yours," I snapped. "There's nowhere you can hide me that my mates won't find. Nothing you can subject me to will make me leave them or pull out of the running for chancellor. You see, *father*, the whole reason I entered was to get out of this deal. I figured if I won, you had what you wanted, so why would I have to marry any of them? But I learned something over the trials, something you tried to smother in me—I'm actually a good leader. I'm strong enough to withstand and still have enough humanity to not run Earth and Emerald into the ground. You taught me how to read people and negotiate so that I could assist a man, when in reality all I actually needed was the confidence to step up and do it for myself. I won't be upset if I lose, because running a House is a lot of fucking work I imagine—but I won't back out either, since thanks

471

to you, there's not many decent candidates left that can do the job. I can, though, and I'm not going to let you stop me."

My father lifted his dark brow at my audacity to speak to him that way. He stepped around the desk, more than a foot taller than me.

"Leave us, son. I need to speak to your sister. Alone."

"Why? So you can hit me like you do mom when she doesn't agree with you? Or are you going to bring another one of your hired thugs here to finish the job the shifter—Lucifer—couldn't?" I lifted my brow in return. The anger I sensed just beneath the surface reflected in his eyes and I took a step back.

"Ty. Out."

My back touched a hard chest just as cool hands grasped me around the forearms. My brother pulled me closer. "What is she talking about?" I'd heard that tone before from him, but it was very rare. He never used it on his family. *Especially* not with my father.

He didn't know?

"Oh so you didn't tell him?" I taunted, unable to feel fear even though I really should. Maybe the adrenaline was just riding me, overpowering whatever feelings I had. "Must be because even *The Sadist* has lines he wouldn't cross, unlike you—"

"Get out!" My father snapped at my brother once more.

Ty's lips came close to my ear and the only way to describe his voice was that it sounded like death.

"What did he do?" he asked me, the words barely audible. But my brother wasn't dangerous when he was yelling. Oh no. He retreated inward, and that was when the real danger surfaced, except it wasn't being aimed at me. "Tell me, Nikki."

"He hired some asshole to *rape* me because he wanted me to learn my place. Because he was pissed off that I wasn't giving into his little threats. Jokes on him, though, my mates had a fun time getting information out of him before leaving his ashes in the alley." Ty stiffened. The scent of seawater, salt, and coming storms perfumed the air. That I could smell it at all didn't bode well. "And now he's got the gall to act like I owe him *anything*. The only thing you deserve is to rot at the bottom of the ocean, *Father*." I spat the name he didn't deserve, with every bit of the vitriol behind it palpable.

Phaon lunged at the same moment Ty shoved me behind him.

"Ty, you are my heir, and for that reason I will give you one chance to step aside—"

"And let you taint her further? Damage what good is left of her soul?" My brother's voice was infused with the power of his beast. The monster of monsters. I didn't need eyes to tell that he was very close to the edge of losing it. Normally I would try to calm him down. To stop the shift. This time, I said nothing. "You were willing to trade her to any of those mongrels in return for a House that we don't need. You made the deal to begin with and lied to me about it."

"Typhaon," my father dropped his voice, lowering his head. "I know I've looked the other way with you, with this thing you have—"

"You said Lucifer was dealt with. I covered for you when I found out you let that snake steal them because you said she needed it. That if she found out you allowed those monsters to kill Marissa so her phoenix would emerge, she'd leave and be hurt more. You promised that you wouldn't let anything happen to her again . . ."

Whatever else he said, was lost as blood rushed to my head.

You said Lucifer was dealt with.

You let that snake steal them.

You allowed those monsters to kill Marissa so her Phoenix would emerge.

You allowed those monsters to kill Marissa.

Kill Marissa.

My vision turned red as each of the dreams I'd had, the flashbacks, the memories played through my mind.

We were with my father in Central Park when he stepped away to take a call. A man approached us. A gun. Marissa let out a squeal. A dart stuck out of her chest. An uncomfortable stinging started in my arm. I looked down to see a dart there as well. Then we woke up and the torture began.

The drowning.

The burning.

The breaking.

They burned her alive like a witch.

I shattered when she died.

My phoenix was born.

Niall escaped and carried me to safety. Even when I couldn't process anything, the warmth of his naked chest and the distinct scent of his dragon calmed me. Kept me from burning more. Kept me from burning *everything*.

Standing in my father's office, I blacked out, my psyche being ripped back to that place and time.

In the darkness, there were voices. My father's. My brother's.

"You swear she won't remember anything? The shifter claiming to be her mate? The kidnapping?"

"Nothing," my father agreed. A calloused fingertip ran down

474

my cheek. "She'll know her sister is gone, and she'll feel the phoenix. Everything else will be what we tell her."

"And if the memories come back in time?"

"They won't. She won't want to remember. She won't be strong enough to break the spell."

Ty sighed, like he wasn't sure he believed it. "You can't do something like this again."

"Excuse me—"

"This is it. My line. You hurt her, but she's not yours to hurt—"

"Ty—" My father warned.

"I'm your heir. Your only true heir. If you want me and your legacy, that's the price. She's mine."

"She's your sister," my father said, disgust filling his tone.

"Let me worry about that. You wanted a phoenix, you got one. You wanted an heir, you have it. Keep her mates away and don't pull something like this again."

"Or what?" my father asked, anger vibrating as he spoke.

I knew that emotion well.

Anger was pain.

Anger was what I felt in the worst moment of my life.

Anger equaled Marissa dying.

So I retreated. Only hearing the last wisp of conversation.

"Or you die."

CHAPTER 45
NIALL

No, no, no.

This was wrong. Very, very wrong.

Adrian and I suddenly appeared back on the Brooklyn Bridge. It was the same place we'd been when they'd magically transported us to the portal field.

Panic assaulted me as Nikki's emotions exploded into a kaleidoscope of red and black.

I didn't know until it was too late.

She was separated from us. From me. Alone. Something I'd promised she would never be again. I rarely made promises, and I did *not* break them.

Four years ago when I'd left her, it was complicated. I felt the need for my mate, but I didn't know her. I wanted her for what she was, not who. That changed during the trials.

Something in me had changed. She wasn't just my mate anymore. She wasn't just the woman whose singular existence could keep me sane. Whose scent made my blood burn. Whose skin made me crave every inch of her.

I didn't *know* Nikki before.

Now I did, and I was completely and utterly in love with her.

But she was alone and angry and scared.

I could feel the distance in our bond, but the strength of it was no less intense than when she was standing beside me. Emotions poured through with greater anger, sorrow, and despair than I've ever felt from her before. I turned, bracing myself against the wind, to face Manhattan.

"Those fucking pricks! I can't believe they split us up. Now Nikki is fuck-knows-where in Manhattan with that piece of shit that tried to have her assaulted—"

"Her home," I said, my feet moving without thought. "Ward territory. Odds are she would have been home when they pulled her out." Adrian rushed to stay by my side. While tall and strong, the fae weren't made to keep pace with creatures like me. "I can feel her. That connection I told you I had with her? It's stronger now. We just have to follow the pull and it will lead us to her."

I was a dragon. A messed up one that didn't know what it meant to be a dragon, but a dragon all the same. I wasn't sure if it was what they did to me and my DNA, or what I was that caused it, but the first time I touched Nikki, some part of me fused with her.

Four years ago, I reached through a cage and touched her fingertips with my own. It was like her soul imprinted on me. It left a mark. A shadow. A string of magic that acted as a lead that I could follow straight to her, letting me know exactly where she was at all times. Since bonding, its strength had only thickened, becoming unbreakable. There wasn't a place in any world or realm Phaon could hide her. I'd never been thankful to be an experiment, but if that was the reason I could track her across any distance, then I would be.

Adrian was her mate, and while he could feel her emotions, he'd never have the same link to her that I did. In this moment, he showed no jealousy. No sign of feeling lesser. Instead, he knocked on my arm, realizing what I meant. "Yes! That! Good," he said, through heavy breaths. "If she's in the Ward mansion, it's going to take us half an hour on foot—and that's without running into guards."

Which we both knew we would.

Phaon would never leave his home unguarded. He might be arrogant, but there was a difference between arrogant and stupid. Her father was not the latter.

Brooklyn neighbored Manhattan, but where we needed to be was far from where we were on the bridge.

The subway wasn't an option with all the stops. The ferry was slow. Getting a witch to do a portal would take too much time, and with Nikki's growing anxiety, I wasn't sure it was time we had. My mate needed me *now*.

She needed *us*.

I stopped in my tracks, and Adrian turned to me in shock. "What are you doing? We don't have time to stand here and think—"

Inside, I burned. If I weren't a dragon, I would have collapsed to my knees as a feeling I'd only ever experienced once consumed me.

"We're not going to stand here," I said through gritted teeth. This was going to hurt. A lot. "We're going to fly."

CHAPTER 46
MALACHI

A ROAR ECHOED OVER NEW YORK CITY.

I looked up at the sky, lungs burning and heaving from how fast I'd run to get out of my underground fortress in Queens.

Tylea was hot on my heels, yelling behind me. "Malachi! Where are you going? Why are you running?"

I wanted to answer her questions, but I didn't have the time. Not when every single fiber of my being was focusing on getting to Nikki.

"Stop, dammit! I can't breathe trying to keep up with you. What the hell is wrong?"'

I stopped dead in my tracks.

A sight I never thought I would see hovered over central Manhattan.

A dragon.

A massive, white scaled beast with an arrow shaped head, bat-like wings, and wicked sharp talons. The creature rained fire down on New York City.

"Holy shit!" Tylea swore as she ran into the back of me. If I weren't so firmly planted to the ground staring in awe, I might have been thrown off. Her sharp nails bit into my biceps as she steadied herself and then let go.

"Jesus Christ," she said when the dragon opened its gaping jaws to reveal two sets of very pointed teeth.

"Nope. That's no god."

"Is that . . ." She struggled to say his name.

"Niall," I affirmed.

While I'd never seen his shifted form, the blood red eyes that glowed like flaming rubies in the sun were a dead giveaway.

He was a motherfucking dragon.

"Is that Adrian, on his back?" she asked. I lifted my hand to shade my eyes and squinted.

"I'll be damned." The fairy was riding him, bareback and all.

I might have made a joke, but the fact that Niall shifted at all in front of the entirety of New York City and was currently unleashing hell was only because something truly awful was happening to our mate.

"I have to go—" I broke off, the breath hissing between my teeth.

Pain crackled over my limbs, splintering, breaking apart, casting small fissures in every muscle and bone of my body as it traveled from the bond outward, looking for an outlet to ground itself and finding none. I felt as if I were shattering into a thousand pieces.

"How?"

"I don't know," I answered through clenched teeth. "But I have to. She's in pain—"

I was whole.

Fear curdled in my stomach because it meant Nikki very much was not.

But unlike Niall, I couldn't turn into a dragon. I could

control fire, but I couldn't sprout wings from the flame. I couldn't teleport. Any witch that I could get would take far too long to set up the spell.

"I can do it," Tylea said. "I can get us there."

"Are you sure?" I grunted, trying not to collapse to my knees. "I know that you've gotten good at it, but I'm heavy. If we fall—"

"I know," she said. "But I've been practicing. I can do this."

A drop from that height may not kill me, but it would make me utterly useless to help my mate because every bone in my body would be crushed.

But she said she could do it.

I trusted Tylea with my life.

My second threw her hair up in a quick ponytail before taking a power stance. Her good wing snapped out, stretching out the muscle suddenly. She hummed a dark tune under her breath, calling on the dark magic in the wing shaped ring on her finger.

Black strands took shape around her shoulder. The inky magic stained her fingers and the veins around her eyes made her look every bit the demon she was.

Tylea had lost her second wing as a child, but she didn't let that stop her from quite literally making a deal with the devil—the ability to conjure a phantom wing and fly.

The creature she'd struck a deal with crafted her wing using black magic, her own blood, hair, feathers and bone.

Sweat beaded her brow as she kept humming. The black tendrils solidified, creating a skeletal wing of flesh and bone.

Copper scented the air when she finished. Tylea bit her lip to hold in her scream as the transformation finished. The price she paid for such a thing was incredible pain.

The creature she bargained with fed on despair. Every time she used her shadow wing, it was given a meal through the bond of its magic that allowed her to fly again.

"You good?"

My second straightened her spine after a long second and took a sharp breath and cracked her neck to the side.

"Let's do this."

CHAPTER 47
NIKKI

THE VISION OF MY PAST FADED BEFORE MY EYES, LEAVING something far darker in its place.

Rage.

Pure. Potent. Profound.

It filled me so swiftly, so fully, that I didn't stand a chance.

The intensity felt like grief and hate and love and sorrow—like *all things*—just too much of them. It was all too much.

My father. My brother. They broke me for their own selfish means. They killed Marissa and tore our family apart.

For four years now, I'd been afraid of my own power—afraid to embrace all that I was. The creature inside of me was born from pain and suffering—and I feared it. Before its arrival, I was a latent shifter. All the signs of a phoenix had been present, but not the creature itself.

I was the daughter that everyone doted on. Marissa was a void, someone incapable of magic. She repelled it.

That made her a disappointment. A mistake.

Our father wasn't fair to her, but I'd always thought he at least loved her—that he'd mourned her as I did. I never would have imagined that he would've had her killed.

My hands had erupted in fire.

Indigo flames danced along my skin, flickering between blue and purple hues.

Dangerous. Lethal. Destructive.

To all except me.

My father and brother were so busy arguing amongst themselves, posturing against one another, that they didn't notice.

"For so long, I made excuses for you. Both of you." My voice no longer sounded like my own.

It was higher. Sharper. Colder.

My father paused, and silence fell. Their eyes weighed heavy on me, keeping me grounded to the spot as my heart began to race.

"I knew that you were shitty people, but I loved you because you weren't shitty to us. To your family. You loved me and Marissa, and so what if you were bad. You weren't evil. That was what I told myself. I let my love blind me into believing that the few good qualities you had made up for everything else about you that was rotten."

Tears of flame ran down my face. Periwinkle droplets fell to the floor, burning holes in it.

Smoke filled the air, but I didn't choke. Not the way my father did. He coughed lightly, then commanded me to cut it out. To stop. To put the fire out. To *calm down*.

I looked down at my hands as the fire spread to my forearms, past my elbow, and up my bicep.

"Nikki!" My father yelled so loud that I could have sworn the room shook. "This is ridiculous. Stop being overdramatic!"

Overdramatic?

I would have laughed if I could. Instead, I stared at him blankly.

My thoughts raced. A cycle of whispered words and memories goaded me.

Kidnapped.

Tortured.

Killed.

Marissa . . .

So many feelings coursed through me. I thought I knew what anger was—that it was comparable to rage. Synonymous.

I was mistaken.

This was so much more than anger.

It was an uncontrolled and vengeful *hate*.

Shifters often said that they felt like an animal in their human form.

I'd never felt trapped in mine until now.

"You're the *worst* kind of monster. You pretended to care, to grieve—"

"I did grieve!" My father roared. His eyes flashed black from his beast. "Marissa was my daughter. Useless as she was, the girl was my blood! I didn't want her to die. That's why I hired Lucifer. I couldn't do it myself."

"Lies," I hissed. "There was no reason for her to die—"

"For the phoenix to rise, first it must fall," he said. "The only phoenix shifters that have existed were born in pairs. One truly immortal. One human. Marissa had to die so that you could be reborn in her ashes. Without that, your phoenix would never surface."

"I don't care," I said. I didn't scream or yell. In my mind, we were so far beyond that. "I'd rather be a latent shifter with no animal than have my twin murdered—"

"Twenty years." The words were little more than a roar as they spewed from my father's mouth, but his animal was taking over. "I gave the girl twenty years," his beast said. "She would have died in another fifty anyway if sickness or an accident didn't take her sooner. I gave her the best years a human has. It was a mercy."

My skin tightened.

Everything inside of me pushed against its confines.

I began to crack. Crevices formed between my fingers, and the crease of my arms, and where my collarbone jutted out.

All over my five-foot nothing body, tiny fissures appeared, leaking with fire. It burned hotter than anything ever could.

"Nikki. *Sister.* He was wrong in thinking you were so weak," Ty said quietly. "But I see you. I've *always* seen you. The light in my dark." He was attempting to use a soothing voice, but neither my phoenix nor I cared.

Ty moved closer, edging around my side while the king of monsters and my phoenix stared each other down.

My brother stepped to the side, close to me, but not touching. He wasn't an immediate threat, but he wasn't safe either.

Not for me.

Not from me.

"I know that I'm a cruel man," he whispered. "I do cruel things. Lose my temper. Kill the occasional person. That's only because I was born wrong. Separated from my soul. It twisted me. *He* twisted me. It was ten long years before you followed me into this world, and he murdered what good there was. Just like he murdered Marissa."

I knew he was manipulating me, but in this place it didn't matter.

"Are you going to challenge me, bright bird?" My father's beast asked. Thunder boomed from beyond his office window as rain began to pour outside. "You won't win, but nor will you die. I can't kill you. I don't want to, but your insolence deserves punishment." Turning to Ty, the creature continued, "You disgust your father, but I've tolerated your demands because I understand the desires that powerful beings feel. You need a strong enough mate to couple with, or we grow restless. It was unfortunate she was born as your sister. Stop now, side with me, and I will let you have her."

Beside me, Ty scoffed. "No. I think not. You've outlived your use, old man."

My father's creature sighed. "Children. This is the reason I got rid of Echidna. You're more hassle than it's worth."

His suit ripped as the beast shifted, taking over his form.

"You'll find I'm not so easy to kill," Ty replied with a growl, his own beast taking over.

"I very much hope not. It's been too many centuries since I've had a good fight."

Between the two monsters of legend, I stood.

A slip of a girl breaking apart at the seams.

Anyone else would have run. A fight between the only two Typhaon monsters in existence would only lead to death.

But I couldn't die.

I was the phoenix. The phoenix was me.

Our wants were the same. Our desires were the same.

For the last four years, it was content to sleep— remaining dormant until I needed it.

While very little was known about my kind, I'd learned

bits and pieces from the immortal soul inside me. To live forever was exhausting. The power it held was soul extinguishing. To be that entity, it needed a reprieve—choosing to sleep for long periods of time in between.

I could still use my powers while it slept.

Healing. Enhanced eyesight. Fire. Claws.

But my true form—the immortal being behind my flesh and bones—only surfaced under emotion so great that I couldn't handle it.

My mind would break if I remained in control.

So I didn't.

I let go.

And I became the fire.

CHAPTER 48
ADRIAN

PILLARS OF BLACK SMOKE CLOGGED THE AIR, CREATING A hazardous sky. We had almost no visibility.

I coughed, waving a hand in front of my face as we flew. The rain was pouring down heavily, but it didn't cleanse the atmosphere.

Niall took a steep turn as a black plume appeared out of nowhere. My hands split on his scales from how tightly I gripped.

"What the hell?" I shouted, taking in the scene before us.

Giant, yellow-eyed creatures snapped at us midair. They looked part dragon, part snake, with extensive protruding fangs that must have been longer than my arm.

If we weren't impaled, their enormous jaws would crush us instantly.

Niall was able to right himself for a brief second when he was forced to rotate his body again, narrowly missing the countless serpents that were attempting to strike him.

When he pivoted, he was able to grab one by its body,

tearing it in half and the move allowed me to get a better look at the monster's face.

As the light faded from its eyes, the color shifted from a dark yellow to a dull gray.

Fuck.

These weren't serpents. They were Typhaon.

"We need to land!" I yelled. It did no good as the dragon continued to swerve and bite, swerve and bite.

My hands were cut to hell. My left pinky was barely attached anymore. Niall was killing them one by one, but it seemed never ending. There were simply too many.

Dammit, we really needed to get to the ground.

"Niall, tell this overgrown lizard to land. I've already lost one finger trying to stay on, and I'd rather not have to regrow another!" I wasn't sure if he heard me or if my voice got lost in the storm.

Niall dipped again, hitting something hard enough that my bones themselves threatened to come free from my body. I bounced once before flying off his back. I was expecting to freefall and die, but I didn't get any time to feel afraid or have those last thoughts you always see in movies. The ones where the guy says something stupidly romantic like, tell Nikki I loved her, then dies.

Real life wasn't like that.

There were no last words, or deep, thought-provoking realizations. I was flying and then I wasn't. My body hit the ground hard. I could feel a connection to the earth beneath the concrete. Nature welcomed me back, saying I should never leave the solid ground again. If I lived through what-ever hell we were in, I wouldn't be flying anywhere ever again.

Dragon rider I was not.

Niall would sooner eat me than want to regularly fly me on his back anyway.

I rolled, groaning for a second as I tried to convince myself that nothing was broken, and I wasn't actually Jell-o.

Lifting my head was as far as I made it.

A body landed on me; two hundred pounds of weight smashed me into the floor. I shouted as the stranger let out an "oof".

"Adrian?"

"Malachi?"

"Oh shit, I thought you were a rug." He moved, helping me turn over. I glared at him through narrowed eyes.

"What the shit, asshole? A rug? Who has a rug that's shaped like a person? We're outside!"

He twisted his mouth. "You do realize you're in the Ward's living room right?"

I blinked, sitting up straight. My head swam, but I clenched my teeth and pushed through it, waiting until the dizziness abated. It was then I took in my surroundings. Broken furniture littered the ground, and a gaping hole split the building where the Ward family lived. The multi-level penthouse was exposed to the elements.

It also explained why I didn't fall further and die on impact.

"How'd you get here?" I managed when my vision started to settle. "You don't have wings."

"But I do." The newcomer's voice was feminine, and I saw the fuzzy outline of a familiar redhead.

"Tylea. Fancy meeting you here." If I could still remember her name, then my head didn't have much damage, and it was enough for me to get moving. "Didn't know you could fly," I grunted. She only had one wing, so I figured the odds of her flying were about as good as me taking flight.

"Maybe I teleported."

"Above me? Don't people generally teleport into a standing position rather than dropping on top of someone?"

"You were laying down." She shrugged.

I glared at her, getting to my feet. "I wasn't lying down, I fell." Another roar rent the air, and I looked up as Niall's dragon form flew by. "Off of that, thank you very much. You're the one that should work on your landing."

She rolled her eyes, muttering something about me being a baby.

A deafening reptilian shriek caused us to clap our hands over our ears.

"We need to find Nikki," Malachi yelled.

No more than a hundred feet away two giants dueled on the edge of Central Park. Their serpentine bottom halves were covered in shiny black scales. Their bodies transformed at the waist, forming a masculine chest with muscular arms. Their skin was as gray as the storm clouds. Bat-like wings with serpents hanging from the ends of them made the sky seem darker. It was certainly more dangerous.

Typhaon Ward was the king of monsters. A being as much myth and legend as his daughter. His son's name wasn't just handed down to him for being the firstborn. While neither of them hid it, none of us had ever seen them in full form.

They were both as hideous as they were monstrous.

"What are the odds that flame trick of yours will work here?" I asked Malachi.

"Given they're both literal giants, not great," he

answered without looking away from the scene straight out of a Godzilla movie. "Even if it did, they'd heal too fast. Typhaon has a dozen hearts. There's a reason I've never picked a fight with either of them."

"Great. The giant lizard men are bigger and harder to kill than a damn dragon. Anything else you want to share while we're looking for Nikki? Maybe a secret hideaway she could be in or—"

"Guys," Tylea shouted in alarm. The pitch of her voice hit a shrill note that made me wince.

"What?" I snapped, my sarcasm failing under the gravity of our situation. We were in a literal hellscape and Nikki was nowhere to be found. Their entire home was demolished and unstable, not leaving anywhere to even look besides the rubble.

I couldn't entertain that thought.

She was a phoenix. She couldn't die.

Tylea pointed into the sky, and as I looked, my stomach roiled.

I saw my mate.

Captured.

Writhing.

Burning.

One of the Typhaon's giant fists wrapped around her body as the phoenix thrashed. I couldn't tell the difference between father and son, only that one of them was squeezing the life out of her and I was helpless.

I'd seen a lot of bad shit in my life, but nothing came close to this.

Panic. Fear. Terror.

They clawed at my inside, threatening to eat me alive.

The monster tightened his grip.

I couldn't see her eyes as the light of her fire faded.

Logically, I was aware she would live. She had to. She was a phoenix, for fuck's sake. That didn't stop the pain from nearly splitting me open from the inside out.

Without warning, the bond snapped.

What was once so pure and full of life within me, shriveled and died.

I collapsed to my knees, grasping my chest. The grief and agony seemed to go on forever, even though it had to have only been seconds.

I felt my soul drawing back and crumbling into nothing, decaying with every passing moment.

Between one beat of my heart and the next, something incredible happened.

In the ashes of our bond, a newer and stronger connection flared to life.

A sonic boom tore through the air.

Fire filled the sky with the wrath of a vengeful god. Rain evaporated into steam when her phoenix fully emerged, burning through the water. Clouds combusted in the sky, as lightning and fire clashed.

The wind blew me back, threatening to knock me on my ass once more.

My skin warmed beneath the heat of a living sun.

Light erupted from Nikki's body, blinding me.

My mate burned brighter in her rebirth.

It happened so fast, there was no time to think or recover or act. One moment it was hell on Earth, then came the moment of reckoning.

When the light diminished enough to see without burning my retinas beyond measure, I opened my eyes. Black ash rained down on us. Massive wings of glowing embers and flame framed Nikki's form. The bird swooped down to the ground, stopping a few feet from where Malachi and I stood, then she stared.

Surrounded by the phoenix's fire, her coal-black eyes and matching dark feathers created an otherworldly aura.

To be in her presence was astonishing.

Though she had an ethereal quality to her, her form was very much corporeal, her flame wasn't something one could touch.

The Typhaon didn't respect her power, thinking he was capable of containing her fire within his palm, and he'd paid for his arrogance with his life.

She'd incinerated the beast, burning the giant so thoroughly that nothing but his ash remained.

The second monster was shrinking rapidly and disappeared into a pile of rubble below. As if the phoenix sensed the danger had passed, our firebird shifted as well. Bronze skin and long dark hair replaced her feathers as she regained her humanoid body. Her eyes were open, but they were not quite Nikki. While the phoenix had stepped back, it was still very much in control.

I stepped forward and the creature surveyed me.

"It's safe now. You can let her go," I said gently.

Nikki's head tilted to the side as she regarded me.

"I killed the father. She isn't strong enough to handle the son."

"What? How?" Malachi demanded as he touched her shoulder.

The phoenix didn't look at him, never releasing me from its hard stare.

"One day, we will be unstoppable. Today is not that day. My soul is ancient, but the body we share is not. She is young and cannot remain in this form for long. When I let go, we will be weak. You must protect her."

"I will—"

"He must die today."

"Ty?" Malachi asked, beating me to the punch. "He has a dozen hearts. We can't burn him up instantly. If there's a way, we'll need to find it, but we need time—"

"No," the phoenix said, still watching me; still assessing. "The earth can kill just as swiftly as flame."

Her eyes fell shut and Nikki fainted. We both went to catch her and ended up falling to the ground. I moved to one side of her body while Malachi went to the other.

"What was she going on about the earth? Do you know?" he asked me, brushing a thumb over her cheek bone. I held her wrist, timing her pulse like it was my own lifeline instead.

"I have a feeling," I muttered, but before I could elaborate, Nikki's eyelids fluttered open.

"Why am I naked?" she mumbled, voice hoarse.

"Um . . ." Honestly not what I expected to be her question.

"Wait." She looked between us. "Why are you not?"

"You see . . ." Malachi started, but he shrugged and looked at me.

"What do you remember?" I asked.

Her brows pinched together in concentration. "We were sent back. My dad; he was so angry. But so was I. We fought. I lost control and—" she broke off with a sharp squeak and a small gasp. "The phoenix surfaced." She looked between the two of us, eyes wide and waiting for confirmation of what she already knew to be true.

I nodded. "Your father. He—"

"Killed Marissa."

"Died," I said at the same time she spoke.

Her eyes widened. "Did I . . .?"

496

We nodded.

"You went supernova," Malachi said. "Scared the shit out of me. Let's not do that again."

She swallowed, taking it all in. "What about Ty?"

"Worry not, Sister. I promised I would be there to protect you and I will."

The devil himself strolled out from behind a crumbling wall. He'd even taken the time to put on slacks, saving us all from that image. Though he had bloody smudges and smoky streaks across his chest, he otherwise appeared fine. There was no sign that he'd shifted into his alternate form, except for the lack of white in his eyes.

He looked like a demon.

Worse.

He looked like a monster.

The pleasant tone dropped from his voice as he said, "Step away from her."

"No," Malachi and I growled in unison.

Ty cocked his head. "My sister has been through a very trying experience. In an effort to not further traumatize her, I will give you one more chance. While you're her mates for now, she will survive your eventual deaths. Ultimately it benefits me to have you gone sooner, but right now, killing you would be upsetting to her. So I will say it only once more, let go of my sister and step away. She's mine."

My jaw slipped.

He couldn't mean . . .

My eyes slid to Nikki, and she grimaced, her lips turning down and her nostrils slightly flaring. Without speaking, she confirmed the truth of his words. She'd apparently already learned just how deep his depravity ran.

"You sick fuck," Malachi started. He went to snap his

fingers, likely calling on the flame. A strong gust of wind slammed into his chest, throwing him through the air.

"Don't try me, demon." Ty sighed dramatically. "She was always meant to be mine. It was just a curse of fate that we were born in a time that considers the union taboo. Not that I will let that stop me."

Nikki's lips trembled. She clutched my hand holding hers.

A piercing roar sounded as Niall's dragon came flying toward us, but it didn't matter. Typhaons controlled the very wind, and with a wicked smile, Ty knocked the beast out of the air.

Nikki screamed in outrage as the white dragon slammed into a pile of rubble.

"I am sorry for the pain this will cause you, my dear, but it was inevitable. The phoenix needs powerful mates. If yours die, she will choose more."

"It'll never choose you. You're her fucking brother!" Malachi shouted, standing up from where he'd landed. Ty lifted a brow.

"Half," he said sharply. "The Sea Empress birthed me, not the woman I call mother. Her blood makes me all the more worthy. Even if my sweet doesn't see it at first. If the phoenix doesn't choose me, I'll simply kill those it does—again and again—until it realizes that its only true equal is me. I don't care if I have to rid this world of all other options for her to recognize that she's mine. The only reason the phoenix takes multiple mates is because it needs other beings to ground it and keep its soul here when it dies. She is the only one that could hurt me, ergo, I will never die. This makes me the best—and only—mate for her."

As Ty finished speaking, Malachi's dark skin flushed as

the whites of his eyes began to turn red. He clutched his throat, seemingly choking on . . . air.

"Close your eyes," I mouthed to my mate. Nikki frowned, not understanding. Desperation clawed at me. "Close them no—"

A gust of wind picked me up, throwing me. I hit something hard, my head cracking against it with violent force.

Dots scattered across the backs of my eyes. Copper filled my mouth. I may not be a dragon shifter like Niall, or a demon-fae hybrid like Malachi, but I wasn't weak.

"Let me go!" she yelled, terrified and angry.

I tried to force myself up, but it felt impossible. My mind screamed at me to move, but my body refused to listen—and then I understood. I couldn't feel.

My bones slowly repaired themselves, knitting back together. My nerve-endings would reconnect, but when still remained unknown.

Malachi dropped to his knees, teetering on the edge of suffocation.

"Shh," Ty said as she struggled. "You'll understand soon."

"I understand perfectly well. You're a sick piece of shit—"

Smack.

The sound of his palm cracking against her cheek made my leg twitch. A tingling sensation was spreading up my calf as my body healed at a glacial pace.

I just needed to take off the glamour and open my fucking—

Eyes.

Her pleading eyes stared at me as Ty stuck a needle in her neck. Nikki shuddered as he pushed the plunger, filling her bloodstream with whatever crap was in it.

He grabbed her by the nape of her neck. Without seeing her face, he seemed to know where she was staring, and his angry gaze fell on me.

"Remember this?" He held up the syringe. "You gave us a little demonstration of it before my lovely sister and her band of misfits ruined your plans." Nikki jerked and Ty pulled her closer as a smile curled on one side. "She thought she was so secretive. I didn't have the heart to stop her, and it didn't hurt that they were giving her valuable lessons our father didn't approve of. I covered her tracks when Gavriel couldn't, but even I didn't expect that little stunt she pulled. Bombs? Genius. She thought she was saving the pathetic duck shifter when in reality she gave me the out I needed to take a case of this. It won't last forever, but I don't need it to. Nikki will comply in the meantime, and you and the other filthy mongrels that defiled her will be long gone . . ."

Ty continued monologuing. It would have made Hamlet proud.

When it became clear he was just going to spew dramatic bullshit, I blocked it out. Hearing it wasn't going to give me more motivation to heal faster. I didn't give a shit what disgusting ideas he had about mating with Nikki. If I could have laughed at him, I would have. What he didn't know was that "drug" wouldn't work on her.

It was just ground up dragon scales and water.

It did in fact work on others. It allowed temporary control of someone else—that much was true—but Nikki was the one person that would have a natural resistance to it.

It was her mate's scales, so unless Niall himself was the one controlling her, it wouldn't do a damn thing.

She wasn't in a trance.

He had no power over her.

So all that twisted idiot accomplished was likely terrifying the ever-loving shit out of her with all of his talk about sister-fucking. She was going to need a lot of therapy after this.

A familiar piece of me returned, restoring my connection to deeper parts of my magic.

I still couldn't move, but I didn't need to.

I was going to end it.

Looking directly at her, I squeezed my eyes shut, then reopened them, pleading with her.

Close your eyes, I said, pushing the silent command through the bond.

Nikki's brows furrowed and she snapped them shut.

I lifted the glamour from mine.

The earth can kill just as swiftly as flame.

Typhaon Ward didn't have time to fear. He didn't have time to react.

It was an easy death for him, but it was death all the same.

We had all been keeping secrets.

Nikki was a phoenix.

Niall was a dragon.

Malachi possessed fire that made you want to consume it.

And me?

I was Medusa's heir.

CHAPTER 49
NIKKI

STONE.

Gray, porous cracked stone.

My once living, breathing brother was now a statue. His face was forever frozen in an angry scowl.

It was a befitting expression.

I rubbed my neck where the fine grains of dust from his fingers had rubbed off on my skin. I didn't know how Adrian did it. My eyes were closed, but I knew that he was somehow responsible.

A rough hacking sound startled me out of my motionless state. Malachi pushed himself up into a sitting position. "God damn, dude," he choked out in a hoarse cough. "Would it have killed you to do that before he choked the life out of me?" He cleared his throat, trying to take in deeper breaths.

Emotions battled inside me.

Relief. Sadness. Love.

There were too many trying to take the lead, but confusion certainly stood out.

I questioned whether or not I was supposed to grieve

the loss of the father and brother I thought I knew. The reality was I didn't feel grief. The family I thought to mourn didn't exist. They had each played a part in Marissa's death. They'd each played a part in mine. What I'd heard my brother say about me . . . about being *with* me . . . that was a whole level of gross I didn't want to think about. Where was my brain now, protecting me from that trauma?

I couldn't unhear those words.

The world was rid of them. I had no remorse. No regret.

What mattered the most was that they would never hurt *anyone* again.

It was a relief, and that was the emotion I would accept. That and love.

I smiled at Malachi as he stretched his neck, still griping about being choked. "He's got a point, you know," I said, extending my hand to Adrian as he pulled himself up.

Adrian's lips parted in disbelief. "Seriously? I turn him to stone—which is truly the best I've ever seen him—and I don't even get a thanks? Just a 'could ya have done that sooner?'" he said in mock outrage.

"Thanks," I whispered, pulling him to me.

Tylea moaned, sitting up and pushing a piece of furniture off her. "This day sucks," she muttered.

"What happened to you?" Malachi asked, going to her and offering to help her.

"The rage monster huffed and puffed and blew me down, asshole." She scrubbed her hands over her face, and looked at the statue of my brother and she hummed in approval. "Nice."

A deep groan vibrated from below us.

"The building took a lot of damage," I said, shifting my weight. "We should probably get out of here in case it goes down.

KEL CARPENTER & AURELIA JANE

"Where are your teleporting skills, now?" Adrian muttered, and I looked at him in confusion. "Nothing. Tylea . . . never mind. Had to be there."

An intense cracking sound ricocheted from the streets below. We all turned as one, and I ran to what used to be a window.

A great white dragon lifted itself out of rubble, shaking its mammoth body like a cat to rid itself of the concrete bits that were trapped beneath its scales. The creature turned its face to look up at me with glowing red eyes that I would know anywhere.

"Niall," I said softly.

I couldn't see anyone nearby, but it was impossible no one spotted him.

My mate. My beautiful, scarred dragon mate; taken before he was even born and tortured for most of his life because of what he was . . . It brought tears to my eyes.

I didn't know if the day would ever come that I would get to meet his dragon because of the fear he lived in that someone would discover him and attempt to trap him again.

He was powerful. Incredibly so.

But all the power in the world couldn't stop people from hunting him. All it would take is one hunter to be successful and he'd be chained and imprisoned once more.

But for me, Niall unleashed his beast on Manhattan.

I hadn't seen him during the fight, but I knew it to be true.

I bit my lip, smiling as I looked at him.

Then I bolted for the door.

Adrian, Tylea, and Malachi called behind me, but I didn't stop. I couldn't. I flew down the stairs, holding the railing as I sped around each corner in the stairwell.

I flew out of the building and came to a sudden halt when I saw him outside. The dragon moved slowly. Cautious. He was worried that I was scared. Me. The woman who'd just killed her own father.

I smiled at him and took off running.

Bits of glass and hard stone cut my feet. The dragon stilled as I flung myself at him. His head was so massive I could only wrap my arms part way around the bridge of his nose. I turned my face, pressing my cheek to the spot between his eyes. A deep rumbling purr vibrated through him and into me, echoing around us.

Niall's dragon collapsed to the ground in a heap. His tense muscles went loose and lax as he allowed me to explore more of his giant, scaly body.

"You're beautiful, aren't you?"

My dragon purred in delight.

"Such a pretty boy."

He grumbled.

"Man," I corrected. "Manly dragon."

Adrian and Malachi came out of the building with Tylea at their back, huffing out of breath.

"Why didn't you just ask if I could have flown you down?" she gasped, putting her hands on her knees and sucking in gulps of air. "I wouldn't have, but at least we wouldn't have to chase you down a million flights of stairs."

"Nikki, you're n—" Adrian started, but my grunting drowned him out as I climbed onto Niall's back, straddling it as best I could.

"You can't be serious!" Hearing my best friend's voice made me snap my head up. She and Lindsey were jogging and began to slow down as they approached us.

"What?" I asked, genuinely confused. I pointed at the buildings behind me. "That wasn't my fault."

A burning tree in the park came crashing down with a thundering smack, and Malachi snickered. "Okay, that one is on me, though," I mumbled, wincing and looking away.

Sam gestured with her hands as she spoke. "We could see the battle from miles away. *Miles*. I just bartered with pixies to get here so we had the element of surprise from underground. But you're good. You're about to go for a ride on the back of a giant lizard." She shook her head, then jutted her thumb behind her. "Oh, and I brought reinforcements."

"What the hell happened, Nikki?" Alexander said, his voice rising in surprise as he caught up and stopped abruptly. Gavriel halted beside him, his mouth falling open in shock.

"What are you doing here?" I asked, directing my question toward my brothers. "And why does Gavriel have a black eye?"

"Pixies," they answered in unison.

Alexander gave a half-hearted salute to Adrian and Malachi, then blew out a long breath. "Sam came to us as soon as you were blipped out of Earth and Emerald. She knew where you were and that we needed to get to you," he said, surveying the damage and rubbing the back of his neck. "Didn't take much for us to find you. Even the buildings couldn't hide the Typhaons." Then he returned his gaze to me, looking between me and the dragon. "And here you are . . . sitting on a dra—"

Niall's light purring had turned into a low growl. Steam rose from his nostrils. With the Typhaons gone, he was the biggest, baddest beast on the playground, and he wanted to show it.

It took me two seconds to see why.

Jackie came running up behind them.

"From the looks of things, I think I'm late to the part—" she said, then stuttered as she stopped in her tracks.

"That's a dragon, right?" Jackie said cautiously. "My eyes aren't deceiving me?"

"Yep," Sam said, popping in the P. Her arms were crossed, but she used a hand to point at Niall. "That there is a dragon."

"What I want to know is what my sister is doing on it," Gavriel said, rubbing the overgrown stubble along his jaw.

"Gavriel, meet Niall's dragon." I introduced them like we were an ordinary couple meeting the family for Sunday brunch, and not their naked sister sitting on a dragon's back like some sort of *Game of Thrones* wannabe.

My dragon is way cooler. He turns into a man that knows how to fuck me really, really well.

Sam and Lindsey burst out laughing as Gavriel pressed his lips together and looked away in awkwardness.

Oh shit.

I had apparently said that out loud.

The dragon beneath me began to purr happily about his prowess. At least that was my guess. He could be digesting a dead body for all I knew.

I stroked two scales idly with one hand and the side of my foot. There was a lot to learn about dragons. Particularly how one acquired a saddle . . .

"Nikki, I love you and care about your happiness deeply, but I really didn't need to know that, *especially* while you are buck ass naked and sitting on its back," Alexander said, opting to be the adult of the group.

"Good point," Sam said, covering Lindsey's eyes.

"Hey!" she protested. "Worry about your own eyes."

"Nikki is like a sister. Ew," Sam told her.

I smiled so hard my cheeks ached.

"Well, apparently her family rolls that way," Jackie said, just loud enough we could hear.

My smile faded into a hard glare.

"What?" Jackie asked. "Too soon?"

"One would think you'd be more upset about Ty's death," Adrian said in a hard voice. "You were his second, after all."

"He chose me when he announced himself. I didn't exactly have a choice in the matter," Jackie said defensively.

"You were there, though. At the pier that night. You did business with him. With all of them," I argued. "When they were going to kill Lindsey."

She raised her brows. "You're the duck shifter?" Lindsey nodded. "I'm sorry about that. Probably gave you a hell of a scare. My affinity is air, but my brother's is water. I wasn't going to let you drown yourself that night."

"You were still doing the deal with him," I countered.

"So were they." She pointed at Adrian and Niall. "We're all syndicate, Nikki. We've all played our parts one way or another, but that doesn't make me bad. Ty was my ex, but there was no love between us." She bristled. "Also? Fuck him. He tried to shoot me so he could win, so even if there had been loyalty between us, it would have ended with that bullet."

"All right, that's enough." Malachi dusted himself off before removing the T-shirt from his delectable chest and striding toward us.

The dragon looked at him and let out a sigh, not bothering to move as he walked right up to it without hesitation.

He tossed the shirt at me with a look that brokered no room for argument. Pssh. Like I would argue about covering my bits in front of *my brothers?* Like Sam said. *Ew.*

"Speaking of Ty," Lindsey said, looking around. "Where is he?"

"And where's Dad?" Alexander added.

"I, uh . . . Dad's . . . dead," I said, holding my chin up.

Adrian tilted his head to the side, then ran his fingers through his hair and shook it. Little bits of black ash fell to the ground. "There's some of him right there," he said with a crooked smile.

"Oh, snap," Gavriel said, a grin appearing on his face. He was almost too excited when he added, "Ty as well?"

"Yeah . . ." Malachi scratched his jaw glancing at Adrian. He wasn't sure how much he was supposed to say—or not.

Happiness filled me that they respected and protected not just me, but each other.

Alexander searched around us. "Where is he?"

Adrian pointed up at the building. "Your living room."

When my brother glanced at Jackie, she realized why and she rolled her eyes. "Fine."

She summoned wind and gracefully lifted herself up to the exposed floor of our penthouse.

My jaw dropped.

That was way more than an affinity for air.

That was some comic book superhero-level control, and I had questions.

She disappeared, then came back over to the side, holding her hands up and controlling Ty's stone figure. She struggled with the weight, it seemed, and she managed to set it down on the grass by the sidewalk with a great thud.

"What in the actual fuck?" Alexander whispered in awe as he stared at Ty's rocky form.

Jackie floated herself down to the ground with us, crossing her arms and assessing the statue alongside my brother.

Seriously. So many questions.

"We found him that way," Malachi said after a beat.

Behind him, Tylea smacked her palm into her forehead at the obvious lie.

I wasn't sure where she had been during that final showdown.

All of my attention had been focused on Ty and Adrian, but it was clear she was aware of what had happened and knew Adrian was the cause.

Flashes of her face and mismatched wings filtered into my mind, but I couldn't place the memories into a series of events.

It wasn't the same way I'd lost my memories when my father had erased them, nor were they completely clear. Inside of me, my phoenix seemed to watch with tired eyes. With a silent understanding, I accepted that the entity was keeping the worst of it from me.

I'd reached my breaking point, and she knew it. Until I was ready and wanted to remember, I wouldn't.

I could live with that.

"Weird when that happens," Alexander mused, playing along with the explanation.

"What can I say?" Adrian shrugged.

"Ty really hit rock bottom," Jackie quipped, not even cracking a smile and Tylea barked a laugh.

"He was arrogant and took his powers for granite," I blurted and snorted loudly at my terrible pun, then Malachi burst out laughing. Lindsey cackled so hard, she quacked, and that sent Sam tumbling to the ground.

"Mom always told him not to get stoned," Gavriel added, and we lost ourselves in a fit of giggles until we cried. Even Niall's dragon found it funny and joined in, shaking me as I sat on top.

"Where is Mom?" I asked, wiping the tears from beneath my eyes. Logic told me she was safe, otherwise my brothers wouldn't have been lighthearted about anything.

"She's with Earth and Emerald," Lindsey said, clearing her throat from her laughter-induced duck call. "I found out shortly after you were summoned to the final trial that you'd be sent back, and I knew that was going to be bad. I reached out to Gavriel through the same network he used to get me out of here. We were trying to get back here before . . ." She looked around at the city block that had been destroyed. "It seems that things escalated faster than we thought they would."

"That's an understatement," Adrian grumbled. "A little warning about all this would have been nice."

She gave him the stink eye.

"For your information, I couldn't. I never lied. Hekate's assistants are bound by magic to keep House secrets. I couldn't tell any of you or your seconds—not even my own wife. I had minimal time. The best I could do was reach out to my contact, who would reach out to his contact, who would reach out to Gavriel, and relay a vague message about your mom and him needing to leave. In case you've never played telephone, it takes time." Sam wrapped her arm around Lindsey, pulling her close. "We're lucky they moved as quickly as they did."

"You did good, babe." Sam smiled like Lindsey was the center of her world. "No one's hurt except the assholes that deserve to be."

Lindsey returned her smile with nothing short of adoration. She wrapped an arm around Sam's waist and squeezed.

"What happens now?" I asked, looking around. "I don't want to stay here, but . . ."

Malachi seemed to know where my thoughts were going. "You owe them nothing, Nikki."

"And even if you did, we can't stay here," Adrian added. "We kind of agreed to be part of Earth and Emerald when we entered the trials. There's no going back on that unless we choose to leave through the official channels."

"You're also candidates, and there's no withdrawing from that. Until the voting concludes, you're Earth and Emerald residents. They returned you where you started so candidates could spend time with their families during the reprieve, but options for permanent residences are being organized behind the scenes," Lindsey added. "There are locations all over the world. Even if you don't win, you'd have your pick of where to go."

Hope swelled within me. I knew my mates would follow me anywhere, but the rest of my family?

"Sam?"

"We're waiting on you. Lindsey got us set up with a temporary apartment, but as your second, I've been told there's some great benefits. Apparently relocation is covered for us too."

"Gav? Alex?"

The latter sighed. "Gav is going with you and Mom, but I'm staying here." Alex's expression softened, but the conflict he was experiencing couldn't be hidden.

"You didn't choose this life," I told him. "You don't have to take over—"

"I'm not," he said, tilting his head to the side. "Jackie is."

I looked between them, frowning. "Jackie?"

"Our family has destroyed so many lives. We've ripped Manhattan apart." Alex motioned toward the rubble around us. He had a point. "The shifter syndicate doesn't

512

need another Ward. It needs someone that can work with the other syndicates."

"But Jackie?" I questioned, still not sold on the concept. "Maybe it's better that no one takes over this mess."

"The absence of power is chaos, and the people of Manhattan don't deserve that," she said, and then nudged my brother with her elbow. "We came to an understanding a while back and it's been in the works to dethrone your father, but it was no easy task. The Wards couldn't remain in power, but Alex wanted to stay. I'm willing to look the other way while he handles his business, and I'll handle mine."

"She's also one of the few people strong enough to hold the position when challenged and isn't completely batshit crazy," Alexander added.

"Thanks," she said sarcastically.

He rolled his eyes.

"If Jackie is taking over, why can't you leave with us?"

He rubbed the back of his neck and stretched it, but he looked at me with gentle eyes. "I have to take care of some things first, and she'll likely need me to help the transition go smoothly. Dad had a lot of shifters loyal to him, and a lot of them will either refuse to accept her as the alpha unless I tell them to, or they'll fight for it themselves." I didn't like that he was staying behind while the rest of us were moving on and starting a new life. "Someone has to right the wrongs, Nik. He and Ty . . . they damaged this city. I can't fix it singlehandedly, but we need to try. You have sacrificed more than any of us to do the right thing. You and Gav. You guys earned this. I . . . I have some work I need to do first."

While I didn't know what else it was that he needed to do, I could tell there was something he wasn't saying. I didn't need to know what it was to understand and respect his reasoning. Alex was always gray. He didn't smuggle people out like Gav, or work with the Movement like me, but he also wasn't anything like Ty. With our father gone and no longer influencing him, he needed to make reparations in his own way and figure out who he was.

"So . . . not to be an asshole here," Tylea started, "but what are we going to do about that?" She pointed to Ty's statue.

We all shared a contemplative look, but the real answer came from Niall. The dragon slowly got to his feet, letting me adjust so that I wouldn't fall. He looked over his shoulder at me to check if I was good.

I patted one of the scales, not quite sure if he could feel it.

Were they reactive and sensitive like skin? Or were they more like a turtle's shell and just transmitted vibrations? These were important questions I would have to ask him at another time.

I dipped my chin in case the patting wasn't obvious. The dragon parted his jaws in what I could only describe as a feral smile.

Then he pounced on Ty.

A dozen times.

Everyone stared at him in shock, as he reared back on his hind legs to grind the stone into the ground. I hung on for dear life while cackling at his enthusiasm.

He pounded the stone until it was little more than dust. I wasn't sure if Adrian or anyone else had the ability to turn him back. But if they did, there was nothing to change anymore.

"We should burn the ashes. Now," Malachi said. "Put them in little baggies and spread them across the world."

Sam rolled her eyes. "This isn't *Twilight,* dipshit. I think it's good."

"How do you know?" he replied.

They started bickering lightheartedly, like old friends—or frenemies, really. As long as I'd known them both, they'd always fought for my attention. Just for different reasons.

Something in me settled for the first time since Marissa's death. I'd felt lost and confused. Like I was missing my soul.

Grief was like a crack in the foundation. The bigger the crack was, and the more it spread, the more unstable the structure.

My grief wouldn't ever disappear. That's not how it worked.

A crack in the foundation could be patched, but its scar would always be there, forever marking its presence.

I'd still miss my sister every day, and I would always have that scar, but stability would eventually return. My mates, my friends, my family: they couldn't fix me. They didn't have to. That was my responsibility.

However, in the short time my mates and I had been together, they'd helped me learn that the foundation would be repaired, and I wouldn't do the work alone. They'd give me their love and support as I rebuilt what had been broken.

They helped me find that sense of purpose I was looking for these last four years, and they quite literally had slayed my enemies—with my help, of course.

I never really was a damsel in distress.

Princess never suited me.

After all, I did fuck the dragon.

515

CHAPTER 50
MALACHI

NIKKI STOOD IN FRONT OF THE MIRROR PICKING AT HER DRESS, smoothing wrinkles that weren't there.

I closed the door to the ladies room behind me, flipping the lock. Her dark eyes snapped up to meet mine.

"Nervous?"

"You're not?" she asked, voice rising in pitch.

"No," I said with a smile. "I'm not."

She narrowed her gaze, looking adorable, sexy, and irritated all at once. If I thought she'd let me bend her over the vanity and fuck her until she couldn't remember she felt anxious, I would do it in a heartbeat.

"You're gorgeous. You could go in there in a potato sack, and you'd still look beautiful."

She groaned, wiping at a non-existent smudge in her eyeliner.

"What if they hate me?" she asked, voice wavering slightly. "What if the ones that voted for me were wrong and I'm going to make a terrible chancellor?"

I walked up behind her, settling my arms around her waist. I pulled her back flush against my chest and ignored

516

my already hardened cock as it pressed into her backside. "Well, then I guess it's a good thing it's only ten years, now isn't it—"

"Malachi!"

I chuckled, pressing my lips to her hair. "What if you do amazing?" I said, lowering my voice. "What if those people that voted for you saw what I see? What if you're the best thing that has ever happened to Earth and Emerald?"

"You're ridiculous."

"Says the youngest chancellor in history—"

"Only because my family killed half the candidates."

"Semantics."

"Facts."

"Unrelated facts."

"Relevant facts."

I let out a sigh of exasperation. "You successfully negotiated a deal with the sea witch. That has nothing to do with who else was running. No other candidate or chancellor has done that before, and you did it on your own. Accept the praise, princess."

She rolled her eyes, then the corners of her lips curled in what I took as concession.

Another success as her first mate.

It wasn't an official label. Niall also insisted he was the first mate because they'd bonded first. He was clearly mistaken. I was her *very* first back when we were teenagers and that made me the *real* first mate.

I was going to have cards made that said so too.

Adrian refused to engage in the debate saying that he didn't care what number he was, as long as he was her mate—at which point Nikki went all googly-eyed over the bastard for being so mature.

I might have thrown up in my mouth a little bit when it happened.

"You're only saying that because you're my partner."

"That doesn't make it any less true."

Nikki laughed. "It's like when your mom tells you you're beautiful. It doesn't count."

I squinted at her. "That still doesn't make it any less true."

"You're biased."

"*Still* true."

"I can't with you right now."

"Look, Nik." I leaned down to let my lips trace the shell of her ear. "Your self-esteem is too high for you to be doubting yourself. You're a badass, remember? You've got this."

Her expression softened again. She tilted her head back against my shoulder, relaxing into me.

"Sometimes I can't believe this is real," she said quietly. "That we're actually mated."

"I never gave up on us mating, but I can agree in a way. It's surreal at times to think this is our reality. That we actually got a happily ever after like the sappy movies you're in love with."

She let out a cackle a witch would be jealous of, and gods did I love her for it. "Newsflash, I'm pretty sure none of you are Prince Charming. If anything, I got a bunch of Flynn Riders."

"Okay, one, Niall is a dragon, so he can be Toothless. Two, how can you compare me to Flynn? Rapunzel could have done so much better than his fake ass. I can see the correlation between him and Adrian. I mean, they're both pretty obsessed with themselves, but—"

Nikki snorted. "Uh huh, right. *He's* the self-obsessed

one." She lifted a brow in a teasing manner. "Even though you spend over an hour in the bathroom every day doing gods knows what—"

"I like to be clean for my woman, is that a crime?" She smiled as the door handle jiggled.

"For fuck's sake," Adrian grumbled. "Niall, are you seriously fucking her? Right now? Her inauguration starts in ten minutes—"

"Not Niall," I called back.

"Malachi?" Adrian said. "I expect this shit from him, but not—"

"We're not fucking," Nikki said, elbowing me playfully as I chuckled silently. She twisted around me to flip the lock. Adrian opened the door, taking us both in, particularly the mischievous grin plastered on my face. "He was talking me down from running out the back door."

"If I need to fuck you to help you calm down, that was my next step," I added with a wink.

Adrian wasn't amused and muttered, "Keep it in your pants until later."

"Well I wasn't going to take it out while she was onstage." Now I was just being an ass for my own entertainment.

Nikki rolled her eyes and he looked at me in confusion.

"Tell me you don't want to fuck our mate right now," I challenged. "Tell me she doesn't smell delicious, and that you don't want her pretty lips wrapped around your cock."

She flushed, and his eyes darkened, but it wasn't in anger. Her scent was getting to him too. I smiled.

He glanced at her, then looked back to me and took a deep breath. "Right now I would love nothing more than to kick you out and fuck her until everyone in this building could hear her scream. But she is being sworn in as chancellor in a matter of minutes and they are waiting on her."

"Kick me out?" I tisked at him. "Sharing is caring, Adrian."

"Oh my god. You are *both* Flynn Riders," she muttered, pushing herself between us to exit in a huff.

Adrian glared daggers at me, but I inclined my head toward her with a smirk. Understanding crossed his features, and he nodded. "She's not focused on nerves anymore. Nice work."

"Thanks." I smirked, then gestured for him to leave ahead of me. "I'm not opposed to sharing her later, though."

"Oh that is *one hundred percent* happening," he whispered, adjusting himself. "Give me a warning next time. We need a code word. The images that came to mind . . . I can't go out there with a raging hard on." He cleared his throat.

We followed her a moment later, content to watch as she made her way through the back hallways to the side of the stage.

"Finally!" Sam exclaimed. Her long blonde hair was pulled back in a sleek ponytail. She wore a fitted women's suit that gave her the flexibility needed as Nikki's official bodyguard. An Earth and Emerald ring adorned her finger; a gift from her wife.

Lindsey was the new supernatural syndicate liaison, a position Nikki implemented immediately to help families who wanted to leave.

After the Battle of Giants, as the Typhaons' fight had been dubbed, the council felt the syndicates were too unstable. That belief was reaffirmed when three of the five syndicates declared the trials were rigged, so therefore the deal was voided.

If the council really wanted to push it, they could have. There had been a contract. As the newly appointed chancellor was intimately familiar with the syndicates, they asked for her input on the subject. While Nikki hated all that the syndicates stood for, she was worried the very people she wanted to help would be those caught in the crossfire. It was what happened every time a House attempted to take New York City by force.

The syndicates fought dirty and called in every favor they were owed. Which often overlapped with people in powerful positions within a House.

Funny how that happened.

When they called her name, Chancellor Nikki Ward, I couldn't help but beam. I was so proud of her. We all were.

A strong hand clapped me on the shoulder, pulling me from my thoughts. "What do you have to be thinking so hard about?" Niall said. "We both know your job is to smile and look pretty."

"I thought that was Adrian's job."

Niall considered that. "That's fair. He is the third mate."

I nodded in agreement. "Might as well be a spare."

Niall snorted. "You both are."

"I had her first—"

"You rejected her first too."

"Two words. Fuck. You."

"I did that to her first." Niall grinned. "Claimed her first too. Which is why I'm—"

"Oh my god," Sam whispered harshly. "My ears are bleeding from the sound of your arguing."

"Agreed," Adrian said, watching as Nikki was escorted on stage by Hekate. "Especially when *neither* of them are the first mate *nor* the best looking."

We both stared at him dumbfounded.

Of course *that's* when we were announced. Adrian grinned over his shoulder, enjoying that he got the last word.

Sam laughed under her breath at our expense as Adrian walked on stage—and was indeed announced as the first mate.

"He's sly for a pretty boy. I'll give him that," I said, walking on stage next as my name was called. Before I passed the curtain, I quickly shot Niall a look and mouthed. "At least I'm not *third*."

Niall, Adrian, and I stood on the terrace, waiting for Nikki to come home. We'd poured drinks for ourselves and had dinner in the warming oven. Niall had made lasagna for us, and he'd made some sort of chili pepper fire version of it for her.

Adrian and I had to leave the kitchen when our eyes started to water.

Somehow we fell into a domestic life with each other without difficulty. I thought it would have been harder than it was, but the fates knew what they were doing when they tied our souls together.

We were a family, and she was the center of our world.

When we all loved the same woman and wanted what was best for her. Adrian was right.

Chancellor was a busy role and a big responsibility. Nikki was learning the ropes, and many days we refused to leave her. No, we weren't her official bodyguards. We were her mates. But we also had to give her space to be the leader, especially in the beginning. It was important for her to establish herself and her authority amongst the council and the constituents. We couldn't take up the room so that she became our shadow.

It was us that had to fade into the background. We were the shadow, and we were happy to be there supporting her.

As hard as it was for us to stay away from her for long lengths of time, we didn't want to do anything to jeopardize how she was viewed. We wanted to respect the boundaries she needed.

Didn't make it easy, though.

Sam begrudgingly gave us hourly updates on days we weren't there with her. Lindsey had told me that while Sam grumbled to us about being forced to "provide the stalkers with updates," she completely understood as a mate herself.

I silently twirled the ice in my glass, taking another sip of my whiskey.

Adrian glanced at his watch and said, "She'll be here any minute."

"I'm here now."

We all turned to see Nikki walking through the double doors. Setting a bag down on the chair, she went to Adrian first. Standing on her tip toes, she reached up to give him a kiss. She went to Niall, pressing her lips to his, then came to me and did the same.

"Sorry I'm late," she said, sniffing the air. "Whatever is in the kitchen smells amazing."

"We have to eat it out here," Niall said, pointing at me. "This one almost started to cry."

I rolled my eyes.

"That's a shame," she said, one side of her lips curling in a smile. "I have a surprise."

"Oh?" Adrian raised his brows. "Which movie did you pick out tonight? *Ferngully* or *The Land Before Time*?"

She scrunched her nose at him in a playful way before going to her bag and pulling out three movie boxes. Holding them up, she said, "I thought we could have a movie marathon tonight. Unless there's an emergency, I told them that I would be in late tomorrow."

The front of the covers read *Mad Max*, *The Proposal*, and *The Day After Tomorrow*.

Adrian clapped his hands together once. "I'm game. Dinner and a Sandra Bullock rom-com? Hell yes."

"*Mad Max*? Are you serious?" Niall asked, looking a bit too excited over his action film as she handed it to him.

I was one to talk. She held up my all-time favorite disaster movie.

"I figured we could take a break from what I watch. I know I've been working a lot and I wanted to make it up to you."

While the guys had turned their movies over to look at the back cover, I was knocking back the rest of my drink, and she added, "*All* of you."

The husky tenor of her tone didn't escape any of us.

I raised my eyebrow, setting my glass down. "Not that you owe us anything, but for argument's sake, let's say you did. How exactly would you like to make it up to us?"

She shrugged. "You tell me," she purred, reaching down and grabbing the hem of her dress. She tugged it over her head and tossed it to the side.

She had nothing on underneath, and our mate stood before us, as beautiful as ever. My body reacted instantly, and her mark on my chest flared to life.

"You're mine, princess," I growled.

As I started forward, Adrian put out his hand to block

me in a friendly manner. With a smile, he dipped his chin. "Ours."

I looked at Niall, and we nodded and spoke in unison. "*Ours.*"

Nikki smiled coyly. "Then come get me, *mates.*"

The End.

9 781957 953